Malevolent Desire

Rob McWilliam

Also by Rob McWilliam

House of Shadows

Cover image: iStockphoto

ISBN: 0987596209
ISBN 13: 9780987596208

ONE

Sanderson perched on a barstool in the Lord Nelson while his colleague, Dave disappeared among the throng of customers. They were on their third round of beers. Tension seeped from his neck muscles as he settled in for a good night. A plasma TV on the far wall had a footie match on. Perfect.

He felt a touch incongruous in a suit in this pub, Australia's oldest. Dave favoured this place built by convicts over some of Sydney's swankier establishments. Whenever Sanderson saw this hotel's solid sandstone and the welcoming glow of the wrought iron lamp above the corner door, he relaxed.

Melding with workers and possibly a criminal element didn't faze them after five years working together in Homicide. Edgy tattoos and body piercings were more likely in this domain than Armani suits and leather briefcases.

Sanderson noticed Dave's chunky handsome face emerge, frothy schooners in each hand.

'Took your time, mate. Could die of thirst.' Sanderson's hand enveloped the glass and he took a swig. 'Ahh. Thank God our caseload allows a bit of drinking time tonight.'

'Bloody busy here.' Dave's voice was loud above the cacophony of patrons. 'Just ducking outside, Sando. Ringing the missus to say goodnight to the little fellow.'

'Sure, Dave.'

He turned his attention back to the game. A try was scored. Shouts roared. Despite the distraction, Sanderson thought, Dave's got it all. Jen was never bitchy and Billy, nearly three, loved gabbling on the phone. Would the right woman ever cross his path? Somehow he just didn't have the knack of settling down.

Dave returned, a smile lighting up his eyes. Sanderson filled him in on the footie then his mobile rang. His teeth clenched as he listened to what he could of the tirade.

'Helen. Past history that dame. She's at my place. Hysterical. Says she's moving in. Got to go.'

'Pity, Sando. The game's hotting up. I'll finish my beer. Surprise Jen, go home early.'

After a hasty cab ride to Surry Hills, Sanderson was in no mood to deal with Helen's tantrums. He'd just talked her into leaving in her laden car when his phone rang. Ear to his mobile, the words sent a chill through him, 'Officer down in the Rocks.' For a moment he considered jumping into his car but he didn't dare risk driving after so many beers. Helen's taillights were a distant blur. He raced towards Oxford Street where he snared a cab quickly. The warm night air made him hotter, adding to his unease. All the way through the city he was on edge. He wasn't usually called out to brawls. Then the words registered, northern end of Kent Street. Right near the Lord Nelson. Dread encircled his stomach.

Sanderson was out of the cab running towards the barely illuminated crime scene tape. Patrol car lights, red and blue, intermittently lit up the dark end of the street. Weird shadows. Gloomy trees.

Uniformed cops were standing in the road, heads down. A torch's glare showed a figure askew on the bitumen. A squeal of tyres and a piercing siren announced an ambulance. He surged forward. The circle of light flashed on an attractive square-jawed face. The eyes didn't react. Then he saw the slashes in his mate's shirt. An ever-widening stain. Almost black. The metallic smell of blood assaulted his nostrils.

He turned to the constable and noticed his own business card in her hand. So that's how they knew to call him.

'Christ. What happened?'

'A witness thinks he intervened in a drug deal gone wrong.'

They stood aside while ambos checked for vitals. Sanderson overheard the other uniform say, 'Think you're too late.'

'Not Dave, not Dave,' he moaned. He tried to detach, remain professional when a raging heat ripped through his body. Saliva flooded his mouth. He made it to the gutter, heaving. His stomach contents rushed out. Throat and nasal passages burned.

After, he fumbled for a card and handed it to the constable. 'Ring him, he'll take charge of the investigation.'

'Right, Sir. Will you be able to advise next of kin?' Her voice was soft.

'Yeah, I'll do it.' Sanderson wiped his mouth. 'Fucken junkies.'

A murder call summonsing him rarely came in working hours. Rapid dressing, driving whilst outlining the job to his sergeant was all part of the caper. But when it was a colleague, a mate, knifed by some druggie, pain seared every nerve ending.

Insidious guilt. What if he hadn't left Dave? Why had he succumbed to Helen's emotional blackmail? This was so much worse, Sanderson thought, than the usual Sydney scene of devastation: fresh artwork of human blood, perhaps a weapon and the ubiquitous lifeless body.

Half an hour later he stood on his former friend's doorstep hoping like hell he knew what to say. The Homicide Squad commanded his life. And, of course, embroiled him in death.

TWO

Storm clouds obliterated the last rays of sunlight as Jill left the university. Greenish grey thunderheads indicated hail, a common phenomenon in late March. Sydney's farewell to a sticky summer could be ferocious with balls of ice the size of walnuts skittering to earth. She drove faster. Five minutes and the refuge of her carport would avoid an insurance claim.

Thunder rumbled and raindrops splattered the windscreen as she wheeled into her street. The radio blared a storm warning. Tension circled her stomach. When she got out, clutching a pile of essays, the long cotton dress clung to her thighs. Relief. Her Honda's black duco was shiny and unscathed.

Inside, Jill turned the air conditioner on and poured a glass of iced water. A month here from Canberra and she still hadn't adjusted to the stifling heat. On the lounge she let the cooling blast of air do its magic. She imagined her mum's red lips pursed in disapproval. Extravagance was something Mother never allowed herself. At thirty-five Jill was determined to break away. She wondered if Mother's new audience at the retirement village would be accommodating.

After a shower she still lacked the energy for real cooking. A microwaved pasta would do for dinner. Jill emptied the powdery contents into a bowl, stirred in milk, water and butter then zapped it. Meanwhile she chopped ham, an avocado and tangerine curls of sun-dried tomatoes to give the dish an exotic tang. A final couple of minutes and the meal was ready in time for her to eat while watching the evening news. The hail had been light in her suburb but others were not so lucky and a smattering of dents on exposed cars paraded across the screen.

She marked tutorial assignments and spent an hour researching Fiji's offer of cession to Britain in 1874, before making a late night cup of tea to take to bed. Beside a lamp on the limed cane table a stack of novels threatened to topple. Reading well into the night was enjoyable but it was also a coping mechanism. This was the hour she always felt uneasy. In time Jill hoped she'd get used to living alone.

Outside the night was wild. Shrubs in the tiny garden swayed as gusts hit them. Occasionally lightning struck an eerie glow. The sliding window was locked open leaving a ten-centimetre gap. Wide eaves meant no rain could enter and she enjoyed feeling wafts of fresh air over her as she slept. Jill pulled the cord, angling the Venetians against the darkness and assured herself she would be safe in this townhouse. But if someone scaled the garden wall they'd get in easily enough. Perhaps she should have bought in a high-rise block.

Jill padded into the bathroom to complete her nightly routine. Clothes shed, she put on the shiny aubergine nightie she'd left hanging on a door hook then cleaned and creamed her face. A smell of damp foliage permeated the bedroom. In bed, she picked up *Alias Grace*, a Margaret Atwood novel she was half way through. Beautifully written but she found it unnerving to read of grisly murders late at night. Discarding it, Jill turned off the light and stretched out across the double bed with just a sheet covering her.

Sometime in the night a scraping noise woke her. Eyes opened wide to the room's darkness, she lay rigid waiting for it again. All she could hear was rain trickling in the downpipes. How she hated waking like this. Jill breathed deeply but her imagination already had an intruder inside. Her body sweat soaked as her mind grabbed at possibilities. She always felt threatened; scared her demise would come in the dark of night.

Adrenalin surged. Slipping out of bed, Jill slithered home the bolt she'd put on the bedroom door. Alert, she listened. Now no one could get in and stand over her.

The scene of that night long ago reared up. She could see the dingy flat where she'd lived with her mum when she was ten. Remembered that loud banging on the door, the raucous drunken voice. One of Mother's boyfriends.

'Make yourself scarce,' she'd hissed as Jill scuttled under the dining table. Concealed by its hanging cloth, she waited.

Mother could usually handle men and would send them away with curt words. But this one was frightening. She'd pleaded, 'Please, go home.'

'Not till I get what I came for.' His voice slurred. He was pawing at her as she pushed him away. Then Jill heard a loud slap and her mum reeled backwards slipping on the linoleum. He was on top of her, pulling at her dress and grunting like an animal. She struggled at first then lay quietly as he started lurching. Her head was turned to one side and Jill remembered seeing her tears. Finally he slumped on her body. When he came to his eyes looked straight at Jill. They were bloodshot and the black stubble of his beard gave him the scariest look. Would he come after her? Jill clung to the floor in panic, face down. She heard him get up and come closer. He flipped at the tablecloth and she smelt his beery breath. Then he left. Her mum was kneeling as Jill crawled out. She scooped her into loving arms. Jill was shaking.

'Jilly, forget what you saw. That was a bad man.'

They moved to a new flat and Jill had a sitter whenever Mother went out after that night. But that raging drunk's ferocity had engendered a fear of men. And Jill blamed her father. What kind of man was he leaving the two of them alone? Why did he never see them? She recalled coming home from primary school saying, 'Why haven't I got a Daddy?' Mother's lips thinned in anger stopped her asking again.

Next morning the weather had cleared, only a few clouds streaked the sky. As the traffic edged along she went over the adjustments she'd have to make in order to live alone. Sleeping properly was a priority so as to be clear-headed for her lectures and tutorials. While students might stumble in hung over or near asleep it wasn't acceptable for her. Fancy not realising her insecurities would surface. The bedroom door lock was step one. Perhaps she should buy one of those personal alarms. Jill definitely didn't want someone moving into the spare room. She'd filled it with a computer, files and books so even Mother couldn't stay over.

Leaves crackled around the car park as she lugged her briefcase towards the humanities building. The seven-storey edifice towered behind two humps of sun-seared grass. Jill shared the lift with Professor Mitchell's research assistant, Paula. She was chatty and always immaculately groomed. Large breasts bulged her beige jacket. Jill noticed her sensuous lips were mulberry this morning.

'Coming to staff drinkies this evening, Jill?'

'Oh, I'm not into socialising.' She felt dowdy in a long denim skirt beside Paula's smart suit.

'You must come. The Professor's been asking about you. He likes to check out new staff members.'

'I'll think about it.' Jill smiled and left the lift.

Her tiny office was a haven. A narrow window looked down over the car park. Bookshelves, neatly packed with reference books, lined the walls. Their presence gave her comfort. She slid into a chair, its castors moving noiselessly over royal blue carpet. On her desk was a flyer elaborating on tonight's function. The wording meant attendance was mandatory. If only she'd asked the researcher more. Why do colleagues have to mix socially? Academia is a safe world but she wanted to be left alone to work. She'd have to go once then no more. Jill had become quite adept at avoiding staff interaction at the Australian National University, her last workplace.

That evening the humidity returned. She slipped on a long shapeless purple dress. Fawn flowers splashed across the filmy fabric. Her limp blonde hair pulled back, she fastening it with a butterfly clip, added a touch of make-up then drove back to the university.

Jill was hardly in the room before the Professor was at her side. He handed her a glass of white wine.

'Good to see you, Jill.'

His voice was melodious, confident, making her feel uneasy.

'Thanks, Professor Mitchell.'

'Call me Duncan. We don't stand on ceremony here.'

He stood back as if appraising her, brown eyes behind rimless spectacles. His hand massaged the short grey stubble of a beard. He must be over fifty, she thought. Jill couldn't believe he was wearing a black leather jacket in this heat. Perhaps that was part of his image, a slim man trying to add bulk.

'Aren't you hot?' slipped from her mouth.

At this his sweaty hand took Jill's and she detected a twinkle in his dark eyes. 'The night is young,' he said suggestively.

She saw a tray of hors d'oeuvres and tried to escape his grasp. 'I didn't have time for dinner,' Jill explained.

'Have some caviar,' he oozed, presenting a square of rye bread cascading red eggs. 'Now, I hear your specialty is Pacific History. You'll need my help publishing your articles. I'm the most prolific at Phillips University, you know. It's so much easier when you're shown the ropes.'

Duncan leaned closer patting her shoulder as she tried not to flinch. How she hated touchy feely men. Perhaps he envisaged late nights working together. She'd heard he seldom went home to his whining mouse of a wife.

'I'm sure everyone will be a great help. Perhaps you could introduce me to those I've not met.' She cast a glance around the room of chattering people.

'Of course, Jill, can't keep you all to myself.'

Duncan winked at her before his sweaty hand swooped. Jill gulped wine, gorged on savouries and spoke to a few colleagues. Later, when she saw the Professor careering in her direction she scuttled out of the room.

Outside, the evening air was cooling. Jill sped home. Thank God the main staff function for the year was over. And as for Professor Duncan Mitchell or God's gift to women as he obviously thought himself. Yuk! Sleep was a welcome relief.

Preparing lectures and seeing the odd student with essay problems kept her absorbed. Jill had spent enough time settling into her townhouse. This weekend she was looking forward to seeing the city. Several of the staff had been horrified she knew no one here. For her it wasn't a problem. Jill liked life uncomplicated.

She made time for a cappuccino at the cafeteria before the last tutorial of the day. Tall gums swung in the breeze as the massive concrete union building appeared. As she passed the lecture theatre a noisily flapping tape caught her attention. Jill walked down the pathway that led over the culvert to the gymnasium. Uniformed police prevented students pushing closer. Only then she realised the blue and white chequered tape meant a crime scene. She left the path, trying to see further down near the drainpipe. The ground smelt musty. An officer stood inside the tape, his arms folded defensively.

'What happened, Officer?'

'A girl's body has been found.'

'Was she murdered?'

'I'm sorry, madam. Can't give any details.'

His tone was far from chatty so she moved away. Then half hidden in the grass she saw it. A scalpel smeared with dried blood. Curly blonde hairs stuck to the blade. Her hand hovered above it as realisation struck. The murder weapon?

'Don't touch that,' the policeman bellowed.

He'd been watching. Jill retracted her hand, dropping to her knees, the folder scattering papers. Others came running as she stared at the implement as if mesmerised. Her stomach felt queasy. Jill wiped a sweaty forehead hearing her breath charging in and out of her nostrils. The officer helped Jill to her feet, turning away as gloved hands seized the scalpel.

'Are you all right?' he said.

Jill looked at him, uncomprehending. His firm hands were on her shoulders supporting her weight. Did he think she was going to faint?

'I … I'll be okay. Going to get a coffee.' Jill made it to the path and didn't look back.

THREE

Detective Inspector Gary Sanderson admired his muscular torso in the bathroom mirror. Curls of golden chest hair set off his late summer tan.

'No wonder babes find you irresistible,' he crooned, patting on aftershave. Sanderson went into the bedroom for his clothes. He tucked a grey shirt into black pants then returned to the mirror putting his arms through his shoulder holster and adjusted the leather straps firmly. His fingers trailed across the dimpled butt of his Glock 9 mm automatic. He orchestrated a quick withdraw with his right hand to show he was ready for action. Putting the weapon back in place, he knotted a silky mauve tie. A hanger swung noisily in the robe as he retrieved a charcoal sports jacket. He enjoyed his reputation as the best-dressed D around and never mentioned the time and dollars it cost. He grabbed a pair of black jocks for his car kit, went down the narrow stairs and deadlocked the front door of his terrace.

Riley Street was relatively peaceful for an inner city location. That had been its attraction three years earlier when he'd pulled up outside the burgundy front door. The regimentation of the wrought iron spears in the same colour seemed so smart in front of fawn walls. Huge plane trees flanked the street; their branches arching over the roadway provided a cool sanctuary for his white Commodore. Yet, mere blocks from here were the flurry of nightclubs, shops and restaurants of Oxford Street. Sanderson found its location perfect for walking home after a drink.

Dead leaves scattered in the gutter as his car alarm beeped off. He flung his jacket over the passenger's seat; the jocks went into the glove box. Then he checked his battery shaver and aftershave. Never know when you have to freshen up for some lady, he thought. He headed north over the Harbour Bridge to his regional office. The sky had cleared after yesterday's hailstorm. Traffic was slow but not as bad as the barely moving lanes making for the CBD. Day after day cramming into high-rise offices wasn't Sanderson's idea of life. He envied high-flying financiers and legal eagles only their huge salaries.

Working in Homicide, he never knew what his day would bring. Any moment a call could come to drag him away from inquiries, briefs and court work. He thought of his new offsider. Sergeant Fyurk needed a mountain of training before he'd handle a case. Fyurk. Where'd he get a name like that? And he always had bits of clothing hanging out. He'd have to smarten up. Sanderson had forgotten how he learned to be a detective yet now he was showing others. He had to focus on developing the boy's observational and deductive skills if he was going to be any good. Still, Fyurk appeared to be a communicator so people might open up to him.

Sanderson parked and was walking to his office when he saw Janine. He took in her cute face, those big breasts straining her uniform before giving her a seductive wink. Pity things had never got started there. He'd been seeking out the delicious Janine for a coffee break when he'd overheard the other female cop's warning.

'Don't go drinking with Sanderson, darl, he's a real pants man. You want every detail of your bedroom gymnastics known?'

He'd sidled round the doorway.

'Janine, time for a coffee?'

'Not now, Gary, lots to do.'

The younger woman had scurried out, leaving her hefty colleague with an amused smirk on her face.

Sergeant Fyurk, in his rumpled state, was poring over files on Sanderson's desk. The senior detective hung his coat on a stand, grabbed a marker and tossed it to Fyurk.

'Catch.'

Fyurk fumbled for the pen looking bewildered.

Sanderson continued, 'Richard, do me a flow chart of this drug overdose.'

He spent fifteen minutes directing the younger man as the marker squeaked across the shiny surface of the whiteboard. Arrows connected victim and supplier. He hoped his offsider was catching on to this main tool for solving cases. Here he got down a visual representation of everything known about a case. Big red question marks probed the unknown. His usual practice was sipping coffee, feet on the desk, allowing his mind to run through scenarios. Focusing on the whiteboard with its marks and squiggles would often reveal the next line of inquiry. Fyurk stood staring dumbly at the pattern. Sanderson wondered if it was possible to train another to work the way he did. Resentment threatened to overwhelm him. Dave's loss and having a new partner thrust on him brought sharpness to his voice, 'Richard, copy what's on the board and then add something to it. First, get me another coffee.'

'Sure, Gary.'

His phone rang. Sanderson nodded at regular intervals and jotted information in the black-and-red notebook he used in the field. He had one arm into his coat sleeve when Fyurk returned.

'Let's go. We've got a dead'n at the uni. A girl.'

They joined the three-lane highway snaking north.

'Ever been to this university, Richard?'

'No. I went to ANU.'

Sanderson turned off. 'Well, here we go into the hallowed halls of learning.'

'You go to uni, Gary?' Fyurk glanced at him.

'No. In my day, boy, we learned on the job. So let's see if your fancy education can make you a better cop.'

Showing the gateman his badge, the senior detective noted the directions to the nearest car park. They had to go through the history building, around a lecture theatre before the path came into view. Fyurk, camera slung round his neck, followed. The walkway led down over a culvert. On the left a stand of trees shadowed the area. In the distance were more buildings. Must be a creepy place at night, Sanderson thought, noting only a few lights, ball-shaped on poles some distance apart.

Uniformed cops already had the crime scene tape up. The familiar ribbon fluttered noisily in the breeze. Several students, trying to peer from the walkway, were hurried on. At least the entry and exit points were secure, Sanderson noted.

'Phew,' said Fyurk as the first waft of death became evident.

They put on overalls and shoe covers before stretching paper caps over their hair.

'Very attractive,' said Sanderson, smiling. 'Our attempt to leave nothing of ourselves.'

Ralston, head of their squad, had just emerged from the huge concrete pipe below the pathway. Ruggeri, a familiar face from the SOCO team, escorted him to the tape.

'Morning, boss,' Sanderson said.

'Not good, take a look. This one's yours, Sanderson.' Ralston gave him a snapshot of what he'd found out from the uniforms.

Ruggeri removed his cap and ran fingers through dark curls before shaking Sanderson's hand. 'Sando, good to see you. Pity we never meet under better circumstances.'

Sanderson smiled at the swarthy Italian in his navy uniform. 'My offsider, Richard Fyurk. Pete Ruggeri. Runs the forensics team. Muck with his crime scene and you'll hear about it.'

Ralston gave an approving nod before moving off.

'Hi, Pete.' Fyurk straightened his lanky frame.

Ruggeri motioned them towards the body.

Sanderson's shoes slid on the damp clay despite the covers. His mind ran through the first tasks to be allocated.

'Keep to the track.' Ruggeri's tone was serious.

'See, Richard. He's a prickly bastard.' Sanderson gave the leader's shoulder a friendly pat.

'Okay, Sando. Lay off. Detectives have been known to stuff up. Let me get on with collecting evidence.' Ruggeri went to check on his team.

Fyurk got out the camera, 'You think he'd mind if I take a few shots?'

'Can't hurt. So long as you don't disturb anything.'

Ignoring the stench, they went inside. The pipe, concealing the victim, was large enough to stand in. Light entered from both ends. The girl's body must have been here several days. Her neck was a series of dark striations, blood encrusted. Her mouth was open as if still screaming. Bending down, Sanderson could detect movement behind her teeth. Maggots.

The pink top, probably torn in the girl's struggle, was smeared with mud. He had a feeling the killer had positioned her. Her lower body was naked, legs opened in a V drawing your eyes to her pelvis. Pubic hair had been slashed off in a final desecration. The darkened wound was seething with insects. A sick bastard, Sanderson thought. He noticed the girl's hand trailing in water, the glint of a silver ring on her finger.

'Okay,' said Sanderson. 'Move carefully around the body. Check for shoe prints at entry and exit of the pipe. SOCOs might get a cast.'

They put on latex gloves. Fyurk's camera whirred, capturing the body placement and surrounds. The girl's bowels had released and her body was bloating. Sanderson heard a gurgle in his offsider's throat. The mix of odours was too much for Fyurk.

'Stop.' Sanderson yelled to halt his departure. 'Stand still. Breathe slowly. Your nose will get used to the smell in a couple of minutes.'

'But I need fresh air,' Fyurk gasped.

'It'll be just as bad when you come back in, Richard.'

Fyurk stood rigid, obviously wishing away the convulsions his body had instigated.

'For Christ's sake, focus! Did you get a shot of the lividity?'

Making a note of it, Fyurk nodded.

'That indicates the body hasn't been moved,' Sanderson added.

Ruggeri tracked them out again. Sanderson could see Detective Superintendent Ralston waiting on the embankment. A burly bloke with bushy black eyebrows, his booming voice echoed in the gully. His superior cast a glance over Fyurk's dishevelled appearance. Lines of annoyance tightened his face. Sanderson knew his insistence on professionalism and efficiency on the job. Was Fyurk going to be a liability? He realised Ralston had sized up his offsider as a young dill who could contaminate the scene.

'This one's a sicko,' Sanderson said rejoining the others.

'We're up against a nasty killer. Liaise with Ruggeri over the evidence collected. We don't want the crime scene jeopardised. Find out what you can from those kids,' Ralston pointed, 'and get the bug man to help determine time of death. You saw the maggots? Call up reinforcements to doorknock the surrounding areas.'

Sanderson nodded. He didn't need reminding of the bleeding obvious.

'I want a full situation report after the post mortem's done. Then we'll have a review. I'll let the Chancellor know what we're doing.'

'Fine, boss. He'll be rattled having a killer on campus.'

'She. I'm going to see her now to ensure full cooperation. Get on with it, Sanderson.'

As he watched his superior stride away, Sanderson punched numbers into his mobile. 'Dr Levy?' he began and detailed his requirements.

'The bug man?' Fyurk asked, noting Sanderson's nod in reply. 'Can't the SOCOs deal with them?'

'Levy collects the critters himself and examines them in his lab. Those maggots can be the best indicator of how long the body's been there. Don't go back near the girl until they've videoed and photographed. If you do anything wrong before Ruggeri's finished, he'll have your arse. Get your notebook and keep a running sheet. I want everything: time of day, temperature, weather, and names of officers present. I'll find someone to replace you as soon as I can. I'm going to question the kid who found the body.'

'Fine,' said Fyurk.

Stripping off his paraphernalia, he left his offsider near a dimpled metal case belonging to forensics. Sanderson walked up to a trio of students standing with an officer. He hoped they'd not talked it over. Eyewitness testimony was often devalued if versions were exchanged. Five minutes with them and he had the picture. All three had smelt the scent of death from the walkway. The girls talked the young bloke into investigating. The sight of the body had shaken him, his white face stark against the black T-shirt.

'It was gross.' The lad scuffed the path with a huge sneaker.

'What did you do then?' Sanderson asked.

'The girls didn't believe me at first. I told them not to look. We rang triple O on the mobile. Then we waited till the cops arrived.'

'That was me, Detective. You want my number?' broke in the pert redhead.

Provocative piece, Sanderson thought. He shook his head. The other girl flushed.

'Constable, take these three to the station for signed statements. And get an imprint of the boy's jogger. Thanks for your cooperation, kids.' He waved them off seeing Levy had arrived promptly. Sanderson greeted him before Ruggeri took the scientist to the body.

'The kids any help, Gary?' asked Fyurk.

'I doubt they're persons of interest. We need to concentrate on what the victim has to tell us.'

Fyurk noted the comings and goings on his running sheet.

Sanderson ambled over to watch Levy pack away his samples.

'Should have an idea how long she's been dead in the morning, Gary.' The balding man said.

'Thanks, Doc.' Officers were still processing the scene. Near the tape a group of uniformed police awaited him. Sanderson organised two teams, one to doorknock the street nearest the university's perimeter, the other to interview anybody in nearby buildings. He denoted which ones were to contact him with information. The sun made him hot and he craved a coffee. It'd still be a while before they could move the body. Time out could be useful. He surveyed the crime scene. He knew the procedure: not think of the victim as a person, retrieve the evidence before it was lost, and devise a strategy for the case.

Despite attempts to focus, his mind wandered. Observing the sauntering jeans-clad students took him back to his own youth. He'd never considered continuing his education in this leisurely fashion. No sooner had he dumped his schoolbooks after the HSC than he heard his father's words, 'Get a job, son. There's no room for bludgers round here.' Several years as a labourer on building sites had bulked him up. He'd had a few blues and thought he was tough. None of the trades particularly interested him despite his mother's pressure to find an apprenticeship. Then he'd seen the ad. Being a cop was tough.

He glanced around for Fyurk. Would lectures make him any good at this? Sanderson was curious. He hadn't really talked to him. How he'd become a cop. Why Homicide? Fyurk appeared to have dragged his own way through life so far. Sure, he'd been rough with him over the body's ripe odours. But you couldn't have a detective vomiting on a crime scene.

Relieved from keeping the running sheet, Fyurk called out from an area beyond the tape. 'Over here, Gary, this might be something.' They alerted a member of the team in charge of collecting who put the cigarette butt in an evidence bag.

Mid-afternoon, Fyurk brought Sanderson a dried ham sandwich and a weak coffee in a Styrofoam cup. They sat on a bench seat in view of the crime scene. The afternoon sun had plenty of sting. Shirtsleeves rolled up, Sanderson was glad to be out of the overalls.

'Richard, did you see the Government Medical Officer arrive? You'll get to know the cast of characters soon enough.'

Fyurk nodded, taking his colleague's rubbish. Sanderson went to speak to Hazelton, the Forensic Pathologist, who'd also come to view the body in situ.

Returning, Sanderson said to Fyurk, 'The autopsy will be in the morning. Hazelton's mob is flat out with a bus smash. Meticulous old bugger. You coming?'

The younger man nodded.

'Find anything significant?' Sanderson asked.

Fyurk shook his head whilst chewing. He screwed up the sandwich wrapper and wiped his hands on his pants.

Sanderson grimaced then continued, 'He must have dumped the rest of her clothes. Jeans possibly and undies.'

'Forensics has searched all the forest area and the gullies on either side of the pipe.'

'Say our man came up behind her on the path, got the ligature round her neck then dragged her down to the pipe. Today's Thursday. With decomposition and maggots it had to be Monday or Tuesday night. Have we missed the drag marks?'

'Remember, Gary, the hailstorm yesterday. That'd be enough to obliterate those and bugger up footprints. SOCOs did a partial cast of one near the body but it'll most likely be the boy who discovered her.'

His mobile chimed. 'Sanderson here … We're nearly done, Sir … Right.' He put the phone in his shirt pocket. 'Ralston's arranged for campus maps and the schedule of night lectures to be faxed to the office. We still need those clothes, Richard. Go search all the garbage bins.'

'Nice job,' said Fyurk, raising his hands as if dirt was foreign to them.

'Evidence, Richard. There's got to be more of it somewhere on this bloody campus. Jeans, underwear, ligature, possibly a torch. Maybe he didn't do that mutilation in the dark.'

'If he dropped the scalpel over there,' Fyurk pointed to the grassy area, 'maybe he had it wrapped in her clothes. A uniform said some woman nearly picked it up then almost fainted.'

'Must track her down.'

Fyurk pulled on latex gloves, gathered the cups and wrappers and made for the nearest bin.

By late afternoon Sanderson heard the zip of the body bag. What a relief, the atrocities were finally covered. He'd assigned an officer to accompany their grim finding to the morgue. Staring at where the girl's body had been, he wondered at the malice behind this event. Brutal death never failed to shock him. Despite the insatiable curiosity of the students he still had no idea of her identity. Someone had to have missed her in class. Assuming she was a student and this wasn't just a dumpsite. Sanderson noted a few ideas kicking around in his head. Fyurk returned empty handed.

Ralston must have been successful in convincing the Chancellor. None of the media had made it past the gatemen. Then the noise of a chopper took them by surprise, a reverberating whoomph before they felt the down draft. Sanderson saw the news cameraman's huge lens capture a shot of the body bag as it was taken away. Only the height of the gums kept the vultures from descending lower. Just as suddenly the disturbance was gone.

'Took them a while,' he said to Fyurk, 'that's why we use mobiles instead of police radio.'

'That footage will be all over the TV screens on tonight's news.' Too late, Fyurk tucked in his shirt and straightened his tie.

'Now we've worked the crime scene, I'll use the media.' Sanderson rang through a holding statement with the briefest of details. Police media would hand it on. Girl's body found at Phillips University, blonde hair, wearing a pink top and a silver ring. He hoped a response would be at the office when he got back. Maybe the Crime Stoppers number would be ringing hot. Checking missing persons would be a priority. The girl should be ready for identification shortly after the body reached the morgue.

Nose crinkling, Sanderson erupted as soon as Fyurk got into the car, 'Those garbage smells have added to your perfume. Open the bloody window.'

'Nothing a shower won't fix. Pity I didn't find anything related to the crime.'

'Oh, Richard, an incident room has been set up at the nearest cop shop at Chatswood. It's a 24-hour station so the exhibits will be locked up there. I've assigned tasks to the local Ds already.'

'Guess we'll be working late, Gary?'

Tired of instructing, Sanderson went straight to the washroom on their return to his office. Second stop was for a strong coffee. He flipped the whiteboard over, marking what had happened so far with this case. Sending Fyurk off to get the crime photos done gave him time to focus on the campus maps. He marked the site of the body. There was an evening lecture in the theatre near the gymnasium on both Monday and Tuesday nights. It'd be dark for those returning to the main area. Surely, girls don't walk alone round here then. There's no record of attendance at lectures so it won't be easy to confirm it's a student.

At his computer, Sanderson selected a name for the investigation. Artemis. Referring to his notebook he began the arduous task of logging in all the information as well as his early thoughts. Close to midnight, he drove across the Harbour Bridge. Chunky steel cast shadows over the roadway in the artificial lighting. Neons delineated the tops of glass skyscrapers against a black sky. By the time he pulled into Riley Street he was looking forward to a drink. Walking briskly through to the rear courtyard he stripped off his clothes. How he missed Dave, his sick jokes, the debriefing beers.

He began his ritual to remove the odours of death. He left the trousers slung over a chair outside then took shirt, jocks and socks to the tiny adjacent laundry and put a load on. In the sink he scrubbed his shoes, dried and polished them. Nude, he bounded up the stairs locking his gun in the cabinet in his wardrobe before showering. Wearing jeans and T-shirt he returned, taking the pants to the corner store. Their dry cleaning agency proved handy. The Korean owner no longer asked about the strange smells. He'd taken on caring for the detective's clothes as part of his service to the community.

Fortunately, he lived in a part of the city that stayed open into the early hours of the morning. Sanderson bought milk and a small jar of apricot jam. He continued another two blocks to Oxford Street for Indian takeaway. Korma curry was a favourite when he couldn't be bothered eating out. Totally drained of energy, he was glad of a short wait. Back in his terrace house he finally opened a bottle of semillon, emptied the carton onto a plate and collapsed on the lounge to watch TV. It took a while to unwind.

Next morning, the drive to the Department of Forensic Medicine, was brief. Sanderson's shoes squeaked on rubber tiles as he made for the autopsy room. He peered through the door's glass panel. Several bodies were visible covered by white sheets, one with toes pointing rigidly towards the ceiling. Rigor mortis. No pathologist was present so he went in search finding Ruggeri along the way.

The procedure was in progress when Fyurk arrived.

'Sorry, Gary,' he murmured, 'overslept.'

'That's why they invented alarm clocks, Richard. Phew, you stink. Don't tell me you haven't changed your clothes from yesterday?'

'Well, er, no.'

'Bloody hell, Fyurk. I'm training you as a detective. I shouldn't have to be nursemaid as well. Sorry, Doctor, this is my offsider.'

Fyurk looked at the recently cut abdomen. Sanderson heard gurgling in the younger man's throat as he ran from the room. Ruggeri raised his eyebrows.

'New?' asked Doctor Hazelton.

Sanderson nodded.

FOUR

Barbara heaved herself out of bed and slipped into a slinky teal robe.

In the kitchen she held a pineapple firmly and sliced off its thorny skin. She'd already laid out a bowl and cereal container for her husband's breakfast. He was the type of man who ate fresh fruit only if it was cut up for him. Water rumbled in the kettle. She prepared tea for him, wanting to be ready.

Beau hovered at the kitchen's perimeter. Barbara regarded her adorable dog as a 'bundle of fluff'. He knew not to get under her feet. She tipped pellets into his bowl and he crunched away.

Hugh bundled into the family room and sat. His poorly knotted tie was a sign of his usual rush to get to his practice. While he gulped a bowl of cereal was probably not the best time to discuss window and door-frame colour, Barbara thought, as she endeavoured to steal his attention from the morning paper. Sliding the colour chart closer, she said, 'I had in mind this lovely taupe colour for the frames.' Her perfect peach nail was poised above the shade.

'What sort of colour is that?' Hugh replied.

'A brownish grey. The only problem, it's quite a bit extra. Not a standard powder coat colour.' Barbara noticed his grip on the spoon tighten.

'What's wrong with the grey?' he said.

'Nothing really.'

'Well, Barbara, go with that. You're letting this house thing get out of control.'

Hugh gave his wife a customary peck on the cheek, grabbed his medical bag and left.

Barbara sighed. Why did she marry a man so mean with money? The long-held dream of a new home had kept her going over the last difficult year. That officious little man from Council was in the past. Now as brick walls rose higher each day she could see her precious ideas coming to fruition. She looked over the colours again, trying not to let disappointment seep into her day. Colours were her forte. They had attracted Hugh into her life in the first place. The grey did have a lovely name, Notre Dame, like the impressive Paris cathedral.

Still, Barbara pondered, a lesson learned. Hugh was so busy with his patients, why present him with choices over the house? He'd said the project was hers. The man could barely select socks to match his pants. She didn't really want him interfering with her colour scheme. All the PC items would be within budget. She wouldn't mention money again. Ring the builder, was added to her list of chores.

Madeline blustered into the kitchen.

'Morning, Mum.'

'Morning, Maddy. I've sliced some pineapple and there's a carton of yoghurt. Do you want toast?'

'No thanks. First lecture's at ten.'

Barbara watched her daughter slide onto the stool at the breakfast bar as she poured her a glass of orange juice. The tight jeans and skimpy tops Madeline wore as a new uniform were taking some getting used to. University attire was obviously casual. She preferred the image of the private school girl of last year, a neat tunic and wispy blonde hair tied with a bow. Madeline rushed breakfast like her father.

'Isn't this your late night?' Barbara asked.

'Yes, Mum. Evening lecture. Maybe a drink after. Be home tonight by ten.' Madeline picked up her backpack laden with books then gave Beau a quick scratch behind his ear. The dog scampered off and Barbara could hear his nametag tinkling against the ceramic water bowl as he drank.

'All right, Maddy. I'll keep your dinner. And do be careful. I don't like you wandering around the university after dark.'

'You worry too much.'

Her daughter flew out banging the door. There was no point suggesting Maddy cover her midriff. Barbara imagined the glinting fake diamond of the navel ring drawing male eyes to that part of her daughter's body. She felt it was unnecessary advertising. Madeline's perky breasts and youthful curves made her sex patently obvious. A mother could not voice concerns without being picky. Barbara felt the heat of her large bosom resting on her stomach. Let Maddy enjoy her body while she's young.

The craving for coffee was strong. Barbara liked to wait till her family had gone. She'd recently bought a new machine on special at David Jones, all black and shiny stainless steel. The packet crackled as Barbara poured the Rockpool beans into the electric grinder. This new brand was the one served in Neil Perry's restaurants. She gave the beans a buzz then compacted the grounds for a single shot. The screeching probe frothed the milk. Piling it on top of the dark liquid made the crema rise around the cup's rim forming a golden border.

Glossy *Home Beautiful* magazines fanned across the coffee table. Barbara placed her cup beside her notebook ready for the day's planning. The first sip of coffee revived her senses. The aroma took her back to Florence, a vision of the Duomo dominating the city. She realised those heady months in Europe almost twenty years earlier were responsible for the adoration of this drink.

A pat on the sofa encouraged Beau to bounce up and snuggle onto her lap. One hand strayed across his tight white curls. His company always seemed to make coffee time relaxing. She flipped through a magazine on the never-ending search for fittings to enhance her new house. In her imagination she saw the rooms decorated not the bare brick compartments they were.

Barbara loaded the dishwasher and wiped the benches. She still felt anxious about Madeline and wondered why she'd gone into medicine. Hugh had not seemed to push her. Was she meeting some silent expectation? It was a hard career choice. Perhaps her pretty daughter would not have the stamina. Yet she was strong-willed and confident; traits that Barbara lacked even now. Sheer determination would have to bring Barbara the house she'd always wanted.

After showering, Barbara decided to cut the size of the mirror in the new ensuite. Middle age came with unwanted flesh in the body's mid regions and a proliferation of fine lines around mouth and eyes. She pulled on elastic-waisted orange pants then buttoned up a beige linen shirt. Finishing her make-up, she checked her hair in the mirror; short with blonde streaks as she liked it. The high cheekbones, her daughter had inherited, still made her feel attractive. Her list of suppliers tucked neatly in her handbag, she sashayed out to her car. There were so many things to select for a new home. Who would have thought it could be such a delight?

She drove through the Parkway, tree shadows dappling the bitumen. In the tile shop at St Ives she pondered her challenge. The spa bath only came in white or ivory. White was out, it reminded her of hospitals. Set in the bay window overlooking the lake, a white tub would also be too bright. But what tile would blend ivory, a warmer colour, into the grey window frames? After scanning a myriad of tiles, she shared her predicament with the saleswoman.

'I certainly haven't seen anything like that,' the woman replied vaguely.

No help whatsoever, Barbara thought, as she got back into the hot car. She blasted the air conditioner on her face as she drove to Mona Vale. Coming down the escarpment she glanced out to sea. All was calm after the hailstorm last evening. How lucky she wasn't driving when the deluge began.

At her second destination a bright young woman offered assistance, 'We've just got some polished porcelain ones in. Beige with a touch of grey and a darker one you could use for the floor.'

Barbara followed her to the display. 'They're perfect.' She trailed her fingers over the shiny tiles. 'My husband will think these stylish. He's a doctor, you know.'

'That's nice.'

'Can I take samples to show the builder?' said Barbara, her enthusiasm rising.

Once in the car, Barbara decided to go straight to the site. She pulled up near wire barricades, picked her way past a yellow dumpster and called out, 'Yoo hoo, Glen.' The two-storey shell was imposing. Roof timbers had arrived. She found the builder squatting beside a length of timber pencilling marks on it. When he straightened, she noticed his dark eyes matched the trim moustache.

'What brings you over, Barbara?'

'These,' she said, laying out two large tiles, 'for the walls and floor of the ensuite. Found them today. See they blend beige and grey together.'

'Pretty expensive,' Glen said.

'I must have them,' Barbara's face shone, 'but I can't find a border tile.'

'Why don't we tile to the ceiling and do a strip of the darker floor tile? That'll look classy,' Glen suggested.

'Wonderful,' said Barbara, 'and don't mention costs to Hugh. I'll deal with it.'

Almost skipping over the rubble in her sandals, Barbara continued in her car to the plumber's suppliers. Pity she hadn't seen any of her future neighbours. Her new home would definitely improve the streetscape. Amidst the bathroom displays she found and noted the brand of her spa then selected a toilet and basin in ivory to match. What an ensuite she'd have.

The phone rang as she came home. Someone from the hospital asked if she'd come in an hour early in the morning.

'Fine,' Barbara said, hiding her annoyance. At times she wondered how efficiently the physiotherapy department was being run.

She splashed teriyaki marinade over the steaks for dinner as the garage door opened. A dash of red wine was added to the meat.

'Hello, Barbs. Had a good day?' Hugh skimmed past her to change his clothes. He returned to the kitchen in faded stubbies and an old T-shirt. Hugh insisted on wearing dreadful clothes around the house. His legs looked skinny despite the regular rounds of golf. His receding hair emphasised the craze of lines on his forehead. He was not ageing well. But with her weight problem she couldn't criticize.

With barely a nod he took the glass of red and small bowl of peanuts she offered. Nothing could get in the way of the 7 pm news on the ABC. Any exchange attempted would be unpleasant. Afterwards she could ask him to barbecue the steaks.

Whisking the salad dressing, she then sliced Chinese cabbage while three solitary potatoes spun in the microwave. Formerly she'd do a potato bake with lots of cream but Hugh had niggled about diet again. Barbara brought the meat to him on the balcony. She leant on the balustrade, enjoying the colours of dusk: mauve, peach and the deep blue of the sea. After many years perched on this cliff edge above Bilgola Beach, she wondered if she'd miss such an expansive view.

'We won't be living among the gum trees much longer. No more chirpy lorikeets.' Hugh glanced at her while turning the sizzling steaks.

'But we'll have pelicans skimming across the lake and see them poised on the light poles by the bridge.'

Barbara sipped a wine during dinner and related her tile find. Hugh was largely unresponsive. She gathered their plates.

'I've been thinking of buying you a treadmill,' he said, his eyes scanning her rotund figure, 'I know you won't go to a gym.'

'Hugh,' her tone exasperated, 'I can't stand getting overheated. Pounding myself to death on one of those things is not my idea of exercise.'

He raised his hands. 'Just an idea.'

'Look,' she said wielding the plates dangerously near his face, 'I'm trying to diet but most menopausal women stack weight on. I get enough exercise running around at work.' Barbara clattered the dishes in the kitchen.

They watched several shows on TV. Barbara periodically checked the time. Still Madeline hadn't come home.

FIVE

Rattling dishes and garbled conversations in the busy cafeteria brought some sense of normality. From her first visit here Jill loved the maze of steel girders supporting the glass roof. The whole café was slung on a mezzanine level above a vast room with shiny timber flooring. Observing others would help erase the image of the scalpel. Her weird reaction was upsetting. When those physical sensations of nausea and weakness overwhelmed her, she felt her body was out of control.

After shuffling in the queue she took the coffee and caramel slice to a just-vacated table. Only ten minutes before the tutorial. She savoured the creamy sweetness of the treat. Rewarding herself after any unpleasantness was a habit she couldn't break. The warm coffee was relaxing. Thank goodness the policeman had returned her papers. Jill perused the notes, willing her mind back to the islands she loved.

Jill found it strange, this fascination with the Pacific Islands. She watched every travel show. Any brochure that featured palms and an arc of white sand edged with turquoise water had her instant attention. Not that she was a beach addict. Perhaps the idea of escape appealed to some undeveloped part of her psyche. Maybe it was her mum's influence. As a teenager Mother watched 'Adventures in Paradise' on TV. Every week she couldn't wait for Adam Troy's steamy looks. She'd say, 'He's so handsome and sexy I go weak at the knees.' Jill could envisage her now, eyes looking up in ecstasy, embracing herself. And then she'd tell her about his stunning ketch the *Tiki*. The romance of sailing through the islands had infected her soul. 'I want to be kissed like that,' she'd continue, her eyes misting at the memory. Mother was such a romantic. Pity men never lived up to her expectations. Jill had seen enough of the blokes Mother went out with to adopt a healthy cynicism.

She recalled her coach trip to Europe: image after image of amazing buildings and artworks to take her breath away. Yet the attraction of Mother's islands had been subtle. They became her specialty once she'd begun history studies.

When she arrived at the tutorial room Jill expected the usual array of students lounging around the table. Instead they were animated, chatting noisily and she overheard the words 'body' and 'murdered'.

'Have you heard, Jill?' asked Liam, his dark eyes intent.

She nodded.

'Someone saw you near the tape. Said you fell down.'

Her face beaded with sweat.

'Did you see the body?'

'I heard you found the murder weapon.'

'Okay, enough,' she said. 'It's terrible but we're not going to spend the hour speculating. We've got work to do.'

Liam leaned back in his chair clasping his hands across a black T-shirt. His top hat was propped askew on his scruffy backpack. A black coat with tails hung over a vacant chair. He ponced around campus with the air of a nineteenth century scholar. Only a psychology major could get away with that. The others took his lead, relaxing as well. A pleasant group, most did their preparatory reading. One student began texting on her mobile.

'Turn that off.' Jill's voice was sharp.

The girl swished her burgundy hair, turning her face away. 'Only checking where Madeline was,' she mumbled.

With some concern, Jill realised Katie was missing as well. 'They're running late. Most likely still in the library reading up on today's topic.'

The discussion focussed on the differences between Melanesians and Polynesians. Most students were entranced with the early accounts of sailors arriving in Tahiti especially the beauty of the women and their idea of free love. After months at sea the men couldn't believe their luck. But the Melanesians on island groups in the South Pacific north east of Australia had been far less welcoming. The darker skin, frizzy hair and fear of strangers meant a different experience for new-comers altogether.

They'd gained some valuable insights from the primary documents. The slant was often changed slightly in the many books written later. The former encouraged students to think like those early sailors dis-covering the islands, encountering cultures radically different from any-thing in Europe. Jill checked the students' progress with their research topic. Each had a four thousand-word essay to hand in before the end of semester. With up to thirty sources to read to get a comprehensive understanding of the issue, they had to be organised. Some students just couldn't plan their work. She was always disgusted by last minute efforts, obviously scrawled the night before the deadline.

Deliberately, Jill took a path back to her office that avoided the crime scene. The rest of the afternoon was taken up with administrative tasks. On her way home she noticed the heat was less oppressive. She planned to cool down on the lounge escaping into a novel. If that didn't work a few wines with dinner would take the edge off the day's horror.

Jill woke early next morning and walked to the nearby service station for a paper and milk. GIRL MURDERED AT UNI was emblazoned across the front page of the newspaper.

Over breakfast she read the scant details the police had released. The girl's death had been brutal, mutilation was mentioned. The body had been there three days. The name would not be released until fam-ily members had been notified. This would instil fear in all the girls at Phillips University. Until now, Jill had felt perfectly safe on campus.

Today, pulling in to park, she realised her new workplace seemed dif-ferent. She knew nothing of violent crime except through newspapers. Duncan Mitchell sidled up as she waited for the lift. Thankfully, he kept his hands to himself.

'Jill, are you okay after yesterday? Terrible happenings.'

She nodded, not wanting a detailed reminder.

'Oh, a detective's in your office. Everyone's being questioned.' He sauntered off as the doors whooshed open.

The detective was slouched in a chair, whistling softly, peering down into the car park. He rose to introduce himself, displaying his ID. Jill tried to cover her nervousness by placing files neatly on the desk.

'You know about the murder, Ms Ashworth?'

'Only from passing the scene yesterday and this morning's paper.'

He rolled the chair over as if remembering this was her office. 'Here. You sit. I've a few routine questions to help our inquiry.'

Detective Sanderson perched on the desk edge, notebook ready. 'I believe you saw the scalpel.'

He could see her discomfort and gave a reassuring smile.

'Was that the murder weapon? The paper mentioned mutilation.'

'No, Ms Ashworth. The victim was strangled. That scalpel may have been used on the body. We're waiting on DNA tests.'

'What was it used for?'

'To cut away the pudendum,' he replied.

'The what?'

'Exterior of the girl's genitals. All the flesh with the pubic hair has gone. We're dealing with a pretty sick killer, Ms Ashworth.'

Jill must have gone white for he put his hand out in case she fainted.

'Sorry,' she murmured, 'I keep overreacting.'

'My mistake. I shouldn't have gone into that much detail.' He glanced around at the books as if imagining a totally sheltered existence. 'Details leaked out could hamper our inquiry. We're focussing on Medical Science students first as they have easy access to scalpels. You have one, a Madeline Harper in your Pacific History course.'

'Yes.' She replied.

'I believe on Thursdays she catches up with her friend Katie Foster, who was absent yesterday?'

'Oh,' Jill gasped, 'You don't think ... Both didn't come to class.'

'We haven't made a formal identification yet,' he said, 'but Katie's not answering her mobile. She lives on campus and no one's seen her since Monday. Madeline fears the worst.'

The detective stood up and presented his card.

'I'll be back as soon as we know the victim's ID. In the meantime if you think of anything useful about the girls, who they mixed with, call me. And Ms Ashworth,' his fingers squeezed his lips together momentarily, 'do not discuss case details with anyone.'

'I can be discreet, Detective,' Jill's curt tone surprised him.

He smiled. 'Call me Gary. I've not had dealings with university lecturers before so bear with me.'

His amiable manner softened her response. 'Okay, Gary. I'll help any way I can. The whole campus is reeling over this murder.'

When Gary left, the office felt empty and somehow less safe. She scanned over scenes from yesterday: the shadowy culvert, a blood-smeared scalpel and almost fainting. Katie and Madeline's absence at the tutorial had been a mere annoyance at the time. The girls usually came in late, boisterous and chatty, avoiding Liam's disapproving looks. They'd only attended three weeks of classes. It wasn't as if she knew them well. Perhaps Jill could remember something of note. Being involved meant she had to do something to help. Her fingers flew over the keyboard as ideas came to mind.

Then she really had to work: two lectures, a tutorial and a mountain of research. That afternoon she received an email from the Chancellor forwarded to all staff advising everyone to assist with the police inquiry. It ended with a warning to students and staff to be more vigilant with regard to safety.

Before leaving Jill printed out the statement about Katie: the little she knew of her interaction with other students in the tutorial especially Madeline. Jill mentioned Katie's dislike of Liam. In his weird attire he stood out as strange. He appeared relaxed then any small incident would send him into a sulky silence. Jill felt guilty pointing the finger at Liam as she liked him.

A policewoman was alone at the station. To Jill's surprise, she said, 'Gary, the charmer, is not here. But he'll be in touch.'

Embarrassed, she left the statement. Heading home to a Friday evening alone and nothing planned made her aware of holes in her life. Gary's message on the phone was brief. Jill couldn't believe what he'd suggested. She'd have to give it consideration over the weekend.

Jill had a restless night. The scant details of the murder kept intruding into her thoughts. Did she know anything about Katie to help find the killer? She was young and blonde with a flirtatious manner. Madeline was too but her sharp intelligence made her appear streetwise.

Thrashing over this wasn't helping. Unable to relax in bed Jill made tea and toast, taking it to the balcony. She shivered in the cool morning air. The sun, barely risen, revealed the hail-damaged foliage in the court-yard garden. She almost decided on a day at home. If she kept putting it off she'd never discover Sydney. Today Jill needed a greater distraction than gardening.

A hot pink one piece was her sole swimwear. She covered it with black three-quarter length pants and a rose T-shirt. After packing a beach bag with towel, shade and water bottle, Jill was on the road by ten. Saturday morning was chaotic as she drove past the towering glass and chrome shopfronts of Neutral Bay. She found the turn off to Balmoral and headed down Awaba Street.

The harbour shimmered. All the homes round here had views to die for. A massive cliff to the north shielded the harbour's entrance. Waves created a white froth at its base. A green and yellow ferry plied its way between a myriad of yachts.

Along the waterfront Jill was lucky to find a car pulling out and secured a spot and paid for parking. Bag in hand, she breathed in the fresh salty air. It did her good. With extra zest in her step she headed for the sand. Time to explore after a swim. A month into autumn meant the opportunity would soon disappear. She sunbaked for a while, enjoying the warmth on her skin. Jill tried relaxing to the rhythmic sounds of water. The netting of part of the beach allayed her fear of sharks. The water was chilly so she swam along the shoreline, lifted occasionally by tiny swells. This inner harbour beach suited her better than raging surfs. Gentle pleasure was more attractive than struggling for survival.

Tingling after exercise, she lazed in the sun until hunger pangs drew her to the nearby café. The yellow stone building with fret worked win-dows was the old Bathers Pavilion. Jill walked through one of the tall doors swivelled open and sat in a cane armchair. The atmosphere was busy cosmopolitan: young couples, mums squeezed in with prams and elegant Mosman ladies. She was used to doing cafés solo but always had a book handy.

A waitress wearing a long black apron tied below her tanned midriff took the order; a focaccia with Mediterranean vegetables and a latte. Lunch was tasty, giving her the stamina for more exploring. Jill had seen a stone bridge leading to an island but decided to save it for last. She wandered over to the rotunda supported by a circle of columns and imagined an orchestra playing there in earlier days. Crimson rose petals carpeted the steps, signs of a wedding. A short distance away was a plaque on a sandstone plinth naming the beach as Edwards Beach. A retired whaling captain had built a stone house here in 1839. Then she came across the statue of Billy, a dog that frequented the park for many years. Balmoral had a quirky sense of history that appealed to her.

Continuing along the promenade amongst the melee of people, Jill meandered as far as the jetty before turning back. Sounds of halyards jangling on masts showed the breeze had freshened. Childish squeals came from those playing on the beach. Seagulls swirled above. Lazy days like this were a tonic for the soul.

She crossed the stone bridge at dusk. A few couples were lying out on flat rocks or on the grass under the gums. The sandy path crunched under foot as she followed a track. Jill heard a soft foot tread behind her. She jumped. Instantly, images of attackers surfaced. She spun around.

'Sorry,' the young man said, jogging by.

He knew he'd scared her. Heart racing, she headed straight for the car. Her mind was back with the murder. In a dreadful moment, all the day's restoration vanished.

SIX

Autopsy is precise work. Detective Sanderson had observed many where the remains gradually revealed how lives had ended in violent ways. The skin of this girl's face was almost translucent, her pert nose and full lips undamaged, slight compensation for the parents who'd soon be identifying her.

Doctor Hazelton's monotone voice resonated behind his Perspex mask as a lapel microphone recorded each detailed step and his findings. This last-stop medico was a daunting sight; greying beard and sunken eyes gave him an air of highly developed detachment. His long white apron, already smeared with bodily fluids, emphasised his excessive height.

Ruggeri was leaning against the adjacent table, fingers tapping on the stainless steel. His dark looks often matched his mood and Sanderson felt no need for communication.

After the torso incision, Hazelton snipped the ribs allowing access to the organs. A glistening liver slipped from his gloved hands onto the stainless steel scales. Next came the heart.

'Weight above normal range.' Hazelton noted. A blue marker pen squeaked as he jotted the result on a whiteboard. 'Also strange discolouration. Further examination required. Possible congenital heart disease.'

Behind the pathologist, a technician sampled and sliced parts of the brain's intricate folds.

Sanderson glanced up letting his mind wander. Had the young woman been raped? Was semen present? Could he get the DNA of the killer? The swabs and fingernail scrapings would have gone off to the laboratory before the body was cleaned. He hoped they'd got rid of the maggots too. Keeping a body in the freezer overnight would kill them. Hazelton had spent time on the throat lacerations. The ligature, he believed, was braided nylon like the ropes used for water skiing. Sanderson put that in his notes.

He was impatient for the scrutiny of the genital area. If sexual intercourse had taken place perhaps a pubic hair of the attacker was present. He couldn't fast track the process just to get evidence. This body held clues to the moment of death. Waiting for an orderly examination was a necessary evil. The Coroner, too, had to be satisfied by a full report. Sanderson's gaze strayed to the other four bodies covered in white sheets. The nearest had feet splayed outward, a toe tag dangling a printed name. He glanced at the door wondering if Fyurk was coming back in, when his mobile rang.

'Sanderson speaking,' he said. Madeline Harper was so distressed it took him some minutes to make the connection. Between sobs she babbled about drinking at a bar on campus last night. Katie hadn't turned up. She'd spoken to the boy who'd found the body. He'd mentioned a pink top and a silver ring. They'd both bought rings last week. Then she'd seen Jill Ashworth and realised Katie had missed her lecture as well. 'I got your number and came to Katie's room at the college.' Her voice almost broke but he heard, 'She's not here. Her bed's not been slept in. I think it's Katie.'

'Listen, Madeline. Stay where you are, give me directions and I'll get there as soon as I can. Okay.' Sanderson turned to the doctor. 'Sorry Hazo, got to go. Could be the break on her identity.' He nodded to Ruggeri.

His offsider was sitting outside, head in his hands.

'C'mon, Richard. Got a lead.'

They were in his car in double quick time. Sanderson turned back onto Parramatta Road, sped past the ultra-modern building he'd just left. After the gloomy room of bodies its caramel and ochre coloured walls were bright in the morning sunshine. He shot down Harris Street to get back over the Harbour Bridge. On the highway north to the university he felt he'd make an effort with Fyurk.

'What's with this vomiting?'

'I'll be all right,' Richard snapped.

Despite his lanky frame, Fyurk slumped towards the passenger door.

'Not everyone in this business has a cast-iron stomach.'

Fyurk didn't answer.

'I suggest you go observe a few demo autopsies. Behind the glass you don't get the smells. Get used to seeing what they do. Put some eucalyptus oil in your nose. That'll smother those obnoxious smells. Then go back into the main room.'

'Righto, I'll do that.'

Sanderson weaved past several trucks hogging the outside lane.

'And while I'm on it. Your clothes. When you're around bodies, particularly where decomposition has set in, the smell gets into the fabric. Your hair too. Lemon scented shampoo is the go.'

'I guess that's obvious.' Fyurk sat up straighter as if paying attention.

'Well, Richard, you need to change your clothes. When I've been at a crime scene like yesterday I wash mine as soon as I get in. My pants go to the dry cleaners.'

'Dad and I don't do the washing till the weekend. With him driving buses and me running around it's too hectic.'

'So you're still living at home?' Sanderson asked.

'Yeah, Ryde.'

'And Mum? She shoot through?'

'She was killed.'

Sanderson detected a tightening in Fyurk's voice betraying emotion.

'Killed? When was that?'

'Eighteen years ago. I was at primary school. Called out of class when they found her.'

Sanderson waited for him to continue.

'She was a teller in a bank. Taken hostage after a robbery. She tried to escape and they killed her.'

'Bloody tough on a kid.'

Fyurk stared ahead. His voice faltered. 'You're right there. It hit Dad hard too.' He composed himself. 'But we've done okay.'

Sanderson turned up the police radio. He'd just had the longest conversation ever with his offsider. Finding this much out put a few things in place. The sloppy dressing. No mum from a young age. And he seemed a touch squeamish for a detective. But he had determination. He's out there to get the bad bastards who put his mum away. Strange how an occupation is picked for you, he mused. And he just wanted to be seen as tough.

Turning into the university he flashed his badge at the gateman. A road skirted around the central core of buildings before he saw the sign for the residential colleges. Beyond a screening of trees the concrete high rises appeared. Sanderson checked the name Madeline had given him. Once out of the lift they strode down a dim corridor till they found a door ajar.

Curled in a foetal position on a narrow single bed was their caller. Amidst a crumple of blonde hair he saw her face as she heard them. Tears had smeared her mascara. She sat up. Sanderson showed his badge. Fyurk hovered behind.

'Thank God, you're here.'

She was shaking.

'Madeline, you'll be okay.' Sanderson patted her shoulder. The gesture released the floodgates and she babbled again.

'Hey, slow down,' he said.

'But I keep thinking about Katie and I ...' she broke into sobs.

Fyurk plonked himself beside her on the bed and leaned back against the wall. He began to ask simple questions about her friend and succeeded in distracting Madeline. Sanderson took notes and within ten minutes felt a call to Katie Foster's parents warranted. They lived at Nowra on the coast south of Sydney several hours drive away.

'I'll meet you at the Department of Forensic Medicine. It's on the main road so park in the street behind. See you around noon, Mr Foster.' Sanderson concluded.

He glanced back at his offsider. The formerly distraught Madeline was now at ease. Good one, Richard, he thought. Must remember to use this technique again. It gave him time to observe and gather useful information. If Katie was the victim, Sanderson wasn't hopeful this sparse student accommodation would reveal much.

The doona cover was a dark olive brightened by pink and purple cushions. Ornate and sequinned, they could be bought in any homeware store. A basin, with a mirror above took up one corner. In the other were a desk, computer, texts and notebooks. Bluetacked to the wall was a poster of the Britpop band Supergrass.

Sanderson noticed a family photo on a bedside table near the window. A gathering of Granny, Mum, Dad, Katie, brother and a black labrador. The girl's features were instantly recognisable as those he'd seen on the slab at the morgue. Madeline watched him examine the image, a questioning look on her face.

He nodded. Slow tears ran down her cheeks. She remained calm. Fyurk made a move and pulled the girl to her feet. 'Was Katie in any kind of trouble recently?'

'Not that I know.'

'Go home,' Sanderson said. 'I'll be in touch later. You had a key?'

Madeline retrieved one from her jeans pocket, handing it over.

'Any others have one?'

'Don't think so, Detective.'

They left the room, Sanderson locking the door. Fyurk saw Madeline to her car. The senior detective was studying the campus map when his offsider joined him.

'Bloody shame losing a new friend like that. Nice girl, Madeline.'

'Sure is. You handled the situation well, Rich.'

Fyurk's face brightened. He tucked in his shirt. 'Do we head back to the morgue, Gary?'

'Not yet. We'll go look at the lecture theatre near the gymnasium while we're here. And there's a few staff members I want to interview.'

They drove back out the main entrance and along a side road. Once there, they walked inside and Sanderson peered through a glass panel, seeing tiers of seated students busy note taking. The lecturer, absorbed in his spiel, didn't notice them. Outside a path led past tennis courts joining another where the attack had probably taken place. Looking towards the tree-filled gully Sanderson was quiet as if mentally re-enacting the crime.

'C'mon Fyurk. Why would a girl be walking back there on her own in the dark?'

'Night lectures are often for part-timers so they'd have cars. Some may go to the gym. Late night pumping iron wouldn't be unusual here.' The younger man took the map. 'My guess is she got talking to someone so few walkers were left. She must have been heading for the library.'

'Fair enough. Let's see what the staff has to offer.'

An hour later they were back at the office. Janine came straight for Sanderson proffering a note.

'What's this Janine? Your phone number at last.' He flashed a grin at his offsider.

'I'm afraid not, Gary. Looks like you'll be busy tonight. Cyndi Steele wants to meet up with you.' She flounced down the corridor.

'Cyndi Steele,' repeated Fyurk, 'isn't that the call girl we found with that dead bloke some weeks ago?'

'Yeah, wasn't she a stunner?'

'What does she want to see you for?' Fyurk's face showed distaste.

'Who cares.' Sanderson swivelled his hips suggestively. 'Richard, I don't know your sexual preferences but ladies like Cyndi know how to make a man's night. This is one date I'm going to keep.'

'Let's hope you don't end up dead.' Fyurk shrugged his shoulders.

Sanderson winked. His smile widened as he patted the weapon in his shoulder holster.

SEVEN

When Barbara woke the house was strangely quiet. Unsettled sleep waiting to hear Madeline come in left her with a foggy head. Teenagers' peak hours were when most people slept. She hoped her daughter wasn't being carried away with the social side of university life.

A glance at the clock showed she had an hour to make it to work. Barbara checked for activity in the kitchen. Hugh had gone leaving his breakfast dishes in the sink. She strode into Madeline's room. The usual mess assaulted her. A hastily pulled up doona and yesterday's top tossed on the floor showed her daughter had been home. Barbara wasn't aware of an early lecture today.

On her way back to the kitchen she noticed Beau on the balcony, his tiny tail wagging. She let him in. Sounds of his claws on the timber floor followed her. Damn, she thought, no time for a real coffee. Barbara ate toast and tidied up. At least Madeline's dinner plate was in the dishwasher. She'd have to remind Hugh of the machine's use. If he mastered medicine, stacking a dishwasher couldn't be hard.

'Morning, Barbara,' Bronwyn's chirpy voice welcomed her to work.

She replied, checking the list for the day. Thinking of patients in terms of their complaints had become the norm. Her colleague was off to deal with a recurring back injury.

Barbara massaged her knobbly fingers wincing in pain. Seven years earlier her hands had betrayed her. Arthritis forced her into a less hands-on role and part-time hours. Pain shot up her fingers as she applied pressure during massages. A physio with a valuable background in rehabilitation, she was not prepared to leave her career behind. Fortunately, the hospital cooperated. Barbara now assisted in administrating the department and could use her experience advising the younger physiotherapists. She updated some records on her computer while planning a detour to a nearby café for a long black on the way home. During the afternoon Barbara found herself humming a familiar tune. Work always cheered her up.

An unexpected bonus was more time to herself despite the lower income hindering her shopping habit. Buying was an art in her estimation. Wandering through glitzy centres it was easy to find items she simply must have. Homewares, clothing and shoes to die for were her main extravagances. Occasionally, she'd steal off to a gallery to buy a painting. Hugh complained they'd run out of wall space.

She battled the Friday afternoon shoppers in the supermarket. Her daughter's bubble Mazda was parked in the street outside their home. Laden with shopping bags, she deposited them in the kitchen.

'Maddy,' she called, receiving no answer.

The bedroom door was shut. Barbara opened it to see Madeline asleep on the crumpled doona. Beau had been curled up with her. He bounced off the bed causing the figure to stir. Her daughter's face was puffy, her eyes reddened as if she'd been crying. Madeline slumped back, totally disheartened.

'Maddy, what's wrong?'

'Katie's dead.' Her daughter sobbed.

'Katie, your new friend?' Barbara recalled the blonde teenager with the bubbly personality. Last Sunday she had stayed for a barbecue lunch before the girls went to the movies.

'Murdered.' Madeline sniffed and wiped her eyes with a tissue. 'The detective came to her room on campus this morning while I was there.'

Barbara reeled in shock. Confusion flooded her face. How could something like that happen? Her poor darling.

'Maddy, what's all this about?' Barbara sat on the bed drawing her daughter into her arms. 'Now tell me from the beginning.'

Madeline's jumbled words conveyed the horror at the university. How could a place of learning become a murder scene? And what if ... Barbara held her daughter as dread filtered into every fibre of her being.

Deliberately calming her rapid breathing, while her mind raced, Barbara forced herself not to think it could have been Maddy. Her daughter pulled away, propping herself on pillows.

'What about Katie's parents? Is there anything we can do to help?' Barbara asked.

'They're driving from Nowra. Meeting the detective at the morgue. I don't think we can do much, Mum.'

'Is there anything you want?'

Madeline shook her head.

In the kitchen Barbara sought comfort. Cellophane crinkled as she tore open a packet of melting moments. She devoured two while making a strong coffee. The sugary sweetness brought its usual surge of satisfaction. She had to focus on the here and now not what could have been. Keeping her mind active quelled the fear of losing Madeline. She wondered how Katie's parents would handle identifying their precious daughter.

Hugh, in his manner, would have been strong. He was used to guiding people through sudden upheavals.

'It's just a fact of life' he'd say with his look of calm acceptance when he told her of a patient's cancer diagnosis. And the calls at home would come as he helped them through their passage to death. But this situation was entirely different. A quick savage cessation of life. How would this affect Madeline?

Barbara packed away the shopping while waiting for her husband to come home. He would cope with the crisis. She remembered the hospital where he'd first noticed her. Barbara, tanned from the European summer, brought abundant energy into the physio department. Then thirty-two, she realised most of the men she'd been attracted to overseas were drifters. After many dalliances of the body she'd been pleasantly surprised by Hugh's intellectual appeal. He loved her colourful outfits and absorbed her appreciation of the Continent's art and culture.

When Hugh came in she kept the story to the facts. Pouring himself a wine, he said, 'These things happen. Don't assume it could have been Madeline. What's the point of worrying what could have been?' Barbara, relaxed by his sensible approach, diced vegetables for a stir-fry while he went to check on their daughter.

For once Hugh missed the TV news. Barbara could hear their voices in Madeline's room. Her husband had always been better dealing with their daughter when she was upset. He used his 'patient' voice reasoning with her until she could see beyond her temperamental stance.

'Hugh, Maddy. Dinner's ready.' Tonight Barbara had not set the table preferring to eat while watching TV. This would avoid further discussion of the murder. Hugh had changed his clothes and Maddy's face was free of make-up when they came. During the ads Barbara prattled on about the building progress but Hugh gave her a look. Feigning a headache, she decided to retire early.

'Night, Maddy. See you in the morning.'

'Oh, I'm going to breakfast in Manly with the girls.'

'Okay, darling.'

'Night, Barbs. I'm off to golf early. Don't forget dinner with the Rivers tomorrow night.'

'I haven't forgotten, Hugh.' Barbara watched Beau curl up again at Maddy's feet.

She slept better knowing Maddy was home. The morning sparkled, drawing Barbara out onto the balcony. Beau followed her inside. Sun streamed in as she ate breakfast. On impulse she planned a swim at the beach pool. She had to drop the tile samples back first.

Barbara tracked down the same young woman who had served her before.

'These are fabulous. Could you jot the details for the builder, please?'

'Sure, madam.' The assistant placed the samples next to a similar one in grey. Barbara's face lit up. She loved these porcelain tiles with their glossy sheen. They had none of the problems of marble and were within her budget.

'Add the grey one too,' she said, 'it's perfect for the guest toilet.' Then she spied a shiny black border and smiled. Another room fixed. Now all she needed was a vanity unit and mirror. Things were dropping into place. Not that she had anyone to share her interest. Her family and friends would admire her taste when the house was finished.

In Newport Barbara pulled up at the bread shop for a cheese and bacon roll. She'd need a decent snack before her swim. Nearby, a home-ware shop caught her eye. The temptation to browse and imagine articles in her new home was too much. A Balinese influence dominated: statues, elaborate cushions and bamboo ladders to drape scarves and bags on. This was not the style she envisaged so she just bought two expensive stainless steel coffee cups. Avanti, made in Italy. They kept the heat in. She'd explain to Hugh they were essential since she had her own machine.

One end of Bilgola Beach was carpeted with kelp giving off an unpleasant odour. As she parked, Barbara hoped the pool was clean. Wending her way through shrieking children she found a spot to leave her clothes and towel. The water was a pleasing temperature as she breaststroked her first length. By the second she was heaving for breath and gave up. She was happy to leave the noisy pool behind.

During the journey home she became despondent. How could she be so unfit? All her life she'd worked with the body, taking her own healthy functioning for granted. In just a couple of years her arthritis medication and the onset of menopause had brought a plumpness she despised.

Cleaning chores took up the remainder of her afternoon at home. She played rock 'n' roll to boost her energy. Hugh walked in the door; his face flushed from one too many drinks at the nineteenth hole. She'd be driving them to dinner.

'Hugh, you'll be pleased to hear I had a swim today.'

'Good. How many laps?'

Barbara smiled. 'Only a couple.'

'That won't do you much good.'

'Thanks for the support, dear. I suppose you had a pleasant round of golf.' She left the room before an altercation developed.

Madeline had been working on an essay before she emerged from her room ready to go out. Barbara could see flashes of skin between her top and jeans.

'Maddy, couldn't you wear a jacket or something?'

'Mum, I'm only going to the pub.' The impatient adolescent shook her head.

'All right, Maddy, have it your own way. But please be careful.' Barbara went to shower. She'd order something outlandish and expensive at the restaurant tonight.

EIGHT

'Ah,' Sanderson sipped the strong brew, glancing around the dingy incident room. He preferred his light-filled office. The rest of the team would soon be with them and no doubt looking for direction.

Fyurk reached for his mug of coffee amongst the clutter on the desk.

'We've two hours before meeting Katie's parents. Wonder if Reeves and Abbot found anything in Katie's room. C'mon, Rich, let's see what we've got.'

They immersed themselves in the paperwork. The kids' signed statements weren't much help. Sanderson flipped through the crime scene photos then checked what reports had come in from the SOCOs team. An email from Dr Levy estimated time of death; most probably Tuesday evening. Flies rest at night but would have found the body early on Wednesday morning, as it was hot. Some maggots he collected had developed three slits, which took about thirty hours. Levy was certain it was less than five days as no beetles were present. Sanderson knew the creatures he'd seen in the girl's mouth fed on the soft protein rich parts of the body, leaving the drier bone, hair and skin for insects arriving later.

'Here, Rich, see what our bug man has to say.'

Fyurk perused the report. 'Quite useful even if it is a gory task collecting maggots. I did read up on Forensic Entomology during my course, Gary. I do understand that particular insects on or around the body arrive in a predictable order.'

'So, you were a good student?'

'All right.' Fyurk focussed on the photo depicting the genital mutilation.

'You ever dealt with a signature killing before?' asked Sanderson.

'Only scenarios from past cases in training. Specialists in sexual homicide behaviour like Ressler in the US are the gun guys in this area. I'll look up some references over the weekend.'

'Good, it helps to understand how these whackos think.' Sanderson finished his coffee. 'We'll have the interim report from the post mortem on Monday. I hope our killer's not too forensically aware and has left us some of his DNA. Maybe some rapist has just got out of clink. He's escalated to murder. His scalpel work doesn't look too proficient.'

Fyurk acknowledged this reasoning, moving over to the whiteboard, making several additions. Sanderson felt encouraged by his offsider's actions. He'd seen how Fyurk gained information from people this morning and now he was thinking through the case. Perhaps the boy would be an asset not the dill Ralston figured. He made a note of several things to follow up. Sanderson could imagine Ralston's puffy face asking exasperating questions at Monday's meeting.

Jill Ashworth's statement was of most interest. She'd found Katie and Madeline chatty but pleasant. Katie was studying journalism and lived on campus; Madeline's major was health sciences. If she performed well she'd transfer to Medicine at Sydney University to be a doctor like her father. The history course was just an interest. The girls got on well with all the others in the tutorial except for Liam, an eccentric psychology student. Jill noted he also lived on campus and left details how he could be contacted. She concluded he was a likeable boy but intolerant with giggly girls.

Good one, Jill, Sanderson thought, any lead's useful. He conjured an image of the lecturer he'd seen briefly. Wary, blonde and mildly attractive, she gave the impression of not making the best of herself. He had no idea what academic women were about. Did they all hide behind ordinary clothes? Perhaps they led a sheltered existence in universities, buried in books, dealing only with students.

Sanderson broke his reverie to examine Fyurk's scribblings. He pointed at gardener listed under persons of interest. 'Who's that?'

'Oh, I met Bob when I was going through the bins. Nice bloke. Gave him your card. Told him to let you know if he found anything unusual round the grounds.'

'Umm,' Sanderson rubbed his chin, 'Might track him down when we talk to Liam this afternoon.'

'Liam?'

'The psych student in Katie's tutorial. They didn't get on.' Sanderson gathered the running sheets and the reports in a bundle. He compared Fyurk's photos with the official crime scene ones. Fyurk's had notations of camera type, film ASA even the f-stop used. His offsider had taken shots from both sides of the pipe looking up then down from the pathway. The photos of the body were well detailed too with close ups of the neck and pubic injuries.

'I'm impressed, Rich. Make sure Janine types these notes and they're attached to the photos. We'll put them up on a board for Monday's meeting.'

'Thanks, Gary. You think mine are good enough for court?' Fyurk bent his lanky frame to collect the material.

Sanderson nodded. 'Photography an interest of yours?'

'Yeah, since high school.'

The older detective noted the flare of enthusiasm in the younger one's flecked hazel eyes. His offsider left, closing the door quietly.

Fyurk returned with the latest from missing persons. Most recent was a man with Alzheimer's disappearing in the bush near his nursing home. No one matching Katie's description. Her parents wouldn't be aware she hadn't been in her room on campus.

Sanderson checked Ruggeri's sketches of the crime scene that would go to the Photogrammetry Unit. Thanks to their stereo photographs accurate scale plans of the scene would be prepared. Evidence of the Italian's thoroughness boosted his confidence, made him glad he had him on this case.

Senior Constable Reeves' shaved head appeared around the door-frame. Abbott sidled in. Of equal rank, the pair worked well together. Abbott wasn't a talker so Sanderson directed his enquiries at Reeves.

'Nothing,' Sanderson repeated. It took the best part of an hour getting them up to pace then he assigned more duties.

On his and Fyurk's way back across the harbour Sanderson thought of the task ahead. Bloody terrible telling parents they'd lost a child. Perhaps it was one of the reasons he'd never married or had any of his own. As they sped along the freeway curving westward, he glimpsed Darling Harbour with its straggle of tourists. One day he must find time to wander through the Maritime Museum.

Turning off at the Glebe sign, Sanderson soon parked opposite the Department of Forensic Medicine. The insignia was a snake coiled around the scales of justice etched on the glass door. Whatever did that mean? A reptile squeezing for the truth. Fyurk followed like a shadow. He sent him off to check in with Hazelton.

Despite the heat outside, this room with blue walls always seemed subdued. The few chairs facing the counter were empty. Tatty pot plants in cane planters were the solitary attempt to brighten the place. The wall clock showed noon.

A door opened. Angela, the grief counsellor, came towards him. She was a large woman with an expressive friendly face. Just the sort you imagined hugging people.

'Hi, Ange. The Fosters haven't arrived.'

'I'll wait. Good to see you, Gary. So what's on your agenda for the weekend?' Angela tucked a strand of dark hair behind her ear.

Sanderson knew that look. She was hoping to be asked out. Why did he overdo the charm? An image of Cyndi Steele flashed into his mind. No comparison with Angela, the motherly type.

'Big bad detectives are no good for nice women like you, Angela. It'll be full on work anyway.'

She glowed momentarily, as the door opened. The couple were overweight and underdressed; matching tracksuits in a washed-out grey. Mrs Foster looked terrified, the lines on her face taut. Mr Foster's nicotine-stained fingers brought a cigarette to his lips. He inhaled deeply then found a bin.

'Mr and Mrs Foster, I'm Detective Sanderson. This is Angela Kouris, a grief counsellor. She'll stay with you.' Handshakes were exchanged.

'Detective. Angela.' Mr Foster replied.

'Do you both want to do this? One will be sufficient for official identification,' Sanderson said.

Mrs Foster clung to her husband's arm.

'Then I'll get things going.'

Angela led the pair through a door labelled Relatives Waiting.

When he found Fyurk and Hazelton, Katie's covered body was on the trolley beside them, her pretty face serene. Wheels squeaked on rubber tiles as they stopped. The attendant pressed a button on the wall. The curtains covering the window in the waiting room drew back. Sanderson watched the couple peer forward. Mr Foster nodded slightly. His wife's face collapsed, she turned away crying into Angela's arms.

Fyurk had hovered in the background. He seemed shaken.

'The ID's done,' said Sanderson, 'now we have to find out what led to Katie's death. The Victims Support Group will do what they can for the Fosters, Rich. Come on.'

On the drive to the university Fyurk was quiet. Perhaps the morgue scene made him think of losing his mother. Sanderson wished his offsider would lighten up. Jokes and a bit of fun helped in Homicide.

Sanderson was stopped on a red turn arrow when a loud whoosh of a semi's airbrakes filled the car. The huge transport juddered to a halt beside the Commodore. Fyurk glared up at the truckie as their car moved off. Back at the residential colleges they searched for Liam's room. Sanderson knocked. A student in grimy jeans and a red T-shirt opened the door.

'Liam Davidson?'

'No ... er. This is his room. I'm just using his computer. He's gone to the library.'

'Didn't think it was him,' Sanderson told Fyurk on the way out, 'Jill Ashworth said he only wore black and a top hat to boot.'

Fyurk produced a rare smile. 'A top hat. Does he think he's in another century?'

'Who knows? Psychology students are a breed of their own, I believe.'

Sanderson pulled out a campus map, studying their quickest route to the library. They walked over a crossing and along a path. A strong afternoon breeze whipped the branches overhead and sent papers scuttling around the quadrangle. The façade of the library was chunky concrete squares. Students clustered near a bronze statue by the doors.

'Wait here, Rich. I'll see if they'll page Liam.' Sanderson returned. 'We'll give him ten minutes.'

Fyurk looked beyond a row of liquidambars. 'There's the gardener, Gary. I'll just check if he's found anything.'

Sanderson waited, watching the continuous stream of students. He recognised Liam instantly from Jill's description. Weird attire. Did weird behaviour go with it? He walked up to the black-clad figure.

'Liam Davidson?' The top hat moved up and down. 'I'm Detective Sanderson. I've got a few routine questions regarding Katie Foster.'

The boy stiffened and a wary look crossed his pimpled face.

'Okay. What?' said Liam.

'You were in Katie's tutorial. You both live on campus. Is there any-thing you can tell me to indicate why she was murdered?'

'Slut got what's coming to her. But I had nothing to do with it if that's what you're thinking. And I'm not saying any more without a solici-tor present. I know my rights, Detective.' Liam spun on his heels and disappeared back into the library.

Fyurk re-emerged through the trees. 'Any luck, Gary? Oh, Bob con-firmed the bins were emptied on Wednesday.'

'Liam showed but he's not talking. We might put him under surveillance. Surly little creep. Find out where the rubbish went? Maybe our evidence is not yet dozered into oblivion.' Sanderson yawned. 'While we're here I'll just thank Jill for her statement. The history building's five minutes away.' He straightened his tie and ran his fingers through his hair.

'You sure see a lot of women in a day.' Fyurk hurried along beside him.

'Many as I can, Rich.' Sanderson enjoyed winding him up. The walk-way provided cooling shade. Tree and birds nest ferns sprouted green fronds below the paperbarks. A white statue of a woman stopped him. Leaning nonchalantly against a red steel doorframe, she was twice nor-mal size, moulded in plaster, her miniskirt barely covering the top of long legs.

'Why put something like that in a garden?' Fyurk shook his head.

'Art, boy. She certainly got my attention. Fancy dealing with a woman that big. The silent type more to your liking, Rich?' Sanderson laughed.

Fyurk gave him a wry look. 'Stop fishing, Gary. I'm not into mixing work and play.'

They had reached the high rise.

'Well, you wait here then. Jill's a little nervy round cops.'

Sanderson knocked lightly.

'Come in.'

Jill rose from her desk. 'Ah, Detective.'

Her hair was caught back in a knot.

'Jill, just a quick thank you call for your statement. Saw Liam. Not the most cooperative lad.'

'Oh, I find him eager to help.'

'Not everyone wants to assist the police though, Jill.'

She sat on the edge of the desk. 'But I do, Detective. The sooner this thing's over the better.'

He detected a flash of fear in her eyes. Something made him want to allay that; to convince her not all men were fearful. Hard in his business. The majority of homicides were perpetrated by his gender. Sanderson decided to keep her involved.

'There is something. Liam's suspicious. Do you think you could surreptitiously get a hair of his?'

'I'll certainly try, Detective.'

'Gary.' He winked at her and left.

At home he watered his bonsai then took off for a run in Centennial Park to clear his head. He'd be up half the night working. Hot and sweaty on his return, he shaved and showered. He patted on a touch of the CK cologne his last girlfriend had given him. Babes must like it. Cyndi, being in the business, shouldn't be too fussy.

Sanderson dressed in his best jeans, a yellow shirt and a black zippered jacket. Downstairs, he put on an Emma Pask CD. Her voice was smooth. He liked the sensuality of jazz. Pouring a Scotch, ice cubes clinked in the glass. His stomach wanted food. He hadn't eaten since the hamburger on the way home. After Cyndi, he thought.

The evening air was pleasant as he walked to the pub in Woolloomooloo. A fringe of iron lace hung from the awnings and its yellow exterior was tiled in the manner of old hotels. He arrived at ten. The place hadn't started thumping. But she was there. Cyndi walked towards him in a figure-hugging black dress. Red strappy stilettos matched the colour of her lipstick. She was a looker, all right. He'd pondered her previous predicament on the walk over. Being found with a dead client was not good. Still, she'd rung the cops. After investigating, they'd found his death wasn't suspicious. He'd just had too much excitement.

This woman had fucked a man to death. What a way to go.

'Gary. Thanks for your help last week.' Cyndi smiled and ran a red nailed finger over his lips. The gesture was a deliberate turn on. And it worked.

'Glad to help. Sorry to keep you waiting, babe.'

She had a chardonnay, he another Scotch. He followed her to an upstairs room where a solitary lamp scattered light over the Spartan interior. Cyndi put her glass on the table and slipped out of the dress.

Wow, he thought, this woman knows her lingerie. A black lacy suspender belt partly concealed crimson panties. A matching bra barely constrained honey coloured breasts. Sanderson stepped out of his jeans and jocks.

'Let's feel the man you are,' she said. Her smile was wicked.

'You're every detective's dream, Cyndi.'

She liked him playing along. He pulled her toward him by her hips and they kissed, slow and exploring at first. Cyndi slid her hands up under his shirt and felt the restraint of his shoulder holster.

'Oh. I like a man with a weapon,' she murmured.

'And you're just the woman to disarm him.' His tone was jovial.

Cyndi giggled. He felt her slide a condom over his erection. Her mouth followed and he revelled in the sensation. She stood, grabbed a chair and raised a high heel onto its seat. She parted the red lace of her crotch-less panties. He could see only a strip of pubic hair. Brazilian, he thought? Her red-nailed fingers became busy arousing herself.

Needing no further encouragement, Sanderson moved in.

NINE

The message light blinked on the phone. Mother's anxious voice: 'Jill, darling are you all right? I didn't hear till this morning. Murder at your university. I can't believe it. Ring me as soon as you get in. As if I didn't have enough to worry about. Bye now.'

Jill couldn't handle Mother's histrionics at that moment. After dinner, she told herself. Draping a beach towel over the balcony chair, she made for the shower. Water sluiced the crusty salt from her skin. Splatters of foam surrounded her feet as she shampooed her hair.

Famished, she padded into the kitchen barefoot. A search of the fridge did not inspire her. A flyer for a local Chinese restaurant was here somewhere. She located it amongst the sections of *The Sydney Morning Herald*. Home delivery was advertised but Jill didn't want some male casing her home while dropping off a meal.

Five minutes in the car and she found the place. Neon pagodas lit the façade. Jill noticed there were several shops in the strip including a video store. Perfect. A Bridget Jones evening on the lounge appealed. But first, food. Inside, enticing aromas wafted from the kitchen at the back. She ordered honey king prawns, Mongolian lamb and a small fried rice. Far too much food for one meal but she wanted variety. She'd tidy up the leftovers tomorrow. Instead of waiting she went to pick a video. No dramas. The week at university had been way too much. *As Good As It Gets*, a Jack Nicholson movie, caught her eye. He's usually funny. She joined up and took Jack to pick up the takeaway.

Back at home Jill poured a white wine, put on the movie and sat down to eat. She crunched through the prawns savouring their sweet coating. The lamb was spicy, a definite improvement on anything she could whip up in a hurry. Entertained by the twists in the film, she was refilling her glass when the phone rang. She stopped the tape.

'Mother,' Jill said, 'just got in with dinner.' The mass of questions over the murder left her exasperated. Mother made her feel as if she were somehow responsible for the horrible event. Jill changed the subject.

'Made any new friends yet?'

'Not really, Jill. They're mostly widows in dowdy clothes. I wear something colourful and they look down their noses. And the conversations, glorifying their dear departed husbands. Some are such fearful snobs I wonder if I'm in the wrong place.'

Mother's tone became a whine. Jill held the receiver further from her ear.

'Well, Mother, you must give them a chance. Got to go. My Chinese meal's getting cold. I'll keep in touch. Bye.' She hung up before the tirade could start again. The rest of the movie failed to lighten her spirits. Talking with Mother was seldom good. Before she went to sleep she replayed Gary's last visit in her mind. Why did he want her involved? If Liam was a suspect she should be wary.

On Sunday Jill attacked the hail-damaged garden. Secateurs in hand, she snipped off the half torn leaves. A palm frond lay on the lawn. She stuffed it in a garbage bag with the debris. The activity had kept her busy but mentally she still felt uneasy. University work had to go on despite this murder investigation.

Next morning, according to Gary's instructions, she wore an electric blue top that accentuated her breasts. Figure-hugging pants and careful make-up completed the outfit. Her intellectual image could be blown away. Jill often bought racy clothes on holidays but wasn't inclined to wear them when she returned.

Gary insisted the new persona was necessary. Yeah, she thought, he's using her as bait. She'd never met anyone as streetwise as this detective. He really seemed to know people and what to expect of them. He'd quashed all her reservations and somehow Jill trusted his judgement. Or was she just weakened by the sparkle in his deep brown eyes?

As she walked from the university car park the liquidambars atop the grassy banks in front of the building were resplendent in their summer foliage. A melodic call of a currawong made her reluctant to enter the portals of academia. Dressing up made her feel like going somewhere exotic. Jill directed her mind back to the task. Somehow she had to get Liam to her office. Gary would be watching on a television screen from next door. She didn't want to disappoint him; had rehearsed the performance.

Later, on the way to the tutorial she noticed the crime scene tape was still present. There was no sign of police guarding the area. She thought of asking Gary when it could come down. Her stomach tightened. Katie was gone. A chair would be empty again this morning. And Jill was already nervous over Liam's reaction. He would have been questioned by now and must realise she'd been an informant.

She tried to move with confidence threading her way through sauntering students. Handling Liam might not be easy but she had to or else let Gary down. The detective seemed to have more trust in her people skills than she did.

Liam was waiting outside the room. Leaning against the wall, his scowl was as dark as his attire. Role-play, she told herself.

'Okay, Jill, what did you tell that detective?'

Jill was stunned by the malice of his tone. Eventually, she answered, 'Now, Liam. Calm down.'

'Calm down. That bloody D came on to me like I was a suspect.'

'The police need to question everyone they can in a murder case. Something that's seen or heard might be vital in their investigation. I reported on the whole group. Sure I mentioned you were irritated by giggly girls but also that I liked you and found you a valuable student.'

The scowl softened as he thought this through. 'So he wanted my help?'

'Yes.'

'There's plenty of weirdos watching girls on this campus.' He took off his top hat, tapping the crown on the wall behind him.

'Did you tell that to Detective Sanderson?'

'No. He's so smart let him work it out for himself.'

'That's not the right attitude, Liam. Murder is serious. What if he kills again? We've all got to work together to prevent that happening.'

'You really think so, Jill?'

'I know so. Now let's get into class.'

He followed her into the room. Jill felt strong till she saw Madeline's listless face. Three days of grief had taken a toll. She heard an appreciative whistle.

'Wow, look at you. Got a new fella?'

Mark, with the spiky hair, had noticed her new look. They all watched her sit. Avoiding embarrassment, Jill placed her books precisely on the table and looked up at the students. She had to take the lead and get on with their history course.

'The topic we're looking at today is blackbirding. As you know whalers first brought trade goods to the islands north of here. Missionaries followed. Islanders were captured and shipped back to Queensland in the 1860s to work on sugar plantations.'

'But weren't the Melanesians aggressive and wary of strangers?' Liam interjected.

'Yes but these captains were unscrupulous. Imagine a schooner sailing into a lagoon on the island of Lifu, lying between the New Hebrides and New Caledonia. The anchor is dropped and the crew wait for the muscular young men with black, woolly hair to paddle out in their canoes. Each was worth six pounds a head on the Queensland labour market. They entice them below with trade goods and sail away.'

'It's hard to believe they continually got away with it. Have you ever been to any of these islands, Jill?'

'No, Liam.'

'Why not? Isn't it your field of expertise?'

'Good point. I'll consider it.'

The atmosphere in the room improved as the hour progressed. Even Madeline contributed from her research under gentle coaxing. Liam's eyes had flickered across Jill's body many times. She hadn't felt so self-conscious in an aeon. He hadn't noticed her earlier when consumed by anger. When Liam asked if he could talk over the references for his essay she made a time before lunch. He almost bounded out of the room. That was too easy.

Only later when awaiting his knock did she think of being alone with a possible killer. Jill couldn't let him sense her wariness. There were only two ways out of her office: the door and a solitary window four floors up. But the surveillance camera had been installed that morning, easy to conceal when the walls were bookcases sprawling with references and files. She meant to come in to tidy up but hadn't got around to it.

'Come in, Liam. Take a seat.' Jill was glad the desk separated them, as he appeared edgy. 'Now how can I help?'

He opened a folder. 'I'm not going to get through all these references. Could you steer me to the most useful ones?'

She picked up a pen and walked round to his side. 'Sure.' And she leant closer than necessary and marked the appropriate ones. He'd chosen the essay on blackbirding. Perhaps sailing ships and islands had got to him this morning. He breathed in deeply as if absorbing her perfume. She lingered. He became flustered and gathered his notes.

'Th ... thanks,' he murmured.

'Don't worry, Liam. You'll do okay with the essay.' Her hand just touched his shoulder before he left. He became agitated.

Leaning back against the closed door Jill sucked in a breath. She wanted to rush in to Gary. Seek approval. But she had a lecture to give.

That night he called her just as she was getting into bed. The timing was as if he had a camera inside her bedroom.

'Alone?' he said, 'pity.' Was he flirting? She had given Gary no encouragement. But the timbre of his voice echoed in her mind, soft and sensual. Jill couldn't help wondering what he'd be like in more intimate situations, could almost feel the confident touch of his tanned hands. Heat seeped through her only to be instantly chilled by the memory of a fumbling academic's pasty body.

When she walked to the carport next morning a note was under the wiper blade. *Thanks for the help, Liam.* Jill froze. It was all right playing up to him at work. This meant he'd been at her home. She thought they had him under surveillance. Why wasn't she told he was so close? Then Jill remembered she had more to do. Gary had revealed the previous evening they'd found a dark hair on the victim's top. They wanted one of Liam's for a DNA match.

Liam was waiting for her outside the lecture theatre in his regulation black garb.

'Jill, those references were great. I was half the night at the library.'

'I got your note, Liam. You shouldn't have come to my home.' She'd always worried how easy it was for someone to follow you.

He hung his head, dejected. 'But I was so stoked I had to thank you straight away. Can I tell you how my angle's developing on the essay, please?' His appeal was almost childlike and she considered the new agenda.

'Okay, Liam. Let's grab a coffee in the atrium.'

They strolled past the library and down the wide steps. Liam chattered the whole way about cargo cults. Jill could barely hear him as they approached the fountain. Someone had put blue dye in the water. Columns of water surged and fell causing a mass of frothy bubbles. The food court wasn't busy.

'Liam, you get us a table. Cappuccino?'

He nodded; obviously not keen to break his discourse but she needed a breather. Over coffee they discussed his ideas. Jill glanced at her watch. She couldn't spare much longer. Gary's offsider was watching them. He had this unkempt look so was not out of place amongst the generally scruffy students.

'You like living on campus?' Jill asked.

'Not really.' He didn't elaborate. She sensed he was uncomfortable talking about his life.

Then Jill saw it. Her eyes focused on the solitary dark strand on his shoulder barely discernible against the ubiquitous black T-shirt. She reached out as if to groom him. He knocked her hand away brushing at the spot himself.

'What're you doing?' he demanded.

'Sorry, Liam, removing a hair. Habit of mine.'

He'd thrust his chair back noisily and fled through the chatter. She was glad that hadn't been on camera. Jill looked between her fingertips. Nothing. But down on the white tiles was the prize. She placed it in the tiny plastic bag Gary had given her. Mission accomplished. A kick of adrenalin surged through her. Liam was proving unpredictable. What would make him crack? He obviously didn't like being touched. As she left the cafeteria Jill slipped the bag to the assisting detective.

TEN

On Sunday morning Barbara made her usual short black. Seeing the coffee in one of her new stainless steel cups made her feel as if she were in a swanky café. She took it to the deck chair on the balcony where the ocean shimmered blue below. Thunderstorms were forecast so she'd better enjoy the early part of the day.

A pair of lorikeets zipped past, squawking. They settled on the bird feeder causing it to sway. One bird husked and ate the wild birdseed while the other switched its head from one side to the other as if wondering what Barbara was doing there. The brilliance of their feathers, apple green with flashes of orange and purple, delighted her. She almost forgot the bad mood of last night. Leaving Hugh snoring in bed, she needed solitude this morning.

Dinner with the Rivers had been a bore. Hugh's golfing friends didn't have much conversation beyond their common obsession. At one stage she felt like screaming as the talk of pars and birdies continued. Barbara had broken in with details of the new house but no interest ensued. Even happenings at the hospital had brought a rebuke from Hugh. Anything medical was talking shop to him. So she'd ordered lots of seafood and enjoyed the tantalising tastes of the sea instead. Hugh's face was more crinkled than ever with embarrassment when it came to splitting the bill and his attempt to put in more money was rebuffed. On the way home he'd had a go at her.

'Why did you order such expensive seafood?'

'Hugh, darling,' she'd replied sarcastically, 'the price for eating with your golfing cronies.'

'Really, Barbara. You've become such a bitch.'

A stony silence filled the car for the remainder of the trip.

Barbara sipped her coffee, planning how she'd avoid Hugh for the day. At least Madeline wouldn't surface before noon after she'd been out nightclubbing. Her daughter was so touchy since her friend had died, Barbara wondered about counselling. Madeline had known Katie only since the start of the semester so it wasn't too strong a bond. Yet reactions to death varied. If anything, Barbara was the one accused of over-reacting. But there was some whacko murderer on campus.

She wished the family dramas would subside so she could concentrate on the new house. Leaving the chair, she sought out her magazines. Beau was scratching on the back door. Barbara let in her white fluff ball and gave the dog a cuddle. She returned to the balcony with an armful of *Home Beautiful* magazines.

An hour later Hugh emerged dressed in smart shorts and polo shirt. Barbara was surprised, as he'd planned to tidy the garden. Weeks ago he'd had a token clean up to refute her request for a gardener.

'Going to the shops,' he said.

'Oh? No good morning?'

'Barbara, please don't start.'

'All right, Hugh. What about coming to look at stoves for the new kitchen later on?'

His face contorted. 'No, not today.'

'Fine,' she said, 'I'll go myself.'

Her husband left and Barbara's eyes returned to her magazine. But the words and pictures blurred. She ached with disappointment. After her recent health problems she hoped this house project might bring them together again. She'd expected more understanding considering his profession. Perhaps Hugh saved this for his patients. What do they say? A plumber's house is the last to have leaks fixed.

No point moping at home. Half an hour later she opened the garage door. She felt wanted again at the sight of her silvery BMW. Two years earlier this was Hugh's birthday surprise.

Barbara took a sketch of her kitchen layout into the showroom. Bright lights made the satiny finish of the stainless steel appliances glow. Cook tops were first on her agenda. She liked a smaller style as it allowed for more bench space. The Smeg had three gas and one wok burner. The latter was essential with Hugh's fancy for stir-fry. European names impressed everyone. The ovens to match were too small and didn't have a separate grill. They certainly didn't suit the way she cooked. How could you have a roast sizzling away and grill the cheese topping on cauliflower au gratin? Then she came across the double oven. Stunning. Barbara envisaged the separate grill at work with space to warm plates for a dinner party or cook a dessert. It was so practical she ignored the expense. She grabbed a brochure showing its measurements.

Glen had squashed her idea of a kitchen designer and talked her into using his mob. This had pacified Hugh when he'd last ranted about costs. Barbara had worked out what suited her during the planning of the house. The sink was in an island bench facing the view over the lake. An open plan meant she could also watch the news while preparing dinner.

The showroom was relatively quiet for a Sunday. A few couples rattled oven trays and opened dishwashers. When a woman pushing a stroller with a crying baby entered Barbara decided to leave. Hugh had already agreed to a double door stainless steel refrigerator. The icemaker appealed to him. Imagining these shiny new appliances in place gave her a jolt of pleasure. No wonder retail therapy was good for the soul, she thought.

Her trip home was slowed by beach traffic. So many people from beyond the coastal strip came to enjoy the late summer days. Barbara glanced down over Long Reef with its wide green fairways where her husband spent several days a week amusing himself.

In the house a note awaited her: *Mum, gone to the beach, love Maddy.* This was a good sign her daughter's life was more normal. Barbara placed the brochures with her magazines and went to the fridge. While dicing and skewering chicken for the evening barbecue, she scoffed several Tim Tam biscuits. She chided herself for continuing to buy them. They were hidden at the back of the pantry. Over the kebabs she poured a marinade of honey, soy sauce and ginger. She'd make a Caesar salad later.

Hugh came home holding a distinctive black and white David Jones bag. He tried to slink past the kitchen.

'So what've you been buying?' Barbara raised her eyebrows.

Hugh had a guilty look on his face. 'I saw some new jeans. My old ones are hanging off me with the weight I've lost.'

'But Hugh, you never shop for clothes on your own. Show me.'

Reluctantly, he pulled them out. They were black and the designer label screamed expensive.

'Cost a pretty penny. No doubt,' she said.

'Well, you don't hold back in the spending department.' He returned them to the bag. 'By the way I'm going to the Hunter next week. A seminar on Alzheimer's.'

'What a nice break. But Hugh, you know I can't get days off with so little notice.'

'I realise that, Barbara. I'm going alone. It's just a night.'

The Monday drive to the hospital was a relief from the weekend tension at home. The previous evening Hugh avoided any mention of his trip, Madeline evaded the Katie issue and Barbara focused on the preparation of dinner. The aroma of barbecued chicken drew her family. Father and daughter had been engrossed in a medical discussion. Barbara served herself salad, contemplating a safe topic. Low grey clouds finally released heavy spattering drops sending the family inside. Somehow it seemed easier to succumb to TV than restore harmony.

Most of the way to work she'd been on automatic. Slowed by the many traffic lights in the seaside village, Barbara accelerated up the steep hill. The Cardinals Palace on her left with its solemn sandstone presided over the populace below. In earlier times trainee priests walked the dingy hallways. Now hospitality students had the run of the place, enjoying magnificent views over Manly Beach.

Within moments of arrival Barbara was absorbed into the busy physio department. Her first case was a shoulder reconstruction. With one arm strapped and supported, he sat with a pinched look on his face.

'Good morning, Mr Watson. I'm Barbara Harper.'

As he stood, she noticed he was lean and muscular, obviously an active man now stiffened by his injury.

'Morning, Mrs Harper,' he replied, his face flinching with pain, disturbing the shape of his grey moustache.

'I understand it's been six weeks since your surgery. It's time we got some movement back.'

He rubbed his arm. 'The muscle's quite wasted after all this time. I hope it's not too long before I can get back to playing golf.'

'Another golfer. My husband's mad about the game.'

'It does fill in the days of retirement.'

He looked lost. Barbara felt this man's dissatisfaction with life was almost palpable.

'Well, Mr Watson, let's waste no time getting that arm going again.'

Barbara took off the sling and avoided further chatter. She directed his movements choosing to ignore the gasps of pain. Before taking him to the hydrotherapy pool she explained exercises. The smell of chlorine pervaded the room as she assured her patient the warm swirling water would bring pain relief. Everyone was different, she thought. She preferred working with younger athletes who were used to pushing through pain barriers in intensive training. Barbara found older women with hip breaks the most tragic. She worked to get them mobile only to hear of a further fall and complications leading to death.

There she was thinking about death again. Katie's death had impinged on her own work and family life. Its repercussions on Madeline might be severe. Move on, Barbara told herself. Don't sink into morbid scenarios. Her job was in recovery, the body's renewal. She brought people through to a new beginning. The laughter of the younger physios cheered her at break times; her extensive experience impressed them. A smile came at last bringing a tinge of optimism. Here she did make a difference. On the way home she'd drop in at the new house to see whether Glen had the roof timbers up.

ELEVEN

Despite only two Scotches, Sanderson woke feeling seedy. Lack of sleep was the most likely culprit, hours tapping away on his laptop after he got home. Weekends did not exist at this stage of a murder investigation.

His fingers ran over fine stubble on his chin. The buzz of his shaver sounded overly loud. While devouring cereal, feet propped on the coffee table, Sanderson noticed his mobile had a message. He turned down the TV and retrieved Fyurk's voice: 'Just checking to see if you're okay, Gary. Ring me.'

Sanderson couldn't understand his offsider's concerns. A babe like Cyndi wasn't risky. He thrived on a thrill every so often. Life wasn't all twin sets and nice girls. Maybe Fyurk didn't have a life. Still, with his sloppy appearance he was perfect for the task last night. In grungy jeans and T-shirt, Fyurk was to hang out at the campus bars to get a handle on their victim. Madeline hadn't given them much to go on. Perhaps Katie's behaviour had made her a target.

He put a call through. 'Richard, how'd it go last night?'

'I could ask the same thing.'

'Mine? Great. Enough said. What'd you find out?'

'More about the uni culture these days than I care to know. The girls play up to blokes, drink too much then come across in the toilets in return for ecstasy tablets.' Fyurk sounded far from impressed.

'Any talk of Katie?' Sanderson continued eating.

'The word is she was a slut.'

'That's a bit harsh isn't it, Rich?'

'No, drugs and nice behaviour don't mix. I figure some creep's been watching and tried to crack onto her. She's told him to piss off and he's gone after her.'

'Mmm,' Sanderson pondered this. 'Did you find out which bar staff were working the night Katie was murdered? What about the cleaners? Maybe they can shed light on this.'

'I'll try and get that info tonight. I'm going into the incident room soon. The summaries of the door knocks and uni interviews may reveal something more.'

'Good, Rich. I'll see you there. Need a lift?'

'No thanks, Gary. I can walk that far.'

Sanderson put the phone down and finished his breakfast. No watching sport on the lounge today. His gaze rested on his bonsai plant in its tiny Asian pot. Mesmerised by the intricacy of miniature branches, he wished his fallen colleague was with him.

After Dave was knifed his wife brought Sanderson his prized bonsai. It linked them in death. Sanderson felt compelled to keep the plant alive. On hot summer days it dried out quickly. Some evenings he stared at its gnarled features, even confiding in it as he had with Dave before his death. Sanderson gave it a liberal watering before heading off on a run to finally clear his head.

He passed through the sandstone portals of Centennial Park and proceeded around the shady track. On hearing the clopping of hooves behind him, he moved over. Equestrians, cyclists and all manner of athletes trained here. Sanderson glanced across the expansive grassed area to a group of mothers picnicking. By the lake children fed a mass of honking geese. A light breeze cooled his sweaty skin. Running here brought balance to his life. These everyday activities often drew his mind away from crime scene images.

After a shower, he put on his Billabong board shorts and a white T-shirt then jumped into the Commodore. The bridge had more walkers than cars crossing it today. Near Archer Street, the caramel police station dominated the corner. This metal clad monstrosity with its hideous lattice would soon be demolished, Sanderson thought. The new building under construction on the opposite corner, all concrete and glass, would keep out the incessant traffic noise of this busy suburb.

The detective swiped his card and watched the spears atop the motorised gate move aside. Most of the spaces had cop cars in them. By the time he entered the incident room Sanderson felt refreshed. He asked for the physical evidence to be signed out and brought in. Everything had to be in order before Monday's review. They now knew the pink top and ring belonged to Katie Foster. Where were the rest of her clothes, he wondered? Probably buried in landfill somewhere. Had Fyurk followed that up?

He glanced at the small plastic bag containing the solitary black hair Hazelton had found on the body. Liam had black hair. Could it be that simple? Sanderson doubted it. The shoe cast and cigarette butt were slim pickings. He sent it all back to be locked up.

Graphic photos covered several of the whiteboards set up in a U-shape round the room. Fyurk's head rose above mountains of paper on one of the desks.

'Hi, Gary. I've been going through the summaries from the door-knocks and uni interviews.'

'Good, Rich. I'll sift through them as well. Often it's one insignificant detail that matches with a later one, which opens up a line of inquiry. With all the trees round the uni's perimeter I don't expect people in the houses to have heard anything.' Sanderson sat in the spare chair rolling it towards the desk.

'Quite a few remember the hailstorm. Reckon hot sticky weather brings out the nutters. Maybe someone around the uni noticed odd behaviour. Janine's been sent over to help with data entry. She's got a good eye for detail.'

'She's easy on the eyes, Rich,' Sanderson winked at his offsider.

'What is it with you, Gary? Janine's way too young for you.' Fyurk's face showed disgust.

'Lighten up, Rich. No need to play the knight in shining armour.'

Janine entered carrying two cups of coffee for the detectives.

'Thanks, babe,' said Sanderson.

'Thank you, Janine,' Fyurk added.

'That's okay, boys.' Janine returned to work on her computer at the end of the room.

'Here's something of interest, Gary. Forensics found fingerprints on cellophane from a cigarette packet. It was retrieved from the gully not far from the body. Our killer could have been smoking while waiting for his victim. They checked the prints in the AFIS database. No match.'

'So.' Sanderson looked puzzled.

'There's another report here saying Professor Mitchell was seen smoking on a balcony in the vicinity one night last week,' Fyurk added.

'Wasn't there a staff do Wednesday night? It could have blown from there. Think the professor could be a suspect?'

'No, Gary. But we should get his prints to eliminate him.'

Sanderson gulped his cooling coffee. 'Okay, I'll get on to that. We'll be at the uni Monday.'

'Liam's a strange one but I don't know if he's warped enough for lust murder. Mutilation, especially of the genitalia, is often done by lower class blokes.'

'Where'd you hear that?' Sanderson asked.

'Read it. Here's an article by Turvey I brought in. It profiles the type we're after.' Fyurk went over to talk to Janine. He certainly looked spruced up today. The jeans appeared new and the striped casual shirt suited his tall frame. Sanderson noticed him smell her hair and heard the word 'apples.' Janine's reply was softer. Sanderson stopped watching them and absorbed himself in reading.

The article pointed to the obvious: collect physical evidence, reconstruct the crime scientifically then profiling can follow. Turvey had a go at investigators faced with disturbingly violent crime scenes being unable to overcome their own reactions. Sanderson felt affronted but went on to the definition of profiling: letting the physical evidence tell what behaviours occurred then thinking what was intended.

He knew his type of offender was driven by fantasy; going over it many times in his mind before acting. Because of the crude cutting and the carelessness of leaving the scalpel at the scene this might be a first time murder. His killer had overpowered Katie quickly. There was no sign of torture or prolonging her death. Gaining control, he was free to master the corpse by post-mortem mutilation. He was probably masturbating over the pudendum as he relived his fantasy.

Sanderson was familiar with this scenario and knew pressure would cause the killer to attack again. No one had voiced this fear. The urgency of their investigation made him feel strung out. And the papers always wanted a quick result. He knew to look for someone with a veneer of personality that enabled him to blend with his peers. Someone who got off on his victim's suffering and terror. Fyurk may be right. Sex offenders desire intimacy but lack the skills to achieve it in a healthy form. Not that this toilet sex the students were having sounded healthy. An outsider could observe what was going on and try to join the action.

His offsider returned as Sanderson finished the article. 'Interesting stuff, Rich. You could be on the right track. Back to the bars for you tonight. Scour the campus. See if you can find out about Liam's sex life.'

'Right, Gary. That could be a tall order.' Fyurk smiled, waved to Janine and left the incident room.

Sanderson stood behind her, peering at the computer screen. Janine moved her chair slightly away from him.

'Don't be that way, babe,' he said. 'You seem pally with Fyurk.'

Her luscious lips were tightly pursed.

'Stop calling me babe.'

Sanderson was still fuming as he drove to the university late Monday morning. Sunday had been a blur going over every detail of the case. Ralston was a hard bastard to please and this investigation could turn into a nightmare, he thought. Fyurk remained quiet. Perhaps he too was mulling over the meeting. Their superior's voice had filled every corner of the long incident room. Questions, probing and interminable, were met with feeble answers. Ralston's eyebrows worked overtime with frequent frowns. Sanderson acknowledged they had few direct leads. His boss did seem impressed with Fyurk's crime scene photographs. He'd caught Ralston glancing at the younger detective.

Relieved by the interruption, Sanderson took Jill Ashworth's call regarding Liam. This looked good to his boss. He and Fyurk made a hasty exit. Twenty minutes later, at the university the two detectives were safely ensconced in an adjacent room with the surveillance team ten minutes before Liam arrived to see his tutor. They watched on the screen as Liam's agitation increased with Jill's closer proximity.

'See that,' whispered Fyurk.

'What?' Sanderson asked.

'Those little involuntary jerks of his fingers, Gary. Could be a sign of brain damage.'

Sanderson nodded, giving Fyurk an approving look before watching their suspect leave. Chairs squeaked as surveillance packed up.

'Rich, we ran a police check on Liam. Zilch.'

'Gary, if he's our man there's got to be a record of assaults or possibly arson. We need to access Liam's medical and school records. If he suffered childhood abuse and I'm right about the brain damage we have two predictors for violent behaviour.'

Ralston had blasted them over not getting to the tip earlier. Sanderson flashed his badge while stating his mission to the attendant in the booth. The boom gate rose and they drove to where a dozer was operating. The detectives left the Commodore and watched a mountain of rubbish being levelled. A microwave disintegrated and a headless doll rolled clear.

Sanderson hailed the driver; the machine's roar subsided. 'Detectives. We're looking for the clothes of a murdered girl. The contents of bins from Phillips University came here last Wednesday.'

'Be over there, mate.' The man's face, made more gruesome by a missing tooth, turned in the opposite direction. He revved up the dozer. Fyurk and Sanderson followed. His bucket dug and clawed through the muddy debris for five minutes before stopping.

'Take a decko,' the operator said, 'not many clothes in this rubbish. Most put it in the Salvo's bin.'

The smell of putrefying matter almost set Fyurk off. Sanderson scowled at the muck on his shoes but proceeded to search.

'The chances aren't good, Gary.' Fyurk held a handkerchief over his largish nose.

Sanderson shook his head. 'At least we can tell Ralston we checked it out. No sign of jeans. Maybe he'll be interested in the amount of disposable nappies in landfill.'

They waved to the dozer bloke and headed back to the car, then wiped mud off their shoes with newspaper.

'Where to now?'

'Wish I bloody knew.' Sanderson turned the keys violently to start the car. 'An outdoor location, no DNA and one black hair. Damn few suspects. Not much to catch a killer.'

TWELVE

Tuesday evening Jill waited for Gary's call. Trying to focus on preparation for a lecture on beachcombers, she repeatedly glanced at the wall phone. This reminded her of teenage angst. Hanging around in the house, willing the phone to ring, hoping it would be the new flame.

This was business. Gary wanted that hair but didn't want to spook Liam by asking for one. Failing to understand why he'd involved her, she still deserved to be thanked. Liam mustn't find out her involvement. He'd taken some calming after the last confrontation. Nobody knew how dangerous he might be.

In the last week Jill had questioned her ability to read character. Gary had warned against trusting Liam while they investigated his background and processed the evidence. In her company he was mostly the avid student keen to impress with his intellectual reasoning. Occasionally there were flashes of aberrant behaviour. The phone rang.

'Jill?'

'Is that you, Liam?' Jill clenched the handpiece.

'Yes.'

'What are you doing ringing me at home? How did you get my number?' Her tone put him on the defensive.

'I … I'm sorry. I saw it on paperwork in your office. I couldn't work on my essay thinking I'd upset you.'

He sounded distraught. 'Liam, it's okay. You misunderstood and overreacted. Forget it.'

'Really. You've been so helpful and kind. You're my favourite lecturer.'

His words defused her anger. Perhaps this was manipulative behaviour at its best. 'Now you're laying it on, Liam. But seriously, you mustn't ring me at home. It's not appropriate.'

'Night, Jill. I won't do it again.' He hung up.

Slowly she replaced the receiver. A chill swept through her despite the warm summer night. Jill's immediate reaction was to arrange a silent number. Liam, a murder suspect, had been to her home and now had rung. Tense, with shallow breaths she cowered in the kitchen.

The phone rang again. Jill jumped.

'Hello,' she said.

'Jill?'

'Thank God it's you, Gary,' she told him about Liam's call and her concerns. He thanked her for the hair Fyurk had brought in for matching with the one found on the body.

'I guess we'd better get you out of the house,' Gary said, 'Have dinner with me tomorrow night. Nino's, a little place in Chatswood. Do you know it?'

'Yes. I love Italian.'

'Good, be there at seven. And Jill, try not to worry about Liam. We're right on to this case. Ring me if you need to. See you soon, babe.'

The sound of his voice lingered pleasantly as she tried to expunge the earlier call. And no man had ever called her babe. Jill felt a certain thrill at the thought of dinner with Gary. Helping a detective with a case was proving interesting. Who knows what might happen? Her fingertips tingled with anticipation.

Jill scanned her wardrobe pondering what to wear to a detective dinner. The dress she'd worn to the staff function was too dowdy. So she tried on a lacy top with jeans. Too casual. Jill figured Gary liked women smart and sexy. Her choice: the red linen suit with the too-short skirt, sheer black stockings and stilettos to match. The outfit was another impulse buy on her last holiday. Checking her make-up, she felt more confident. Was she still role-playing?

Gary was waiting outside Nino's, a bottle of red wine in his hand. He swept an appreciative but amused look over her attire. Glad of the dim lights inside, Jill inhaled the aroma of garlic. A candle fluttered in a Chianti bottle. Trails of wax merged with its raffia.

As Gary read the menu she noticed his strong, sinewy hands. Candlelight glinted on the gold links of his watchband, his forearm tanned with fine gold hairs. Aroused, Jill felt a strong urge to touch that arm to see how he'd react. But she was too controlled. She'd never been guilty of inappropriate advances to anyone in her life. This was new territory. What did she really know of the nuances of sexual attraction? Jill covered her scrutiny by raising the menu. The dishes described interrupted her fantasy.

At that moment they both lowered menus and his eyes locked onto hers with an inquisitive look before the edges of his mouth curled upwards in a delicious way.

'What has the learned lady decided on for dinner?'

'Veal Oscar,' Jill answered. The hovering waiter squiggled on a notepad.

'Ditto,' Gary said, 'and garlic bread please.' He poured the red. 'To our shared endeavour.'

Glasses clinked. Jill wanted to lose herself in Gary's eyes. Deep brown and enticing. She wondered if he made a habit of involving women in murder cases.

'Will it take long to catch this killer?'

'Depends. If Liam's hair matches the one on the body it puts him at the scene.'

'If not you move on to other suspects?'

Gary nodded.

Jill continued, 'Liam shares a room on campus with another young man. He told me they both transferred from ANU.'

'I don't suppose you could keep a lookout some nights?'

'Me, wander the campus after dark?'

'I thought you liked playing detective. Not frightened are you?' He gave her one of his grins.

'No,' she lied, 'I can take care of myself.' Why should she reveal her fears, especially to Mr Streetsmart? Taking a mouthful of wine, Jill tucked a wisp of hair behind her ear.

She observed him cut into the meat and push cheese-covered asparagus with it onto his fork. Starting her own meal, she thought, he's always ahead. His business must be fast thinking. He doesn't even slow down for food. As if intuitive he picked up his glass for a long sip. Sighing, he said, 'So tell me what it's like working at a university.'

When she related the usual routine his attention made her face colour. Jill took another gulp of wine. She rallied on trying to make living at an earlier time sound as fascinating as it was to her. The details she fed into lectures took the students on an emotional journey. Jill finished with: 'People are driven by different things. Today it's the latest mobile phone. Back in the nineteenth century in the Pacific it was axes and mirrors.'

Gary gave a silent clap. His job seemed so vibrant in comparison. His eyes wandered to a poster of Naples with its volcano hovering above the city. Did she detect boredom?

'Aren't more police trained in unis now?' Jill asked.

'Yes and think they're smarter. But learning on the job still produces the best cops.'

His knife and fork clattered onto the plate. Was this a sore point?

'Gary, have there been any similar cases at other universities?'

'No matter how gorgeous or intelligent you are, Jill, I can't tell you details. What if you leaked it to the press? Often they get hold of something too early and it jeopardises …'

'So you don't trust me?'

'Come on, Jill. Don't be offended. I'll order cappuccinos and tiramisu to sweeten you up.' He sauntered to the bar in search of a waiter leaving her seething.

Why had she reacted so personally? When Gary sat down he raised her chin with his finger. 'Smile,' he said.

Jill's face responded.

'That's better. I appreciate your help but becoming involved with police procedure is a bit tricky. Enjoy your dessert.'

She found the layered cake sensational. There was no point being petulant. Perhaps she could charm information out of him. After cappuccinos they left the restaurant.

'Night, babe,' Gary said, 'Don't overdo the image.' He was gone.

Jill strode to her car, gripped by fury as she drove home. Gary had made fun of her, delighted in treating her as if she were a novice with men. Jill supposed the sort of woman he usually mixed with had educated him in every ruse. With his ego he probably couldn't conceive of a woman with a mind. She saw herself back at dinner defending intellectual pursuits. Smiling at last, she realised she'd never been in that situation before. Gary had confronted her comfortable existence with a hard look at the real world of crime, violence and desperation.

Too keyed up to sleep, she welcomed the cooling breeze wafting in the window. Jill lay in the dark. Her mind wandered through every scenario with Gary since the day he'd appeared in her office. That tranquil academic existence seemed gone forever.

Gary stirred her hormones, upsetting her focus on career. With her cerebral occupation it was like moving ever forward on automatic. Now her emotions were a jangled mess. Perhaps that part of Jill was underdeveloped. Was she just trying to be the sensible girl Mother had moulded? Mother was aware how difficult life could be in a swirl of feelings.

Whatever it was, Gary appealed to her physically. Her body at 35 was long overdue for the sexual workout that his presence evoked. She'd tried turning from the screen in movies when a hot melding of figures was shown. Intervals between touching were as long as droughts. Was she dry and parched?

Finally a man her body yearned for and he didn't take her seriously. He flirted and when she reacted he laughingly brushed it aside. Jill felt like shaking him. Her moods seesawed: elation to anger.

Who was she kidding? A detective. She couldn't tell Mother she'd had dinner with one. Mother put them in the sleaze category. Jill could almost hear her diatribe. Detectives have connections with the underworld. Their informants are crims. They see people at the worst times of their lives if not dead. There must be some nice professors on campus. Calm men with good steady careers.

Gary excited her. She found his world scary and intriguing. A determination to pursue this new path had taken hold. A single question perplexed her. How does an academic woman wangle another date with a detective?

Next day she didn't hear from Gary. Jill felt used, annoyed after helping to be cut out of the action. Suppressing her feelings, she walked into the lecture theatre. Students were slumped in chairs ready for note taking. A pen dropped and rolled from one concrete tier to the next. She launched into the lecture.

Beachcombers interested most students. Many probably dreamed of living on a tropical island. No doubt it had appeal but not many dreamers make it reality. The majority in this room were only after a piece of paper to assist them into a career.

Jill held up a copy of E J Banfield's *The Confessions of a Beachcomber.*

'A classic,' she said, 'showing how he lived on Dunk Island, mingling with aborigines that visited and developing his own philosophies.

'In September 1897 the sickly 45 year old journalist moved to this uninhabited isle with his wife. After being told by doctors he had six months to live, he remained on Dunk for 25 years.'

Jill went on to explain how the Australian naturalist with a passion for freedom and fresh air was different from the usual South Sea island beachcombers. They were mainly seaman who had little affection for western society. Dressing native style, often tattooed, they paved the way for traders. Apart from occasional work on ships, they were dependent on the locals and had no wish to change lifestyles. This made beachcombers unpopular with the missionaries. The hour flew and she headed back to her office.

Late in the afternoon she passed the still-blue fountain on her way to the library. Its frothy gushing obliterated the noisy chatter of students. Inside the sanctuary of learning, Jill heard sneakers shushing on the carpet. Several wide-leafed pot plants adjacent to the information desk decorated the stark interior.

She borrowed some primary documents from reserve and took them into a tiny office. Every year Jill read a selection of first-hand accounts of life in the Pacific Islands. Traders, plantation owners, ships' captains and missionaries had differing versions. She was absorbed for several hours before needing a comfort break.

On her way back she caught a glimpse of Liam. He'd left a desk and was proceeding downstairs. His dinner break, she guessed. Jill snuck behind a pillar so he wouldn't see her. Curious, she was drawn to Liam's desk. Scattered on it were psychology texts and a notebook.

A paperback, *The Jigsaw Man* by Paul Britton, grabbed her attention. Checking in the direction of the stairs, she picked it up. Jill scanned several pages of the biography of one of the UK's top forensic psychologists. Details of the weird behaviour of a serial killer made her shudder. She put the book back beside Liam's signature top hat. It looked as if it was guarding highbrow literature from another era. His black coat with tails was slung over the chair back. Surely he'd take these to the cafeteria. They were part of his persona. She pictured Liam's dark straggly hair, his palest of blue eyes and wondered if he was out there, incognito, stalking another girl.

Jill retreated to the office, thinking about the book. Why was Liam reading it? Was it part of his course? She sat down and tried to concentrate on her work. Beads of perspiration formed on her forehead. Her thoughts wouldn't settle. She kept wondering if Liam was researching for his own agenda. If he'd killed Katie, was he seeking new behaviours? Maybe Britton didn't realise his interviews with killers might be used in a perverted way.

Packing up, she returned the items to reserve and left the library. In the darkness outside, ball-shaped lights led the way to her building. The sound of her leather shoes scuffing the stone pavers seemed overly loud. Few students were around. No young women on their own, she was pleased to see. Jill thought of Gary's dare to walk the campus at night. Ridiculous, knowing a murderer was around. She hurried into the lift. All the doors in the corridor on her floor were shut. Light seeped from under several. Some colleagues preferred working here rather than at home.

She unlocked her office, took what she needed and left. Rustling trees encircled the car park. Pools of light came from steel poles that pierced the sky. A globe was out in one area. Her breaths increased to rapid in the eerie shadows. Why hadn't she left before sunset? Bugger that library work. Her sweaty fingers sought the car keys in her handbag. She saw her Honda in the next row. Then she heard someone behind her. God. She couldn't look around. Her brain switched to panic. Jill grabbed the door handle and felt a tug on her elbow. She let out a gasp.

'Jill, don't be frightened.'

Her startled response eased as she realised it was Duncan Mitchell. 'I ... I didn't know who was there,' she said, attempting to sound calm. He was still touching her. Jill wanted to edge away, get in her car and out of there. His bearded face was too close as he muttered about dangers and how he was her saviour having seen her from his office.

'I have to go,' she said, pulling herself free and getting into the car. There wasn't enough light to see the look on his face as she sped off. Instinct told her Professor Mitchell was a creep.

THIRTEEN

Barbara parked outside her new home beside the huge peppercorn tree. Its lacy foliage wasn't a regular sight in the city and reminded her of trips to the country as a girl with her parents. She touched up her lipstick. Outside the car, she pulled her shirt to cover a midriff bulge.

The roofers had gone but many of the beams were in place. As yet, it wasn't easy to see the various pitches. The wire gates were not padlocked so Glen was still around. She liked to wander through at the end of a workday. Any progress on the house thrilled her.

Scraping her elbow on the rough bricks beside the stairs she let out a gasp of pain. Barbara rubbed her injury as she stood in the corner where her kitchen would be mentally placing the appliances she'd selected. Then she turned to the vista of the lake. Two people on wave skis paddled past on the dull green ripples. Near the bridge over the lagoon, she noticed a pair of cabbage tree palms taller than the light poles. Her reverie of her new life here was broken by Glen's arrival.

'Oh it's you, Barbara. Just checking before I locked up.' Glen brushed cement dust from his stubbies.

'Glad I wasn't shut in. Sprung visualising my new kitchen with the appliances I've picked. Got carried away with the view.'

'Not bad working here with this outlook. Lucky you liked that standard window colour, Barbara. The first lot should arrive quickly and I can get the renderers started.'

'That's good, Glen. I'll get going.' She edged past him down the stairs.

'See you. We'll have a meeting with the kitchen bloke in a couple of weeks.'

Before going to her car, she glanced over at her neighbour's modest weatherboard cottage. Through two overgrown bottlebrush, she could see a mess of pot plants hanging on a stand by the front door. A large glazed pot with a yucca would have looked so much better. What sort of people were they, she wondered? The estate agent had told her more professionals were moving into the area. While pricey waterfronts on Pittwater were out of reach, a lakefront was certainly a step up.

As Barbara drove around the bends, slowing with the traffic, she smiled thinking of the young physios at work. During lunchbreak, while picking at her salad, she'd felt heat surge into her face then move down her whole body. Grabbing a manila folder, she'd fanned the perspiration away.

'What's wrong?' Bronwyn asked.

'Just a hot flush.' Barbara looked at their uncomprehending expressions. 'Wait for menopause. You'll find out what it's like with a buggered thermostat.' They'd all laughed. Barbara made light of any problems at work.

Relieved at seeing Madeline's car outside their home, Barbara immediately thought of asking her daughter about progress in the murder case. Madeline was draped over the lounge watching a quiz show. Beau raced over to Barbara. His eyes stared up, appealing.

'Okay, little fella. Hi, Maddy.' She scooped the dog into her arms then sat beside her daughter. Madeline, in board shorts, looked as if she'd been to the beach.

'You have been to uni today?' Barbara asked.

Madeline sat up and gave Beau a pat.

'Of course, Mum.' Her tone defensive.

'Are you okay? You're too quiet. Not yourself at all.'

'Mum, how would you feel if one of your workmates was suddenly butchered? Not overjoyed I'll bet.'

'All right, Maddy. I do understand. Has anything happened over the murder?'

'The detectives have interviewed everyone in our tutorial including Jill Ashworth. No one's saying much but I think they suspect Liam.' Madeline flicked her hair over her shoulder.

'Who's Liam?'

'He's a psych major student. A bit of a weirdo. Wears a top hat and tails round campus as if he's from another century. Thinks he's a philosopher. Always arguing a point.'

'He might just look different. Do you know why he's a suspect?' Barbara drew Beau back onto her lap, tickled his tummy, then turned the sound down on the TV.

'Katie and I annoyed him. He gave us creepy looks. His milky blue eyes and jet-black hair set him apart. I guess Detective Sanderson found him odd.'

'The boy certainly sounds strange, Maddy. Perhaps he's a modern day Jack the Ripper. I might get that new book of Patricia Cornwell's. She's done a retake on that. Reckons she's solved the case.'

'Mum, isn't that going over the top? You're not getting involved in all this surely. We're trying to deal with it.'

'Well, Maddy, I can't help thinking about it. I've never had any involvement in a murder before.'

'And neither have I. Liam's weird but he's an intellectual. Sure he's a loner. Us girls avoid him. I think he's almost asexual. I'd be surprised if he's capable of killing especially in that sick way.'

'We'll leave it then, Maddy. But keep me posted.' Barbara waltzed off to the kitchen.

Hugh left earlier than usual. Barbara was about to take her breakfast to the balcony when Madeline appeared. Her long hair was a mess of knots. After her daughter's sortie in the fridge, Barbara noticed Madeline's eyes were puffy.

'Had a bad night?' Barbara asked, 'you're upset.'

'Course I'm upset, Mum. Katie's funeral is today.' Madeline sagged on the breakfast bar.

'So it is, darling. I'm sorry. I've been busy organising my errands for the new house. Wondered why you weren't up.' Barbara gathered a magazine and notes, taking them outside. When she returned for toast and a flat white in her new Avanti cup, her daughter's face was fresh with tears. She gave her a hug.

'Oh Maddy, it'll soon be over.'

The girl's body was shaking with sobs.

'Mum, I'm too upset to drive. Will you take me to Katie's funeral?'

Barbara hesitated. Her daughter pulled away. The devastation in her face was obvious.

'All right, Maddy. When do we leave?'

'In an hour.'

Barbara was putting Beau outside with a treat when Madeline came out wearing the usual jeans. At least her belly-button jewel could not be seen.

'Maddy, could you put a skirt on? Jeans at a funeral.' She raised her hands. Her daughter complied without argument.

The whole way in the car Madeline patted her eyes with scrunched up tissues. The Northern Suburbs Crematorium was perched on a knoll after crossing the Lane Cove River. Barbara wove her way through the massive car parks among its gardens. The different sized chapels were laid out on the four points of the compass. Madeline told her the smaller eastern one had been booked as few friends were expected to travel from the south coast. Their shoes crunched over gravel as they moved towards mourners standing in the shade of gum trees. Before leaving her to join fellow students, Madeline pointed out detectives Sanderson and Fyurk. The older of the two looked extremely dapper, Barbara thought. His taupe coloured suit and rust red tie drew attention to his good looks. Patting her hair, she felt she looked stylish in her olive dress. Sanderson acknowledged her with a nod and she detected a slight smile. Fyurk was taller and his navy jacket hung on him. A largish nose dominated his pasty face.

She remembered Madeline telling her how nice he was when they'd questioned her in Katie's room on campus. Looks can be deceiving. Barbara felt she'd prefer being interviewed by the delightful Sanderson.

The student group was larger now with many boys in faded jeans. Barbara was glad she'd asked Madeline to change, as the girls were better dressed. The noise of cicadas rose above murmured conversations. Not knowing anyone, Barbara preferred to stand, alone. Hovering on the periphery of the students was the top hat boy, his black tails incongruous with similar coloured jeans.

A woman in a white suit wearing a smart burgundy hat presented her with a rosebud.

'Thank you for coming,' she said.

Barbara smiled, thinking what a nice touch. On the way into the chapel, Madeline joined her. They were handed a pamphlet with Katie's photo on it. This set Madeline off again. Barbara took her daughter's arm. What a heart-wrenching experience for a young person to go through.

They sat not far from the front in view of the white casket. Yellow and white flowers cascaded over it: roses, lilies and delicate baby's breath. Perfect for the innocence of a life taken early, Barbara felt. The flowers' fragrance was delicate adding reverence to the occasion. Katie's parents and brother were huddled at the front with another woman. How horrible it must be to lose a child especially one on the brink of independence, she thought. And Barbara had only one child. She took Madeline's hand, squeezing it gently.

Organ music rose as the service commenced. The minister did his best to convince them it was a celebration of Katie's short life. Her brother read a poem then her father spoke. Tear-stained faces dotted the small gathering.

As they emerged Barbara heard the melodic call of a currawong. How wonderfully uplifting. Madeline went over to Katie's parents. The mother, a small grey-haired woman, seemed paralysed by grief. Supported by her husband, she was obviously sedated. Unable to speak, she nodded and stroked Madeline's face.

Her daughter told her there was no wake but the students were going to the university cafeteria. Barbara noticed a youngish woman in a long dark dress talking to the group.

'Who's that?'

'Jill Ashworth, my lecturer. Come on Mum, I'll introduce you.'

'Madeline. This must be Mum.' The woman shook Barbara's hand in a confident manner. 'Good to meet you, Mrs Harper.'

Without her hair drawn severely into a bun and a few pointers on dress, the lecturer could be quite attractive, Barbara thought.

'And you, Jill. Pity it's under such circumstances. What's being done about security on campus?'

Madeline winced as she tore her away. 'You're embarrassing, Mum. I'm going off with the others.'

'How will you get home?'

'I'll get a lift and it won't be after dark. Okay?' Madeline raised her eyebrows.

'All right, Maddy. I'll get on with my errands.'

'The new house. It's all you think of, Mum.'

'That's what building is. It'd be nice if you and your father showed more interest.' Barbara marched off to her car.

Daughters, she thought, so touchy. They want your help. Next minute you're an embarrassment. Barbara found it hard to keep up with Madeline's emotions. Perhaps everything was magnified by Katie's death. Madeline appeared to be covering her midriff more. Barbara wondered if that was a reaction to losing her friend. Did she continually think about Katie's last moments of life?

From the car park Barbara watched the cluster of people dispersing after the funeral. Madeline was the centre of her tutorial group. She realised her daughter had something of Barbara's own father's charm. He had put that to good use in his career as a journalist. How many times had his looks and easy manner prised extra secrets from his subjects? Perhaps the trait in Madeline would make her a doctor with an exceptional bedside manner.

Watching those following her brought a quick memory flash. She was about Madeline's age when walking past an outdoor restaurant at Circular Quay. She saw her father was with a stunning younger woman. Heads leaned towards each other and easy laughs told her this was more than business. She was appalled by his duplicity, could never tell her mother. Barbara had absorbed the shock of her father's womanising.

The screech of a cockatoo brought her gaze back to the chapel. That strangely attired boy was talking to Madeline's lecturer. In the distance, the two detectives watched this encounter. Barbara realised they had their own agenda at this funeral. She'd heard the police hoped suspects would attend. From what Maddy had said and her gut reaction, Barbara felt Liam could not possibly be the killer. A young girl's life needlessly lost had brought this gathering together. If only the detectives could catch the culprit it would put an end to this whole murder thing. And Barbara could stop the constant worry over her daughter's safety.

Leaving the funeral, Barbara decided to make the tile shop with the helpful assistant her first stop. Barbara was looking for large tiles for the living area. No more carpet to attract red wine spills. Most tiles were in beige tones so she explained the sea colours of her house. The girl finally produced one with tinges of pale teal. Delighted with the sample, Barbara left; keen to show it to Hugh that night. Damn, she thought, he's at the conference.

Her evening was a quiet one in front of the TV. Madeline had gone to bed with the dog for comfort. Barbara indulged herself with a few Tim Tams. By eleven she felt rather overwhelmed by her day off. The funeral had been emotionally draining. She needed a touch of Hugh's understanding. And she'd tell him of her tile find. She dialled his room at the conference centre.

'I'm sorry, madam,' the receptionist interjected, 'the person you are calling is not in his room.'

FOURTEEN

Nine days since Katie's body had been found, thought Sanderson. In the incident room his navy sports coat hung on the back of a chair. Completely absorbed, he paced around the exhibits. The sheer volume of paperwork this kind of investigation generated threatened to overwhelm him. Still, the first review had gone okay. Ruggeri and his team often had a different spin on things. Their suggestions produced handy leads.

Returning to the desk, Sanderson finished a lukewarm coffee. With shiny shoes propped up on the only tidy surface, he surveyed the whiteboard. Somewhere amongst all this information was a lead. He stared at the names that had so recently invaded his life as well as the arrows connecting them. Surely his capable mind could figure this whole thing out?

Victim. Katie Foster. A girl starting out at university immediately caught up in drugs and sex. The toxicology report had showed her predilection for ecstasy. The parents, living on the south coast, were oblivious. They could never have imagined their daughter brutally murdered.

Fyurk had shown Katie's photo to the bar staff and cleaners on duty that week. Sanderson had read their witness statements. No one had noticed anything unusual. Katie hadn't stood out. He gazed at the victim's photo: vivid green eyes and straight blonde hair. His mind brought back the contrasting image when he first saw this face, the silently screaming mouth seething with maggots. How he hated dealing with lives wasted before they'd barely begun.

He turned to the list of suspects: Liam, the student, Bob, the gardener, and possibly some psychopath roaming the campus. Liam was certainly the most likely. After that first meeting outside the library he had cooperated. At the regional office his appearance with the solicitor had been brief. Liam's alibi for the Monday was working in the library. The bloke Sanderson encountered in Liam's room days later corroborated this. On the Tuesday night he had attended the same lecture in the gym building as Katie. The lecturer remembered seeing his top hat. Liam said he'd gone straight back to his study desk to research and didn't recall seeing Katie. The boy seemed at ease and his explanations were feasible.

Fyurk had tracked him to a bar at the university over the weekend. Liam drank a few beers and sought out male company. Fyurk, overhearing Liam's philosophising, had put it down to intellectual crap. He'd summed it up: 'Gary, I think he's too direct to appeal to those chicks. They're looking for a whole lot more excitement.'

Sanderson placed the evidence bags containing the two dark hairs side by side. One was found on the body, the other belonged to Liam. An analyst had compared them under an electron microscope. No match. He couldn't risk trying to get DNA from the vital one, as it would be destroyed in the process.

Liam definitely was in the vicinity of the scene when the murder took place. Katie annoyed him in the tutorials. But that was hardly motivation enough to kill her. The hair link was a failure. Sanderson walked over to a TV and recorder. He replayed the surveillance tape of Liam. Definitely edgy around Jill but she likes him. Could he trust her character judgement?

If only something had come from the fingernail scrapings and swabs. Nothing. Not a skerrick of DNA. Even fingerprints were bamboozled. The killer had worn gloves, probably latex. That shows organization, Sanderson thought. Returning his gaze to the hairs, he reacted on a hunch and called Ruggeri on his mobile, hoping he hadn't left the station yet.

'Pete, the hair you found on the body is a no match with our chief suspect.'

'Bad luck, Sando. We'll keep working on the evidence. Something will come up.'

'I want one of yours,' Sanderson chuckled.

'My hair? Why?' Ruggeri asked, not at all amused.

''Cause the only other proliferation of dark hairs I've seen is on your bloody Italian head. Maybe you infected your own crime scene.'

Sanderson waited for the response. He heard Ruggeri snort.

'All right. I'll come to the incident room.'

Fyurk and Janine walked in. His offsider was dressed almost neatly. Janine's eyes sparkled in the way that had first attracted Sanderson. But she wasn't looking at him. Annoyed, he interrupted their conversation to report the call to Ruggeri. Janine raised her eyebrows at the senior detective then traipsed to her computer. She hunched her shoulders and let them release before dealing with the mass of data entry. Sanderson watched her until realising his offsider's discomfort. Lines of tension tightened Fyurk's face. Caught out perving, he switched his attention back to the whiteboard. He shared his musings with Fyurk.

'That's the problem,' he continued, 'our outdoor crime scene's revealed precious little. The only footprint was the fellow who found the body.'

'How lucky was our killer? A hail storm of all things to obliterate so much evidence.' Fyurk slid onto a chair, running it closer to the board.

'We're slim on the victimology. Perhaps we should have another chat with Madeline now we know about the drugs. Could kick up the pressure by hinting we'll talk to the parents. You saw Mum at the funeral, swish north shore type. And Dad's a doctor.'

'Okay, Gary. I'm sure Madeline will help.' Fyurk reached over for a file. 'A few of the checks on Liam have come in. Always in trouble at school. A bit of a smart arse. High IQ. No indication of abuse the school was aware of. Also no police record and the medical ones haven't arrived.'

Sanderson scanned the sheets. 'So no real red flags as yet on Liam. Well, we should get back to the office. Other jobs are pressing. That Darlinghurst drug overdose before we found this girl has just escalated to a murder investigation. The autopsy found it was a hot shot. A non-drug user filled with heroin. Remember the man's body was found in a stormwater drain. The scientific section even put a pig in one to simulate the conditions.'

'No kidding.' Fyurk's largish nose twitched.

After the exhibits were locked away, Sanderson grabbed his jacket and waved to Janine. The Commodore rumbled into life as they headed to the regional office. Static crackled on the police radio.

'Rich, it's bloody frustrating having so little to go on in this case. We can only work on suspects we've got.'

'Perhaps we need to come in from another angle, Gary. Over the weekend I read over *Whoever Fights Monsters*, the one Ressler helped write.'

'The FBI's chief profiler?'

'Right. Changed policing forever. Especially in murders of a sexual nature like ours. He went into California prisons and learnt stuff directly from the killers. It'd never been done before. Asked them about their childhood, their environment, how they picked victims, the dumpsites. Ressler really tried to understand the criminal mind, wanted to know why they took souvenirs and returned to the scenes of crimes. Some admitted going back, seeing the blood on the ground turned them on sexually. I know we can't afford the manpower to watch that gully at the university but knowing this type of murder I wonder if he has returned.'

'Maybe we should ask Ralston if an infra-red camera could be installed.'

'Good idea, Gary. The other thing Ressler did was teach interviewing techniques. Persuasion often gets better results than force or intimidation.'

Sanderson glanced at his offsider as the car came to a stop. He recalled Fyurk talking to Madeline in Katie's room. 'How about you call Madeline in for an interview. I'll observe. Seemed to work last time.'

Fyurk's face beamed. His stride into the office was purposeful. Sanderson decided that giving his trainee a longer leash might prove effective. Inside there was a message to call Jill Ashworth. He hadn't rung her since their dinner at the Italian joint, figured she might be trouble. Smart women are scary. Of course, she'd amused him dressing like a beacon, wearing sexy shoes. And getting fired up by all that history was beyond him. He liked a sassy woman who put out. Maybe the time for serious relationships would come. Although, Miss Academia had stormed off to her car. That showed spirit.

Keep the call formal, he decided. 'Jill, Detective Sanderson returning your call.'

'Hello … er Detective. There's a couple of things I thought you should know.'

'Fire away.'

'When Liam leaves the library for a break his jacket and top hat remain at his desk.'

'Interesting. So he could be roaming the uni grounds incognito.'

'Possibly. And the other evening I had a scary experience in the car park. Maybe I'm just jumpy but it was dark. Professor Mitchell appeared out of nowhere. Said he was trying to protect me.'

'It's possible he'd seen someone. I wouldn't be overly concerned but thanks, Jill. Often small things are helpful in an investigation.'

'How's the murder inquiry going?'

Sanderson didn't want to chat.

'No real breakthrough at the moment. Thanks for your input, Jill. Bye.' He hung up. Had he detected nervousness in her voice? She'd said she could take care of herself. Liam ringing her at home was unsettling. Was he stalking Jill? Sanderson wondered if his actions had put her in jeopardy. Jill certainly sounded like a worried woman. Something inside him wanted to reassure her yet he'd just cut her off. How safe was it going to work every day where a murderer had struck? He had to be realistic. The best way to alleviate the distress of everyone involved was keep working the case.

The afternoon Madeline Harper walked into the regional office Sanderson barely recognised her. On their previous meetings her face had been tear-stained and blotchy with smudged mascara. Today, he saw what an attractive young woman she was: eyes a stunning blue, high cheek bones and skin the colour of warm honey. She flipped her long shiny hair over her shoulder and extended her hand.

'Detective Sanderson, hope I can be of some help.'

'I'm sure you can, Madeline. You remember Detective Fyurk?'

She nodded. Sanderson watched her while his offsider explained their reasons for further questions. His thing for blondes was distracting. He noticed the fitted shirt she wore over tight jeans covered the navel jewel he remembered.

They sat in a triangle as he listened to Fyurk's calm voice. In contrast, Madeline's was bright and melodious. Sanderson's pen was poised above a notepad.

'Madeline,' Fyurk continued pushing to the point, 'we know Katie was using eccys and about the promiscuity.'

Shock registered on her face. 'Oh … still it doesn't seem right talking about that. She was my friend.'

'This isn't about loyalty. I understand you've lost a friend but if we're to find out why we need to know more about Katie's last days, how she spent her time, who she might have met. Did she tell you about anything suspicious?' Fyurk eased back in his chair awaiting a response.

In Sanderson's estimation Madeline was obviously struggling with how much to reveal.

'Detective Fyurk, I'd only known Katie a month. Sure we hung out a lot. I knew she was doing eccys and she'd get off her face sometimes at the uni bars. For most of that I wasn't there. I had to drive home and as you know my dad's a doctor. He'd kill me if I took drugs. Katie didn't tell me much. She was fresh from a south coast town. So she broke out a little. I figured she'd settle down to her studies. She never mentioned any weirdos to me.'

Sanderson detected her voice faltering. He felt she pulled herself up before mentioning murder. Fyurk didn't seem to be breaking new ground.

'What about Liam? Do you think he killed Katie?' Fyurk asked.

Madeline considered this for a moment. 'I doubt it. Mum told me to keep right away from Liam. We're in the same tutorial. Anyway, what about innocent until proven guilty? He's an idealist, always sprouting on about higher visions but I really can't see him being that brutal. My bet? It's some quiet stalker that's keeping his rage against women all bottled in. But you detectives are dealing with this gruesome stuff all the time. What would I know?' She flung her hands skywards.

'More than you realise, Madeline. You're moving around the campus all the time so if you see anything suspicious give us a call. Thanks for coming in.'

Sanderson acknowledged her farewell and watched Fyurk escort her out.

'Interesting but not overly helpful,' he said to his offsider.

'Right, Gary, but the seed's sown. Madeline might see something we're missing and I don't get to interview a sort like that every day.'

'Oh I see you're developing quite an eye for the ladies.'

Fyurk's smile taunted Sanderson. 'Probably comes from working with you.'

Sanderson's mobile interrupted. 'Jill … no, no I'm not ignoring you nor discounting your input. Work is a constant pressure.' He raised his eyebrows at Fyurk. Jill's voice continued its assault.

'You got me involved. Life on this campus will never be the same again. You can't just shut me out. I won't let you.' She hung up.

'Whew.' Sanderson wiped his brow. 'What happened to the quiet academic?'

'You certainly have a way with women, Gary.' Fyurk's smile was almost a grin.

FIFTEEN

Life on campus had resumed its usual round of lectures, meetings and tutorials. Her only source of staff gossip was Professor Mitchell's research assistant. Paula's sense of glamour interested Jill and she found her ever ready for a chat in the corridors. Several months had passed since Katie's murder; references to it subsided. In Jill's Pacific History tutorial students had rearranged themselves so there was no vacant chair at the desks. None wanted to be reminded of their mortality.

Madeline's face was a constant reminder. Instead of a pair of blondes giggling whenever Jill entered the room, there was a serious solitary one. Liam's top hat still graced the desk. He was wary of Madeline, at first. If she began to speak he would hesitate. Whenever the opportunity arose he showed kindness as if to make amends for her loss.

Jill didn't know what Gary found out about Liam but the detectives obviously didn't have enough evidence to keep pursuing him. How frustrating not knowing what was going on in the investigation. She had thought when Gary took her to dinner she'd remain involved. Her one attempt had found him in business-as-usual mode. Sometimes at night she wondered at the emotions he'd aroused. A spark of daring encouraged dangerous liaisons in her fantasies.

Sydney's late autumn weather suited Jill. With the heat and humidity gone she could enjoy her courtyard garden. After a blustery week, not a breath of air disturbed the palm fronds. Sprawled on an outdoor lounge she scanned the travel section of *The Sydney Morning Herald*.

Jill didn't fancy spending the midyear university break at Mother's retirement village in Canberra. Inland winters were icy. Paper crackled as she turned the unwieldy broadsheet in search of a short getaway. If she had something booked it'd be the perfect foil for her mum's whinge about not seeing her since she'd moved.

A feature on a square rig ship sailing in the Pacific leapt off the page. Coincidence? Only months ago Liam had taunted her about never actually seeing these islands. As she noted the possibility of flying and joining the boat for various legs of its journey, excitement mounted. Described as adventure travel, Jill couldn't believe she'd been so prosaic in her choice of holidays in the past. Who would she meet? An inset shot of the skipper promised muscled, tanned seafarers.

She checked their schedule. The dates in June fitted into her upcoming break. Fly to New Caledonia then sail for three weeks to Vila in Vanuatu. Racing inside she dialled the number and found there was a place available. Jill could download the booking form from the web and see pictures of the boat.

As images of *Dreamsong* appeared on her computer screen she was spellbound. The brigantine was so like the ships that had rounded up the Kanakas off the islands. Jill could imagine being there in colonial days and blend details into her lectures. Also she might be able to access some primary material from museums while there. Spontaneity was not usually her strong point but this trip seemed preordained.

Jill took a cup of tea back outside. The warmth of sun on her skin made her relaxed and dreamy. She decided to keep the holiday secret from colleagues and students. Part of her wanted to savour the possibilities privately. No one at the university had asked if she was going away.

Gary's suggestion to keep an eye out after dark had taken hold. Barely a month after Duncan had scared her witless in the car park, Jill acted. Earlier in the evening, she researched several articles in the library. She monitored Liam at his study desk. When a mate of his turned up, they left together. Jill followed, clutching a soft bag. Where were they going? Was she stalking the stalkers? Her stomach felt fluttery.

Outside the library Jill drew a brown scarf from her bag. Swathing it around her head, she concealed every strand of blonde hair. She thought the hair colour had been attractive to the killer, drawing him like a magnet. Not wanting to be a target, her action seemed a reasonable precaution. Also she'd be less noticeable in the darkness as she tracked the two students. Jill had worn a brown jumper over black jeans for camouflage.

A light breeze caused a whispering of leaves overhead as she traced the boys to the pathway. It was a Tuesday, the most probable night of the murder. Liam and his mate were a hundred metres ahead. Their shadows loomed out in front of them as they passed each ball-shaped light. The one that had been out on the fatal night had been repaired. There was no area of darkness to hide an attacker dragging their victim down into the gully.

Jill didn't want to think of that event and what he did. Leaving Katie's body a macabre discovery. She wondered if the killer got off on the repercussions his act had on campus life. Even though students said they felt safer, that it was a one-off incident, an uncertainty persisted in their eyes.

In sneakers, soundlessly she followed the two figures heading towards the gym buildings. They passed groups walking the opposite way. Were the two in front hoping to find a girl on her own? The thought reinforced the fact that she was the only solitary walker. How well the message had got through to everyone. But she could hardly ask a colleague to play detective with her. If Jill tried to explain, they'd think she was crackers.

Lengthening her stride, she told herself, don't walk like a victim. Regular glances behind assured her no one was there. Jill was looking for reasons to ring Gary. She felt the police investigation had stalled. That's why there'd been no contact.

Rapid breaths signalled anxiety as her targets entered the complex. Inside the gym, rock music assailed her ears as she scanned young men straining their muscles on various machines. On a row of walkers, young bodies paced their way to fitness, watching late night TV. No Liam or his mate. Beyond the gymnasium area, Jill heard the ping of a squash ball resounding around a court. Through the rear glass wall, she saw the two of them were harmlessly playing sport. They didn't notice her scuttle back outside.

She couldn't face walking that path alone in the eerie light. On her mobile she rang a local cab company and was taken the long way round to her car. So much for the after-dark escapade in the university grounds.

If she spent any more time mulling over her actions she'd never leave her townhouse and the weekend would be over. Jill caught the bus into the city intent on a ferry ride to Manly. The best time to go was after rough weather. It had been blowing a strong southerly for days. On the TV last night waves crashed onto beaches and smashed into headlands.

Circular Quay on a Sunday was a destination in itself. Numerous restaurants and cafés facing the wharves were well patronised. Hearing laughter, chatter and the clink of glasses, she took a closer look. A pang of couple-envy enveloped her. There wasn't a solitary person in the place. She wondered what it'd be like regularly doing the café circuit with a constant companion. Correction: a regular man. One who would be so comfortable in her presence he could read the paper and she wouldn't feel at all perturbed. No point going down that thought pathway; what was wrong with her?

The aroma of coffee had her in its grasp. Jill remembered someone at the university had told her about a café at the Museum of Contemporary Art. Perhaps that'd be single friendly. She headed back around the cove towards the brown rectangular building. Feeling a slight chill in the autumn air, she decided to order chunky raisin toast to tide her over.

Set in the pavement, she noticed bronze plaques denoting Australian writers. Jill found a couple of favourite early women writers: Katherine Susannah Prichard and Kylie Tennant. A stroller obscured the next one. Then a group watching one of those painted people blocked another so she gave up. The object of their gaze was covered in gold paint, representing a rather squat statue of liberty. The spikes surrounding her head were nice and sharp but the light she brandished was buckled cardboard.

Everyone seemed amused by her stillness. Jill wondered if the young woman would get ill from the toxic effect of paint on her skin.

The café had a tiny table vacant on the balcony. Her cappuccino was hot and creamy, the raisin toast slathered in butter the way she liked it. Jill watched the ferries docking and leaving, their horn blasts shrill above the harbour's noise. Behind, the huge white shells of the Opera House were bathed in sunlight. She paid, eager to be on her way.

Jill walked upstairs to the front of the ferry among a crush of passengers. The engines thrummed as they made their way past Fort Denison, the rocky prison of the worst convicts in the colony's early days. Sun glinted off Centrepoint's gold tower. Yachts with limp sails barely moved. Swinging north as the heads neared, she felt the boat rise and fall, shuddering when the propeller came out of the water. Although her stomach lurched, she didn't feel queasy. Around her children squealed with delight. Water splattered the front windows as they came off a swell. The tiny lighthouse on south head had frothy waves breaking on the rocks below. Turning towards Manly the boat rolled to an alarming angle. More 'oohs' and 'aahs' then they were in calmer waters. No wonder the ferries stopped in severe weather.

Following the stream of people up the Corso, her first view of the famous Manly Beach was breathtaking. Waves pounded in and only a few board riders braved the conditions. Glad of sneakers, she set off for an invigorating walk along the promenade to Queenscliff first then back to Shelley Beach. With the clean salty air and towering Norfolk pines, it was a great place to be on a Sydney weekend.

When Jill dragged herself in the door late that afternoon, she made a cup of tea and eyed the pile of essays on the dining table. Not in the mood to attack them, she put on a Nat King Cole CD instead. Swaying around the kitchen to his smooth seductive voice, she gave the area a much needed clean up. Plates clattered as she unstacked the dishwasher. A flurry of spraying, wiping and polishing made her feel virtuous.

The kitchen would not be sullied tonight as she'd finally accepted a colleague's invite to dinner. Suzie Norton, with her office opposite hers, had decided Jill needed to mix more. She'd fended off an earlier suggestion. This time she had to accept or risk alienation. Suzie had such a bubbly personality; Jill expected the night to be fun.

After a shower she put on black pants and an electric blue cashmere sweater. She twisted her hair in a knot fixing it with a tortoiseshell clip and added dangly earrings. This was quite an effort, she thought, applying blusher and a pale frosting of lilac lipstick. Her gaze passed over the swanky stilettos she'd worn for Gary. They would probably gather dust at the base of her wardrobe forever. Slipping on a pair of bronze court shoes, she grabbed her favourite evening bag filling it with necessary accoutrements.

At ten past seven, Jill pressed the doorbell of Suzie's Ryde townhouse. Her husband, Eddie answered, wooden spoon in hand. She'd heard he knew his way around the kitchen but not that he was a dish himself. Accepting a bottle of white with a hearty laugh, he led her into the living room.

Another couple on a white leather sofa were helping themselves to cheese and dips. Duncan Mitchell fairly leapt from a chair to grasp her hands in welcome. When Jill heard his wife was visiting her sick mother, she felt he'd engineered this dinner party. How could Suzie not know he was always trying to get his clammy hands on younger women? She forced a smile.

'A wine?' Eddie asked.

'White would be lovely, thanks.' He disappeared into the kitchen as Jill sat in an armchair at the opposite end of the coffee table from Duncan, hoping distance might alleviate her discomfort. Professor Nicholson, she knew, to be a charming man. His much younger wife surprised her. Jenny, a startling blonde, sat back eating and crossed her long legs in a languorous manner. Duncan did not miss the move. The young Mrs Nicholson might prove a diversion.

'And what have you got up to today, Jill?' her husband asked.

'A ferry trip to Manly. Nice and rough it was too.'

'Good to hear you're seeing something of Sydney. Must be such a change coming from our boring capital. Jenny didn't think the place had anything to offer. Did you dear?' He placed a hand on the shiny fabric of his wife's skirt.

Jenny gave him a cheeky look. 'All those museums and art galleries are so boring.'

Duncan gulped his Scotch as if in shock at her attack on culture. Suzie waltzed in announcing the meal was ready. The lamb shanks on kumara mash with a platter of green vegetables were delightful.

Jill enjoyed the banter between the couples while doing her best to fend off Duncan's attempts at intimacy. When he touched her thigh she made a great kerfuffle over losing her serviette then went to the bathroom. She reapplied lipstick and left her sparkly bag on the end of a bed in a room nearby. Duncan excused himself shortly after. On his return he made a pointed effort to engage Jenny in conversation. With crème caramel for dessert and plunger coffee over, Jill felt it better to leave before his prim beard invaded her space one more time. An embarrassing rebuff would then be unavoidable.

When she got home, the odour from her handbag was revolting. What was that smell? On the table Jill opened the clasp. Inside was a mass of tissue. Toilet paper? Peeling the layers back she recoiled in horror. It contained a lump of shit.

SIXTEEN

Barbara thrust the carpet sample under her arm and left the showroom. Sage coloured and pure New Zealand wool, it had to match her tiles. She snapped the boot shut. Finding this floor covering finished her tasks for the new house today.

Over the last few months this project and her work at the hospital had kept her amazingly busy. Noticing it was past lock-up time for the builder, Barbara decided on a little shopping trip.

Parking on the top deck of the Mall, she entered David Jones. Barbara liked to shop in elegant surroundings and the women who served her here were always polite. Taking the escalators to the shoe department, she slowly browsed along the shelves. She wasn't looking for sensible flatties. There were sparkly evening shoes with heels way too high but they conveyed pain to her mind. Then she saw what she was after: caramel leather, medium heel and wickedly pointed toe. Taking the shoe to the attendant, she said, 'Do you have these in a size eight please?'

'I'll check for you, madam.' The black dress flitted through a door where Barbara imagined shoeboxes to the ceiling.

She tried the shoes on and found them more comfortable than they looked. The wonderfully soft leather made her feet appear so smart. Barbara swivelled this way and that in front of the mirror, realising she must have them. The assistant smiled courteously, taking the box.

'Is there anything else, madam? Boots with skirts are big for winter.'

Barbara glanced at a new display. Before she knew it she was trying on a pair: square toed, burgundy and mid-calf length. The stacked heel was higher than she usually wore but wide for stability. She thought of the handbag at home which matched these finely crafted boots. Barbara felt it'd be fun buying a new skirt or two.

The attendant handed back her card. 'Thank you, Mrs Harper. I'm sure you'll enjoy wearing those.'

Barbara gave her a huge smile and toted the black and white shopping bags to the car. Buying shoes gave her such a buzz she tapped her fingers on the steering wheel in time to the music on the radio. A frisson of guilt passed through her mind at Hugh receiving the account. That could be a month away. Her husband was such a bore over money.

The smell of new leather permeated the car as she drove home. Barbara could sneak her purchases into the house tomorrow when Hugh was at golf. He was bringing home Chinese takeaway tonight. Madeline, no doubt, would be going out after dinner.

Beau was pleased to see Barbara home becoming a boisterous mass of excitement at her arrival. As she swept him up his little tongue left a wet patch on her nose. Oh for a peaceful evening at home.

Barbara knocked on Madeline's door then opened it. Her daughter was propped amongst Indian cushions on her bed. Sequins caught a flash of light through the window. Had she not been reading a modern magazine, she gave the impression of being in a more exotic location. Madeline pulled out one of the tiny speakers pumping music into her ears.

'Hi, Mum.'

'Hi, Maddy. I'll leave you to relax. Dad should be home with dinner soon.'

'Great. I'm starving.' Madeline plugged her music back in.

Barbara almost closed Beau's inquisitive nose in the door. Whilst changing into loose and comfortable attire, she pondered on the appeal of magazines like *Cleo* and *Who*. Girls feasted on the lives of celebrities and sex. How much was learnt from the explicit articles the covers proclaimed? Finding the G Spot and the Sizzling Sex Life of yet another actor. So far Madeline hadn't brought any young men home from university. Barbara felt spared from imagining her daughter's sexual adventures. She hoped, like any mother, that unwanted pregnancies and STDs were kept at bay. Remembering the time when Madeline told her of taking a friend to the doctor for the morning-after pill, she realised how practical her daughter was.

Opening a red wine in readiness for Hugh, Barbara poured herself a glass. She made a small cheese platter and took it to the lounge. A quiz show would be a pleasant diversion till her husband came home. Hugh had seemed busier of late. Golf still absorbed Wednesday afternoons and Saturdays. He often raced in during the week just in time for the news. An odd evening away for conferences was part of the pressure on GPs to keep apace with medical advancements.

A memory of the morning after his last trip slipped into her mind. Barbara had sniffed one of his shirts. The odour, redolent of musk, was new to her. Had Hugh changed his aftershave? Could it be perfume? She'd rapidly dismissed this thought, sprayed the collar and stuffed it into the machine. Hugh was one of the straightest blokes she'd ever met. If she questioned his morals, he'd think her neurotic.

'Hello, Barbs,' Hugh said, depositing the plastic bag of cartonned food on the bench. The familiar lines crinkled around his eyes as he smiled. 'Another busy week over. I'll change before dinner.'

'Fine, Hugh. I'll pour you a wine.'

Over dinner, father and daughter ended up discussing medical matters as usual. Although Barbara was to some extent in the body business as well, she felt excluded. Why couldn't they deal with politics or tragedies like other families? If she had to suffer many more body part descriptions, Barbara would scream. Fortunately, Madeline put on a jacket, kissed them both and headed out the door.

When Barbara and Hugh had finished their meal, she made espressos in the stainless steel cups. Placing them, she noticed her daughter had left *Gray's Anatomy*, a doorstop of a book, on the coffee table. Barbara took the offending item to her daughter's room. On the bedside table a business card caught her eye, Detective Inspector Gary Sanderson. That was the good-looking fellow who'd nodded to her at Katie's funeral.

She wondered if the detectives had been talking to Madeline recently. Barbara would ask her tomorrow.

They sipped their coffee and watched a TV drama. Hugh seemed restless. Later, in bed their coupling was hasty but satisfying. Hugh, asleep on his back, snored lightly. Barbara nudged him to roll over. She started thinking of her new home, how much longer before it'd be finished, imagining them moving in. Feeling the heat under her chin first, then the hot flush sweeping over her body, Barbara had to throw back the covers and discard her nightie. She lay letting the cooling air flow over her. Several times a night this occurred. If she woke Hugh he grumbled, not concerned for her broken sleep. Barbara found the disturbances distressing.

In the morning she drove to the house. Sun, warm for autumn, streamed through the windscreen. At the site, the mottled grey walls awaited the rich taupe colour Barbara had selected. What a mess the yard was with half-filled skip bins and crates of tiles. She stepped over the uneven surface with the carpet sample. Placing it beside an area of aqua tiles, Barbara felt the tones matched to a tee. The carpet's textured pile would abut the smooth tiles. Her colour choices were mirrored in the lake waters beyond the windows. She could hear Glen hammering somewhere and didn't wish to disturb him.

Barbara wandered out to the water's edge. Wavelets met the shore. Reeds whispered in the breeze, their feathery tops swaying. On the opposite side of the lake, the drone of traffic plying through Narrabeen was far enough away not to disturb her. She could just make out the market stalls amidst the trees. It wouldn't be long before she could walk there from her home. Near a sandbank, a heron waded seeking tasty morsels.

She liked the feel of this place and wondered how each day would change. This was like a new start. On her way home again, Barbara felt pleased with herself. Her fingers resumed their dance on the steering wheel in time to the boppy music. She'd shown Glen her carpet choice against the tiles.

Smoothing his moustache with a dirty-nailed finger, he looked at her thoughtfully.

'I don't know how you do this, Barbara but it's working. Most people pay decorators heaps.'

'Colours are my thing.' She sashayed out of there. 'Didn't I tell you?'

Madeline's car was outside. Breakfast with the girls had been shorter than usual. Barbara strolled into the living room. Madeline's books covered the dining table. Beau skittered across the timber floor to prance around Barbara's feet. Madeline glanced up from her writing pad. Her hair was back in a scrunchie and she was wearing a comfy tracksuit. 'Hi, Mum. Hope you don't mind me working on my assignment here.'

'No darling, you go ahead.' Barbara would have preferred to play slow music and curl up with her decorator magazines on the lounge. That's the problem, she thought, with houses having only one living area. Barbara planned to have a comfy armchair as a retreat in the bay window of her new bedroom. With a tiny table she could take her coffee in there for privacy.

The detective's card she'd seen earlier in Madeline's room niggled at her. 'Maddy, have the detectives interviewed you again over Katie's death?'

Her daughter's head rose abruptly, a stricken look in her eyes.

'How did you know that?'

'I saw Detective Sanderson's card in your room.'

'So, you've been prying in my room. Mum, you shouldn't do that.'

'Maddy, I wasn't prying. You left *Gray's Anatomy* on my coffee table again. I was putting it away.' Barbara moved closer to the dining table. 'Have they found anything significant?'

Madeline hesitated, no longer annoyed. Her face had the wary look when she'd attempted to lie as a child. 'It was ages ago. The detectives just wanted to know more about Katie's life beforehand. You know, campus life.' Madeline flicked her hand as if dismissing the importance of it.

Barbara persisted. 'They wanted to know what sort of things she got up to, didn't they Maddy? Whether drugs or alcohol were part of it.'

'I suppose so.' Madeline slumped in her chair. 'Look, Mum, I've got to get on with my assignment. Okay.'

'I understand you don't want to reveal anything. In a murder investigation it will come out. I might even give Detective Sanderson a call.' Barbara turned away but not before catching her daughter's startled glance.

'You wouldn't,' she exploded.

SEVENTEEN

Sanderson's fingers struck the keyboard in a frenzy. Finalising this report for the coroner would free him up for more pressing cases. He hated ones where young children were killed. Another de facto wiping out two infants in retaliation for their mother leaving him. Then the bloke walks in front of a semitrailer. The detective shook his head and clicked the print icon.

As Fyurk entered the office, he blew his nose on a checked handkerchief.

'Still got that cold? Your nose looks red raw,' Sanderson said. He was aware of his offsider's sensitivity over a proboscis that large.

'Got to get over it soon, Gary.' Fyurk eased his lanky frame into a chair. 'Winter's coming. It'll build my immunity so I won't get any more.'

'Keep back, Toxic Boy. I can't afford to get sick with my workload at the moment.' Sanderson touched an ornament on his desk. Lines of tension on his face eased into a smile.

Fyurk leaned over the object. 'Is that what I think it is?'

'Yes, Rich. Fornicating pigs.'

'Where'd you get it? Surely that's an insult.' Fyurk's face showed disgust.

'I don't think that's the message at all. Cyndi Steele sent it. Possibly a compliment on my prowess.' Sanderson couldn't restrain a laugh.

Fyurk sneezed again and half his face disappeared behind the handkerchief.

Janine burst into the room. She sure makes a uniform look good. Cute and curvy was how Sanderson summed her up.

'Just heard on police radio, another body's been found at that uni.'

Shit, Sanderson thought. Before either detective replied, Sanderson's mobile rang. Ralston's voice boomed, telling him to cover the scene and that Ruggeri was on his way. The other two were chatting when he finished the call. He patted the weapon in his shoulder holster before slipping on his jacket.

'Bye … Janine.' Sanderson was pleased he'd stopped himself calling her babe. 'Come on, Rich.'

Fyurk loped after him. They tracked the familiar route to the university. Sanderson felt a tightening in his gut. This time they were directed to a dock area behind the cafeteria. The younger detective had a camera slung around his neck; Sanderson carried a notebook and pen.

There was a waist-high sill of concrete then a closed roller shutter door, its surface a maze of graffiti. Balls of paper were jostled by gusts of wind. The place felt cold and smelled of food scraps days old. Sanderson caught a whiff of putrefaction.

One uniform cop was fussing with crime scene tape while another stood beside a dump bin. Its lid was almost closed over a mass of food refuse. Amongst it a solitary foot protruded. From the delicate shape and blue painted toenails, Sanderson deduced it belonged to a woman. What a way to end up, he thought, surrounded by garbage.

He ascertained what he could from the local police as Fyurk's camera whirred. A few shots before forensics turned up couldn't hurt. Sanderson took up a position alone, a short distance away. Naturally, he wondered if the same killer had struck again. Two months had passed. That was a reasonable cooling off period. This time he'd push Ruggeri harder. The last crime scene had provided no DNA at all. Not even the cigarette butt Fyurk retrieved had been useful. Lack of physical evidence made their job extremely difficult. It went against Locard's Principle. It was almost inevitable that a perpetrator would leave something of himself at a scene. Human failure to find it was more the problem.

Sanderson realised he'd have to examine the body before surmising the scenario. The roller shutter opened onto an area behind the cafeteria kitchen, he'd been told. On this level there was one other door to a storeroom. He slipped on a latex glove and tried to open it. Locked.

With relief, he recognised Ruggeri in his blue overalls.

'Sando, we meet again.'

Sanderson removed his glove and shook hands. 'Hope you're in form, Pete, because I want this scene worked like never before.'

Ruggeri reacted with irritation. 'I'm just as keen to get results. Especially if he's the same killer.'

'If it is we'll be crucified if we don't nail him this time.'

Sanderson watched Ruggeri and his team glove up. The crime scene was properly secured. At least students weren't continually walking past this area. He watched while two men opened the lid with a clanking sound. The rank smell of rotting garbage and putrescent flesh dispersed into all their lungs.

Fyurk kept his distance. Sanderson could see the tendons in his neck rigid, trying to exert control. His offsider's cold would surely diminish his acute sense of smell. Sanderson didn't need the embarrassment of a retching detective at every homicide. He noticed Fyurk appeared under control although the handkerchief was clutched firmly in a fist.

The girl's body was concealed by food remnants and discarded packaging material.

'Hey, Ruggeri. Give us a call when she's uncovered. I'll be in the cafeteria interviewing the chef who found her. I'll bring a key for that storeroom back.'

'Sure thing, Sando.'

Sanderson acknowledged Ruggeri's nod, noticing his dark curls protruding from the checkered cap. 'Keep your bloody hair out of this crime scene,' Sanderson added with a grin, thinking of the solitary black hair in an evidence bag.

Fyurk followed him around the base of the building then up a few stairs to the cafeteria. For a Monday morning the place was abuzz with noise. Students, mostly in jeans and sweatshirts, were munching away at snacks or sipping coffee. The aroma reminded Sanderson a caffeine fix was overdue. When did these people work, he wondered? A continuous stream moved trays along in front of brightly displayed packaged sand-wiches and bulging muffins. Chair legs screeched on the tiled floor.

While walking through, Sanderson's eyes lifted to the steel supported glass roof. Looking over a concrete railing he saw a huge room below. 'Clever idea to sling a café up here,' Sanderson said to Fyurk.

'Yeah. Reckon the roof's better. Great architecture. Where's the kitchen?'

'Through here.' Sanderson ducked behind the counter and showed his badge.

A Chinese youth came from the food preparation area. His hair was encased in a white cap. The apron he wore of a similar colour was besmirched with food.

'You detectives?' he asked.

'Detective Inspector Sanderson and Detective Sergeant Fyurk,' Sanderson replied.

'My name Li Sing. Me find body,' the youth said pointing to his chest.

Sanderson shook Li's grimy hand. 'Now Li. Can you tell us when you found the body?'

Li led them past stainless steel bench tops to where a ramp descended to the dock. Cartons of stores dotted the floor. Sanderson could see the roller door. Li stopped at the top of the ramp. 'This morning go down for delivery. When truck gone I see foot sticking out of bin. Jump down, look closer. Realise no joke. Human foot. So call police.' His smooth face took on an amazed expression.

'What time was that, Li?'

'Think ten o'clock.'

'When was the bin last emptied?'

'No empty last week. Strike.'

'So the body could have been there yesterday?' Sanderson jotted a few notes.

'Maybe. When finish last night just stuff garbage in. Bin full. Main light broken. So pretty dark down there.' Li smoothed his apron and glanced nervously back at the kitchen.

Sanderson realised Li had to get back to work. 'Anything missing?'

'Yes,' answered Li, 'Key to storeroom. Cheryl had it Saturday. She no work Sunday.' Li checked his watch. 'She late coming in today.'

Fyurk reacted immediately. 'What does Cheryl do?'

Li responded, 'She clears tables, cleans up. Tough cookie, Cheryl.' A smile lingered on his thin lips.

Sanderson wondered if the motive was right here. He'd heard chefs were often highly strung. Was that Cheryl in the bin? Had she antagonised the chef once too often?

'Did you like Cheryl, Li?' Sanderson asked.

Li did not hesitate. 'Yes, Detective. Not many here do. She give people lip but got good heart.'

'Do you have her number?' Sanderson and Fyurk followed Li back to the kitchen. He pointed to two numbers on a board. Sanderson rang her home with no result; her mobile was switched off.

'That strange,' Li said, 'Cheryl always on mobile.' The youth's face suddenly distorted showing anxiety. Turning his face towards the roller shutter, he eased out the words, 'You don't think that Cheryl in garbage?'

'We don't know. Sorry, Li. Where can we find her details?'

'Administration block, main office.'

'Is there another key to that storeroom?'

The chef retrieved one from a hook and handed it over. Dejected, Li returned to his cooking.

'Thanks for the help,' Sanderson called out.

'Lucky we know our way round this uni,' Fyurk said.

'Yeah. We may have time to get Cheryl's details and send uniform cops around before they uncover that girl. Li's day is going to be ruined if we ask him to ID the body.' The older detective wove his way out of the cafeteria, Fyurk in his wake.

'Pity. Li seems so genuine. What's the saying – things are hotting up in the kitchen.'

Fyurk slipped on some spilt food, his arms cartwheeled as he regained balance. Sanderson examined his offsider's worn leather shoes. Badly scuffed with unravelled stitching, they brought a scornful look to Sanderson's face.

'While we're on sayings. Shoes are the measure of a man. Rich, get yourself some decent ones with a rubber sole.' Sanderson gestured to his brilliantly polished footwear.

Fyurk's reply was quiet. 'Righto, Gary.'

Sanderson thought he sounded like a chastened child. What could he do to spruce the fellow up?

'I don't mean to pick on you. I've noticed you're better decked out lately. No doubt for our pretty Janine. Buggered shoes won't impress, Rich.'

Fyurk quickened his pace to the administration office weaving among the melee of students. Sanderson detected a reticence in his offsider to talk about women. Janine had rebuffed his own approach but there were plenty more fish. He could take a knock back. Maybe Janine preferred quiet types. Perhaps she saw Fyurk as needing care. His mind switched to Cyndi. Cheeky, he thought, sending those pigs. He'd give her a call.

By the time the detectives returned to the dock area the woman's body was exposed. A couple of plastic chairs had been brought in to stand on. Sanderson climbed up beside Ruggeri. The Italian was staring at the killer's work. He whistled softly through his teeth. 'Strangulation marks on the neck and the pudendum cut away. That's the signature of our previous killer wouldn't you say, Sando?'

Sanderson nodded, quietly taking in the details. The two most obvious things pointed out by Ruggeri reminded him of Katie's body in the pipe. This young woman's body was entirely naked and posed. One leg was tucked under, elevating the genital area. Food remnants had stained her freckly white skin. Sanderson looked for similarities to Katie. Why was this one a victim? The spiky carrot coloured hair was nothing like the attractive blonde they found first. The girl's mouth was open and Sanderson noted a tongue stud. He checked her hands for rings. Nothing but blue painted fingernails.

Leaning over the body, ignoring the ripe odours, he saw multiple gold rings up the outer ridge of her ears. If she was into body piercing, Sanderson wondered if other parts were adorned. A glance at the victim's mutilated pubic region sent an image of what the scalpel might have removed. The cutting was more proficient this time. Had the killer not been rushed or concerned about detection?

Ruggeri stepped down to retrieve evidence bags.

'Richard, come take a look,' Sanderson beckoned.

His offsider, handkerchief clasped to his nose, stood up beside him. Sanderson caught a waft of eucalyptus, realising Fyurk had applied this to cope with the smells.

'Same modus operandi,' Fyurk said.

'Why her?' Sanderson mused, 'She's neither blonde nor attractive like Katie.'

Fyurk snapped on a latex glove and reached forward over the body. He removed a piece of tissue paper stuck to the victim's breast. Ruggeri held up a bag for the item.

'Christ,' said Sanderson, 'he's cut her nipple away as well.'

'That's a progression,' said Fyurk, 'and look at her green eyes. Same colour as Katie's.'

'So they are.'

'And she's wearing a cheap scent.' Fyurk sniffed near her neck. 'Old fashioned. Lily of the Valley.'

Sanderson, stepping down gave his offsider an approving nod. 'How can you smell that amongst all the garbage?'

'I just can. You know this sense can be a problem for me, Gary.'

Sanderson patted him on the shoulder. 'Your big snoz might come in handy.'

Ruggeri and his forensics team busily collected evidence. A finger-print fellow was dusting the bin handle.

Sanderson put calls through to Levy and Hazelton. He told the entomologist the body hadn't been in the bin long as there was no sign of maggots. With the lid of the skip shut and the raw cold of Sunday blowflies would have been less active. Bacterial decomposition of inner organs and soft tissue caused the stink.

The man who would do the autopsy was on his way to view the body in situ and the GMO had just arrived. When his mobile rang, Sanderson spent minutes replying, 'Okay, okay.' The police had found Cheryl's flat empty. The landlady had let them in. She hadn't seen or heard of Cheryl since she went to work Saturday. The rent was overdue and the woman was stroppy.

Returning his phone to his pocket, Sanderson felt the key. He put on a glove and opened the storeroom door. A fluorescent light flickered on. Boxes were stacked around the perimeter. On the cement floor were pieces of screwed up duct tape and splotches of blood.

'Ruggeri, your crime scene just got bigger.'

EIGHTEEN

Anxiety levels rose as Jill drove into the university. She intended dropping by Suzie's office to thank her for a superb dinner. Thinking about the previous evening's final incident ruined her recollections. What a dilemma.

No one but Duncan could have been responsible for despoiling her evening bag. She had washed the satin lining till the colour ran and sprayed it with perfume. Despite leaving it outside, the faeces smell clung. Jill threw the bag in a wheelie bin.

Had she got the message right? Was she being a shit? To be told in such a despicable way meant a complete reassessment of her social interactions. Jill still needed to thank Suzie in a normal manner. Suzie was probably unaware of Duncan's conniving.

While it would give her great satisfaction never to see Duncan's smarmy face again, it wasn't possible. He was head of the history faculty; she had to work with the man. The act she suspected him of was way too embarrassing to discuss with anyone. She'd have to get over it and be more amenable.

In the lift she encountered Professor Mitchell's research assistant.

'Hello, Paula,' Jill said, 'that colour suits you.'

Paula was wearing a russet jacket. Her lips were outlined and filled in with a matching colour. What a distinctive style she had.

'Thanks.' Paula walked out as the doors slid open.

Jill hesitated then followed. 'Could I have a word with you, Paula? In my office.'

Paula appeared surprised that she wanted to talk. Jill figured Paula was the way to Duncan. From her observations Paula managed him so well. They went in, shut the door and Jill placed her briefcase on the desk.

'I haven't started out here well. You're so friendly, Paula, I could do with a few pointers.'

'Oh,' she batted the air with her hand, 'Not everyone has the gift of the gab, Jill. You're doing okay.'

Jill propped herself on the edge of the desk determined to go on. 'Not really. I don't have the touch with Duncan.'

'Touch is the word, all right.' Paula heaved a sigh, her breasts moving in unison under a lacy top. 'Duncan is quite manageable if you fend off his advances with a joke. I know he hired me for these.' She glanced down at her curvaceous cleavage.

'Surely not,' Jill said.

'Afraid so. Duncan likes his titillation. If I laid it on I doubt he'd be up to it.' Paula laughed.

'Has he had affairs?'

'Not here to my knowledge. Like a lot of men, Jill, he's all testosterone and talk. Don't let him intimidate you.'

Jill's smile was half hearted. Paula's advice reassured her.

'Duncan's so prolific with his academic publishing. There's so much more to the man. You understand him, Paula.'

The assistant glowed.

'I do. Been here long enough. As to his work that's where I come in. Duncan's a great ideas man but I do the shaping, footnoting and bibliography. He depends on me as much as I do on him.'

'A symbiotic relationship.' Jill walked to the door. 'Thanks, Paula. I get the picture. A good research assistant is invaluable.'

As she left, Paula's grin boosted her confidence. An hour later, after a pleasant exchange with Suzie Norton, Jill knocked on Duncan's door. With a smile glued to her face, she responded to a curt, 'Come in.'

Sitting there in his leather jacket, he looked wary. What she would have given to know his thoughts at that moment. Behind glasses, his beady eyes assessed her. She'd taken care to dress smartly; a burnt orange fitted top over black pants.

'Jill, do sit down. What can I do for you?'

The smarmy tone was back.

'I want advice on where to send this article for publication.' Jill played the underling whilst trying to eradicate all thought of the bag incident.

He took the pages, glancing over the title. 'Impressive,' he said, 'I'll investigate. Glad to help.'

'I've just thanked Suzie for a lovely meal last night. I don't get out enough. Nice to be included.' Jill watched his face for a reaction. Was there a glimmer of guilt?

His reply was smooth, 'Good company too. A stimulating evening.'

'I've been a little touchy since the murder.'

'It's rocked us all. That Fyurk fellow fingerprinted me. Cellophane from my cigarette packet floated from the balcony into their crime scene. Fancy that.'

'Oh, I didn't know they had any evidence.'

'It was only for elimination purposes.'

'Anyway, thanks for being my saviour in the car park that night,' Jill said in the friendliest voice she could muster.

He rose and took her arm to escort her out. 'Attractive young women need looking after.'

Jill took his smile for a smirk. 'You're very thoughtful, Duncan.'

In the safety of her office, Jill felt she'd handled the situation well. She was slowly emerging from a chrysalis. Tonight she would ring Mother, regale her with stories of the dinner party. Her daughter mixing it with professors would give Mother something to boast about at the retirement village morning teas. Jill would break the news of her forthcoming trip.

On the desk was a book she'd recently ordered. *The Cruise of the Janet Nichol* was Fanny Stevenson's account of a three-month trading voyage through the Pacific in 1890 with her famous novelist husband and grown son. The diary form and historic photos immediately grabbed her attention. Fanny was described shooting sharks with a silver revolver in each hand. Realising the time, Jill could not delve further. She had a lecture to give so reluctantly closed the book.

As she hurried to the theatre, groups of students were clustered in various spots talking fervently. What was going on? A security guard outside the building relayed the news. Another murder. Jill felt cold inside as if her stomach had been clamped. Just when normality returned to the campus, the killer had struck again. Who was it this time? For a moment the subdued face of Madeline Harper flashed into mind. Oh no. Jill scrabbled in her bag for the mobile. It slipped to the concrete.

'Shit,' her voice louder than she realised. Jill retrieved it and rang Gary. No one answered.

The security guard was several metres away looking askance at her actions.

'Do they know who?' Jill yelled.

He backed off. 'Don't think so. Heard from students the area behind the cafeteria is crawling with cops.'

Jill left her notes inside and hurried to the scene desperate to find out. Tape blocked her path. She couldn't see Gary or his offsider anywhere so hit redial. Bloody voicemail. Forensic people in their blue overalls were entering a storeroom. A uniformed policeman stood near a huge bin. Atop the rubbish Jill could make out the shape of a body. Her mind reeled with possibilities. Surely that wasn't Madeline. She felt sick imagining how the girl had died, if Madeline too was mutilated.

An incredibly tall bearded man stepped outside the tape. He put his bag on the ground to strip off overalls.

Jill pounced, 'Is it another student?'

'They don't think so.' He strode off.

With some relief, she returned to give a lecture minus her usual enthusiasm. For the rest of the day the history staff speculated on the new tragedy. Late afternoon the Chancellor's email came. Still no identity. Jill realised the morning paper would inform her along with everyone else. Perhaps she wouldn't be involved. The murderer was not targeting her students. She did give Liam a thought. Where was he?

Jill was quite edgy by the time she arrived home. Instead of leaving her mobile concealed in the car she kept it close. If someone broke in they might cut phone lines. She wasn't a mobile person. It was off most of the time unless she was meeting a friend and kept in the car in case of a breakdown. From now on it'd be on her bedside table, a lifeline to the outside world.

Depositing her briefcase in the hall, she warily searched each room. What if someone was waiting inside? Jill wouldn't know until grabbed as in scary movies. Her bedroom window was locked in the open position not wide enough to admit an intruder. All was as it should be. Her agitation eased. She found a packet of Lindt chocolates and scoffed a few to feel better.

With a new murder she wanted more protection in her townhouse. Jill rang a company that installed burglar alarms. Recounting the murders made her uneasy again. In a placating tone, the representative explained an alarm would ensure no one was in the place and a panic button could be near her bed.

That night she picked up *Love Rat*, a book far removed from the crime genre as possible. She'd heard Wendy Harmer's amusing recommendation on the radio: 'People dump on Chick Lit as vain and vacuous.' Jill needed something light tonight, hoping to divert her attention from the horrible happenings at the university.

In the dreamy state of awakening, she realised it was a workday. Her eyes blinked at sunshine wending its way around the blind. An urgent thought made her leap up and put on a tracksuit. Without running a brush through her hair, she grabbed a purse and left to buy a paper. Jill should have flicked the TV on but somehow scanning print was more satisfying. Who was she kidding? Her thoughts were so jumbled she didn't even think about the radio. This second victim at Phillips University would have all forms of the media jumping.

Her sneakers thudded along the pavement shaking reality into her body. The terror of a depraved unknown skulking around campus was hard to believe. He was still there. Dread seeped into Jill once again, tightening her chest. Fear, uncertainty and suspicion would return to her workplace. Quick detection, she hoped, would lead to this vile perpetrator.

Car tyres squealed as drivers rushed to work. For some the day would be different, especially for the charming Detective Inspector Sanderson. Jill assumed he'd been called in on this new case. Not getting through to him yesterday had been frustrating. Not that she expected he'd have time for her. If only he'd been at the crime scene. Maybe Gary and Fyurk had gone off to interview witnesses and collect statements.

A breeze fluttered papers in their rack outside the service station. The headline: KILLER STRIKES AGAIN wasn't terribly inventive. She folded the front page inwards and walked inside to pay. Before her in the queue was a man, immaculate in his business suit. His glance on his way out made her realise how dreadful she must have appeared. Jill thought of men's comments of how women looked when they wake. Possibly he'd describe her when he got to work. Embarrassed, she paid and scarpered.

Impatient to read the main story of the day, Jill hurried home. Her mind tracked back to Gary and his whereabouts. She decided to dress up in case he was at the university. Remembering she hadn't told him about following Liam and his mate that night, urged her to get involved again. But she had nothing to tell. Two students played squash late at night. So what.

Liam had been the model student in recent months. It inspired her to see a young man so caught up in his work. His words: 'You're my favourite lecturer,' echoed in her mind. Jill gave him a well-earned A in his first essay. The look on his face when he saw the grade was heart-warming. This was the payoff in teaching. Somehow your own enthusiasm infiltrates other minds. Jill could not envisage Liam having a violent side or seeing his intellectual journey cut short by murder.

With another killing she imagined some abhorrent type locked away forever. For some reason her skin crawled reminding her of Duncan Mitchell. The creepy crawly professor she'd just managed to be nice to. She recalled telling Gary how Duncan had scared her in the car park one night. The detective had put it down to jittery nerves. Duncan was the most complex person she'd ever met. His academic star was so bright everyone was prepared to overlook the way he treated women.

Inside, Jill laid the paper on the table, rapidly scanning the newsprint. It appeared the girl worked in the cafeteria. Yes, there was a hint of the same methods being used. Oh God. No use trying to ring Gary. Blood thumped in her temples. Did she have any painkillers?

NINETEEN

On Sunday afternoon Barbara could hear Hugh in the garden, finally trimming the murrayas and buxus. The snip of shears brought a sense of satisfaction. She preferred polishing her nails to getting dirt under them. Tonight they were dining at the golf club and although she wasn't a player, she enjoyed the excellent food. Leaning forward on the lounge she stroked mango colour on her perfectly shaped nails. Barbara looked forward to half an hour with her decorating magazines while her polish dried. She'd rung Madeline to pick up a takeaway for herself on the way home.

Hugh came inside looking hot and cranky.

'Darling, can I get you a coffee or cool drink?'

'No. I'll shower and get ready so I can watch the news.' Hugh wiped his hand over a crinkled brow.

Barbara wondered at a mind so concerned with world happenings.

'That's a good job done, Hugh. I just can't handle shears with my arthritis.'

'Your condition seems convenient. Has your bum left the couch all afternoon?'

'Go and shower, Hugh. Your unpleasantness might wash off with the sweat.' He raised his eyebrows but did not bite back.

When Hugh had finished in the bedroom she went in. Not wanting to emphasise her weight gain, Barbara had bought an outfit a size larger than usual, as the style was clingy. Tiny jewels were glued on parts of the printed top. Sparkles made her feel glamorous. Barbara slipped into the new caramel shoes and picked up her handbag.

In the lounge room the weather flashed on TV; sunny for a few days then rain clouds. Shouldn't hold up building as they were largely working inside now, she thought.

Hugh turned the set off taking her in at a glance.

'That outfit makes you look really big,' he said.

Determined not to show hurt at his remark, Barbara responded, 'You look marvellous too, Hugh. Shall we go?'

He was wearing the designer jeans he'd bought himself. The shirt was the fine burgundy check she'd given him for his birthday. Until recently he'd never taken much interest in clothes. Perhaps now he'd appreciate her choices more.

On entering the golf club, Barbara noticed the Rivers were at the table. After the seafood debacle she decided to be on her best behaviour. Mary Rivers was one of those tall athletic women destined to be forever thin. Her tanned skin was evidence of the three days a week she spent on the golf course but the grey blouse did nothing for her complexion, Barbara thought. She smiled at Bob Rivers although he was pompous and reluctant to talk of anything other than golf and his transport business.

The whole golf thing seemed a touch self-indulgent to Barbara. She felt a sense of achievement as patients resumed their lives. Instead of filling in time playing she was still working and helping people. When she'd seen her shoulder injury fellow this week the pinched look of pain was gone; his movement almost recovered.

Fortunately this evening was some kind of club presentation so conversation could be kept to a minimum. Barbara ordered Atlantic salmon, the flakes of pink fish cooked to perfection. A coriander dressing on the greens added to the flavour. When her crème caramel arrived Hugh raised an eyebrow and started to open his mouth. Barbara gave him a look of death. His cutlery clattered to the plate. Hugh's attempts at controlling her diet only made Barbara more defiant. Food was one of the real pleasures of her life. How dare he try to take that from her. Doctors always thought they could tell people what to do. Well, Hugh could just save that for his patients. Her patience was running out.

Next morning after her family had gone Barbara settled on the lounge to enjoy a leisurely coffee. Beau curled up beside her, snuffling and licking his paws. She glanced over her kitchen design for the new house. She had been to the factory to pick the cupboard door mouldings and had chosen a silvery grey colour. The matt finish would be really smart with granite bench tops. If only she could find the stone she had in mind.

At 11 am she left to meet Glen at the house. The whine of a saw told Barbara tiling upstairs was still in progress. The exterior looked almost finished. When were the painters due, she wondered? She tracked down Glen who presented her with a list: mixer tap for the kitchen, fittings for the other bathrooms, even the style of cornice.

'Picking the granite is top priority, Barbara.' Glen produced a tattered piece of paper from his pocket, the address of yet another specialist.

'I've driven most of Sydney. This one's closer. I'll go there now.'

'Time's running out,' Glen said, 'the cupboards will be ready for installation in two weeks. So we'll need bench tops organised. Maybe you could settle for the black granite.' Glen's face was hopeful.

'Today, Glen, I'll find the right colour. Plain black would be so ordinary.' She tried to keep annoyance from her tone. Why did builders always want to take the easy way out?

'I agree, Barbara.'

In the yard, slabs of granite were stacked like peaks of a small mountain range. A man in dusty overalls appeared. Barbara described the stone she had in mind: large crystals, not too dark with a tinge of green. Rubbing the stubble on his chin, he hesitated.

'Got something like that in recently,' he said, 'be enough to do a kitchen.'

'Bingo,' she announced on seeing it, 'exactly what I want.' Barbara rang her builder on the mobile and conveyed the good news. His sigh of relief was clearly audible.

On the way home she stopped to search for taps. After one place the thought of a new skirt to go with her boots seemed a better use of her day off. Barbara's favourite boutique in Mona Vale was sure to have something.

She made a beeline for the rack of skirts. A gold burnished chocolate brown caught her eye; a fabulous fabric but the net panels were a bit fussy. She adored the wine colour of a crushed silk skirt. Recalling her taupe beaded top, the urge to buy escalated. In the change room she twirled as feather soft material swished her thighs. Definitely, a feel-good purchase.

After Barbara switched off the car's ignition, she heard the end of a news flash. Another girl's body had been found at Phillips University. Oh my God. Maddy. Perspiration swamped her forehead. Her stomach churned. A wave of nausea. What if …?

She ratted through her handbag seizing her mobile. Fingers frantically pushed buttons. It rang. Madeline answered.

'Maddy. God. It's you,' she gabbled into the phone.

'Mum?'

'Another girl killed. I thought it might be you,' her voice trembled.

'I'm fine, Mum. Just heard myself. Sorry, I should have called.'

Madeline's voice placated her. 'Can't you just come home where you're safe?'

'Mum, nothing more's going to happen today. I've got exams coming up. Talk to you tonight.'

Her daughter's voice cut off and Barbara sat trying to recover from shock. She noticed a car behind had an indicator on waiting for her parking spot. Blow them. She just couldn't drive. Her hands covered her face as she leant on the steering wheel.

Lulled back into a sense of safety in recent months, Barbara had forgotten the horror of death. Now she'd be paranoid whenever Madeline wasn't home. Who knew which girls the murderer targeted? Why hadn't the police got him after the first one?

Barbara hadn't contacted Katie's parents after the funeral. She felt on the day her condolences were inadequate. The Fosters had lost their only daughter. At least they had another child. Selecting a card bright with flowers, she'd written comforting words: how the family liked Katie, how Maddy would miss her.

Today more parents would have their lives irrevocably changed. Barbara recalled seeing the father of another murdered girl, Anita Cobby, interviewed. Her parents had formed some victims' association to help others deal with violent crime. She wondered how that filled the void of their missing daughter: no career, no partner, no grandchildren.

Gradually, Barbara felt well enough to drive home. She swooped up Beau and cuddled him. Switching on the coffee machine, she took her bag and purchase to the bedroom. Hugh had left his underpants, yet again, on the ensuite floor. She put them in the laundry basket without her usual annoyance. Once more she thought, what if it had been Madeline? Her life and Hugh's could be overturned. Barbara had read how losing a child often ripped a family apart. Whether it was blame or simply not coping had not been clear. All that wasted potential!

Barbara ground the beans for a double shot of coffee and let the machine gurgle away. She placed two Tim Tams on a plate then filled her stainless steel cup with the strong brew. Sitting on the lounge sipping and nibbling her way to comfort, Barbara switched on the TV. Perhaps the early news would feature the new murder. She sat mesmerised. After twenty minutes there was the merest mention.

Hugh crossed her mind. He'd be busy with patients at the surgery. What if his secretary heard of the incident on the radio? He too would want to know Madeline was safe. Barbara phoned to be told Hugh was busy. She left a message.

Unable to settle on any task, Barbara took a notepad into her daughter's room. The detective's card was still on the bedside table. She jotted his mobile number. Ignoring teenage clutter, she wandered out onto the balcony. The ocean stretched flat and blue to the horizon. Slow moving air jostled the gum tips. A feel of the coming winter enveloped Barbara. A lorikeet flew into the nearest tree squawking. The bird's bright plumage and its actions cheered her a little.

How she'd like to know more about this case. The phone number drew Barbara's gaze. Perhaps this wasn't the right time to call Detective Sanderson. He had another murder on his hands.

When Barbara heard Madeline's car she watched her walk down the path. Shiny blonde hair swung with her stride. Barbara ached with emotion at the sight. Faded jeans, slip-on runners and a bronze top showing her cleavage exemplified the young woman's style. A backpack, heavy with books, was slung over one shoulder. Madeline, precious as a diamond, was growing away from her day by day. This letting go of offspring was new to Barbara. Could she step back and allow her to live her own life?

As soon as Madeline entered, Barbara's arms encircled her daughter. 'You're home,' she murmured. Barbara stood back, wiping tear-filled eyes and no doubt smudging her mascara.

Madeline responded gently, 'Mum, stop worrying. You can't live as though you're going to die. Just because that madman attacked Katie, there's no reason to think I'm next.'

Oh, to be bomb proof like the young. 'I'm trying to see reason, Maddy. Just had that one terrible thought. You know how much I love you.' Barbara's voice trembled.

Beau, awakened from his afternoon nap, skittered up the hallway. Sensing the emotion, his upturned face swung back and forth.

'Hi, Beau,' Madeline gave his ear a scratch. 'Come on, Mum, make me one of your coffees.'

Her daughter's arm swung around her, relieving the tightness she felt inside.

Hugh's look was sombre when he arrived home.

'Got your message, Barbs. Had a rough day?'

'Sure have.' Barbara gave him an unexpected hug. All she wanted at that moment was to keep their little family together, safe.

In the kitchen she diced vegetables for a stir-fry: onions, capsicum, mushrooms and beans. Strips of beef sizzled in the wok as she added the contents of the chopping board. Eventually Barbara poured in a jar of satay sauce and sprinkled some crispy noodles. The whole time she kept her eye on Madeline and Hugh watching the news, talking in the ads. We must do more together, she thought, get back to happier times. Years ago her husband had been besotted with her. When Madeline was young he'd raved about her being a great mother. Life now seemed pedestrian. Then this threat of some killer lurking at her daughter's university changed everything.

Before work next morning Barbara rang the detective.

'Sanderson.' His voice sounded harried.

'You don't know me, Detective. I'm Barbara Harper, Madeline's mum. I did see you at Katie Foster's funeral.'

'Ah, the lady in olive.'

Barbara was chuffed at him remembering. 'That's right, Detective. How observant of you.'

'That's my business, Mrs Harper. How can I help?'

Barbara launched into her fears for Madeline.

'I know this is not what a mother wants to hear, Mrs Harper, but we don't know what the killer's criteria are.'

She heard him hesitate.

Barbara's voice was shaky, 'What can I do to keep my daughter safe?'

TWENTY

The roller shutter clanked open revealing a ledge of a height suitable for a truck to reverse in and unload directly from the tray. Sanderson and Fyurk eased themselves down; Li's was more an agile leap. The older detective stood where he could observe the chef's reaction. Li had been reluctant to do an ID on the body, mumbling something about Chinese omens. Sanderson wasn't having any cultural excuses. He wanted to know who this girl was so he could start tracking her killer.

Fyurk urged Li closer to the skip bin. 'Just stand on the chair and look at her face.'

To Sanderson, the chef barely reacted to the odours emanating from his surroundings. His head was deliberately averted from the body. Once elevated, Li focussed his gaze and a strange moan resonated like in a cavern. His smooth face became a crazy distortion. Grief, Sanderson thought.

'That Cheryl,' he said, turning and stepping down.

'Thank you, Li. That's all for now,' Sanderson directed.

The chef scaled the concrete lip, then closed the shutter.

'What do you think?' asked Fyurk.

'Li definitely seemed horrified by what he saw. Hard to fake. Not a reaction you'd expect from a perpetrator. Maybe his Chinese beliefs are right. Images of the dead haunt you.'

'Isn't that why we detach, make sick jokes?' Fyurk scraped the toe of his worn shoe over a ridge in the cement.

'Yeah. Heard one of the forensics blokes saying she must have been a ripe one to be thrown out with the garbage. But we don't know who Cheryl is, Rich. When corpses start floating through my brain at night I hit the grog.' Sanderson noted the disappointed glance of his offsider.

'Not an option for me, Gary. Only drink the odd beer. Still hasn't happened to me yet.'

'Everyone finds his own poison.' Sanderson pointed to Fyurk's camera. 'You get all the preliminary shots we need?'

A nod from the young detective as he wiped his nose again. Sanderson entered the storeroom. Ruggeri was on his haunches working on the bloodstains.

'Pete, our victim's Cheryl Patterson. Worked in the cafeteria. Going up there now to list all her workmates and start interviewing. Buzz me on the mobile if anything else turns up.'

'Right, Sando. It'll be a few hours before we send the body to the morgue.'

Fyurk hovered at the door. 'You think the killer moved some of those boxes to make room in here? Maybe prints on the packing tape.'

'Oh, our young detective's putting his bit in.' Ruggeri's usual stern look hardened. He waved his latexed hand as if dismissing Fyurk. 'I'm pretty sure our murderer's smart enough to wear gloves but I'll get prints to check it out. Thanks, Sherlock.'

Sanderson noticed Fyurk's pasty face redden. He moved to the door. 'What happened to the Italian charm, Ruggeri?' The dark covered head rose with a challenging stare.

'C'mon, Rich, we'll start with a coffee.'

In the cafeteria, Fyurk grabbed a tray. From a heated cabinet he selected a sausage roll and tossed a tomato sauce packet beside it. Sanderson scanned the display and ordered two cappuccinos. The cashier was a beefy woman in a navy dress. Her ample flesh splayed out over the stool she swivelled on. She pressed buttons and told him the amount. Not the chatty type, Sanderson thought, no joy interviewing her when she comes off her shift.

A cleared table was hard to find. Perhaps Cheryl's stand-in hadn't arrived. Sanderson took his first breather of the morning, feeling the hit of caffeine doing him good. Flakes of pastry adorned Fyurk's shirt. Sanderson watched his offsider examine the steel and glass ceiling. A university cafeteria that was rarely closed must require a heap of staff. He hoped the manager's strength was organization. Everyone who worked with Cheryl would help them build the picture. Li's remark that she gave people lip might be a starting point. He did not anticipate a well-liked person was going to emerge from this investigation.

His mind tracked back to the skip bin. Someone she worked with could have sent her to the storeroom on Saturday night. Down there no one was likely to hear screams as a ligature tightened around her neck. When was the duct tape applied? To keep her quiet if she came to. Sanderson would have to wait for the autopsy to see where else it was used on her body. Using the tape was risky. How easy for the killer's hairs to be pulled out and caught.

On the other hand, the offender could be an outsider waiting in the darkness of the dock. That's two lights out and two bodies. Is our killer super observant? Poor maintenance could be a factor. It'd be easy to wait and see if Cheryl opened the shutter, jumped down and went into the storeroom. Just grab her, move in and shut the door. Why didn't someone come looking for her? Late at night all the other staff were in a hurry to leave. Perhaps Cheryl heard the shutter close before her asphyxiation.

Half an hour later the detectives had a list of twenty employees and their shifts. The cashier, kitchen hand and table clearer were all finishing after lunch.

'Are we going to hang around, Gary?' Fyurk took off his jacket and slung it over a chair.

Sanderson felt his offsider was reluctant to return to the crime scene after Ruggeri's jibe. They really should head back to the office to start lining up interviews with Cheryl's co-workers. Coffee had returned the spark to his brain.

'No,' he said, 'follow me.'

Leaving the clatter of the cafeteria behind, they emerged into a tree-lined quadrangle. Clusters of students lazed on its grassy centre. Sanderson peered in a south-westerly direction above the gums. Fyurk's bewildered expression brought a response.

'Just a hunch,' Sanderson said, 'I'd like to see if Liam's got an alibi for the weekend. You could do with a walk in the sun. Clear up that cold. Put some colour in your face.'

The older detective set off at a brisk pace down a path towards the residential buildings. Multi-storeyed car parks shadowed Sanderson before he emerged into brightness once again.

Catching up, Fyurk's breathy remark sounded peeved. 'Good to know someone cares. Is this the new sensitive Sanderson?'

Sanderson laughed. 'Hardly, Rich. Don't go spreading that around or you'll find I'm a hard bastard.'

They crossed a road and found the familiar building. In the dimly lit corridor Sanderson rapped on Liam's door. Disappointment flooded his face. The same student as last time stood before him. Redness around his eyes told Sanderson he hadn't been studying.

'I'm looking for Liam Davidson. You were in his room last time. What're doing here again?'

The young man didn't respond. He swung the door wide open revealing a second bed against a wall. 'It's my room too.' His arm swept an arc in the air.

The distinctive smell of marijuana wafted towards Sanderson. He glanced at Fyurk, who nodded. In several strides Sanderson flung open the window allowing crisp air to infiltrate. Leave drug busting to the uniforms, he told himself.

'What's your name?' Sanderson's tone was rough.

'Martin.' The student backed towards the computer desk, wary.

'Well Martin, Detectives Sanderson and Fyurk would like to know the whereabouts of your room-mate.'

'Liam's visiting his mum. She's sick.'

'Where?'

'Canberra.'

Fyurk interjected, 'When did he leave?'

'Friday. He's due back soon.' Martin checked a black dive watch on his hairy wrist.

'Is there no one else to look after her?' Sanderson asked.

'No. Liam never knew his father. Shot through when he was a baby. Now his mum's got cancer it's really tough on him.'

Fyurk's face reacted to this revelation.

Outside the building Sanderson entered the number Martin had given him. A woman's voice, weak and weary, answered. Within minutes Sanderson ascertained Liam had a perfect alibi for the whole weekend.

'So, Rich, Liam doesn't appear to be our murderer. I saw you react to the absent father. That blows your theory on violent upbringing. Maybe the medical records will clarify things.'

Fyurk was balling his handkerchief. 'Theories offer new leads, Gary. Not all are fruitful. At least we're able to eliminate one suspect. That's progress.'

Sanderson's face showed disgust. 'Put that snot rag away. It's covered in enough bacteria to bag it. Use tissues for Christ's sake.'

Fyurk followed him to the car in silence.

Back in the office his offsider scooted off to find Janine. Sanderson noticed two documents on his desk. Finally Liam's medical records had arrived. He scanned them hastily. Head trauma from a fall off a pushbike in primary school was the main event. Temporary memory loss meant frontal lobe damage was suspected. This can cause personality changes. No mention of the finger movement. Months later burns to the hands were treated after an arson incident at school. Lengthy counselling had followed. No abuse was mentioned. Interesting, Sanderson thought, Liam's potential for criminal behaviour was aborted before reaching the danger of adolescence. Fyurk would no doubt find this fascinating.

He turned his attention to the other envelope. The final autopsy report on Katie Foster had been sitting on a desk somewhere for two weeks if the date was right. Reading the final page, Sanderson's feelings received a jolt. Katie had a serious heart defect. She probably wouldn't have lived long enough to get her university degree anyway. Tragic. He'd call her parents. Not that he expected this news to make them feel better about their daughter's death.

Fyurk seemed much brighter on his return. No doubt Janine had been sympathetic. He plonked down the file on their second victim.

'Read these,' Sanderson handed over the documents he'd been por-ing over, 'then we'll need to advise Cheryl's next of kin before the media get wind of it.'

In the file a solitary name was listed: Mrs Muriel Carter with a Mosman address. Sanderson rang the number. The woman's voice sounded haughty. As she heard the word detective her annoyance came over clearly, 'Cheryl's not in trouble again.'

'No, Mrs Carter. Are you her mother?'

'Aunt. Cheryl's parents died in a tourist bus crash in Spain two years ago. I took my niece in, Detective. But then she started drinking at home, getting surly with me so I helped set her up in a flat. Lot of thanks, I rarely see her now. What's all this about?'

'I'd rather not go into it over the phone. We'd like to see you in half an hour if that suits.'

'I suppose so. But I do have ladies coming for bridge and afternoon tea.'

'We'll be brief, Mrs Carter.'

Sanderson hung up. He didn't care whether his news would mess up the planned card afternoon. Poor Cheryl. Was there no one going to miss her?

As he drove down Awaba Street, Sanderson was amazed at the har-bour views. Sun glimmered off deep blue water, way out to the heads. The luxury apartment block was painted a sunny yellow. Fyurk buzzed the intercom. At first sight Sanderson summed up Muriel Carter: silver permed curls, prim lips and an expensive scarf to highlight an autumn toned pantsuit. She led them over plush Asian carpet to a beige leather lounge. Settling herself in an armchair, ankles crossed, she asked, 'Now Detectives, what's Cheryl been up to this time?'

'I'm sorry to inform you Mrs Carter that your niece has been murdered.' Sanderson noted the wrinkled face showed a flutter of shock.

'Murdered?' Her tone indicated disbelief. Muriel's lower lip trembled. 'I know the girl was a bit silly at times but why would anyone want to kill Cheryl?'

'That's what we'd like to find out, Mrs Carter.'

Fyurk with his calm voice continued the interrogation. Sanderson took notes. Cheryl's bit of trouble had been marijuana possession and maxed credit cards. After the aunt's initial help it didn't sound like much emotional support was forthcoming for a girl who'd tragically lost her parents. Not wanting to ruin Muriel's bridge afternoon, he signalled their departure.

Victimology, to be useful in a case, needed to be built up from a variety of sources. At the university things did not improve. The interviews with the first of Cheryl's colleagues were far from pleasant. Only Li had a good word to say. Fyurk was unable to work out who was last to see Cheryl alive. Sanderson felt weary as page after page of his notebook filled with details.

By the time they'd finished, the body had been removed from the crime scene. The tape was still in place and a solitary uniform cop slouched on a chair not far from the skip bin.

'Guess we'll see Ruggeri later,' Sanderson said with annoyance. 'Who did Li say Cheryl was going out with?'

'Bob, the groundsman.' Fyurk appeared thoughtful, rubbing long fingers over stubble on his chin.

'Your mate, the gardener, deals with the bins round here, right. Maybe he got rough. Time to do a full check on our Bob. Perhaps he was into the action with Katie.'

'Not likely. With today's MO it's pretty obvious we have a serial killer operating here. Their victims are strangers. That's why these killers are hard to catch and they don't stop.'

At the car Sanderson phoned the university administration office to fax him Bob's employee details.

'I'll see if he's got a record as soon as we get back, Gary.'

Grey rain clouds dominated the skyline as they drove to the office. Lightning cracked. They made it inside as drops splattered on the pavement. Sanderson sent Fyurk in search of Janine to enter the information they'd gleaned on Cheryl's life. He glanced the length of the corridor and recognised Fyurk's silhouette with the busty Janine. Sanderson had been well aware of the increased eye contact between the pair lately and wondered where it would lead. He got himself a coffee and slumped at his desk. Hearing Ralston's booming voice next door, he readied himself for an onslaught of questions on this second victim. How long did he have before his superior bustled in? Sanderson reached for Cyndi's ornament, a wry smile crossed his face. She liked having a cop to call if mugs troubled her. He wasn't sure if Cyndi paid him in kind or really fancied him. Jabbing the digits on his mobile, he left a message suggesting they meet for a drink that evening.

The encounter with Ralston went okay. Sanderson picked up a Thai curry on the way home and went through his clothes ritual. Hours later, after a scrub and a feed, he decided to walk down the hill to the Surry Hills pub. Cyndi was just the interlude he needed before re-examining the case.

He'd bought two white wines when most male eyes swivelled towards the door. Cyndi made an entrance in a tight short skirt. Her hair was swept back from her face and gold curls cascaded to her delicious cleavage. She was all class and oozed sex appeal. The way she sidled up to him elevated his spirits. He led her to a table out the back.

'How's my big Detective?' Her voice seductive.

This woman sure knows how to massage a man's ego, Sanderson thought.

After sipping her wine, Cyndi traced a red-nailed finger down his cheek to the edge of his lips.

'A whole lot better for seeing you.' He winked at her feeling a grin encompass his face. Sanderson felt she was in no hurry. Their conversation took a surprising turn to property. He found himself telling her how he'd bought his semi. On his father's death he'd been left a substantial legacy. With this as a deposit and stretching the term of the mortgage, a detective's salary was enough to cover the deal.

Cyndi owned a luxury apartment in Elizabeth Bay and an investment unit in the city. She had started building an elite clientele when at university. Being smarter than the girls who got into drugs, she made so much money she dropped out. Cyndi's plan included building up a portfolio of properties as security then she'd ditch the punters.

Wow, Sanderson thought, quite an agenda for someone on the game.

Cyndi checked her watch and became the tease she usually was. Before long she led him to a darkened room and fulfilment.

When Sanderson arrived home there was a message to ring Fyurk.

'Gary, Jill Ashworth rang in with information. She wants to meet you in the city. Your mobile's been off for hours. Where've you been?'

'Important meeting, Rich.'

'You've been with that Cyndi again.'

'So. Aren't you getting any?' The senior detective heard Fyurk gulp for air.

'None of your bloody business, Sanderson. Not everyone runs their life around women.'

'I've never had a bad fuck yet, Rich.' He laughed.

'You're incorrigible, Gary.'

TWENTY-ONE

Jill was fifteen minutes early for her meeting with Gary. Time to compose herself.

Driving to Roseville Station and catching a train was a better option than trying to park in the city. After being jostled in carriages and on crowded city pavements the bar provided the peace she craved. Deep leather chairs and the red patterned carpet gave it opulence. Heavy varnished frames around the windows and doors created a feeling of century-old grandeur. Outside, few leaves remained on the plane trees as winter approached.

As Jill checked the entrance yet again her eyes rested on a painting of a square rig ship surging down a wave. Probably a John Allcot, one of Australia's finest maritime artists, its heavily gilded frame representative of that shipping era. In a few short weeks she'd be embarking on one of a similar rig. A rush of excitement washed through her. She hoped the weather would not be as wild as that depicted in the painting. Would it feel like stepping back in time? But she could not let her mind wander when any minute the handsome Detective Sanderson would walk in.

He'd sounded harassed when he finally rang her at work. She imagined the day after finding a second victim would be extremely busy. When Jill told him her information could not be revealed over the phone his voice sounded a touch intrigued. She gave him directions and a time then hung up. What was stronger? The urge to see him or to help with the investigation. Just the sound of his voice, the way he hesitated, picturing his smile had a tumultuous effect on her.

Would Gary think the setting matched the historian? While he might prefer seedy bars, she liked old-world ambience. A place this quiet was hard to find in a busy city. A couple of businessmen were huddled in one corner, their voices a murmur. Finishing her coffee, she relaxed into soft leather. Her mind switched to the time she first met Gary in her office. His confidence, the way he moved had an immediate impact. At the Italian restaurant her treatise on academic life had sent his eyes rolling up Mount Vesuvius. Then the suggestion she'd overdressed made her blood boil. Why didn't she know how to act around men?

When he arrived the room seemed to expand. In a well-cut jacket he sauntered over, his bright yellow tie swaying with his walk. The barmaid's glance signalled envy when he headed her way. Watching him, the barmaid polished a glass and slung it on the overhead rack.

'Jill, good to see you.' He shook her hand and surveyed the bar. 'What'll it be?'

'I don't usually drink during the day.' Jill pointed to the coffee cup as proof.

'Come on. A crisp sauvignon blanc? I need something stronger.'

She nodded and he strode away. Chatting up the barmaid, Gary rested his elbow lazily on the bar. He placed the drinks on coasters; his Scotch and ice clinked. Her glass was chilled, a fine beading of moisture on its surface. Jill tasted. His choice was excellent.

He drank, settled back and gazed at her. 'Now just what information is too hot for our phone lines?'

His straight-to-business attitude was discomforting. Jill's throat felt tight.

'Well, Gary, you know how you told me to keep an eye out round the campus at night?'

'You didn't seem too keen on the idea if I remember right.' A flicker of a smile lingered.

She told him about following Liam and his mate, her disguise, wimping out and getting a cab back to her car.

'I felt so silly when they were only playing squash.'

'Crims play sport too, Jill.'

'Have you looked into Liam's background? He's certainly different but I don't think he's capable of these terrible murders.'

Gary's face flashed a look of concern. 'As it happens you're right. I'll tell you in confidence Liam's got a perfect alibi for this second one. Away all weekend looking after his mum. She's got cancer. Turns out a spill off a bike as a kid is probably why he's unusual.'

Her glass clunked on the table. Jill felt relieved; her instinctive estimation of Liam had been correct. Gary appeared confused. Maybe he was thinking a phone call could have handled this. He took another sip and looked her over, eyes twinkling. His scrutiny made her feel self-conscious. She'd worn black pants and a blue cashmere sweater. New dangly earrings with stones of lapis lazuli made her feel elegant.

Jill tucked her hair back and continued, 'that's good news, Gary. Everyone on campus is freaked out again. So scary the first time and being one of my students. Now knowing a killer's still out there ...'

He reached for her hand. The touch was electric. Instead of calming her, she wanted more of him. Jill looked down at their clasped fingers then drew her hand away as if embarrassed. He, too, must have sensed something as his detective manner returned.

'Jill, you have something further to tell me, don't you?'

'Yes,' she whispered. In a stilted voice the incident of the handbag emerged. When she'd finished, Gary laughed.

'Mitchell's so strange. You don't think ...'

'Highly unlikely. The bloke we're after will be younger not an older groping professor.' Sanderson checked his watch.

A mortified expression crossed Jill's face. 'You believe me about the handbag?'

'Course I do, Jill. That sort of shocking behaviour is laughable.'

'I guess it is.' Jill wasn't up to a smile. 'I try really hard to get along with my boss.'

'So do I,' he said, 'but you don't have to like him.' Gary finished his drink and stood. 'If anything worries you, ring me.'

'Tried several times when I thought the second victim might have been another of my students.'

'Keep trying. I'm a busy man. Don't worry unnecessarily.' His finger stroked her cheek as a caress. He glanced around the room. 'Great place,' he said and left.

Jill sat in a daze thinking how deprived her body was of human touch. Here she was helping in a murder investigation and all she could think of at that moment was the detective. The barmaid put their empty glasses on a tray. Jill thanked her in a soft voice. The barmaid wasn't inclined to chat.

As she left the bar a mesh of commuters enveloped her. Once again on the train, she was surprised at its speed clattering on the tracks. What a relief she didn't have to battle into the city on a daily basis. Jill sighed as she found her car and headed back to the university.

Arriving in her office on campus, she noticed final rays of sunlight through the window. She scooped up research folders including a copy of the Janet Nichol journey and headed to the library. Although the Stevensons' first voyage was wholly within Polynesia she'd read they had Kanaka crew from the Solomons. While Polynesia had captured the European imagination for over a hundred years thanks to the writings of eighteenth century writers and philosophers, her part of the Pacific was Melanesia and Micronesia. Traders, missionaries and beachcombers varied in their impact on indigenous cultures. This had fuelled Robert Louis Stevenson's fiction and he'd brought it to the world.

At the reference desk Jill handed over a list only to find many of the sources were in special reserve. That meant extra time in the library when she was hoping to get home before dark. The young man behind the counter was not prepared to brook any rules even if she was staff. Damn, Jill thought, giving him a withering look as she left with the bundle of folders. She used a research room in quiet away from students.

Leafing through articles, Jill made copious notes. She was constantly drawn back to the photos in the Janet Nichol account. In yellowish tones, like the pages in the book, they told endless stories. She, too, had written about these places, been published in respected journals without having been there. What did she know? Jill realised the shallowness of her academic life. Surety of knowing came from plunging into real events. If Jill couldn't time travel back to that era at least she was going to the Pacific and seeing some of the islands she wrote about. Jill delighted in having fresh and invigorating stories for her students next semester.

South Sea Islanders were enticed from palm-fringed bays on Pentecost and Tanna to work as virtual slaves on Queensland cane farms. In 1863 whites believed they could not labour in the tropical heat. She pondered on the reasons people called Kanakas came to Australia. From the academic point of view 'blackbirding' was not stealing young Melanesians but a migration of indentured labourers.

Jill wanted to interview some of their descendants in north Queensland but felt getting the project past Duncan would be impossible. Any focus on the duplicity of ships' captains over the forty-year period would be unpopular. Mal Meninga, Australia's former rugby league captain, was a descendant of these people. That ought to interest the blokes in class. Possibly not Liam. Would our resident philosopher be above football?

Students were busy doing exams at this stage. Jill would be deluged with papers to mark before the South Seas called. Already she'd started a list: costume, surf towel, sarong. At a boat shop she'd purchased some wetsuit shoes for reef walking. A small torch to get back to the ship at night was another essential. Focused on what was needed, she'd given little thought to the others on board. Perhaps there'd be unpleasant men to deal with. Was this man-o-phobia returning? She'd dealt with one of the owners. Ruth was a real gem; had been reassuring about Jill's lack of sailing experience. After talking to Ruth, Jill could face anything.

Hours had evaporated. She gathered her work papers, returned the references and stood in the semi-dark outside the library. Once Jill left the comforting lights she'd be alone. She waited to see if others were walking her way to the car park. Since the night she'd followed Liam, she'd left the university before dark. Before the killer came out. Jill tried not to think how close the cafeteria dock was. How he dragged that girl to her death. Then no doubt, scalpel in hand, had mutilated her body. Placing his handiwork in that skip bin to show her finders what he thought of her.

As she moved off, a spray of the fountain's gushing water misted her face. Stop thinking and walk fast, Jill told herself. The odd window added to the glow of the barely-lit path back to the history building. She'd go through its foyer to the car park. When almost within its safety she heard running from the direction she'd come. Sweat sprung on the back of her neck. Her hair stuck to the clammy surface. Walking briskly, she heard her name. A killer wouldn't do that, she thought. Then Jill saw a top hat in the figure's hand, his cape flying behind him.

'Liam, you gave me a start.'

'Sorry, Jill. Saw you leaving the library. Just wanted to tell you the Pacific History paper was terrific.'

His zany enthusiasm was infectious. She felt safe in responding to this young man after her talk with Gary.

'Hope you do well, Liam.' They walked comfortably together then paused in light from the foyer of the history building. 'Can you keep a secret?'

He nodded. His pale blue eyes engaged hers.

'In the break I'm going sailing on a brigantine to Vanuatu. Thanks to your jibe I'm finally seeing something of the Pacific.'

'That's super. Won't tell a soul. Cross my heart and hope to die.'

With that word and his gestures her fear returned. Liam must have seen her expression.

'Let me walk you to your car. This campus is a bit freaky at night.'

They chattered all the way.

The drive home was uneventful. As Jill took her mobile from the car she saw a blind slatted open in the unit above. Grabbing the mail from her box, she scurried inside disarming the alarm. A bulging envelope with the word *Dreamsong* grabbed her attention. Her ticket had arrived.

Heating up some left over Chinese food, Jill poured a wine. She smiled at Liam's thoughtfulness. The message light was blinking on the phone.

'Shit,' she said on hearing her mother's whining voice. Jill still hadn't mentioned the holiday. She ate while reading the brochure. Unbelievable photos of the ship under sail racked up her excitement. What would it feel like under those billowing sails? Would the crew accept a landlubber? Never had she felt so adventurous. The itinerary sounded great.

145

Jill marked her first choice upon reaching Noumea: a canoe trip on the Dumbea River.

Jill couldn't wait to get away from the university with all its anxiety over the murders. She loathed the endless fear, the vulnerability of young women. Racing home before dark like a wimp was destroying her. Tonight she'd been saved but she needed something to protect herself.

Digging in the bottom of the wardrobe, she found one spiked stiletto. The black sexy ones she'd swore never to wear again. In the kitchen drawers she kept a few tools. With a file Jill began working the heel tip of the shoe into a point. The rasping of metal on metal sounded satisfying.

TWENTY-TWO

A large 4WD vehicle tailgated Barbara as she drove to work. In her rear vision mirror its shiny bull-bar hovered ever closer. Moron, she thought, always someone sitting on your hammer when you're slowing for a school zone. She felt like giving the driver a four-fingers-up sign to remind him of the speed limit.

Perhaps that wasn't wise in this age of road rage. Cutting someone off could lead to a deadly altercation. Barbara recalled an incident she'd witnessed when roundabouts were first introduced. A man had got out of his car to abuse a woman in the vehicle behind. She kept her door locked; her window wound up and stared straight ahead. In fury, the man slammed his forearm across her windscreen. She ignored him; horns began blaring before he went to his car. Aggressive men were to be avoided.

She accelerated, changing lanes as soon as practicable. The vehicle sped past. No wonder people want 4WDs off the city streets with drivers like that. Hugh's jibes may hurt her but Barbara could not envisage him lashing out physically. He was a wiry man with barely noticeable biceps. His strength was in his personality: calm, capable and caring most of the time. That was why she'd felt safe marrying him and having Maddy. She had first thought his remarks were a reaction to her stressing over Madeline's safety but now realised they represented some deeper dissatisfaction.

Pulling into Manly, Barbara still felt hassled over the traffic incident. She had ten minutes to spare before work and diverted to the beachfront car park. North Steyne at this hour was a melee of walkers, cyclists and skateboarders. A pungent smell of seaweed came from kelp strewn on the sand after a storm. Wind riffled through her hair as Barbara strolled along the promenade. The long stretch to Shelley Beach did not look inviting on this grey morning. Steel coloured clouds on the horizon threatened rain. Across the road a bustling café tempted her to take more time out but she hurried back to the warmth of her car.

This interlude strengthened her resolve to walk into the physio department. There'd be questions about the new murder. The staff knew what university Madeline attended. Barbara rubbed the joint at the base of her thumb. Colder weather made her arthritis worse severely restricting the cases she was given. Feelings of inadequacy mounted as she opened the office door.

Bronwyn was alone; her bright smile cheerful.

'Barbara. Holding up okay?'

Barbara looked into her colleague's expressive brown eyes. Bronwyn was the comforter on staff though she could be feisty when angry. Then she'd tuck dark straight hair behind both ears as if preparing for battle. But now her hand rested on Barbara's shoulder, a light touch of support.

'I'm over the shock of yesterday. Thought it might be …'

'Don't even say it. Terrible times. I've wised the others up not to discuss it.'

'Thanks, Bronwyn. I'll manage. Now any new cases?'

Bronwyn handed her a folder. 'Yes, a spinal injury. Motorbike accident. Only nineteen. You'll need to work out a program for him. He's waiting by the hydrotherapy pool.'

'Okay, Bron, I'm onto it.' Barbara left the office in search of her patient. Immersion in the problems of others released her thinking about her own.

The day passed in a blur. On the way home Barbara stopped for a well-earned coffee at the café she'd seen that morning. How did a simple beverage provide so much comfort? Not to mention the lemon friand. Brochures of taps were fanned out over the tabletop. Selecting something stylish that didn't cost the earth was a challenge. Her chores for the new house were almost over.

Barbara had enjoyed the task but was impatient for it to be finished. Would the ambience of the place match her expectations? Her coffee cup was empty. She marked a tap shop at Crows Nest, a destination for her next day off.

Glancing at her watch, she had enough time to buy a roast and vegetables to cook for dinner. Madeline's favourite. She'd need a break from studying. Hugh's surgery closed a little earlier today so they'd all eat together.

An hour later the smell of roasting lamb swirled around the kitchen. With Madeline in her room, Barbara put on a Gershwin CD. Swaying to the soft melody, she top and tailed beans before setting the table. She matched the music to her actions. In a dramatic brass section her vegetable knife flurried like a baton. Barbara found this uplifting and planned to play CDs more often.

Hugh had not come home. Barbara served the meals, placing his in the oven. Madeline traipsed into the dining area.

'Where's Dad?'

'I don't know. Should be home by now. Hasn't called?'

'Nope.'

'I'll try his mobile.' Barbara dialled and listened. 'Switched off.'

'Can we eat, Mum. I'm starved. Studying makes me ravenous.'

She avoided any mention of the murdered girl not wanting Madeline to suspect she'd rung Detective Sanderson. Her daughter's stroppy attitude was more than she could cope with tonight. Barbara prattled on about the new house while they ate. The evening paper was folded over on the coffee table. Barbara had seen the photo of the victim. Spiky hair and numerous studs in her ear made her look tough. Not a skerrick of Katie's prettiness or innocence.

Watching her daughter almost made Barbara catch her breath. Flawless skin, sparkly eyes and silken curls would be a magnet for any man. She tried to stop her mind heading in a fearful direction by describing the morning's aggressive driver.

'You were probably crawling, Mum.'

'I don't want to get booked.' Barbara sliced the gravy-covered meat. 'What are you doing after the exams?'

'A few of us want to go up the Central Coast. Rob's oldies have a holiday house. Hang out at the beach and sit round open fires at night.'

'That sounds great, darling. Who's Rob?'

'A bloke I'm kind of with.'

'A boyfriend?'

'Maybe.'

Her daughter's face showed nonchalance. Barbara immediately wanted to know a million things: what was he like, what did his parents do? She restrained herself and cleared the table. Madeline asked for a coffee and disappeared into her room. Barbara set out two cups and frothed the milk. She delivered one then settled to watch TV. Most unlike Hugh to be this late, she thought. Restless, she tried his mobile again. Turned off. His roast would be dry and inedible by now.

A cheery Hugh walked in the door at ten pm.

'Where have you been?' demanded Barbara.

'I left a message on your mobile. Lisa's divorce came through. We had a meal at the local Indian to cheer her up.' Hugh took off his jacket and loosened his tie. 'Check your mobile.'

Barbara rummaged in her handbag for her phone. She'd forgotten to turn it on after work. As she did so it beeped a message. Taking Hugh's meal from the oven, she said, 'Beau will get this. Why was Lisa so miserable?'

Hugh poured himself a glass of red wine. 'They'd been trying to start a family for years. She's mid-thirties. When hubby found out he was infertile, he shot through. Injured pride? Who knows? Lisa's been with the practice ten years. The other doctors and the receptionist all thought she needed our support.'

'I suppose you had to go. I'd planned a family dinner.' Barbara shrugged.

'Turn your mobile on in future.' Hugh sat down to watch the late news. Barbara felt he increasingly used the TV to ignore her.

'Maddy's got a boyfriend,' she said.

'About time.'

Hugh was not in a talkative mood. Barbara decided to go to bed.

The following afternoon Barbara stopped off at the new house to see if the tiler had finished. Glen was busy hanging a door to the guest bathroom. He nodded as several screws protruded from between his teeth. She went upstairs to the ensuite. The beige spa bath looked spectacular in its bay window surrounded by dark porcelain tiles.

Barbara could almost feel foamy bubbles around her. In the evening she'd light candles, relax back in the water with the dark lake in view. As she glanced at the controls she noticed something was wrong with the tiles. Where they jutted around this wider panel the joints were uneven.

A stab of panic surged through her body. The tiles would have to be re-done. She couldn't look at this for the rest of her life. Hugh wouldn't be pleased either. Barbara had agreed to supervise, as he was too busy. Until now there'd been no real problems. She sought out the builder.

'Glen, there's something wrong with the tiling in the ensuite.'

He followed her back to the room. Barbara pointed to the area, her fingers trailing over the differing angles.

'Mmm,' said Glen, 'comes from using the cheaper tiler.'

'Does that mean you accept shoddy workmanship, Glen? My husband's a doctor. He can't do that to patients. People die.'

Glen rubbed his moustache. Suddenly he was a man of few words. Barbara looked him in the eye. 'I can't live with tiles like that.'

'Guess I'll have to get him back. Don't know when. Fortunately, I've got a few tiles spare.'

Barbara sighed with relief. 'Thanks, Glen. Let me know when it's happening.' She left without checking the other bathrooms.

On impulse she drove to a shopping centre. The diversion was not for retail therapy but to attend to another matter that had been worrying her. Madeline would never understand. A sense of immortality was strong in the young. Her daughter would fling herself off in a fury if she found out about phoning the detective. He was in charge of the case so he knew the most about the murders. Sensibly, Barbara had gone to the source. Why should Madeline be defensive? Just because she'd been interviewed didn't give her priority.

When Barbara had talked to Detective Sanderson, she'd found his voice smooth and sexy. He was a man who knew how to make women feel special. Presented the package well too. She recalled the snazzy suit he wore to Katie's funeral. Barbara couldn't help wondering what the detective's life was like. Viewing dead bodies, tracking killers had little going for it, in her estimation. Was he an out-of-hours charmer to divest himself of the macabre? Yet when she'd confronted him over her daughter's safety he was lacking in advice.

No point deliberating any longer. Barbara walked into the shop. Electronic gadgetry crowded shelves and hung on twirling stands. Many of the items remained a mystery to her. The well-known Dick Smith had ventured into this type of store years earlier. Bits of circuits and special-ist batteries for a variety of new gizmos had started a wave in technology. She gave up her search and waited at the counter. A pleasant young man with pale long-fingered hands placed Barbara's request on the counter.

On the way home she drove to an oval in Newport. A man was walk-ing a black labrador on the far side. She got out of the car, checking no one was nearby. Most of the grassy area was shadowed; an evening chill crept across the valley. Barbara dangled the black plastic disc in front of her. It could easily be attached to the belt loop of jeans or slipped into a pocket. Then she held it firmly and her finger depressed the button. An ear bursting shrill. The dog's head swivelled in her direction. Its owner watched as well.

Effective, Barbara thought, as she got back in the car. The penetrat-ing sound still resonated in her head. Would it detract a depraved mind? The last thing a person of stealth wanted was this kind of attention. Surely this black disc would keep her daughter safe.

Now how was she going to convince Madeline to carry the device?

TWENTY-THREE

Sanderson woke early and opened the blind. Denuded trees outside made the street seem wintry. His body goosepimpled with cold after leaving the warmth of his doona. Putting on a tracksuit, he bounded down the stairs.

While making a steaming cup of coffee, he noticed his slacks slung over a teak chair in the courtyard. Meticulous at keeping the stench of death from inside his home, Sanderson realised he'd forgotten them this time. If a homicide in this area hit the news the Korean man at the corner store expected him. Cup drained, the detective bundled the odorous attire and headed out his front door.

The wrought-iron gate clanked shut behind him; a taxi sped down the street. This convenience store with extended trading was so handy for workers with irregular hours, Sanderson thought. When he handed the pants over for dry cleaning the owner nodded towards the morning's pile of newspapers.

'Your case?' he asked.

'Yes,' replied Sanderson, grabbing a copy. On impulse he added a carton of eggs and paid.

'Good luck,' the owner said and gave him a wave.

Outside sunshine crept over the terrace houses. What's luck got to do with it, Sanderson thought? Only thorough investigative work and the killer leaving trace evidence were going to lead to a result in this case. He decided on a hearty breakfast before fronting up at the morgue.

Back in his kitchen, he threw rashers of bacon into a pan. They sizzled and spat, the aroma teasing his stomach. He cracked three eggs, watching their glutinous texture turn white around tangerine yolks. Over two slices of toast he spread his feast then drizzled tomato sauce on top.

Sanderson ate his breakfast in the courtyard while reading about the murder. The picture of Cheryl would not evoke much sympathy from the general reader. She looked rough and tough. Her direct stare was confronting. The spiked hair and multiple piercings on her ear labelled her. Not a nice type of girl. Not Katie. Yet Cheryl had been killed just as brutally, her body mutilated post mortem.

He sopped up the yolk with toast and perused his yard. Variegated plants spilled from terracotta pots. Not much of a gardener, Sanderson told himself. He'd do a bit of sweeping and have the boys over Sunday afternoon. With the cover off his stainless steel barbecue, the esky full of beer, they'd let off steam before watching the footie match.

Showered and dressed, Sanderson drove across the city. Passing through the Haymarket area, he noticed the preponderance of Chinese. Although seldom visiting Chinatown, he recalled some recent trouble in their community. Restaurants had been targeted, seafood tanks smashed leaving lobsters pincering their way over carpets.

He found a parking spot behind the Department of Forensic Medicine. The insignia on the door always made Sanderson think of the machinations that were uncovered inside this building. Why a snake coiled around scales? Was it a reminder death could strike unexpectedly? In the museum, shelves along walls displayed body parts in preserving fluids: hearts, brains even a fully developed foetus. Stickers marked the entry and exit holes of bullets through vital organs. Numerous doctors' rooms exhibited their speciality. The one for dental records had teeth mouldings scattered on a desk as if chattering to each other. A model head in another room meant a facial reconstruction was in progress. Beyond the main laboratory was the cool room with its racks of blue body bags. Sanderson found the atmosphere of the whole place clinical and serious.

Fyurk and Ruggeri were waiting for him outside the autopsy room.

Doctor Hazelton opened the door, towering over them. His long apron showed telltale signs of blood. He'd begun his day with the dead. The grey beard distorted into a welcoming smile.

'Come in, gentlemen.'

'Morning, Hazo,' Sanderson said.

Ruggeri confirmed the identity of the body with the pathologist. Sanderson could smell the eucalyptus Fyurk used in his nostrils. He hoped this stopped his offsider chucking up. That would be grist for Ruggeri's mill. They were all here to find out what Cheryl's body could tell them. Niggling over each other's foibles would be an unnecessary distraction.

The girl's form, stiff and naked on the slab, quietened them. Hazelton began detailing the external injuries. All the detectives listened intently as every cut and contusion was pointed out. The pathologist noted; strangulation marks on the neck were most likely caused by a braided nylon rope as in Katie's case. Damage to Cheryl's knuckles showed she'd put up a fight. Her fingernail scrapings and swabs would already be at the laboratory. The scalpel work in removing the pudendum and nipples was much neater indicating the killer had more time with the victim.

Sanderson and Ruggeri took the odd note. The investigating detective's neck ached. He wondered how a man as tall as Hazelton coped with all the stooping examinations like this required. The man's dedication to this job was obvious in every move he made. Day after day dealing with corpses. When the pathologist prepared to dissect the torso, Sanderson watched Fyurk for a reaction. His offsider was doing better today. Hazelton took infinite care with the internal organs.

Finally, the saw in Hazelton's hands whined into action, cutting into the cranium. A mist of bone fragments rose towards his Perspex mask. The laboratory technician squeaked across the tiled floor in his white rubber boots. He assisted the pathologist's deft actions as the brain was eased from the opening.

Its intricate folds always amazed Sanderson as he observed the so-called grey matter settle on the scales. Without this coordinating organ a human is nothing. How often did the brain's malfunction lead to a tragic death? All this talk of brain chemistry gone wrong wasn't satisfying in his job. He'd never understand how something switched in this neuronal mass to make a predator.

The laboratory technician took the organ to begin his sampling and slicing. Ruggeri's dark eyes swept up and down the girl's body. He was usually silent at an autopsy. Hazelton's voice recorded every observation. Fyurk stood straight, his hands clasped behind him as if at a memorial service. Occasionally, Sanderson heard him inhale deeply and watched him peer round the room. A white sheet covered one other body. Fyurk was learning to cope with the rigours of this task. Sanderson knew the examination of a murder victim could take all day in some cases.

Coloured cotton wads filled the brain cavity then the scalp was folded back up over the cranium, revealing Cheryl's face again. The pathologist's stitching halted when Sanderson interrupted, 'Hazo, when can I expect the interim report?'

'I'll fax it through Thursday morning, Gary. See you, Ruggeri. Well done, Fyurk. No gurgling noises this time.' Wiping his hands on his apron, Hazelton picked up the scalpel.

Sanderson led the way out. They removed their gowns and booties, tossing them into a bin. Ruggeri seemed impatient to leave. He'd mentioned a court appearance. Sanderson understood how stressful these could be in the presence of cunning barristers. What seemed clear evidence to the police could be twisted and tangled in a morass of detail.

'Got anything on this Sunday, Ruggeri? Barbecue at my place to watch the footie.'

The physical evidence bloke showed surprise. Sanderson had not asked him before but felt he needed to foster his colleague. Maybe his broody face would lighten up with a few beers.

'Taking a lady on a picnic. Thanks anyway, Gary.'

Sanderson laughed. 'The Italian Stallion. Told you.' He nudged Fyurk and gave Ruggeri a wink.

Back in the car they took the freeway north over the Harbour Bridge. Low clouds obliterated many of the city's skyscrapers.

'The bridge climbers won't get much of a view today,' Fyurk said.

'Sure won't. If this wind builds they might get blown off the coathanger. What about you, Rich, want to come Sunday?'

'Yeah, Gary. Watching the footie with a crowd is always better. There's a good salad bar near my place. I'll bring a couple of salads.' Fyurk straightened in his seat. He appeared pleased. Sanderson felt the lad's form was improving.

'Okay then, see you round one.'

'Must be nice having your own place.' Fyurk rubbed his oversize nose.

'Unexpected bonus. My old man retired at sixty. Was dead within a year. Prostate cancer. Left me enough dough for a deposit. He'd already helped my sister get a house.'

'I don't mind living with my Dad. He's the only family I've got, watches a heap of TV. Leaves me alone to read. This case, Gary, we've got to be dealing with a serial killer. I know it's meant to be three or more before using that term. But same modus operandi, same scalpel work. I think he's territorial. The university is his area. We're looking at a white male, twenties and a working class background. Despite what a friendly fellow the groundsman is, Bob fits the picture.'

'Hold on, Rich. That may be so. But you've got to keep an open mind. We don't want to be accused of targeting. We have no link except that he looks after the bins Cheryl was found in. I'm for calling in at the incident room, checking all her colleagues' statements for clues. Then we'll go see your Bin Boy.'

Sanderson turned off the highway to the police station. He swiped his card and the gate rattled open.

'Phew,' said a constable they passed in the corridor, 'Been at the morgue?'

Fyurk nodded. In the incident room, they walked past the para-phernalia of Katie Foster's death. Cheryl's photos were up. Vivid green eyes were the only obvious feature these victims had in common. Was that their killer's criteria? Perhaps the murderer's mother had irises of the same colour. Fyurk had picked the similarity. Mothers were often blamed for the deranged behaviour of their offspring.

He'd also noticed a perfume, Lily of the Valley. Had they missed that with Katie? The hailstorm and more open location could have dissipated that smell.

Fyurk was sorting the statements. Sanderson glanced at the whiteboard listing their suspects. He picked up a marker. It squeaked over the surface. A red line crossed Liam's name. The detective added 'room-mate' to the list.

They spent half an hour scanning the witness statements. The frumpy cashier was the most scathing of Cheryl Patterson. The others on table clearing duty had found her efficient but seldom customer friendly. 'They're here to bloody learn not chat' was a frequent comment. Sanderson wondered if Cheryl had been into drugs. He rang Hazelton to remind them to check for evidence of ecstasy. Katie's toxicology report had shown this. Perhaps there was a drug link between the two girls. They were both on campus. Could be a pissed off drug dealer.

As the senior detective flipped through the pages, he stopped at Li's account. Only the chef had a good word for their second victim. Sanderson decided another trip to the university's cafeteria was warranted. They needed to probe the drug issue and maybe Li might know what Cheryl did in her time off.

'C'mon, Rich. Time for a cappuccino.'

Fyurk grabbed his jacket and they headed back to the Commodore. The blokes on the gate at the university knew them by now. Barely a badge flash was needed. Sanderson drove around the tree-lined avenue to a car park. A path wove around the concrete and glass buildings to the central courtyard.

'Look at that,' said Fyurk.

Sanderson turned towards the noisy fountain's splashing water. Mountains of bubbles expanded, jiggled and subsided. At that moment sunlight broke through the clouds tinging the bubbles with rainbows.

'The students get their buzz in different ways. I kinda like the fountain as a bubble bath.'

'A couple of months ago the water was blue. Remember?' Fyurk raised his nose, sniffing the air like a dog.

'This is better. What's that snoz of yours receiving?' Sanderson asked.

'Lemon. Crisp and zesty.' Fyurk walked on towards the cafeteria.

Before following, Sanderson watched student reactions as they encountered the bubbly mass. Some things were good clean fun, he thought, refreshing after the gruesome scenes at the morgue.

They sat with their coffees. Sanderson observed his offsider tucking into a meat pie. He wasn't hungry after his huge breakfast. His body itched for exercise. He planned a long run round Centennial Park before sunset.

'Don't let Ruggeri get to you, Rich. He's the strong silent type. Always has a go at young blood. Tests their mettle, he says. A few years from now you'll be having a go back.'

'Yeah, I know, Gary. When we get a breakthrough in this case I might gain some credibility.' Fyurk wiped a dab of mince from the side of his mouth.

Before his hand transferred it to his trousers, Sanderson passed him a serviette. His offsider's piggy habits were taking time to fix.

'C'mon let's go see Li.'

The beefy cashier gave Sanderson a hostile look when he sauntered past into the kitchen.

'Ah, Detectives. Can Li help? I work. You talk.'

The chef took toasted Turkish bread from under a grill, layered cooked Mediterranean vegetables on the pieces and added a dash of some kind of sauce. A sprinkling of mozzarella cheese and they were back under the heat.

'A few more questions about Cheryl,' said Fyurk before continuing his interrogation.

Sanderson scrawled in his notebook glancing up at Li's expressive honest face. The chef openly missed Cheryl although his voice became muted when other worker's opinions were mentioned. Orders were building up as more students came in for lunch. They were about to leave when Sanderson fired one last question.

'Did Cheryl go out with anyone from the university?'

'Not know much Cheryl's private life.' Li paused, placing a finger to his cheek. 'But did see her talking to gardener man.'

'When was that?' jumped in Fyurk.

'Week before she die.' Li's face clouded.

'Right.' Sanderson wheeled round. Fyurk followed in his wake.

TWENTY-FOUR

Jill woke late having read well into the night. With no lectures to give she could enjoy a sleep in. Her thoughts turned to yesterday.

A mere drink with Gary had sent her hormones into turmoil again. Was he aware that his every touch triggered a yearning in her body? She was sure he knew the effect he had on women. His dynamic personality, the way he moved made beginning a relationship seem so easy. As Jill's desire strengthened she became bolder. Hadn't she arranged the meeting? And he'd liked the bar. Perhaps she shouldn't have restricted their conversation to the murders. Why had she not mentioned the sailing trip?

After breakfast she could no longer put off returning her mother's phone call.

'Mother, sorry I didn't ring last night. Got in really late.'

'Jill, you shouldn't be wandering around that campus after dark. Not with a killer about. Saw the photo of that girl in the paper. What are the police doing?'

Jill sighed and stretched the coiled phone cord so she could lean on the kitchen bench.

'I'm all right, Mother. A student walked me to my car. I saw the detective in charge of the case yesterday. There's regular police patrols on campus. What I really called about was my holiday.'

'What holiday, Jill? Aren't you coming to Canberra?'

'Probably not.'

'That's why I've got a spare room. So you can visit me,' she sounded almost despondent.

'I might get down for a day or two on my return. I'm flying to New Caledonia then sailing on a ship for Vanuatu.' Jill tried to make it sound like a regular holiday. For once she hoped her mother would be enthusiastic about her getting on with life.

Mother's voice drilled down the line. 'Sailing? Whatever for?'

'Because I've never seen anything of the Pacific first hand. With those shows you used to watch I thought you'd understand.'

'So you're off to find Gardener McKay. Let me tell you, Jill, men bring you nothing but grief. Not that it's a ball in a retirement place for younger people. Look at my life. There's a silly old bugger in the village at the moment. Thinks he can teach me bridge.'

Jill let her rant about her problems. Her mother hadn't taken the trip too badly. Relieved when the call finally ended, she drove to the university to pick up the first bundle of papers to mark. She couldn't see any reason for tackling them in the office.

The morning at home passed with red pen flicking over the mass of essays. Jill recognised many of the points of life in the Pacific she'd emphasised in lectures and tutorials. First year students often found writing academic essays extremely hard. Taking a stance and backing it with sound research was an art. She'd gone through the technique many times and shown her students how to plan an answer. Some of the results were a joy to read, especially Liam's. Jill gave him an excellent mark and pictured the look of delight on his face next semester.

She made herself a ham and salad sandwich for lunch and took it into the garden. Although winter sunshine took the chill off the air, she snuggled down into her oversize jumper. Noisy mynas flitted around the bushes. When she scattered crumbs on the grass they flew down, beaks pecking away between the blades.

As the building's shadow snuck across Jill moved her chair into the remaining square of sunshine. On a balcony two floors up she noticed a new outdoor setting for two facing west. She wondered who sat there enjoying the sunset. She'd meet the other occupants of the complex in a month's time at the first body corporate meeting.

In a week Jill would feel tropical sun on her skin. That reminded her to do something about fitness before the holiday. In her tracksuit and sneakers she drove to the nearby shopping centre. At 4.00 pm was a free introductory class at the gym. Through glass doors she saw women with amazing bodies. That should be encouragement enough. Jill entered and went to the back of the class. Physical exertion was something she'd ignored in recent years although she enjoyed walking and the odd swim in summer.

The instructor bounded in and introduced herself. Her long blonde hair pulled into a ponytail swished with every movement. Black lycra clung to her toned torso and her limbs had an impossible summer tan. She pumped up the music. Loud and boppy, its beat was paced to the actions. They began with sidesteps and leg curls to warm up. Then did a section of Tae bo boxing. The instructor described how empowering it was for women. Jill envisaged flinging an elbow back into the face of an imaginary attacker would feel so good. These simple moves gave her confidence in self-defence. Really useful on a campus with a resident murderer. By the time they'd completed twenty minutes on step boxes she was sweating. Her body felt invigorated. Must be the endorphins kicking in, she thought. She'd never thought about becoming a gym junkie.

After class, tired but enthusiastic, she window-shopped. These malls didn't do much for her. She'd rather be home reading a book. Jill drove home via the local shops to pick up a takeaway and DVD.

Once inside, she plonked the bag of containers on the kitchen bench. This room of her townhouse was largely superfluous. She'd meant to do some real cooking this winter but here she was arranging food again. In a pasta bowl Jill formed a mountain of fried rice then piled the Peking shredded beef on top. With a glass of white wine and the movie starting, she settled on the lounge. The strands of meat with the rice had a delicious flavour. Why hassle with cooking. Wasn't she typical of singles in her generation? If only she could stop questioning life, sit back and enjoy her comfortable existence.

The film, *Bride and Prejudice*, with all its Bollywood glory took Jill to India. Dark sultry eyes, brightly coloured saris and layers of tinkling jewellery fascinated her. She had no idea how much Indians loved to dance especially at weddings. Bodies jiggled en masse to music with a mystical rhythm. Enraptured by the movie, she found herself imitating some of the steps on the way to bed.

Jill locked the bedroom door and turned on the security alarm. This gave her peace of mind. In the darkness she lay allowing scenarios of the holiday to drift through her thoughts. Would she feel as dreamy and safe in a bunk aboard *Dreamsong*?

Next day at work Paula was in the tearoom. She was wearing a long brown skirt and smart pointy-toed boots. Orange dangly earrings matched the colour of her lipstick.

'Morning, Jill, I was just about to check your office. Duncan wants to see you.'

'Thanks, Paula. You're looking dazzling as usual.'

Mug in hand, Jill entered the corridor wondering why Duncan was summonsing her. Their relationship had remained on pleasant terms since she'd sought his advice on her article. It had been accepted for publication in the journal he suggested. She had begun the proposal for a research trip to Queensland to interview Kanaka descendants. Later in the year would be a suitable time to present that to her superior.

Knocking on Duncan's door, Jill heard him respond. A glint of light from his glasses flashed as he recognised her. He was on the phone and from his oozing voice she deduced it was the Chancellor. Duncan's face was devoid of colour against the black of his ubiquitous leather jacket. Perhaps he needed the break more than any of them. He hung up.

'Jill,' he said extending his hand.

She remained standing. 'Good morning, Duncan. Paula said you wanted to see me.'

'Yes, yes. It's that girl's funeral today and the Chancellor wants several staff to represent the university. I've offered and I want you to accompany me. Won't keep you from exam papers long.'

Jill thought of Katie's funeral and how uneasy she'd felt with crying students milling around.

'But Duncan, I didn't even know the girl.'

'It's for appearance sake. Cheryl was an employee of the university. The service is at 2.30 in Macquarie Park Cemetery. Come back in half an hour. We'll go together.'

'Fine, Duncan.' In the corridor a heavy sigh escaped. He was determined and she wanted to stay in favour.

Jill pictured the girl as she remembered her in the cafeteria. With all the studs in her earlobe, the back tattoo and chopped hair, Cheryl came across as tough. With students she liked she was quite witty. Efficient enough to be running a café, Jill thought. Perhaps her personality was too prickly.

Absorbed in marking, the time came around quickly. Duncan and Jill walked through the car park to his gold Lexus. She couldn't help thinking of the night he'd frightened her in the car park. That incident seemed so ridiculous in daylight.

Leather seats plush around her, Jill breathed in the new car smell. Luxuriating in expensive cars was a rare pleasure. After ten minutes driving they pulled into what looked like a new estate. Fledgling gardens with small shrubs skirted the roadways. Duncan found a parking spot. Jill put on a wool coat as much for comfort as protection from an icy wind. Duncan took her arm as if they were a couple. For the sake of peace, Jill let him. This man took every opportunity to get his hands on women. She tried to relax as they approached an electronic board. Bubbles of orange lights displayed the names of the deceased with the respective chapel beside them. Cheryl Patterson's service was in the Magnolia Chapel.

The room was ultra-modern and lacked the sombre feel of a church. Her eyes fastened on a large screen on the wall above the casket opening, depicting a serene valley with Cheryl's name at the bottom. Nice touch, Jill thought, edging her thigh away from Duncan's on the seat. His demeanour showed suitable grief for a professor. Jill retrieved a tissue from her bag as she usually cried at funerals.

Duncan had briefed her on the family situation. Cheryl's parents were not alive to see this day. They'd been killed in a bus accident overseas. An aunt, Muriel Carter was the only relative which explained the sparse attendance. Jill could see a solitary woman sitting at the front. Downlights made her silver curls shimmer as she bowed her head.

In the curtained alcove sat a white casket topped with a startling floral tribute. Gerberas, fuchsia, orange and vermilion, were flowers Jill never expected at a funeral. They protruded from the display like so many happy faces. Perhaps they were Cheryl's favourites, vibrant as her personality. Imagining her now inside the casket, she felt morbid. Classical music was playing softly as the final few shuffled into seats. Jill stared into the alcove as a man's voice described the highlights of a young woman's life.

'Cut off so tragically in her prime …' he continued.

Such a correct way of describing the whole horrible affair of murder and mutilation. As they stood and mumbled the Lord's Prayer, Jill noticed Duncan's hands clasped in front were shaking. She hadn't expected him to be so moved by the ceremony. He'd certainly looked strained in recent weeks. She recalled Paula telling her Duncan hadn't been the same since his mother died. Possibly he was ill. She wiped away an errant tear.

There was no tribute from the aunt. After the service side doors opened to a courtyard and the small group of mourners emerged. Jill glanced at a young Chinese man with tracks of tears on his face.

Watching her, Duncan whispered, 'That's Li, the chef at the cafeteria. Worked with Cheryl.'

'Oh,' Jill replied as they strolled up the path to the wake, 'Duncan can I get you a drink?'

'Just a coffee, Jill.'

In the reception room, she directed him to one of the few chairs skirting the wall. He sat his face pale as the white wall behind him. Jill ordered Duncan's coffee and took a white wine for herself. People gathered around the food-laden tables. Platters of hot savouries, sandwiches and sweet slices looked enticing. The aunt had a group around her. Jill had watched her walk in, stiff and pretentious. She seemed too preoccupied with her appearance to grieve for her niece. The dress, matching handbag and shoes screamed expensive. Jill wondered if Cheryl had liked her aunt whose face was far from friendly. Sadness for the young girl who'd lost her life swept over her.

With a coffee in one hand and wine in the other, Jill turned to a voice she recognised.

'Hi, Jill.'

She thrilled to the timbre of Sanderson's voice.

'Gary, what are …' Of course, she thought, detectives always check out funerals. He was at Katie's too.

'I was just getting Duncan a coffee.'

'So you're here with the boss.' Gary winked.

'Roped into going.' Jill shrugged and they walked over to Duncan.

'Professor.' Sanderson said.

'Detective, you're everywhere lately.' Duncan sipped his drink.

'Just doing my job. Mind if I have a word with Jill?'

Duncan waved them away but kept his gaze fixed on their faces.

'Have you noticed anything unusual on campus? You promised to keep an eye out for me.' He brushed invisible fluff from her sleeve.

Was he trying to get her involved again? Jill stared into those brown challenging eyes.

'Not much besides blue uniforms everywhere. I'll be gone for several weeks. Sailing in the Pacific.' Jill sipped her wine waiting for a reaction.

'Wow,' he said, 'Sailing's something I've always wanted to do. Balmy nights, bubbles trailing in the wake. Sounds wonderful. Can I come too?' He laughed.

If only, she thought. 'Can't wait to leave our creepy campus behind.'

He leaned closer. She could smell his aftershave and wanted more.

'Want to hear all about the holiday. Ring me when you get back. Have some sympathy for me, stuck here trying to catch killers.' Sanderson glanced in Duncan's direction. 'Last thing I expected seeing you here with Poo Boy.'

TWENTY-FIVE

Madeline wandered into the kitchen as Barbara finished clearing away her husband's breakfast dishes. Hugh had gone to golf for the day and she was feeling deserted. Many golfing widows were glad to see their husband's backs on a Saturday. Just occasionally, Barbara thought, it'd be nice if they could do something together. Go to an art gallery or a city café.

'Morning, Mum.'

'Morning, Maddy. Would you like a crumpet with honey for breakfast?'

'That'd be fine and a strong coffee, please.'

Her daughter's tangled hair and flannelette pyjamas reminded Barbara of when Madeline was little. Before she headed out into the world. Before the murders.

Barbara smeared butter over the cooked crumpet's porous surface then added a dollop of honey. She scalded the milk, spooning froth into the two cups. The coffee aroma eased her concerns slightly.

Beau curled up beside Madeline on the lounge. A tiny pink tongue emerged as he sniffed the breakfast Barbara handed over. She placed the coffees on the table, aware of the personal alarm in her pocket. Possibly this was the appropriate time. Sitting back, Barbara savoured the caffeine fix before bringing out the black disc.

'What's that?'

'A personal alarm, Maddy and I'd like you to take it to uni with you.'

'Mum, you can't be serious. You're taking the attacks too far.'

'Not attacks. There's someone on campus murdering girls your age.' Barbara raised her voice, 'I'm trying to protect you.'

Madeline finished her crumpet. 'Well, I'm not using that.' Her daughter flicked the alarm onto the floor, making Beau jump. 'Over protective mothers are the end,' she said and stomped to her room.

Barbara shrugged. She hoped Madeline would never need the device. Retrieving it, she put it in a kitchen drawer. She dug out a Tim Tam from her cache in the pantry, enjoying the chocolate taste. In an hour she had a meeting with Glen at the house.

In her caramel coloured shoes, slacks and a new tan jumper, Barbara drove along the coast. As she rounded a bend, waves with spray flying broke over the beach below. Several surfers in wetsuits braved the cold sea. She felt a walk would do her good but it was so blustery.

Pulling up outside the house, the exterior paint colour excited Barbara. The tawny mauve was the colour of pale blood plums. The painters were not working today. She sidestepped past wire fencing to the open front door. Glen was in the kitchen examining the granite bench tops.

'They look superb, Barbara.'

He was not wearing his builder's attire. A smart polo top, moleskins and sailing shoes gave him a sporty appearance. She had not noticed how tall he was. Must be well over six foot, she estimated.

Glen's praise of the house choices delighted her. He nodded at the taps she'd marked on the brochure. A mysterious smile flickered under his moustache.

'Love the pointy toe shoes. My wife never follows fashions.'

'Not many men appreciate women's footwear,' Barbara teased. Glancing down, she turned her ankle back and forth. 'You do cheer me up, Glen.'

'Why? Are you down in the dumps?'

His laughing eyes became serious. What a caring man.

'Just had an altercation with my daughter. I bought her a personal alarm because of the murders at the uni. She refuses to use it.' Barbara wiped away a tear.

'Come here,' Glen murmured as his arms enveloped her in a hug.

169

It had been a long time since she'd felt another man's arms around her. She liked his soapy smell. Glen's height made her feel protected. Barbara's hands rested on his biceps. Their strength surprised her. Minutes later as he pulled away, she felt his moustache brush her cheek lightly.

'Better,' he said.

Barbara nodded.

'Come and I'll show you those bathrooms. You'll be pleased with the tiles in the ensuite. All fixed.'

She remembered how upset she'd been when last at the house. Glen was prepared to accept poor workmanship. Perhaps he'd thought her difficult. His change of attitude surprised her. Was this placation part of the finishing off process? Only a matter of weeks and her family would be moving into their new home. Surely Hugh and Madeline would love it.

Barbara, tingling with excitement, paced behind Glen to the spare bathroom. The wall tiles, white and wavy, were spectacular against the terracotta starfish border. The floor was sunshine yellow. Madeline, whose love of sea creatures had given Barbara the idea, would be impressed.

Glen watched her gaze around the room; his expression showed relief at her approval.

'Bold and beautiful,' she exclaimed.

'Just like you,' he added in a whisper.

'Oh, Glen. I wouldn't have taken you for a softie. Cut it out. Now show me the guest toilet.'

'Yes, Mam,' his tone jocular.

Was he seriously flirting, Barbara wondered? They'd spent a lot of time together at the house. Entirely necessary to get things right, she presumed. Barbara had taken it for granted their comfortable relationship would end when the house was finished. Glen appreciated her flair for colour and design, had hinted they could work as a team.

Outside the next bathroom he stood close behind her. Barbara could feel his warm breath on the back of her neck. Disturbed, she focused on checking the room and its fixtures. Grey porcelain tiles with a white toilet and elaborate pedestal basin made the guest toilet very smart.

After examining the ensuite, Barbara was exuberant, 'Thanks, Glen. You don't know how worried I was.'

He beamed. 'Anything to keep a woman happy.' He leant against the doorjamb, relaxed and confident.

Barbara eased past him. The hallways were much brighter since they'd been painted. Her pointy shoes accumulated a coating of cement dust but sea-coloured carpet would soon cover the rough floors.

From the kitchen window, sunlight dazzled the lake's surface.

'Would you like to go for a coffee?' Glen suggested.

That smile again.

'Sorry, I have an appointment.' Surprised, Barbara made a hasty exit wondering why she'd lied. In the car she fanned away a hot flush.

At home she saw Madeline about to leave. At least the turtleneck jumper covered the top of her jeans, Barbara thought. Colder weather meant less exposed flesh.

'I'm going to the movies with Rob. See you later, Mum.'

'Bye, darling.' Barbara watched her daughter jump into the bubble Mazda and speed off.

Glen was still on her mind. He'd unsettled her. What was he playing at? Barbara felt vulnerable, as things with Hugh had been strained. She shouldn't put too much meaning into Glen's attentions.

Her plan had been to start packing for the impending move. Empty boxes at the end of the garage were a reminder. Barbara dragged one into the kitchen, opening cupboard after cupboard. She didn't know where to start. Perhaps some classical music would help. The room filled with the strains of an orchestra. Her mind was as restless as a trapped bee.

On impulse, she decided to go shopping. Winter sales were on at the department stores at the mall. Barbara joined the throng of shoppers. She selected a set of towels for each of the new bathrooms: grey, aubergine and daffodil. With bulging bags she made it to her favourite café. On the terrace, huge white sails shaded her. The chink of cups above murmured conversations relaxed her after the spending spree. All necessary, she told herself. You couldn't put old towels in new bathrooms.

Pecan pie and ice cream arrived with her espresso. Barbara tucked into the treat. She pushed the plate away not believing what she'd just eaten. When she moved into the new house she'd try one of those low carb diets. She emptied the tiny cup.

Once home, Barbara discarded the caramel shoes and put on Mozart. The packing box went back into the garage. She kicked a soft toy and Beau scampered after it. He deposited the bunny at her feet looking up for more. As Barbara played his favourite game, the dog's panting increased. Eventually, he lay on the rug one paw draped over the toy.

In the kitchen, Barbara washed her hands before preparing dinner, the first family one with Madeline's new boyfriend. Marinated pork fillets sizzled. She was turning the baked vegetables when her daughter and Rob arrived.

'Mum, this is Rob.'

'Hi, Mrs H.'

The boy had the physique of a footballer, Barbara thought, muscly but no neck. Towering over Madeline, his hair as dark as hers was fair, he wore a baseball cap backwards.

Rob strode to the fridge and poured himself an orange juice. Her daughter took a can of coke and they wandered to the lounge room. Barbara's music was switched off. Sounds of an action DVD boomed from the TV. Madeline and Rob lay entwined on the sofa. So this is what bringing a boyfriend home is all about, Barbara thought.

Hugh was later than expected. Too much time at the nineteenth hole. Barbara failed to understand why anyone would endlessly relive the activity of a little white ball finding a hole. Irritated, she served the meal and put the plates in the oven.

Sport had never featured strongly in her life. As a physio she'd seen her share of driven athletes and been amazed by recoveries from horrendous injuries. With continued stretching and work, muscles bulked up again and performed. Barbara pictured her motorbike fellow. He'd come a long way. His calf muscle had almost been torn off his leg. Now he was walking with barely a limp.

Friday's mail was still on the bench by the phone. One was her credit card bill. She marked on the calendar when it had to be paid and stuck it in a drawer. The rest were addressed to Hugh. Barbara glanced at the lovebirds then took the envelopes to the spare room. Flicking on the light, she saw Hugh's desk was the usual mess. Only if it were medical would order prevail. Household bills were scattered over the surface. It was a wonder anything was paid on time. Perhaps in the new house he'd be better.

She ran her finger over gleaming timber. Needed a dust as well. Barbara found the cumbersome desk ugly. Hugh had inherited it from his father who no doubt thought it befitting a doctor. She recalled the stern old man sitting in an armchair in the years before his death. Miserable bastard. He always looked askance at her bright clothes. Barbara knew he thought her flamboyant. Still, the money he'd left them had been enough to buy the lakeside block and start building. Then their buyer had insisted on a delayed settlement. Everything was working out nicely.

Noise of the front door opening filtered down the hallway. Hugh no doubt rushing in with another excuse. He'd turned being late into an art form.

A beep alerted her to his mobile on the desk. He'd forgotten to take it to golf. The phone had to be turned off when playing but he rarely left it behind. Without thinking, she picked it up and retrieved the message just as Hugh's agitated face appeared at the door.

The words on the tiny screen burned into her retina: Miss you already, Hewie.

TWENTY-SIX

Sanderson and Fyurk stood some distance from the foaming fountain.

'I've yet to meet this Bob character.'

'Seemed so friendly and helpful when I first saw him Gary.' Fyurk rubbed a reassuring finger along the side of his nose.

'He wasn't real helpful finding Katie's clothes.' Sanderson goaded his offsider.

'You're right. Perhaps he timed things to suit when the skip bins were emptied.'

'Don't forget, Rich. Ted Bundy had all the charm in the world. No problems getting girls in his car then he'd whack them with a tyre lever. Manipulative behaviour is one of the tags of a psychopath.'

Shrieks of delight filtered over to the detectives. More students had come across the latest prank. Sanderson punched Ralston's number into his mobile. Bloody monetary constraints. He quashed his annoyance. If only the public knew detectives couldn't go all out to catch a killer. Blab that to the media and his job would be on the line.

'Boss, we got enough dough for an outdoor surveillance camera? Want to keep a closer eye on the uni gardener, Bob Wilson. There may be a drug link with the murdered girls.'

'Sure have,' Ralston boomed down the line.

At least this time we've got the go ahead, Sanderson thought. He was in no mood to suck up to his superior.

Sanderson outlined his plan to Fyurk. When the maintenance man replaced that burnt out globe at the crime scene one of their blokes would install the camera.

'Let's go take a look.'

Fyurk traipsed down the stairs after him to the dock area. The rotting garbage stank worse than the day before. Sanderson heard raised voices above the rumble of a truck engine. The tray of the vehicle was backed up to the crime scene tape. Steel arms and jangling chains were waiting to take away the bin Cheryl's body had been found in. A bloke, wearing a navy singlet stretched over a massive beer gut, was propped beside the truck. The driver no doubt.

Toe to toe on either side of the tape, a body-builder type faced a skinny constable.

'Hey,' Sanderson interrupted the stand-off. 'Who are you?'

Huge biceps strained the sleeves of the bigger man's khaki shirt. Chords on his neck remained rigid as his gaze switched to Sanderson.

'Wilson, the groundsman. I need to get this bin taken away. It's a health issue.'

'Not so fast, Bob. See this,' Sanderson tapped the chequered tape. 'While this is still up it's our crime scene.'

Tension eased from the bloke's square jaw as he recognised Fyurk. 'Detective, can't you do anything?'

The constable backed off, happy with the intervention.

'Gary, can we check with Ruggeri if it's okay to take the tape down?' Fyurk asked.

Bob snorted and kicked at the cement surface with his work boot. Sanderson made the call and nodded for Fyurk to proceed. He dismissed the constable.

The driver revved up the truck; its reverse beeps echoing around the dock. The detectives watched Bob direct the skip onto the tray. They made a hasty exit for the car park.

'That wasn't exactly Bob's friendly side,' Sanderson said.

Fyurk sniggered. 'If we hadn't come along I think that constable would have shit himself. Bob must spend a lot of time working out.'

'Yeah, some of these fresh coppers aren't tough enough. Right now we need to focus on what Bob does with his spare time.'

As they drove down the highway Sanderson noticed the afternoon had turned grey and dreary. He flipped on the police radio to hear a 7-Eleven had been hit at Chatswood.

Hearing the word homicide, Fyurk straightened up. 'That's only a couple of k's away, Gary. Shouldn't we check it out?'

'Sure, it's our area. You never know, if we get an easy case Ralston might give us a break.'

When they pulled in, a patrol car with lights flashing was blocking the petrol pumps. Motorists hesitated then turned away. Sanderson snapped on gloves and headed into the store. He talked to one of the uniformed constables. The other was standing near a woman visibly shaking. Her words were almost incoherent. Probably in shock.

Sanderson ascertained it had been an armed hold up. The offender had worn an army-green balaclava and toted a sawn-off shotgun. Most likely a desperate junkie.

'Get that woman a seat and a glass of water,' he yelled.

Chocolate bars: Snickers, Mars and Cherry Ripes, dotted the floor in front of the counter. Sanderson made his way round behind it.

'Have you rung the ambos?'

'On the way,' one of the constables answered.

Sanderson saw a large Indian man folded over in the awkward space, his white shirt awash with blood. The smeared spatter pattern meant he had most likely slid down the back wall. He placed a finger on the dusky skin of the man's neck, feeling for a pulse. The ambos would be too late for this one. Poor bastard. Ethnics work horrendous hours in these places. Being shot down was not part of the job description.

Armed robbery was once big and bold, Sanderson thought. Since the new screens, banks had been largely left alone. Now the pricks do amateurish busts like this. He'd probably hightailed it in a stolen car to Cabramatta for his next fix. Bloody addicts.

Ambulance officers rushed in.

'Too late fellas. But check him out to be sure.' Sanderson inclined his head to the counter. The wait seemed interminable. Would forensics ever get here? He returned to the witness as Ruggeri and his team barged in.

'One bloody thing after another,' Ruggeri rushed towards the victim.

Fyurk took notes as he questioned the middle-aged woman. Her glasses were skewiff and blood oozed on her cheek. The crim had biffed her with the rifle butt to stop her screams. Sanderson was piecing the incident together when the door whooshed open again.

The officer's face beamed. 'Got the bastard, Inspector. Thanks to this lady's description of the getaway car we had him in no time. Silly bugger still hadn't removed the balaclava.'

'Good one. We'll follow you back to the station. See you Ruggeri.'

The Italian popped his capped head up from behind the counter and waved. Sanderson arranged for the constables to take the witness to the station. One was to drive her car. Damn, he thought, this could take all afternoon. Was he ever going to get back to his office? Wilson's details would be on his desk by now. He was anxious to see if CrimTrac had him on record.

Sanderson cruised along behind the patrol cars. As they veered off the highway one red light after another delayed their progress. This suburb was one of the busiest shopping areas of Sydney.

Fyurk sniffled and opened the glove compartment in search of a tissue.

'What's this in here for?' he asked holding up a grey tube of Calvin Klein aftershave.

'Part of my Chick Kit.' Sanderson laughed. 'A touch up shave, a dash of that and you're ready for the ladies.'

His offsider raised his eyebrows. 'You're kidding.' Fyurk snapped open the lid and took a whiff.

'That's one thing I never kid about, Rich. Grab a tissue and blow your snoz.'

They swept in through the station's gate into a car spot. Fyurk dealt with his nose and stuffed the tissue into a pocket.

'I've never used aftershave.'

'Perhaps you should. Sends women wild. Of course, I wouldn't know about Janine.' Sanderson winked at him.

Fyurk's face reddened. 'And these?' He held up a pair of hipster briefs whose seams emphasised a bulge in the front. The same brand name appeared on the waistband.

'Some days you need a shower to be fresh all over,' Sanderson's tone was jocular. 'I'm a Calvin Boy all the way.'

The younger detective replaced the item and shut the compartment. He looked thoughtful.

'This stuff's personal, right,' Sanderson said, switching off the ignition. 'We've got statements to video. Let's do the witness first. Give that creep time to stew.'

Darkness descended as the detectives left the station. Sanderson was glad of his jacket as a chilly wind swirled leaves in the car park. Fyurk sneezed and retrieved a ball of tissue from his pocket.

'Not another cold.' Sanderson sounded exasperated.

'Just the night air, Gary.' Fyurk stepped into the car, slamming the door.

The vehicle's engine thrummed into life and Sanderson pulled onto the street.

'That snoz of yours must be a trial.'

Fyurk stifled a laugh. 'Used to drive my mother mad. I was always telling her something was off in the fridge.'

'Let's put your keen sense of smell to work. D's are meant to sniff out trouble. We're going to check on our gardener bloke before calling it a day.'

'Righto.'

Few windows beamed light from the office building. Janine swept up the hallway as if she'd been waiting for them. On seeing Fyurk, she pushed strands of hair from her face.

'You both look buggered. I'll get coffees.'

'That'd be great, Janine,' the younger detective responded.

'Yeah, thanks,' Sanderson added, 'that fax from the uni arrive?'

Janine nodded as she walked away, her sensible shoes echoing down the corridor.

Lights flickered on in Sanderson's office as he slid into a chair. Fyurk had disappeared after Janine. The fax from Phillips University covered a pile of papers on the desk. Quietly, he scanned Bob Wilson's CV. The bloke was twenty-five and came originally from Western Australia. He'd done the HSC at a high school near Cottesloe Beach, a fancy suburb of Perth. Perhaps he didn't have the working class background Fyurk had figured.

Wilson had started some horticultural course then dropped out after two years. A few hotels were mentioned where he'd done bar work whilst studying. Then he'd worked for several landscapers before racking off to New Zealand. No glowing references. Wilson was a pretty ordinary worker. He'd been employed by an Auckland golf club before starting at the university in February. Sanderson wondered whether the golfers ever thought the bloke mowing their fairways was dangerous.

Fyurk came in, placing two steaming mugs on the desk. He sat and rolled his chair opposite Sanderson.

'Okay, so what's Bob's working history?'

'Came from WA, smart suburb. Then preened a golf course in NZ.'

'So let's see if we've got anything on him.' Fyurk led the way into another room so they could access CrimTrac.

What a boon the national database has been to detectives, thought Sanderson. His offsider's fingers flicked over the keys and Bob Wilson's name came up on screen. More than a page of matches appeared.

'Bloody common name,' sighed Sanderson as he searched for a birth date. None matched the one on the CV. 'Often crims just adopt a name like this and make up a birth date. Some are only known by nicknames like Scum and Rooter.'

Fyurk keyed in Robert Wilson. Another page or more. Sanderson ran his finger down the choices. The second last entry had the date he was after. He highlighted this and proceeded.

'Bingo,' Sanderson said. 'A little activity in WA. Possession of marihuana at eighteen, break and enters. A sexual assault conviction just before he pissed off to NZ.'

'Mmm,' murmured Fyurk, 'does Bob keep moving to stay out of trouble? Still, he might not have progressed to murder, Gary. Can we get onto the Auckland cops? Maybe they have a rapist with a penchant for cutting.'

Sanderson returned to his desk to make the call. Fyurk flicked a copy of Wilson's record down in front of him. The senior detective queried and nodded for several minutes before ending the conversation.

'They've got three serial rapists on the go. None with a cutting MO. No homicides in that vein either.'

'Bugger. If it's Bob perhaps Katie was his first victim. We thought that in the beginning. Remember you said dropping the scalpel and the jagged cuts were dead giveaways.'

'Maybe so, Rich. We don't want him to know we're onto him. I'll organise that camera first thing and wise up our campus cops to make his every movement a priority.'

'Fine. I'm off then if you don't need me. My old man will have dinner ready.'

'Lucky you.' Sanderson logged into the Artemis case. Updating the new information would take hours.

'How come you don't have a regular girlfriend? You're set up and it's not as if you don't like women.'

Sanderson winked at him. 'A little too much. Then they start moving in. Lingerie draped all over my place like a cat marking its territory. Then they bring up the biological clock ticking. Loud as. With the de facto laws these days I didn't want to risk losing my place.'

'Surely you don't want to be on your own forever.'

'Course not, Rich. For now I can please myself what I do when I get home. And whatever you leave in the fridge is still there even if it's limp celery.'

'Fair enough. Enjoy your limp celery. See you tomorrow.' Fyurk headed off into the night.

Eventually, Sanderson finished and drove towards the city. Multi-hued neon lights delineated the tops of skyscrapers. Horns blared as a car zipped across lanes on the bridge. He didn't feel like stopping for takeaway.

In the fridge he found a supermarket lasagne, microwaved it then cracked his first beer of the night. Sanderson changed into a tracksuit and fired up the gas heater. He peered into the courtyard. The night would be cold and clear. His limbs itched to release the day's tensions but it was too dark for a run. Pissed off with his huge workload, he punched numbers into his mobile.

'Hi, babe. Got any time for a weary detective?'

TWENTY-SEVEN

After the funeral Jill felt fragile. Death of a young person such as Cheryl caused a shiver of doubt. Also the strain of being with Duncan had drained her. The unexpected pleasure of seeing Gary was the only boon. His interest in sailing, a welcome surprise; they had something in common.

Her briefcase bulged with the last bundle of exam papers to be marked. She heaved it from the passenger's seat and locked the car. The aroma of roast meat wafting near the carport reminded her of rare family dinners at her grandparents' house in the country. Jill glanced at the curtained windows above and wished for once she could come in to a home-cooked meal. Every career woman needs a wife.

Jill dropped her burden near the dining table and took off her coat. In the bedroom gym gear was laid out on the bed. She could make the five-thirty class and do some late night shopping for the holiday. First on the list was a large bag that packed flat and some new underwear. Her mother always reminded her never to travel with old or tatty lingerie.

'Ruins your chances,' she would say with that wry twist of her ruby lips.

Before Jill left, a cursory glance round the lounge room made her realise its lack of style. In the rush to buy furniture she'd thought only of the practical. Her grey suede sofa displayed several insipid yellow cushions. The glass lamp and coffee tables were smart but devoid of flowers or ornaments. The TV and media unit dominated the other side of the room. A minimalist approach meant little to dust.

This living area was probably gloomy due to winter but what if she asked Gary over. Would he think the dull interior matched her personality? While avoiding meaningless social gatherings, Jill could become effervescent with people she liked. The room's drabness stayed in her mind all the way to class.

The same bouncy instructor worked them hard. Jill had bought a grey Lycra outfit: below-the-knee pants and tank top. Looking the part appeared important even if she was still discovering unused muscles. The gym was slightly warmer than the chilly air outside. More rain was on the way promising a wet, miserable evening. As she swung into the Tae bo movements, fantasy images of the Pacific abounded. Music pumped as they dragged step boxes into place. Sneakers thudded on timber floors. Jill was feeling energised again. Maybe activity rather than hibernation was the way to get through a Sydney winter.

After class she retrieved a fluffy jumper and her handbag from the locker. Jill wandered past brightly lit shops inside the complex. One place had bags packed on shelves, scattered on the floor and hanging from stands. A rather glamorous woman with a toothy smile helped to find one ideal for her trip. Practical black, with lots of zippered sections. A department store for lingerie was next stop. She skirted the hot pink G-strings. Imagining those flimsy pieces strung on the ship's line almost made her blush. All the crew would ogle. For every day, white or skin tone knickers with a touch of lace was more practical.

Jill stopped at a mannequin with the latest offering from Elle. She had always liked the range put out by the Australian model known as The Body. She drifted to a nearby stand. A bra of fine black net embroidered with rose petals caught her attention. A petite bow at the cleavage looked chic but sexy. A matching flower on the briefs convinced her. Who knows what might happen on steamy nights in the South Seas? This lingerie was ripe with possibilities.

When Jill tried on the set the transformation made her cheeks hot. In her mind the lights of the change room dimmed to a seductive setting with a certain handsome detective. Her hand took hold of his silky tie pulling him closer. Jill's head swam in the fragrance of his aftershave. Their lips touched. She was a siren.

Loud knocking snapped her from the reverie. People were waiting for the change room. Jill quickly dressed and went to pay. Her purchases in the tiny bag were more empowering than the gym class. What kind of woman did she wish to be? In the past Jill was serious and academic. Satisfying for a career but not for her hormones. It was as if her body had come of age and demanded its moment in the sun. How can the sight of one detective with a sensual inflection in his voice do that? Would Jill spend the whole holiday wishing Gary had come? Was she ready to rush into a relationship with such a mercurial character? Yes, Jill thought. And she bet Gary was a man who appreciated lingerie.

Asian artefacts in the window of a homewares shop made her hesitate. A few knick-knacks would brighten up the lounge room. Silver and burgundy cushion covers sparkled with minute sequins. Their different patterns were stunning. Jill bought four. Her other purchase was a long cylindrical vase, a packet of white stones and an array of false flowers. Birds of paradise with flaring orange beaks, stalks of greenery and tortured willow would look spectacular on the lamp table. Finally, she saw a treasure both enticing and expensive. The head of a Thai goddess on a stand, rather exotic with gold paint and a jewel-encrusted headdress.

Her many bags of shopping were cumbersome. For someone who rarely shopped, Jill was on a high. Was this pre-holiday madness? She passed a bottle shop and then smelt food. From a noodle bar came the sizzling of stir-fries. Several tables were empty. On impulse she walked back and bought a bottle of wine then found herself ordering Singapore noodles. Eating out alone at night was a rare event. She didn't even have a book with her. The steaming noodles tempered with a sip or two of white were sublime.

When Jill struggled in the door with her purchases it was quite late. She put the new cushion covers on and was pleased with the effect. Pebbles clinked in the bottom of the vase as she arranged the floral display. What a lift it gave the room. Then she placed the Thai head on the coffee table, sat and stared at it. With an elongated flattish nose and shut eyes, it brought a peaceful ambience into the living area. Her fingers traced the nubbles of the goddess's head. Somehow Jill felt protected by its presence.

There was no time for television with the preparatory reading she had in mind. Jill had brought home Kerry Howe's book, *The Loyalty Islands*, to refresh herself on their history. The French had annexed these along with New Caledonia in 1853. Violent infighting amongst the chiefs must have seemed terrible to the colonisers. Raids with machetes brought to mind a photo she'd seen of an elderly islander, his arm a stump below the elbow.

In the two decades to the late 1860s the English and Americans had joined the French in building whaling stations on these islands. This would have given the natives a taste for Western trade goods. To a culture based on stone, bone, shell and timber, metal tools must have seemed wondrous. Various missionaries battled to bring the *Bible* to these outposts. Islanders enjoyed the hymns but conversions were few. Eventually chiefs accepted religion when it helped cement their powers.

The whole era of contact must have been confusing for both sides. Colonists with superior attitudes offered what they perceived a better way of life. Melanesians, ever wary of strangers, adopted and used only what they chose. Despite her wide reading of various accounts, Jill found it hard to imagine these initial encounters. To her mind one beneficial change that had lasted over the centuries was the love of church music. Islander choirs with their melodious voices, was an experience she was looking forward to on the holiday.

Later when Jill was ready for bed, she slung the travel bag into the base of the wardrobe. The stiletto with the sharpened heel stared back at her. She stuck it in her uni bag.

Next morning, she woke feeling uneasy. Whether it was the image of the hastily made weapon the night before or pre-holiday nerves, Jill could not tell. She switched on the radio to hear the weather: scattered showers. A perfect day for marking exam papers. As she wandered through the living area the previous evening's touch of decorating astounded her. Why had she waited so long? With uplifted spirits, Jill made tea and toast then changed her pyjamas for a tracksuit.

Her small dining table was swamped with papers but she progressed rapidly. Comments and grades in red biro were scrawled over the pages. Hours passed with barely a squawk from the resident myna birds outside. Jill decided to make a treat for lunch.

Smearing pasta sauce over pita bread, she dabbled on mozzarella cheese. Stripes of capsicum and marinated eggplant covered baby spinach leaves. Her fingers crumbled fetta cheese on top then she put the tray in the oven. Ten minutes later the aroma of a pizza parlour danced into the room. Jill cut the pizza into quarters almost burning herself. Savouring the cheesy taste, she lingered over lunch.

By late afternoon she'd finished all the marking and drove to the university. The papers would remain locked in her office till next semester. She lowered the blind and secured the door. Protocol decreed she wish Duncan a pleasant holiday. Not that Jill had any idea how he spent his time away from the portals of learning. His wife was not a traveller, she'd heard.

Muffled sounds emerged as she tapped on his office door.

'Come in,' he said.

'Hello Duncan, Paula.'

The research assistant was returning books to shelves. Duncan's gaze switched from her behind to Jill's face. His bony hand clasped a mug of coffee. He looked pale and listless. A concern about his health crept back into her mind.

'Jill, you're off. Anything planned for the holidays?' Duncan made an attempt to be cheerful.

Nothing I'm revealing now, Jill thought. 'Not really, maybe drop in on Mother. Just wanted to wish you both a nice break.'

'Thanks, Jill,' Paula chirped in, 'You really should have booked something. I'm going to the Whitsundays. A five star resort. Get away from this horrible weather.'

'Have a great time.' Jill backed out of Duncan's office.

On the way to the library her shoulder bag with its secret contents made her think of the Campus Killer. Jill knew it would be after dark by the time she'd researched that rare book written in 1852. Perhaps stories of early contact in the New Hebrides would help her relate to Vanuatu today. Tonight was the last before flying out. If Jill kept an eye out as Gary suggested, she might have a reason to phone him.

The book absorbed her for several hours in the reading room. Stiff and cold, Jill walked into the glaring lights of the cafeteria and ordered a coffee. She could hear a few latecomers' murmured conversations.

Jill was almost finished her warming drink when she noticed a young man come up the steps from the dock area. He was wearing a hooded sweatshirt. Instead of striding with attitude as most students did his movements were wary. He yanked at the hood further concealing his face. Intuition told her he had something to hide. Her stomach churned. Was this young man dangerous? Was it HIM?

Then a blonde girl swept out of the cafeteria. Going to meet him, Jill thought. But the girl moved on into the darkness as if she hadn't seen him. He hesitated then followed in her tracks along the pathway. Sweat beaded on Jill's forehead. Had this happened to Katie? Her chair scraped noisily on the tiles as she left and pursued them into the night. Outside, Jill took the brown scarf from her bag, winding it over her hair as a disguise. The dark woollen jacket and jeans she was wearing suited her purpose. Her sneakers were almost soundless on the paved path. One hand firmly clenched the sharpened stiletto. It gave her courage to stalk the possible killer. Every nerve ending tingled. Her mind flashed scenarios: saving the girl, being interviewed by the media.

Jill could hardly believe her actions. Had her innate fear of men evaporated? A light up front showed he was closing on the girl. Why didn't she check behind her? If only a night patrol would come along.

Did the hooded monster have his strangling rope ready? Where did he conceal the scalpel? The thought of mutilation made her shudder. Jill started to run. Adrenalin pumping through her produced a surge of energy. Urgent blood pulsed in her fingertips. Compulsion drove her. Jill had to protect this girl before he struck.

She raised the stiletto. Its sharpened point was aimed at his neck. Perhaps to sever the carotid artery. He swung around. Had he heard her heaving breaths? He said something to the girl.

In the indistinct light, the girl's face showed no fear of him. On seeing Jill, her scream ripped through the night air. Something was not computing in her brain. Both faces, one haloed by blonde hair, the other hooded, saw her as the attacker.

The boy raised his arm in defence. He pulled at the scarf.

'It's a woman.' Jill heard him say. She hurled the shoe, wheeled about, running as fast as she could.

TWENTY-EIGHT

'What the hell is this?' Barbara's voice rasped. Hugh's body went rigid. Silence. She thrust the mobile at his face almost scraping his nose. He read the message.

'Oh, that's only Lisa.'

'Since when has she been calling you Hewie? What's going on here?' Barbara's raucous tone made Hugh glance down the hallway. He touched a finger to his lips. Leaning against the doorjamb, he embarked on an explanation in his calm doctor's voice. Lisa, his nurse, was going through a marriage break up. He was concerned she was becoming dependent on him. It all sounded quite plausible.

Barbara felt the tightness in her stomach ease. She set the mobile down, resting her hip against the desk. Maybe she was overreacting. The drama with Madeline and the personal alarm seemed trivial now. She'd been about to accuse her husband of having an affair. Something had stopped her, possibly his ridicule at the idea. At times she'd watched Hugh shake his head at the sexual messes other people got themselves into. For almost twenty years Barbara had lived a sedate but satisfying existence. Some human beings, she felt, wanted too much out of life. Such expectations often brought turmoil and illness.

'We'd better get on with the family dinner.' Barbara said, smoothing her hair, 'Did you meet Rob on your way in?'

'Kind of. He didn't bother to get off the lounge.' Hugh raised his eyebrows and led the way to the living room.

'Mmm. Didn't take him long to find his way round my kitchen either.'

Barbara asked Madeline to set the table. Wearing oven mitts, she brought the meals. When they'd begun eating, Barbara thought Hugh seemed determined to suss Rob out. He found politics was his area of study.

From a woman's perspective, Barbara had to admit Rob was strikingly handsome. Something about those dark chocolate eyes and pointed chin reminded her of the actor Daniel Day Lewis. But it annoyed her that his cap had stayed on at the table.

Madeline's adoring gaze rarely shifted from Rob's face. Her hand snuck onto his thigh every now and then. Repeatedly, Rob got up to help himself to another beer from the drinks' fridge. Hugh offered him a red wine; the refusal was blunt. Again the lack of manners rattled Barbara. For Madeline's sake she refrained from saying anything. She wondered what sort of home he came from. Parents had to be careful when introduced to new partners. Let things ride, she thought. On the other hand, too much approval was the kiss of death. Madeline was so young Rob mightn't last a month.

Barbara collected the plates while the others remained deep in conversation. Beau followed her into the kitchen and stood by his bowl awaiting leftovers. Barbara rewarded him with the plate scrapings. She rubbed his back and whispered, 'At least you've got manners.'

Golden toffee syrup, a drizzle of cream and splayed strawberries appeared rather swish, she thought as she served the crème caramel.

'Thanks Mrs H, that looks delish,' said Rob.

'Good one, Mum. Robbie loves dessert.'

Her daughter's exuberant expression brought a chuckle from Hugh.

After dinner the young couple returned to the lounge to watch another DVD. Hugh and Barbara retired to bed to read. His fingers stroked her forearm.

'Don't worry about that message. The last thing I want is to change my life.' He yawned. 'Night, Barbs.'

Hugh was asleep instantly after his day of golf. Barbara flipped over a few more pages of the magazine before turning out the light. She lay, thinking of her husband's consoling words. The year so far had brought its changes. Madeline starting university had been a step into her future. Barbara knew she had to ease parental ties but it seemed harder with an only child. Barely a month had passed before she was devastated by the fear of losing her daughter altogether.

How did murder come so close? Barbara pictured Katie's face with a pang of anguish. Then there'd been a second victim. She frequently tried to cast aside thoughts of that lurking killer. Clearly, Madeline was not prepared to discuss the dangers. But time after time when her daughter set off for lectures Barbara wondered if she'd come home.

Work had been her saviour. Bronwyn was a salve to Barbara's worries. Her colleague's antics describing patients made everyone laugh. Physiotherapy involved pushing people through their pain threshold. Some patients could not envisage improved movement months down the track. The staff needed the light relief Bronwyn provided.

Barbara had also felt at odds with Hugh in recent months. He seemed to have no time for her. Jibes about her increasing weight hurt her. She'd always felt her marriage ran in cycles. This had been a down time but things would improve as they had in the past. Hugh's breathing was steady beside her.

Her thoughts turned to the new house. Finishing touches were bringing her dream to reality. The carpet was to be laid next week after the painters moved out. Pillars for the front fence would take several days then the landscapers could start. As Barbara imagined herself walking from room to room, sleep enveloped her.

When she woke it was still dark. Pain throbbed in the joint at the base of her left thumb. Had she forgotten her arthritis medication? Barbara pulled the thumb with a steady pressure alleviating the sensation. Upon release, searing pain brought her fully awake. Not wishing to disturb Hugh, she slipped out of bed and tiptoed across the dim room.

Moonlight streamed through the glass in the living area. This provided enough light to find the Panadol. Barbara swallowed the painkillers then found a cool pack in the freezer. Massaging the joint brought no relief so she decided ice was the solution. She stood, staring through the window to the horizon. A moonbeam spliced the dark sea. Where the water and sky met, a faint luminescence told her dawn was not far off.

Barbara crept back to bed. Did this pain in her thumb signal a progression of the disease?

Next morning at breakfast Hugh down played the episode. Barbara knew better than to expect much sympathy. She had only mild discomfort when she jiggled her thumb. Madeline and Rob had had a late coffee. Her stainless steel cups were in the sink. Barbara hand washed them and turned on the coffee machine.

'Do you know what time Rob left?' asked Hugh.

'Must've been late. Maddy's still asleep.'

Barbara ground the beans, put in a shot and frothed the milk. Savouring the coffee aroma, she took her espresso to the balcony. Hugh joined her placing a steaming mug of tea on the table. They sat in companionable silence enjoying the view. Morning sunshine warmed the crisp wintry air.

'Hugh, there's a new exhibition on at the art gallery. Why don't we go today?'

Her husband took a sip before responding, 'Sorry, Barbs. I thought you'd be fiddling at the new house so I put my name down for doubles.'

'Not more golf. You run your bloody life round the game. It'd be nice if you showed interest in the house or doing something with me.' Barbara's knuckles whitened on the handle of her cup.

'Now don't get upset. If you'd only planned this during the week I'd have gone. You're so touchy lately.'

'Fine,' she said, her voice calm, 'I'll go on my own.' Barbara swept inside.

Barbara arrived home from the art gallery mid-afternoon and had just settled on the lounge with a magazine when Madeline burst in. Her daughter's eyes were red rimmed from crying. Madeline rushed towards her, knelt on the floor and put her head in Barbara's lap. Loud sobs echoed round the room. Barbara ran her fingers through her daughter's silky hair.

'Maddy, what's wrong? Is it Rob?'

Madeline looked up.

'No Mum. It's Helen. A friend we hang out with in Manly. Last night she had her drink spiked. She was raped.'

'Oh God. That's terrible. What's she done about it?' Barbara felt a surge of anxiety bring on a hot flush. She fanned her face with a magazine.

'There's no point reporting it to police. These date-rape drugs cause amnesia. All she remembers is talking to two guys in a club then feeling woozy. Helen must have told them where she lived. She's bruised and sore but recalls nothing of them being in her flat. Why are all these things happening to my friends?'

They heard the door open. Hugh walked in and Madeline told him the tale.

'Rohypnol probably,' he said. 'Helen should still report this. The police need all the evidence they can to stop this spiking business.' Hugh's lined face showed concern.

'But Dad ...'

'Do you go to this club?'

Madeline nodded.

'Well make sure you never leave your drink unattended.' Hugh's voice rose well above its usual octave.

'We don't Dad. But I've heard some of the tampering goes on behind the bar.'

Barbara let out a cry. 'Is nowhere safe?'

TWENTY-NINE

Sunday morning brought perfect weather for a barbecue. Sanderson shaved, showered and dragged on grey track pants. He put on a sweatshirt and flicked fingers through his tousled hair before venturing out to shop.

Opening the fridge, he checked for necessities. Beer bottles took up the lower shelves. He retrieved the roll of scotch fillet and sliced it into thick steaks. With several noisy twists, he ground black pepper over the meat adding a dash of teriyaki marinade and red wine. Sanderson had also bought a bag of fancy snags. Beer and meat, the staples of a barbecue, he thought.

Sanderson patted his back pocket for his wallet as he shut the front door and sauntered towards Oxford Street. Activity on the shopping strip was minimal at this time. A few dog walkers were about and patrons were poring over Sunday papers in the café. He heard a fearsome yapping as a white rugrat of a dog strained his leash towards an alsatian. Knowing police dogs, he felt the larger one would have the other for breakfast if the owners let them get together.

Dressed in habitual black, the Greek woman serving in the salad bar managed a toothy smile. A confusing variety of salads, piled mountains on white plates, faced him. Sanderson asked for two large portions of potato and Greek salad as well as a medium tabouli. That should be enough of the healthy stuff, he figured. He watched the grey-haired shopkeeper pack them expertly into plastic containers.

'Hava nice day,' she said, handing them over slung in a bag.

'Sure will.' Sanderson replied, giving her a wink.

The pimply boy at the bread shop packed a crusty loaf and a mass of cheese and bacon rolls for him. Sanderson, laden with supplies, turned away from the rumble of cars into his quieter street. He stopped off at his corner store to buy a *Sun Herald* and pick up the trousers he'd had dry cleaned after the autopsy.

Noticing his parcels, the Korean man behind the counter said, 'Having a day off?'

'Yeah, barbecue with the mates. Watching the footie this afternoon.'

The man nodded and handed over the change. Sanderson thought a copper worked ridiculous hours but that shopkeeper was tied to that business seven days a week. What kind of a life could he have?

Several hours later half a dozen members of the Homicide Squad lounged around the teak table in Sanderson's courtyard. Beer in one hand and tongs in the other, he was standing over the barbecue.

'Sando, chuck us a snag,' Reeves's voice rang out as Fyurk walked in carrying a six-pack of beer in one hand, more salads in the other. Sanderson had forgotten Fyurk's offer.

'Caesar and avocado something,' his offsider said.

'That's good. I picked up a few different ones. Grab a beer, Rich.'

With a bottle in hand, Fyurk hung around while Sanderson cooked the steaks. His offsider hadn't mixed socially with the blokes before. Fyurk was not much of a drinker. Sanderson had rarely taken him to the pub but that was a part of police culture he'd have to get used to. If the youngster didn't join in the do-it-yourself debriefing sessions over booze he'd have trouble handling the dead'uns.

Sanderson wondered if Fyurk had mustered the courage to ask Janine out. He'd certainly taken his advice to smarten up. With a blue striped shirt over the latest jeans, Fyurk looked almost trendy.

'So you think Ruggeri's seeing someone special today?' Fyurk asked, pulling a roll from the bag.

'Maybe. Ruggeri's a dark horse. You won't get much on his private life. His Italian mamma is always on at him to marry and have bambinos. She just doesn't understand a crime scene examiner's life. It's a bugger for families.'

'I suppose so,' Fyurk munched slowly, 'he's good at his job isn't he?'

'One of the best,' Sanderson replied, 'takes a heavy toll though. Many don't last. They not only see the bodies, they have to examine them for all possible injuries. Combing a crime scene for every trace of evidence, making decisions whether it's a suspicious death, suicide or whatever.'

Flames flared. Quick with the tongs, Sanderson moved the steaks before continuing, 'Then there's endless cataloguing, recording and photographing items. Considering all that, Ruggeri does an amazing job. He often has a sixth sense about what's gone on. You should talk to him more, Rich.'

'He hasn't exactly been approachable.' Fyurk straightened up and presented a platter for the steaks.

'Keep trying. We rely on forensic blokes a lot.'

Sanderson followed Fyurk to the table. The others descended on the food like blowflies.

''Bout bloody time,' Ralston shouted. 'Smells great, Sando.'

Amidst the beers and ribald jokes, Sanderson felt relaxed. He loaded up his plate and tucked in.

After they finished eating, Sanderson noted Fyurk was more comfortable watching the match. The blokes had given him a bit of a ribbing. Yells of encouragement finally saw the Tigers win. At dusk, cleaning up the dirty plates and masses of bottles, Sanderson whistled while he worked.

On Monday morning Fyurk marched into the office with a surveillance tape.

Sanderson smiled, 'Let's see what goes on in that dock area after dark.'

Fyurk slotted the tape into the machine and pressed the remote. After a whirring sound, an image of the last crime scene flickered onto the screen. Sanderson leant forward, his face a mask of concentration. With the shutter down, no delivery trucks and a dump bin, it was a gloomy space of practicality. Not at all like the sunny morning he'd first approached the overflowing skip bin for his nostrils to be assaulted by the mingled smells of death and garbage. The pungent odour of putrefaction invaded clothes, the pores of the skin and the mind. That smell could quickly take him back to a crime scene.

He could clean his clothes, scrub his body but expunging some of the homicides from his brain took kilometres of running or slabs of beer. At his annual medical Sanderson hoped he'd clear the liver function test. Perhaps he should talk to his offsider about methods of coping.

Fyurk watched the screen just as intently. He'd drawn up a chair and draped his lanky body across it. Sanderson peered as the shutter rose. He recognised Li, the Chinese chef, jumping nimbly down from the ledge. The young man threw a bulging bag of rubbish into the skip allowing its lid to bang. Then Li unlocked the storeroom and retrieved a cardboard carton. The door slammed and Li set the carton on the dock, glancing around.

'Wonder if he's thinking of Cheryl,' Fyurk said.

'Poor bloke. I liked Li. He's the only one who had any time for her.' Sanderson reached for his coffee, tilted the cup and found it empty.

'Except for her killer,' added Fyurk.

'Yeah. Right. The very bastard we're trying to catch here.' Sanderson picked up his ornament of fornicating pigs, turning it in his hands as a distraction. On screen, Li leapt up heaving the carton of produce onto his shoulder and the shutter rattled down.

Fyurk fast-forwarded to the next action. A hooded figure appeared.

'Back it up,' urged Sanderson. They both watched for the first sign of movement.

Sanderson saw a fellow move warily into the dock area. With hands in the pockets of low-slung jeans, the figure mooched around as if waiting for someone. The hood made him unrecognisable.

'Damn,' said Fyurk, 'that hood doesn't help us identify him. Perhaps he's wise to cameras.'

'Doubt it. Here comes someone,' mused Sanderson.

A short nuggetty man strode in confidently. His features were not concealed.

'Guess who?' said Fyurk.

'Wilson. Let's see what he's up to.' Sanderson returned the ornament to the desk. The words on the tape were too muffled to hear. The hooded bloke handed over notes; Wilson gave him a small package. Each moved surreptitiously as if this was little more than a handshake. Sanderson had seen enough of these encounters on tape to recognise a drug deal.

'So our gardener's doing a touch of dealing on campus. I'll alert the drug squad but we don't want to move in too quickly. Drugs mightn't be his only game. Can't be a coincidence Wilson's deal site was also a dump site for a body.'

'Figures, Gary. He's been done for possession of marijuana. No record of dealing. Bob's just landed more trouble. Did we find out what gym he goes to?' Fyurk sped through the tape, which showed no more activity.

'No,' Sanderson answered, 'that's where you come in. Wilson seems to have taken to you. Go have a friendly chat. See what you can get out of him.'

The office door opened and Janine walked in. Sanderson watched Fyurk jump up to greet her. He gave her a wave. Her darkly lashed eyes flitted back to the younger detective's face. Their words were softly spoken as if exchanging some intimacy. Let them have their moment, Sanderson thought. His gaze rested on Cyndi's gift. He smiled.

Fyurk left to make fresh coffees as Janine walked over to Sanderson's desk.

'There's a report from one of the officers on campus,' she handed him the papers.

Janine spun around and left the room. She was probably aware that Sanderson observed her exit. Didn't he have a reputation to uphold? Women were high on his list. Details of what they wore, how they looked was part of his job. Fyurk was making an impact on Janine from what he'd observed. Perhaps he should warn his offsider mixing sex and work was not a great idea.

He turned his attention to the report. The Friday night incident it described was a strange one. A university student had informed the constable the day after. She'd been walking down a path towards the history building about 9 pm that night. A male friend caught up with her. They heard someone behind them. Turning, she saw a person with their head swathed in a scarf. Her friend had yelled, 'It's a woman.' The woman's arm was raised brandishing a weapon. It was too dark to see but she thought it might be a shoe. She screamed fearing her male friend was being attacked. The object flung into bushes; the woman ran off. The informant described herself as shaky so the friend escorted her to her car and returned to a residential college. A Constable Stretton had signed the report.

Sanderson rang to speak to him but was told he was patrolling the campus. This new piece of information was bewildering. Here he was trying to track down a possible serial killer and he gets a report of a woman attacker. In 99 per cent of cases, those who murder young women and mutilate their sexual parts are men. This just didn't fit. If the person they were after was a woman this case would be world news. But hang on a minute he told himself. The girl said the attacker threatened her male friend.

Fyurk brought in their drinks. Sanderson handed his offsider the report.

'A woman attacker. What next?' Fyurk's surprised voice echoed round the office. 'Finish your coffee. We're off to the uni. You have your chat with Wilson. I'm going to help our cops search. I want that weapon found and the area near the residential colleges scoured. There's got to be more clues on that bloody campus.' Sanderson sipped then added the report to the expanding paperwork of the case. He decided they'd visit the incident room on the way back to refresh his mind on every bit of evidence so far. He'd sift through everything they had since finding Katie's body.

The whiteboard would get a work out developing directions for further inquiry. He spoke to one of his colleagues on the drug squad regarding the tape and Wilson's involvement. Ralston would no doubt want a full update this week. Fortunately the media pressure had backed off. They couldn't keep printing the Campus Killer was yet to be found.

A gatekeeper gave a friendly wave as Sanderson drove into the university grounds. The senior detective sent Fyurk to track down Wilson then headed for the room assigned to the police. A constable suggested he use her walkie-talkie to talk to Stretton. Sanderson made the fountain a meeting place.

He straightened his tie and was thankful he'd worn a wool-blend suit. Yesterday's sunshine had given way to masses of grey cumulous cloud. Sanderson wanted to get the searches underway before any rain fell. Students clustered around him. His thoughts were as jumbled as the fountain's frothing cascades. Preoccupied by this latest report, he barely noticed a pair of uniformed officers approaching him. A tall burly man stepped forward with a woman who looked sixteen.

'Stretton?' Sanderson asked the man.

'Yes, Sir.'

'Detective Sanderson. I read your report. Interesting to say the least. Can you show me the area where the incident took place? I want that weapon found.'

They walked along a path Sanderson was familiar with. He chatted to Stretton about his observations on campus. As they neared the history building the young constable began her search among shrubs below the windows. The bulky officer stood on the path as if estimating where a thrown weapon might land. Then he led Sanderson to a tangled garden further away.

The woman's voice rang out. 'Found it.' She emerged with a dead leaf on her collar, holding up the shoe. 'A stiletto. Hey, would you believe this? The metal tip's been sharpened. Perfect weapon for a woman.'

'Well done, Constable.' Sanderson beamed and brushed off the leaf.

At that moment Fyurk arrived and produced an evidence bag.

'Phew. A filed heel. That'd hurt.' The young detective sealed the bag and wrote on the label.

Back in the car, Sanderson suggested Fyurk deliver their latest piece of evidence to Ruggeri. He felt this might foster their relationship. Sanderson would have liked more time to examine the bag's contents but couldn't risk contamination. Something about that shoe worried him.

'Did you find Wilson?'

'Sure did, Gary. Had our chat. Found out he goes to a gym in the city. He thanked me for help with that bin incident. I told him we have to follow procedure in homicides. Bob got a touch edgy at that word. "You're not trying to pin anything on me," he said. "Course not", I assured him.'

'He's a hard one, Rich. Charming one minute, agro the next. It's bloody near impossible finding out if he fits the picture of a killer. Sounds like he's suspicious. We just don't have the resources or enough evidence to put him under full surveillance.'

Fyurk showed Sanderson the name of the gym in his notebook. 'You could check it out. Mustn't be far from your place.'

'Will do.' Sanderson changed lanes and turned off to the police station. 'I instigated a search of the bush area near those residential colleges. Too many things seem connected with them one way or another.'

'Wasn't Bob seen talking to Cheryl on the path near there?'

'He was. Which gives him the opportunity. But what motive? Could Cheryl have been in on the drug business and they fell out?'

'Not likely, Gary. Psychopathic killers don't need a motive. The pressure of their fantasies builds up till they go looking for a victim. It's usually a stranger. Chances are those were the first words Bob Wilson spoke to her if he's our man. She was probably dragged into that screen of trees and dumped later.'

'Which gives us further reason to check that area thoroughly.'

Inside the incident room the usual array of gruesome photos greeted Sanderson. His mobile's ring was shrill, the message short. He stared at Fyurk.

'This case just got a whole lot more complicated. That was Stretton. At the search site near the colleges. They've found another body. And Rich, it's skeletonised.'

THIRTY

Jill awoke feeling agitated. The memory of the previous evening flickered into her mind. She wanted to pull the covers over her head. Had she really tried to attack someone with a stiletto? This behaviour seemed utterly ridiculous in daylight. If only Gary had not encouraged her involvement. But Katie was her student. Katie's death gave her no choice.

Her breath came in rapid gasps. Jill sat up. Stupidly, she'd thrown the shoe into bushes. Jill gulped for air. If anyone connected the incident with her what could she say? In flannelette pyjamas, she leapt out of bed. In the lounge room Jill stood near the coffee table trailing her fingers over the Thai goddess's bobbled-timber head.

Initially, Jill worried about using a sacred symbol as a decorative ornament. But then she read if a Buddha image is seen as a thing of beauty that was fine. After further research, she decided to call her Dharani. Before her purchase Jill knew almost nothing of Thai religious beliefs. Apart from life-enhancing blessings, these goddesses protect against enemies and danger. Calmness flooded through Jill as if Dharani sensed her troubled state.

Forget everything to do with the university, she told herself. The murders, Duncan's difficult manner, exam papers and students could all wait till next semester. Jill played panpipe music and prepared breakfast. Her flight left in four hours.

A leisurely shower was just what she needed. Suds spattered the shower screen as she washed her shoulder-length hair. Jill had given little thought to its impracticality on the boat and made a mental note to pack scrunchies. With legs shaved and nails manicured, it was time to concentrate on last minute packing.

Jill had purchased a Goretex jacket fearing the foul-weather gear the ship supplied would be too heavy. Her gaze scanned the list as she ticked items off. Mostly she'd be wearing shorts and T-shirts on board. A few colourful pants and tops were sufficient for dining ashore. Jill zipped up her bag and filled in the luggage label.

Her toiletries bag was wedged into a backpack with reading matter, notebooks and camera. A bumbag contained passport, tickets, a travel brush, lip balm and a purse with both Australian dollars and Pacific French francs. No handbags to tote around for three whole weeks. Jill clipped the bumbag over a polar fleece top. Its warmth would no longer be needed after escaping Sydney's winter.

Bags ready, she meandered through every room checking that all windows and doors were locked. She would set the alarm when the airport shuttle arrived. As she heard the blare of a horn, her final glance took in the goddess. Dharani's serene expression sent Jill on her way to the Pacific.

After a two and a half flight she could see the reef-fringed island of New Caledonia surrounded by an aquamarine sea. An islander wearing a red hibiscus shirt waited outside the airport, holding aloft a sign with the name *Dreamsong*. Around a dozen people gathered near a minivan, their bags forming a growing pile. Steve introduced himself. He had the tan and exuberance of a fitness instructor. Many of her fellow seafarers were part of a diving group from South Australia. Steve was their dive master. Jill nodded around the circle not concentrating on the names.

The bus driver's frizz of dark hair jiggled as he counted the passengers. They loaded up and drove at a reckless pace through the streets of Noumea to the wharves. Opening a window, Jill smelt warm tropical air with a tang of salt. After years of studying and lecturing on the Pacific region she was finally seeing it for herself. Stomach tense, Jill realised with excitement this journey could be life changing.

Their vehicle came to a juddering halt. The sight of the magnificent brigantine captured her attention as others fussed over luggage.

Dreamsong was more impressive than in the brochure. With bag hoisted on her shoulder, Jill heard the creak of hawsers holding the vessel at the wharf. Atop one of the masts a triangular flag snaked in the breeze. Furled canvas, a maze of ropes and huge wooden blocks kept her gaze skywards. Jill felt she'd stepped back through two hundred years of history. Almost last to negotiate the rickety planks, she stepped aboard her first tallship.

Ruth welcomed them. Jill warmed to her voice. Ruth was wearing a pink sarong and no shoes. Her hair was a mess of black curls streaked with grey.

'Follow the girls to your cabins,' Ruth said with a wide smile, 'then come up to the saloon for a cuppa.'

Ducking her head to step inside, Jill slid her bag down the winding staircase to one of the galley girls. She turned to descend backwards, her sneakers squeaking on each step. Below, timber gleamed in dim light. The skylight, a glass prism set in the deck, brightened the cabin. Her bunk was the lower one opposite the basin and mirror. Shelves covered with curtains provided stowage for gear. Above the pillow were a reading light and a small fan. The latter no doubt to help them sleep in the steamy tropics. She'd shed her jacket at the airport but the heat made her clammy in jeans. Jill ditched them and the sneakers for a pair of shorts.

The rest of the gang were making tea and coffee, pouring water from a large dented kettle. With a mug of English breakfast she slid along a timber seat beside one of the huge tables. From the saloon she could see activity on the wharves. Ruth began her introductory talk on the ship's routine. She told them they carried enough water for a quick hot shower each day. What a luxury! Jill thought of her saltwater shampoo for bucket showers on deck. Shortly they'd have a demonstration on how to work the heads, the ship's jargon for toilets. Hygiene was an issue too. Through her reading she knew dysentery could ravage a ship's crew but Jill had not expected its relevance today.

They would adapt to shipboard life over the next few days before setting sail, Ruth assured them. Jill sipped tea as the various shore excursions were described. Tomorrow they would meet the skipper and crew for initiation into sailing and the watch system. Those around her began to buzz with excitement. Jill was looking forward to getting to know some of her shipmates but not before a wander around *Dreamsong*.

The dive group stayed to plan their first foray underwater while she went aft. The monstrous spoked wheel evoked another era; the compass was encased in shiny brass. Climbing down the rear stairs she found herself in a vast lower saloon. With wall lamps and cosy cushions, it had a comfortable feel. A glass fronted cabinet held the ship's library. Jill noticed a few trashy airport novels among older books about the islands. With no time to delve, she continued her inspection.

Up on the bow a black winch held fast huge links of the anchor chain. Jill stood on a ledge to see the long bowsprit. Below it hung a cradle of knotted rope where she pictured herself lying while drifting across smooth seas. She had to clamber onto the wharf to see the carved figurehead with its cheeks puffed fit to burst.

That evening Steve was serving cocktails on the poop deck. He had changed into short shorts and a yellow tank top that displayed both tan and muscles. Wanting to include her, he handed over a glass of something white and frothy. Most of the dive group knew each other and were chatting amicably. Steve liked to be the centre of attention. His voice was always an octave louder, his laugh hearty and his eyes roved over every female body including hers. She noticed his eyes were a soft grey.

'Come on, Jill, drink up.'

She tasted the refreshing pineapple and coconut flavour.

'Lovely,' Jill said, her gaze slipping to Steve's prominent Adam's apple. Something about his manner reminded her of Gary. Perhaps the lazy confidence of knowing he was attractive to women. She hadn't thought of her detective all day. Too busy with the possibilities of the holiday.

Her mind flitted back to Professor Mitchell's office. What had that kerfuffle been about? Jill wondered just what Paula had to put up with to keep her job. The thought of Duncan's sweaty hands made her shiver. Damn him. No way was she going to be touched up to keep her position at the university.

The next afternoon they finally met the skipper. A barrel-chested man, he was powerfully built. He wore a red bandana to keep unruly grey curls from his face. From his voice Jill could detect his absolute devotion to *Dreamsong* and the seafaring life. His nickname was Banjo, which seemed incongruous with his work-toughened hands. He pointed to a chart, tracing a forefinger over the course they'd sail to Vanuatu. Her mind drifted, wondering what it would be like at sea.

At first the noisy flapping of canvas and yelled orders was bewildering. Jill could feel *Dreamsong* leap ahead as the sails set. Gradually the crew inducted them into the mysteries of tallship sailing as their island-hopping venture progressed.

Only the throb of the diesel disturbed the cooling evening as they approached the anchorage. Chain rumbled out then all was quiet. Jill wandered to the bow and sat on the Samson post. Twilight in the tropics had become her thinking time. Solitude wasn't easy with twenty-eight people on board. Something in her yearned to absorb this atmosphere: the warm breath of Pacific air on skin, the darkened peaks etching their reflections in glassy water. Her body seemed to be imprinting the peace of the islands. Jill was only too aware her escape from academia was temporary. How many years had she taught Pacific History from a theoretical point of view?

Steve arrived late to dinner and eased his tall muscled frame in beside Jill. Easily the most popular person on the boat, he was everyone's ideal fun bloke. His grey eyes engaged hers.

'Glass of white, Jill?'

As she sipped he continued, 'Maybe she'll tell us how that academic imagination is going. I caught Jill at the bow in deep contemplation.' Steve often set up the dinner conversation but so far he hadn't picked on her. His glance was a challenge.

'Actually, I was enjoying the serenity. I've been avoiding thinking about the university at all.' Then Jill blurted, 'Two girls have been brutally murdered there this year.'

A communal gasp meant she had their attention. For the rest of the meal Jill was pestered for details of the crime. Steve put a protective arm around her shoulders.

'We'll have to see Jill has a good holiday to forget all that nasty stuff.'

She could feel his body warm against hers.

'Thanks, Steve,' Jill whispered.

Over the following week Steve's popularity grew with his famous foot massages. Jill watched one of the galley girls ooh and aah in delight as his fingers moved across her toes. Steve's gaze drifted in her direction. She sensed his growing interest in her.

One evening Steve took her foot onto his lap and began stroking. As he worked the joints with his firm hands she succumbed to the sensation. Waves of lassitude swept up her body. He continued till everyone had gone, then gently taking her hand led her below.

Inside the dark cabin, Steve held her close. He smelt good. Jill felt his hands rub up her back to undo the knotted sarong.

'I'd better go,' she whispered.

'Not yet,' he murmured, 'you don't have to do anything. Just let me give you pleasure.'

They were against each other. The feel of his body was intoxicating as his lips traced her neck. Then their mouths met in the darkness. Her whole body responded to his kiss, like a whirlpool being drawn ever deeper.

He let her covering slip to the floor and lay her face down on the bunk. Feather-soft, his fingers ran down her back to her legs. As if hypnotised Jill relished his touch. He turned her over, caressing with his hands and lips. Her breasts quivered. His fingers moved over thighs barely skimming pubic hair. Gentle and teasing, she yearned for their exploration. Jill moved his hand and he began a massage of a different kind. She felt so moist. A wave of heat rose to her cheeks as her body shuddered against his hand. Never had she wanted a man inside her as she wanted Steve at that moment. Jill barely heard the crinkle of cellophane before their bodies melded, fast and feverish. His lips brushed hers afterwards, as they lay entwined drifting into sleep.

In the early hours Jill woke to the ship's soft creaking and Steve's breathing. During the night they'd become disentangled. She tiptoed up on deck. Shivering, with just a sarong for warmth, she saw the first fingers of dawn break the horizon.

The next night Jill lay on her bunk thinking. Having satisfied its natural urges, her body tingled all over. Steve had performed magic. She made a mental note to take this holiday one day at a time. Her fantasies drifted. What would Gary be like in bed?

During disturbed sleep, images of Duncan and Paula in compromising positions interspersed with his hands reaching for her. If only she didn't have to go back and deal with her creepy boss.

Next day was near perfect. Jill was off watch as the vessel surged along leaving a frothy wake. The tang of salty air, the occasional flap of sails, made her feel so alive. In the week away her skin, no longer wintry white, had taken on a pale honey hue. Without the trappings of suburban life, she'd begun to see herself differently. Seafaring suited Jill. Her short escape was proving more enticing than she'd envisaged. How would she settle back into academia after this experience?

One afternoon when she was on bow watch, clouds on the horizon took on a firmer shape.

'Land ho,' Jill yelled as sailors had for centuries.

Arriving at a new place excited everyone. Thrilled at being first to see Vanuatu, Jill watched its peaks become clearer. Within hours they entered a quiet bay on Efate Island away from towns or villages. The anchor chain rolled out to the bottom and all on board could enjoy tranquillity once more. Jill went to help make piña coladas, the favourite cocktail.

Next day Jill was on deck wondering why she hadn't succumbed again to Steve's meaningful glances when he appeared.

'I've talked to the elders at the village and told them we have a history lady on board. You wanted to talk to someone about the impact of men taken to the sugar plantations in Queensland. One ancient fellow says he remembers stories handed down. Do you want to talk to him?'

'That'd be great, Steve. Thanks so much.'

He smiled. 'I'll arrange it.'

Jill slinked off to afternoon tea. A certain detective's face flashed into mind.

Thunderheads threatened a tropical downpour.

'Will we still be able to go to the village?' Jill asked Steve.

Rain pelted hard on the awning overhead. The sea around *Dreamsong* was pitted with the spatter of huge drops. This deluge would not last long. Soon the sun would come out and they'd be back to the steamy heat. Steve and Jill climbed into the dinghy as the outboard sputtered.

Jill followed in Steve's footsteps along the well-tamped track, jungle foliage dancing out of their way. On the outskirts of the village, children in raggedy clothing spotted them immediately and came running. The whiteness of their teeth bright in dark-skinned faces. Encircled, they made slow progress towards the huts. One pubescent girl reached out shyly to touch Jill's blonde hair.

'She's not sure it's real,' Steve said looking at the girl's frizzy mop.

Reaching into her pocket, Jill withdrew several balloons. They blew them up, tied off the ends and batted them into the air. The children, shrieking with delight, scattered after bright orbs of orange, blue and crimson. One popped, causing a toddler to cry. Jill prepared another and placed it in his tiny grasping hand. With a beaming smile, he ran off with his prize. She handed out the rest of her supply and they left the giggling youngsters to their new game.

Stones marked the pathways. Hens skittered around the supporting poles. Many of the dwellings were open sided to allow breeze through. A few women in colourful sarongs watched them with curiosity. On the veranda of a larger hut sat an old man, his back propped against a wall. As they joined him he rose in a slow and careful manner. His grey hair was frizzled like steel wool. Dark eyes engaged Jill's as Steve introduced the elder.

Hayde shook her hand. He wore what looked like a sheet with some traditional pattern wrapped around him. A necklace of shell clinked as they all sat cross-legged.

Steve explained, 'Jill work in university in Australia. She study your ancestors taken there for sugar plantations.'

The elder nodded. Nearby, a younger man picked up a coconut and impaled it on a spike, tearing its fibrous coating off. With a few clean swipes with his machete he opened the top and handed it to Jill. Hayde mimicked a drinking action and said, 'Welcome.'

'Thank you.' Refreshed, she sat back to allow Hayde to continue. His English was quite good with only a few lapses into Bislama, the local language. Jill listened to stories that had been passed down to him. Trade goods enticed on board so many young men. The ships had then sailed away. He mentioned some family names and Jill wished she'd brought a notebook. Consigning them to memory, she'd jot them down the minute she got back on to the ship.

Perhaps an hour had passed before Hayde scrabbled for a piece of paper. 'My place,' he said, pointing to an address. 'You find some of my people in Australia you write me.'

'Sure, Hayde,' Jill said, sensing a mission to his request. 'Thank you so much for sharing your stories.'

Jill's mind buzzed with ideas. A research project was forming out of Hayde's desire to find more about his ancestors. She'd have to win Duncan over but it was perfect for someone with a Pacific History major.

Leaving this quiet bay behind, they finally motored into Port Vila. The sea had barely a ripple; fluffy clouds hovered above the town.

The following morning, tinged with sadness, she packed her clothes and said goodbye to the crew. Ruth gave Jill a hug.

'We've made a sailor out of an academic,' announced Banjo.

To receive acknowledgement from the normally quiet skipper made her blush. The image of him in his bandana would stay with Jill. A true seafarer.

'Thank you,' Jill said, 'it's been great.'

As those leaving were whizzed ashore, the outboard's scream prevented conversation. Jill was overwhelmed with sadness at leaving the tallship behind. Her adventure was over.

Once airborne, the islands of Vanuatu became less distinct in a turquoise sea. Jill couldn't believe how quickly three weeks had passed. Bound for Sydney's cold she wondered if she would ever return. Sailing had seeped into her blood. How would she explain her love for the islands? The intoxicating effect of atolls, palm trees and crystal clear water would be with her forever. Perhaps Jill could pass it on in her lectures.

Jill handled the chaos of arrivals at Sydney airport in a dreamy state. After paying the taxi driver, she walked to the apartment block. Her car was still in its carport sporting a veneer of grime. She found the keys, entered and turned off the alarm. Leaving her gear behind the closed door Jill wandered through checking everything was as she'd left it. Relieved her haven was safe; she caught sight of Dharani. Her serene expression welcomed Jill. An aura of calm pervaded. Fingers brushed the talisman. The place felt like home with those recent decorating touches.

The light on the phone flashed messages. The first was Mother's voice, her tone unpleasant. 'When are you coming to see me, Jill?'

A beep. Then the timbre of another tone altogether. Gary's was sexy and teasing. Jill's body reacted with a kind of yearning.

'Hi, babe. Love to hear how the sailing went. Call me.'

THIRTY-ONE

Barbara drove into the garage at home. She felt strung out. Work had kept her worries at bay; planning programs for their current list of patients absorbed her completely.

In the office, she'd noticed Bronwyn being particularly chatty with one of the new physiotherapists. The two were in their early thirties; they probably had heaps in common. Barbara acknowledged a surge of jealousy. She couldn't expect Bronwyn to be as close with her. A sigh escaped as she glanced down at her knobbly fingers, a reminder of arthritis and old age hovering like a shadow. Chubby menopausal women were not the ideal companions for women twenty years younger. If she didn't work, Barbara realised, she'd have no contact with these vibrant young people. Where were the girlfriends her own age?

Whilst endeavouring to blend career and family, Barbara had let them fall away. The realisation of this void brought a sudden wave of anxiety. Lack of a confidante, a true friend, had not bothered her before. At parties she'd been drawn to male conversations often dismissing clusters of women. After morning tea she'd emptied her cup in the sink, patted her curls into place and got on with the job.

Outside the house there was a vacant space where Madeline's car should be. Her daughter was on a mid-year break from university and supposed to be packing for the move. At least a month without lectures meant Madeline was away from that unsafe environment. The murder of those two girls was never far from Barbara's mind. Though her daughter avoided mentioning them, she was sure there would be lasting effects.

Outgoing, intelligent and brash, Madeline had begun to see the world as an insecure place. Last year a tear-stained face was a rarity but yesterday had brought another outburst. These drink spikers were a new type of predator. Men were always looking for sex but in her day were more open about it. Having sex with a comatose girl was sick.

Fortunately, Rob was on the scene. A boyfriend would surely be some protection from lowlifes. If only he had a few manners, Barbara thought. Once they were back at lectures Madeline would be moving around the campus alone. Stressing over remote possibilities was ridiculous, Barbara told herself.

She checked her daughter's room and saw several boxes packed. Beau scampered around Barbara's feet till she swooped him up for a cuddle. He strained towards her cheek, his tiny tongue wet on her face. Her spirits lifted. Dogs were so good at giving unconditional love. Relationships with people were just too difficult. Barbara relinquished Beau's warm body and turned on the gas heater.

Through the balcony windows the sky was leaden, reflecting its sombre grey on the sea.

'We're in for a cold night,' she told Beau.

Barbara changed into comfy slacks and jumper, washed her hands and put on a classical CD. In the kitchen, she diced pumpkin to make soup. When Hugh and Madeline came home they'd enjoy its hearty warmth. She sliced spring onions and a leek, sizzling them in butter before adding the orange-coloured cubes and chicken stock. Barbara happily hummed along with the music. The freshness of vegetables combined into flavoursome meals was like artwork to her. As a painter wields a brush she stirred the boiler with a wooden spoon. She soft shoe shuffled across to the spice drawer, adding lemon pepper to her concoction. Love of cooking just made it too hard to diet.

The phone rang and she could just hear Glen's voice.

'Give us a tick. I'll turn down the music.' Barbara heard him chuckle.

'Sounds like a full orchestra.'

She twiddled the knob on the stereo. 'That's better. What's the news on the house?'

'Carpet's being laid tomorrow. Thought you might like to call round in the afternoon.'

'Great news, Glen. See you then.'

Barbara amped up the decibels and checked the bubbling soup.

An image of the tall, friendly builder persisted in her mind. Barbara hadn't thought about him as much as she'd expected after he made a pass at her. Instinct told her Glen had done this before. Had other women he'd built houses for responded? Yet he'd made her feel so great about her choices and colours. Following the incident she'd allowed her fantasies to stray momentarily. What if she succumbed to his charm and they built magnificent houses together? He could use his flair for building design, she her colour sense for the décor. Maybe she could write articles for the home magazines she read.

She'd always taken pride in telling people she was married to a doctor. Somehow a builder didn't have the same ring to it. Besides breaking up her family was a ridiculous idea. Discarding the reverie, Barbara made a decision to be more distant with Glen.

At six o'clock she still hadn't heard from Madeline. Barbara switched on the evening news. The lead story was another body found at the university. Barbara couldn't believe it. For a second she thought it could be Madeline but the newsman said skeletonised. That meant the death had to be some time ago. She watched as the camera flashed onto bushland near the residential colleges. And for the first time the media used the term serial killer.

The words spread a sickening chill through Barbara's body. How could she let her daughter go back to that place? All year some maniac had been mingling with students and staff seeking out his next victim. Sure there were police patrols around the campus but the manpower to keep everyone safe was not possible. She rested her hands on the back of the lounge as the news team switched to another story. Soon more parents would learn the fate of their missing child.

Barbara would have to discuss this with Hugh. Perhaps he could get Madeline transferred to another university. What was that Detective

Sanderson doing? She wavered. Would contacting him again do any good?

At that moment Hugh bundled through the door with his medical bag.

'Hi, Barbs.'

'Oh, Hugh.' Barbara's face crumpled as she related the news item. Hugh dropped the bag, placing his hands on her shoulders. Her voice trembled. 'You … you must get Maddy out of there.'

'I don't know if that's possible. It's not how universities work.' His hands fell to his sides and he shrugged.

'But Hugh, don't you see? If we don't do something we could lose Maddy.' Tears blurred Barbara's eyes.

'We're not going to lose her.' His tone was as definite as a slap in the face.

She smelt the soup catching and fled to the kitchen. Hugh disappeared to the bedroom. By the time he returned to open some wine she felt better. Not one to continue intense conversations, Hugh drifted to the lounge, glass in hand.

Madeline flounced in the door clutching a shopping bag.

'I was wondering where you'd got to, young lady.' Barbara turned off the cook top.

'Met Rob at the Mall. Look at these.' Madeline drew a sort of cut down sports shoe from the bag.

'Haven't you got ones like those?'

'Mum, really. These are Eccos. They're the best.' Madeline shot her an excited glance before rubbing her fingers over the striped leather.

'They look expensive. I've told you to tell me before putting items like that on my credit card.'

Her daughter's face tightened, the blue eyes becoming icy. Madeline stepped back. 'I've been studying for months. You said I could go shopping after the exams. You're always buying shoes.'

Madeline stomped off to her room. Barbara felt defeated. She usually enjoyed seeing purchases and realised her worry over the latest death at the university caused her to snap.

'That didn't go too well,' said Hugh, refilling his glass.

'No. Pour me another. Sometimes I think we're not going to make it through the teenage years.' Barbara set out the bowls and ladled in the soup she'd blended.

'Oh she's all right. Looks like I need to curb the Imelda tendency in both of you,' he smirked. 'I'll have a word with Maddy. Tell her you're uptight about the uni situation.' Hugh scuffed down the hallway in his worn slippers.

Barbara opened the oven to a whoosh of warm air. The casserole that had been frozen was simmering. As the family sat to eat, Barbara relayed the schedule of moving house. Over the main course father and subdued daughter veered to their usual discussion of medicine.

While many of Hugh's patients were elderly women wanting little more than a chat Barbara knew some lived in violent relationships. Battered wives, abused children, old people forced into nursing homes by avaricious offspring were just a few of the problems general practitioners encountered. Was Hugh trying to prepare their daughter for the tougher side of medicine? Barbara would be happier if Madeline specialised in obstetrics. There was a need for more women doctors in that area. Bringing babies into the world was surely a more joyous occupation.

The following afternoon Barbara parked in the driveway of her new home. A landscaper was carrying a staggering pile of empty black pots to his ute. Chocolate soil awaiting mulch was rich and dark in contrast to the plants. She had no time to examine the garden. Her heels clinked on the tiles in the foyer. The carpet layers had gone and Glen did not appear. With a tinge of disappointment, Barbara realised she'd thrived on his praise.

She climbed the stairs to the main bedroom. A milky sea of carpet replaced the raw hardness of concrete. Its pale turquoise stretched to the bay window. Barbara slipped out of her shoes to feel the luxuriant pile under her toes. Through the window she saw wind ruffling the lake's surface. Beyond the distant bridge two lone cabbage tree palms waved in unison. Several pelicans scooped low over the water almost skimming the wavelets. How amazing, Barbara thought. She couldn't wait to wake up to this every morning.

Back in the car Barbara checked her diary. Two days after they moved in would be Hugh's birthday. She wanted his present to be special, something to tie in with the new house. An idea flashed: a kayak, shiny and yellow, for him to explore the lake. Hugh would love being here and Madeline might take to paddling as well.

Barbara turned up the radio dancing her fingers on the steering wheel as she drove to Mona Vale to arrange the purchase.

THIRTY-TWO

Sanderson cast aside the initial report on Cheryl's autopsy, called his superior and told him what the searchers had found.

Ralston's voice boomed in his ear. 'Get over there, Sanderson, before the media turn this thing into a bloody circus.'

The detective ended the call and slipped the mobile into his jacket pocket. Fyurk, camera bag slung over his shoulder, followed Sanderson back to the car park. Traffic on the highway moved steadily as Sanderson took the usual route to Phillips University.

'I've been to this place so often they ought to give me a degree.' He winked at his offsider.

'You don't need it, Gary. You've done okay in the uni of life,' Fyurk reached to turn down the police radio hushing the crackle. 'Three bodies gives us serial killer status. Now we'll get more back up.'

'Only if it's the same bloke. We don't know how long the body's been there. Might be years. Could be male.' Sanderson changed lanes, leaving the blinker clicking. A familiar expanse of trees to his right signalled their destination was close. He waved his badge and the gatekeeper acknowledged. Sanderson waited as the balding man approached.

'Can I help you, Detective?'

'Another body. Keep the press vehicles out.'

'No problem. I'll lower the boom gate and check everyone's credentials.'

'Good man,' Sanderson said before driving on.

He pulled into the car park near the residential colleges. Timber beams creaked under their weight as they crossed the bridge. Fyurk pointed out several police standing near bushland. Crime scene tape was already strung between tree trunks. A clear day with no breeze made their visit seem like a jaunt in the park but the older detective knew better. Something insidious awaited them even if the victim had been there a long time.

'Ruggeri got here quick.' Sanderson pointed to the forensics' wagon.

As their shoes munched gravel, Fyurk reached into his pocket for the tiny bottle of eucalyptus oil. Sanderson patted his offsider on the shoulder.

'You won't need it, Rich. The pong stage is over.'

'Of course. Habits die hard. I've never seen a skeletonised body before. Won't most of the physical evidence be gone by now?'

'Not all. Let's see what Ruggeri thinks.' Sanderson talked to Stretton and made sure another officer kept the scene secure. At least there was no constant stream of students past this spot.

They were led in through gloomy undergrowth. Sticks cracked and mosquitos whined. Sanderson estimated they'd gone more than fifteen metres when they came to a small clearing. Ruggeri was peering over an area of disturbed soil covered by a broken branch with long-dead leaves.

'Hi, Sando. We've got an interesting one here.' Ruggeri pointed to a sector where the bones of a hand emerged from brown earth.

In the indistinct light, Sanderson thought it looked like someone reaching for help. He hunched down as he heard Fyurk's camera fire off a few shots.

'It sure looks like a human hand. How do we retrieve the body Pete?'

Ruggeri brushed dirt from the knees of his blue overalls. 'We'll have to call in a forensic anthropologist. Only an expert can help us with evidence from a skeleton. I'm assuming this is another murder victim rather than an unrelated crime. If so that would mean Katie was not number one. Who knows there may be others?'

'Yeah, no point jumping the gun with theories at this stage. Who do we use?'

'Dr Arabella Steele. Old Faraday died. She lectures at Sydney uni but may be away on holidays. An outdoors type. Always off somewhere.'

Ruggeri fumbled for his phone, selected a number and handed it to Sanderson.

His voice rang through the scrub as he outlined his requirements. Fyurk and Stretton stood as silent witnesses to the macabre sight.

'Beauty,' Sanderson said, 'she's on her way. Not going away till next week. Thanks, Pete. No point us all hanging round. Give me a buzz when it's time for the body snatchers.'

Fyurk raised his eyebrows. 'The what?'

'C'mon, Rich. Don't tell me you haven't heard what the government contractors are called?'

'I just thought they were weird men in green vans.'

Sanderson saw the amused smirk on Stretton's face and headed back through the bush. Leaving the tall officer in charge, Fyurk traipsed after him to the Commodore. The senior detective used the drive back to the station to mull over possible links. If that skeleton was the remains of another young woman it meant the killer had started his spree before March. Before Katie. Her body had been found only days after her death. The perpetrator wanted to be noticed. Strangulation and bodily mutilation was not the modus operandi of your every-day murderer. A drug link was tentative to say the least.

Differences from Cheryl's death only added to the confusion. When peering at the crime scene photographs, he felt as if he were seeing a crazy kaleidoscope. Jagged pieces didn't seem to fit. Sanderson knew when they had enough information and evidence, a discernible pattern would emerge. Stick to procedure, he told himself. He needed to add to Cheryl's victimology before even contemplating this new find. Still an image of a girl being dragged into that bushland with a ligature round her neck haunted him. Had it been as far back as January when all was quiet on campus? Sanderson thought of Bob Wilson; if he was their man they were getting closer.

Fyurk interrupted Sanderson's musing. 'Gary, is there anything we can start doing on this new case?'

'Not at the moment. We'll need the big four from Dr Steele first. Sex, age, race and stature.' As Sanderson accelerated from traffic lights he was aware of Fyurk rubbing the side of his nose. His offsider's habit usually indicated the grey matter was working overtime.

'Won't dental records be important?' Fyurk asked.

'Sure will, if we can track them down. Then we can try the Missing Persons Unit. In the meantime it's back to the whiteboard. There's an avalanche of paperwork on Cheryl to get through let alone the other cases.'

The motorised gate at the station clunked open and Sanderson parked near a row of police vehicles. Coffees made, the two detectives headed for the incident room. Someone had turned the air conditioner way up. It spewed overly warm air. Sanderson removed his jacket and readjusted the temperature. Fyurk wandered past his labelled crime scene photos. Sanderson watched him read the labels on exhibits that had been laid out on desks. Katie's silver ring was dull in its plastic bag. A larger paper bag looked like the battered one the stiletto had been placed in. He'd forgotten to ask his offsider what Ruggeri had thought of it. Perhaps the shoe was back from testing already. Sanderson couldn't wait to re-examine it. Was it connected to the Campus Killer?

He downed his coffee, rolling the chair, castors squeaking, nearer the desk. Hazelton had faxed him some of the initial findings from Cheryl's autopsy. A fractured hyoid bone and lacerations to the neck substantiated strangulation. Mention was made again of a braided nylon rope. The new documentation was daunting. Nothing different so far from Katie's circumstances, he thought.

Sanderson flicked to a couple of reports from the Analytical Laboratory. Zilch from the swabs could mean their killer did not sexually assault his victims. Or he was careful with condoms. Maybe he was impotent or penetrative sex did not fit his fantasies.

Cheryl had put up a fight so Sanderson's main hope was the fingernail scrapings. Those results weren't back yet so they had no DNA samples to go on.

'Damn,' Sanderson muttered. He checked his watch. Ralston and the rest of the squad would be here for a review in an hour.

He strode over to the few exhibits they had on their second victim. Most were stored in paper bags to prevent mould growing with any dampness. The gold rings of Cheryl's multiple ear piercing nestled in a plastic bag beside her tongue stud. On a brown bag, he read, duct tape from storeroom. To one side was another plastic envelope with a tiny torn piece of black leather. Why hadn't he noticed this before? What had Cheryl been wearing that night at work?

Sifting through the pile of papers he found Li's statement. Cheryl's body had been dumped naked. No doubt to remove any chance of fibres or hairs from the killer being found. They'd had no luck finding any of her clothes. Sanderson's finger ran down the page till he found the paragraph he was looking for. Li, the chef, was observant. His description of Cheryl's black chunky boots was priceless. 'She very noisy clumping round cafeteria. Look like she work in massage parlour.'

Sanderson's brow furrowed. Did her murderer drag the body across concrete scuffing and tearing the leather? Perhaps a piece adhered to Cheryl's skin as he removed the boots. He turned to the toxicology report. Cheryl had no evidence of drugs in her system. But then she was working. Other tests could reveal if she had a habit. Sanderson still couldn't fathom whether this victim had any relationship with Bob Wilson. One person had said she was going out with him. Li had mentioned Cheryl was attracted to Wilson's physique and he'd seen her talking to him once. That wasn't a lot to go on.

He proceeded to the report from the Fingerprints Section. Only Wilson and Li's prints were on the bin handle. Both had a reason to be there. Nothing incriminating about that! The duct tape Fyurk had suggested Ruggeri get checked had no prints either. Sanderson scanned another sheet. The blood on the storeroom floor was Cheryl's alone. He shoved the file aside in frustration. With so little physical evidence it was like searching in a snowstorm. As if in a time slip he glanced around expecting to see Dave. Anger surged through Sanderson as he remembered his mate's senseless death. Repetitive tapping of his pen drew a quizzical look from his offsider.

Markers in hand, he and Fyurk spent an interminable time adding every detail to the whiteboard.

Fyurk's stomach grumbled. 'Time for lunch. I'll go. What about a chicken tandoori wrap?'

'Sounds good, Rich.'

While they ate lunch, Sanderson's mobile rang. Expecting Ruggeri's smooth Italian intonation he was surprised to hear Li's broken English.

'Detective, find Cheryl's shoulder bag. Slip from hook. Stuck behind stove.'

'Have you opened it?'

'No.'

'Don't touch anything inside. See what's there.' Sanderson swivelled on his chair during the silence.

'Detective, can see wallet, brush, phone and tissues.'

'We'll be right over. Leave the bag closed. Good job, Li.'

The chef sounded pleased with himself as if assisting with the ongoing mystery of Cheryl's death had given him a boost.

Fyurk screwed their lunch wrappings into a ball and shot it at the wastepaper basket. A direct hit brought a smile to Sanderson's face.

'Let's go. We need to be back. New evidence might appease Ralston.'

'Sure hope so, Gary.'

After driving to the university, they hurried past the fountain, dodging students.

Li beckoned them into the cafeteria's kitchen, pointing to a bag on a hook. Narrow and flimsy, its burgundy fabric was patterned with gold sequins. It looked like cheap gaudy stuff from India, Sanderson thought. Opening the bag, he retrieved a slim wallet. Cheryl's licence photo was similar to the one printed in the paper following her death. He showed it to Fyurk then turned to Li.

'How come this wasn't found till now?'

Li's expression wavered between surprise and shock. 'Me tell Cheryl not leave it there. She no listen. Bags kept in locked cupboard under counter.' The chef indicated a cupboard then took the bag leaving the wallet in Sanderson's hand. A demonstration of the bag slipping from the hook and snagging on gas lines to the cook plate took no more than thirty seconds.

'If it fall right down I find it washing floor.' Li continued, 'It missing so I think Cheryl gone home that night. Today keys fall, catch in bag. Ring Detective straight away.'

Fyurk nodded as Li returned the bag to him. Sanderson, not as easily convinced, further examined the location. Reluctant to kneel on the grease-spattered floor in his slacks, he used a clean tea towel as protection. He could see how the wire-braided lines could trap an object.

Straightening up, Sanderson said, 'Well, Li, you're off the hook for now.'

The chef wiped his hands on his apron as if adjusting his attention back to cooking. Fyurk gave him a friendly wave as they left.

'You were a bit hard on him, Gary.'

'Not really. I think Li's okay. But racking up the pressure often reveals something more.'

'Wonder why Cheryl didn't keep her bag in the proper place. Maybe there's something in it she wanted to keep an eye on.' Fyurk held the bag aloft, its sequins flashed in the sunshine.

'We'll examine it thoroughly in the car,' Sanderson added, his pace quickening.

Once seated in their vehicle, both detectives snapped on latex gloves. Sanderson began searching the contents: a brush with strands of red hair, one dark purple lipstick ending in a sharp apex, the wallet with licence and Visa card and a mobile phone. At the bottom was a carefully folded tissue. Opening this revealed two pink tablets each with a tiny symbol.

'Ecstasy,' Fyurk said.

'Cheryl was planning to party after work. Who with? If only we could get some direct link with Bob Wilson we could bring him in for questioning.'

Sanderson returned all the items to the bag except the phone. He switched it on scrolling down the few contacts. Auntie's name brought an image of Muriel Carter to mind. He'd promised to bring the old hag up to date on her niece's murder. Initials only designated several of the contacts. A solitary B was a mobile number.

'Do we have Wilson's mobile number?' he asked.

'Sure, Gary. On his CV back at the incident room.'

'Okay we'll check for matches later. We've just got time to check on the exhumation. That Arabella Steele had a sexy voice.'

Fyurk snorted. 'Here we go again. What about the bag? And we'll need to check Cheryl's phone records.'

'I'll get that underway.' Sanderson rang the office giving the operator Cheryl's number. 'The bag can go to the lab. They might be able to lift Wilson's prints off those tablets.'

Fyurk pacified, Sanderson put the phone back and got out of the car. Dumping the evidence bag in the boot, he stripped off his gloves. Fyurk did the same.

'Let's walk,' Sanderson suggested. They crossed a road amidst students rushing for a bus. Then Fyurk found a pathway between multilevel car parks to the residential colleges.

A constable led them through the bush to the burial site. One of the forensics team leant on a shovel beside the half-exposed skeleton. A woman with a small trowel added to the mound of ochre soil. Twirling a brush, she flicked grit from a curving rib bone. He noticed she was wearing a white business shirt over jeans when she stood up.

'Ah,' the anthropologist said, 'Detective Sanderson, I presume.'

Sanderson nodded taken aback by her formality.

'Dr Steele, my offsider Detective Fyurk.'

The woman before him had eyes as dark as her shiny hair drawn into a ponytail. Her face, cold and serious, reminded him of classical beauty. How had he found her voice appealing? In reality, it was superior, mocking.

'Have you come to any conclusions yet?' Sanderson asked cautiously.

'This is not an operation to be rushed but after examining the pelvis and pubic symphysis I can tell you the body is female.'

'Was she young?' rushed in Fyurk.

'Can you tell if she was strangled?' Sanderson added.

A look of distaste flickered across the doctor's face. 'Detectives, don't push me. Hasty assumptions lead to mistakes. Please allow the dead to speak for themselves.'

Sanderson stepped back. Her voice had the mettle of her surname. Fyurk had already turned to leave.

Before dark, Sanderson went for a long run in Centennial Park. As his joggers pounded the path, thoughts of his day reverberated in his mind. His body built up heat against the evening chill.

A young woman slid past him, curvaceous in spandex. He noticed the wire of her earphones wriggling and wondered if he should get an iPod. Deciding that music blasting his brain was not his way of relaxing, he ditched the idea. It would cut out the crunch of gravel and the whisper of wind that brought him peace.

Sanderson figured another lap might erase Arabella Steele's cold superior voice. Dismiss the bitch, he told himself. He'd deal with her in a polite professional manner. For all he cared the iceberg could remain forever frozen.

'Allow the dead to speak for themselves,' he mimicked. Sanderson hoped Steele was as good as she thought she was. He wanted answers and fast. This switch of a body killed way before the other two victims had thrown him into a quandary. For the first time on this case a doubt flickered. Was he up to the job?

He felt suitably sweaty as he arrived at the gym off Oxford Street. In a queue of beefy blokes, Sanderson waited as the girl behind the counter swiped their membership cards. A tiny sparkle of a nose stud caught his attention as she extended her hand. He surreptitiously flashed his cop ID.

'I need to see the manager.'

A worried look flooded her flawless face. Tapping on a door behind her, she mumbled a few words to the occupant. After escorting him to the office, she hurried back to her post.

The fellow who ran the place looked like a champion skier, svelte and tanned, with a shiny bald head.

'Detective, how can I be of help?' The manager leaned across the desk and shook hands. His fingernails were a touch too manicured in Sanderson's opinion.

'I'm investigating the movements of Bob Wilson, one of your members. Seems he spends a lot of time hanging out here.'

'People like to keep up a certain level of fitness.'

Sanderson realised the manager was assessing him and was glad he'd worn his running gear. The bloke probably thought most cops were slobs who never exercised.

'Wilson's record of attendance might be useful in our inquiries,' Sanderson added.

The manager bristled in his chair. 'You must understand, Detective, our records are confidential.'

'Not if I get a warrant and bring a shitload of cops in here.'

The fellow's tan paled. 'Well if that's the case.' Facing his computer, the manager zoomed his mouse around clicking hurriedly.

Within minutes Sanderson was back in the evening air, a copy of Wilson's visits to the establishment concealed in his pocket. Once home, he showered and hightailed it to the pub where the rest of the squad drank. Ralston dominated the circle nearest the bar. Sanderson found he wasn't in the mood for laughter tonight. He turned to Ruggeri and was about to ask him about the shoe found at the university when Fyurk arrived.

'Rich, can I buy you a beer?'

His offsider nodded. While Sanderson waited for the barmaid to pull three schooners, he watched Fyurk deep in conversation with Ruggeri. That's good, he thought, the kid's gaining acceptance. Perhaps Fyurk's reading and thirst for knowledge will get Ruggeri on side.

'The skeleton's in a private room at the morgue. Already been X-rayed for evidence of bullets or knife wounds,' Ruggeri said as Sanderson handed round the beers amidst noisy chatter and the chink of glasses.

'The anthropologist's told us it's female. How does she determine race and height?' Fyurk asked.

Sanderson, reluctant to intervene, sipped his lager and waited.

Ruggeri considered his reply. 'There are three sorts of skulls. Negroid, Caucasoid and Mongoloid. The latter covers mainly Asians; the middle one includes Aussies. And there's some formula to work out height if they have the femur.'

'This stuff is amazing,' beamed Fyurk.

Ruggeri continued, 'You're a reader. Get the book *Death's Acre* by Bill Bass. He started the Body Farm. It'll fill you in. Now Sando, you had a shit of a day I hear.'

'Not as bad as some. Perhaps your Italian charm worked on that woman of steel.' Sanderson's tone sounded bitter.

'You're slipping, mate. Bet she pissed you off.' Ruggeri chuckled.

'Can't help himself. Always trying to impress women, aren't you, Gary?' Fyurk added.

Sanderson bit back. 'You're so slow, Rich, they get away.'

'Not after working with you. Gotta go. I'm taking Janine out for dinner.' Fyurk placed his empty glass on the bar and walked off. Sanderson's mouth gaped.

When he left the bar, Sanderson made for the nearest hamburger joint. His order filled, he sat on a chair outside and ate hungrily. The blend of meat, egg, bacon and tomato tasted great, he thought. His hasty dinner brought other appetites to mind. He stabbed the numbers on his mobile until he heard Cyndi's honey voice. Nodding, he hung up. Their meeting half an hour later was fast and furious. The arrangement, Sanderson felt, suited him famously.

Next morning he wasn't so sure. He'd ducked to the corner store to buy milk. The Korean had a newspaper by the till.

'This you,' he said, pointing at a photo of Sanderson with his arm around Cyndi in a bar.

Sanderson groaned and paid for the paper. Was that look on the shopkeeper's face a smirk or not, he wondered. Bloody media. In their frustration at no progress to report on the Campus Killer they'd written a scathing article about the detective in charge of the case on the ran tan. It also mentioned Cyndi being found with a dead client.

'Bloody great,' Sanderson said. He could bet Ralston would be onto him as soon as he heard. How had they got that shot? He had no recollection of a camera flash when he was with Cyndi.

During breakfast, he mulled over the situation. Was his association with a high-class hooker too risky? He could be thrown off the case if this got embarrassing. Cyndi was sweet; sex on a stick. In his mind he fabricated a suitable story for his boss.

As he made another coffee he thought of Jill. The few times he'd seen her smile her whole face came alive. She seemed so clean and wholesome, a regular take-home-to-mum girl. Spirited too, when she thought he was making fun of her. He hadn't seen her since she'd been lazing away in the Pacific. Hopefully, she'd missed this issue. An image of Jill in a bikini floated into his mind; he imagined her rubbing lotion on his back. Jill had been amazed when he'd told her he wanted to go, revealed his love of sailing.

Sanderson pictured Jill walking off from him the night they'd had dinner, heels clacking in anger. Christ, he thought, that's where he'd seen that stiletto before. He was sure it matched the one found at the university, now in an evidence bag in the incident room. It could have been discarded the night before she left. Had Jill thought she'd found the murderer? He must contact her.

This would remain between them. Imagine if Ralston found out. Had he really encouraged Jill to intervene, Sanderson asked himself. In so many words, he had. But with what motivation? A reason to keep seeing her. He didn't understand. Guilt settled heavily on him. Had he been that stupid? Sanderson leant his face into covering hands, sighing as he exhaled.

In his mixed-up mind he'd wanted Jill to overcome her fear of men. Asking her to keep an eye out at night caused the shoe incident, he had no doubt. The outcome could have been different if she'd confronted the real killer. How could he have put Jill in such danger? He had to capture the bastard before Jill returned to campus.

His phone rang. The volley of abuse was Ralston at his best. Sanderson was to report straight to the boss's office. He donned a navy sports jacket, checking his appearance in the hall mirror. On the drive in, he felt his jaw tighten. The worst that could happen, he told himself, was getting booted off the case. Sanderson had always found Ralston to be fair-minded. Perhaps this time the boss had it in for him. Names of those likely to take over flashed through his brain. His reputation would be buggered. He'd have to convince Ralston to let him stay in charge. Sanderson's breathing was tight; he barely noticed the traffic around him.

As he knocked firmly on the boss's door, Sanderson hoped for a reasonable hearing. Ralston slumped at his desk, buttons of his white shirt straining across his beer gut.

'Sit down, Sando.'

The voice not overly loud and the use of his nickname was positive, thought Sanderson. He sat and focussed on Ralston's untrimmed eyebrows.

'Now let's get a few things straight.' The boss leant forward, clasped hands resting on the desk. 'The Police Force doesn't need the sort of media attention your stupid behaviour's brought to light. I've already had a call from the Commissioner. Told him I'm not taking you off the case. He's got Public Relations working on damage control.'

Sanderson felt the tension ease between his shoulder blades but kept his face serious. 'Thanks, boss.'

'Don't thank me. You're a good detective. When you catch the killer the press will make you a goddamned hero. Make no mistake. The hooker has to go. No more bad publicity. Right.'

Sanderson nodded.

The frown unbuckled Ralston's face. 'Now tell me where you're up to.'

'Our most likely suspect is Bob Wilson. Got a record. He's on tape dealing drugs at the uni. We were trying to establish a link between him and Cheryl, the second victim, when this skeleton was discovered.'

'You thinking the same killer?'

'I am. Soon as we find out more from the anthropologist I'd like to bring in a profiler if that's okay.' Sanderson sat back in the chair.

'Fine,' Ralston replied, 'the Commissioner has given the go ahead to any resources you want.'

After a hasty knock, Fyurk's head appeared. 'Sorry to interrupt ...'

'What is it?' Ralston waved Sanderson's offsider into the room.

'Gary, they've lifted Wilson's prints off one of those tablets and his number is in Cheryl's mobile under 'B'.'

Sanderson leapt up. 'Good, Rich. We'll get the drug squad to pick him up. Mind if we get onto it?' He glanced back at Ralston.

'Go. Call me to observe the questioning.'

'Will do, boss.' Sanderson followed Fyurk outside. Elation surged through him at the thought of Ralston's support, not to mention this breakthrough.

Within the hour the three detectives were watching their person of interest through one-way glass. Wilson sat cockily in a chair wearing khaki shorts. Sanderson wondered if the groundsman was going to flex his biceps in front of the trim men from the drug squad.

'Let's see how Wilson does in the hot seat,' Sanderson whispered to Fyurk and Ralston.

The interrogation began. 'Let me put it to you that on the night of May 20 you were observed dealing drugs.'

'No way, mate,' Wilson answered.

A portion of the videotape was played showing Wilson with the hooded man.

Momentarily surprised, Wilson continued, 'Just paying a debt, he was. You gotta catch people with drugs. mate, I'm not into dealing. Okay.'

Wilson's torso stiffened.

Sanderson studied the accused's face, every movement he made.

The interrogator threw a small plastic bag on the table.

'This cannabis,' he said, 'was found in the glove box of your ute.'

'So,' answered Wilson, 'that's not enough for dealing.'

Sanderson left the others watching and entered the room. His presence was mentioned on the videoed interview. He decided to hit hard to see if he could rattle the smooth bastard.

'Can you explain how your fingerprints came to be on ecstasy tablets found in Cheryl Patterson's handbag?'

'Cheryl who?' Wilson countered.

'C'mon Wilson,' Sanderson raised his voice an octave, 'you know this victim. Your mobile number's in her phone. Supplying her too, were you?'

For the first time Sanderson detected a flicker of fear pass across the groundsman's face.

'You're trying to pin these bloody murders on me,' Wilson growled, 'No way. I'm no fucking killer.'

Sanderson noticed Wilson's powerful fingers gripping the edge of the table as if he meant to snap the wood.

'Why would we do that, Wilson? I just want to know where you were on the night of …'

'I want a lawyer,' Wilson's hoarse voice screeched.

Sanderson tried placating. 'Settle down, man. We're just asking a few questions.'

'No comment.' Wilson spat.

Sanderson left the room, returning to his colleagues. Ralston's eyebrows flitted up and down.

'Interesting,' added Fyurk, 'psychopaths can talk about dismembering bodies without showing emotion. Wilson lost his cool.'

'What makes you think we're looking for a psychopath?' Ralston asked.

Fyurk straightened, almost matching the boss's height then answered, 'Serial killers usually are.'

THIRTY-THREE

The morning of the move Barbara woke to the sound of drumming rain. Hugh made a snuffling sound before turning over, dragging most of the doona with him. Barbara slipped out of bed and pulled aside the curtains to confirm her worst fears.

Outside, a grey dreary day confronted her. Gum leaves, wet and dripping, jiggled with the constant patter of drops. Barbara eased into her dressing gown and slid her feet into fluffy slippers. She tiptoed out to the living room. Searching the sky through rain-spotted windows for a break in the low clouds, she realised the dreadful conditions were going to make moving house even more stressful.

Their furniture looked strange devoid of any knick-knacks. Not a cushion, ornament or photo frame could be seen. Cartons, sealed and labelled, were piled like huge building blocks at one end. All the kitchen benches were bare too. Wistfully, Barbara gazed around the rooms that had been the hub of her existence for so many years. Without the homely touches it was spartan. Her wonderful new home was waiting. Barbara's mood soared.

She knew it was time to rouse Hugh and Madeline for a light breakfast before the removalists arrived. Barbara retrieved some old towels to protect the new carpet from a carton in the laundry and put them in her car. She knocked on her daughter's door.

'C'mon Maddy. Wakey, wakey. Moving day.' Barbara heard a muffled response then proceeded to her own room.

Hugh was dragging on a tracksuit. 'Rain for the move. Not good.'

'We'll just have to make the best of it.' Barbara skipped off to the shower.

Breakfast dishes had been dried and packed when the doorbell rang. Before her, stood three men. One was short with ginger hair, a contrast to his lanky mate. Hovering behind was a huge Maori complete with muscles and tattoos. Barbara hoped he was a gentle giant with her belongings. The formalities attended to, she left them to start loading the truck.

Hugh packed the smaller cartons from his office into his car. Madeline lugged her treasures out to her Mazda. As each room was emptied, Barbara hoovered the floors, skimming over indentations left in the carpet. Slowly the house became a shell. She glanced out on the balcony and saw the Maori pick up one of her pot plants. The tub was so heavy Hugh couldn't move it. Yet the New Zealander marched it through the house with seemingly little effort. No wonder he was in this job.

Within hours, Ginger Hair told her the truck was loaded. Barbara had to lead the way and direct where the furniture was to be placed. After informing Madeline, she found Hugh in his office on the phone. He waved for her to wait and hung up.

'What do you want? I'm off to the new house.'

'Sorry, Barbs, but I'll have to duck into the surgery. Emergency. Patient will only see me. Domestic violence. She's pretty bad, Lisa says.' Hugh raised his hands in resignation.

Barbara tried to cover her annoyance. 'Didn't they explain you're moving?' Hands on hips, she waited for an answer.

Ignoring her, Hugh checked his medical bag then looked down at his attire.

'Your spare clothes are in the laundry,' Barbara said with a sigh. 'Get to the house as soon as you can, Hugh. I'll need you.' Her voice echoed down the hall as he strode away.

She slammed the door and raced for her car. Semi-soaked in the short distance, Barbara then drove timidly; the massive pantechnicon trailed her. Rounding the bends, she saw the sea was up. Waves, the colour of sage, smashed onto the deserted beach. She turned her wipers to a faster speed as rain slashed the windscreen. This must let up, she thought. Thank God the new living area was tiled. Mud would inevitably be tramped in. She could feel tension in her shoulders already. How was she going to stop the blokes trashing the carpet? Lots of towels and she'd insist they take their boots off.

Arms laden, she unlocked the front door. Barbara could hear the truck beeping as it backed into the driveway. After wiping her flatties, she placed the towels in strategic spots and waited for the removalists.

Puffing and straining, two men appeared with a sofa draped in plastic sheeting. In the entry, the Maori removed the cover with his spare hand, depositing it in a crinkling heap. Barbara, eager to set the rules, reminded them to wipe their feet.

Ginger Hair swept droplets from his brow. 'We'll try, lady. But it's a bugger of a day.' The Maori made the effort and flashed her a smile.

He's not as scary as he looks, Barbara thought. She directed them to the lounge room. Over the next hour as if to pacify her, the men cooperated in moving pieces this way and that.

Madeline arrived, Beau pattering behind, his muddy paws dotting the tiles. Barbara raced to clean them before he followed her daughter up the carpeted stairs.

'How's it going, Mum?' Madeline flipped her long hair and headed for her new room.

'Quite well, Maddy. Sorting the kitchen will be the worst after the men leave.'

Minutes later, Barbara was almost nose-to-nose with the Maori.

'Take your boots off, please. You'll dirty the carpet.'

With a heavy bed head precariously balanced, he shook his head and complied.

By the time Hugh arrived, the removalists had gone and open cartons surrounded Barbara in the kitchen.

'How'd it go?' Hugh's glance took in the chaos.

'Not too bad. Managed to keep the mess to a minimum. I'd kill for a coffee.' Barbara rummaged for her machine. With Hugh's help they were soon enjoying a break. After their brief reviver, they made the beds and Barbara established some order in the kitchen. When Madeline descended from her room, all three devoured wedges of the pizza they'd had delivered. Exhausted but happy, Barbara began to fantasise about life in her new home.

Preoccupied with the move, Barbara found her mood slumped the next day. Stacking plates and placing wine glasses on shelves failed to distract her. The problem of Madeline's safety was uppermost on her mind. Since Barbara had seen that last newsflash of a skeleton found at the university, she'd been urged to act. This recent gruesome find meant some maniacal killer had been preying on the campus all year. The police were apparently powerless to stop him. She'd got nowhere with Hugh; total rebuttal of her idea to get Madeline transferred to Sydney University. Her daughter had thought this completely over the top.

As the university holidays drew to a close, Barbara found her agitation increased. She refused to believe she was overreacting. Her arthritis had been worse, possibly due to anxiety. Rubbing her hands together, a thought crossed her mind: was the disease contributing to the whole situation?

'Damn it,' she muttered and strode to her bedroom to change. Barbara dressed in black slacks and a plum cashmere jumper. She tied a matching velvet scarf in a loose knot. In the bathroom she applied make-up and tweaked her curls.

The drive to Phillips University took no more than forty minutes outside peak hour. Barbara recognised the concrete building adjacent to the tree-studded quadrangle as the one where she'd been with Madeline on enrolment day. In summer, the grass had been lush. With the chill of winter it looked decidedly uninviting. The atmosphere matched the grey of the woman's hair behind the counter. Barbara noticed her fussing with the chain dangling from her glasses.

'I want to transfer my daughter to Sydney University,' Barbara began.

The woman sighed and compressed her lips. 'Transfers are rarely possible, madam. Often the courses are ...'

'There must be some form, someone in authority I can see,' broke in Barbara. 'This campus isn't safe.'

'I understand your concern for your daughter, madam, but only the Vice-Chancellor has the power to do what you're asking and he isn't here.' The woman raised her hands.

'Is there no one I can talk to?' Barbara's tone impatient.

The woman pointed behind her. 'You can add your contact details to the list. You're not the only parent requesting a transfer.'

Barbara turned to see a clipboard being passed between adults seated along one wall of the office. She waited, scribbled her details and left. Ineffectual as it was, her visit brought some relief. Others wanted their daughters out of here. She wasn't the only paranoid parent.

On the way to her car, Barbara saw two men in suits join the pathway ahead. One was tall; the other moved with a purposeful gait she recognised.

'Detective Sanderson,' Barbara called out.

Both men spun round and waited for her to catch up.

'Barbara Harper. We haven't officially met but I rang you regarding my daughter Madeline.'

'You remember, Gary. Katie's friend. Helped us with our inquiries,' the other detective added.

'Oh, yes. Mrs Harper. I saw you at the funeral.'

Barbara recalled his acknowledgement and was glad she'd taken trouble to dress smartly. The detective's brown eyes seemed busy taking in every detail. His manner was smooth and friendly.

'What brings you out here?'

'I'm trying to get my daughter transferred to another university. I don't want Maddy to be the next victim.' Barbara's voice trembled.

The younger detective's face registered shock. 'It's not as bad as that. Campus security has been stepped up.'

'I've already spoken to Detective Sanderson about my daughter's safety and there's no guarantees.' Barbara shivered as wind whipped her scarf across her face.

'Mrs Harper, we're doing everything we can. I can't promise you we'll have him caught before the next semester starts but we are working on a major breakthrough.' The senior detective glanced at his watch. 'Now I'm sorry but we'll have to get back to our crime scene.'

Barbara watched them go. If only they could get their man she could stop worrying about Madeline coming back to this place. As she spun around she bumped into a youth wearing a hooded top. A backpack slung over his shoulder had a skull on it. He loped away without apologising. A shiver ran through her. That could be him, she thought. The Campus Killer.

Barbara's knuckles whitened as she gripped the steering wheel. Every finger joint felt her frustration. Each step to make Madeline's world safer had the feel of quicksand.

Hugh wouldn't make the effort to get their daughter transferred to another university. Perhaps he was right. Barbara hadn't held much hope for a successful visit to Phillips University. But she had unexpectedly seen the two detectives. And Detective Sanderson mentioned a breakthrough. If they caught the killer before lectures resumed, Barbara would feel less pressured.

A vehicle cut in front of her without indicating. Annoyed, she blasted the horn. The male driver extended a raised finger out the window. Even driving was becoming stressful. Barbara dropped back behind the offender. Her mind felt ready to burst. She pressed buttons on the radio in search of classical music to soothe her.

As she drove down the escarpment, Barbara took in the vista of the coast. Houses clustered on headlands above a sea that stretched to the horizon. Chopin and the scenery brought a touch of calm. Not for the first time, she considered finding something to alleviate her stress levels. Popping a pill wasn't easy with a disapproving husband for a doctor. Bronwyn, her work colleague, was always on about meditation.

Barbara decided on her usual quick fix. She parked in Narrabeen and walked to a café facing the lake. Ordering a double-shot coffee and a lemon friand, she sank into a wicker chair. Walkers littered the public path on this side of the waterway. Children tottered on tiny bikes with trainer wheels. Beyond, an old man sat on a milk crate at the water's edge, a fishing rod held lazily. Barbara envied his peaceful pastime. Ducks waded in and swam off among the reeds.

Coffee restored her sanity. Why flounder in negativity when across the lake was her stunning new house? Barbara had only this afternoon for more titivating before work tomorrow. The cake's tart lemon flavour obliterated any whisper of guilt over the treat.

At home a clunking garage door shut out the streetscape as she went inside. Beau scampered around her feet. Madeline must have let him in. Barbara expected to see her daughter sprawled on the lounge watching soapies on TV.

She climbed the stairs, unwound her scarf and called, 'Maddy.' A muffled reply came from behind her daughter's closed bedroom door. What if Rob were in there too? She had avoided thinking about the stages of her daughter's romance. Madeline was old enough but Barbara hadn't contemplated the issue of sex under her own roof. She marched into the master bedroom, the heat of a hot flush searing her face. Was her imagination working overtime again?

Barbara's gaze fell on the gigantic shopping bag from David Jones. Unpacking her new doona and pillow covers would distract her. Plastic crackled as she removed the packaging. She flung the large cover over the bed like a fleece, its brocade-like fabric revealed flowers of teal, aqua and mauve. Rich and vibrant, it gave her bedroom the exotic touch she'd planned. Stripping the doona, she transformed it with a new covering. She piled the pillows luxuriously in front of the bed head. Pleased with her choices, Barbara stood admiring the effect.

She heard footsteps on the stairs.

'Hello, darling. You're home early.'

Hugh placed his medical bag in the walk-in robe and began removing his work attire.

'Hi, Barbs. Going to hit a bucket of balls before the competition this Saturday.'

'There's still boxes I wanted a hand with. Couldn't golf be put on hold for once?' Barbara saw the frown of determination as her husband finished dressing. He didn't seem to care when the chaos of moving found order. Waltzing in and out as if this were a bloody motel. Emotions churned. She'd had such hopes for their happiness in the new house. Change the subject, she told herself, letting a sigh escape.

With a sweep of her hand at the bed, she said, 'Do you like the new covers?'

His glance lingered on the marital bed. 'Be more appropriate in an Indian bazaar.' Hugh turned to leave.

Barbara hid her disappointment, wishing she had a friend to pop around and tell her the bedroom looked gorgeous.

'Maddy home?' he asked.

Barbara followed him into the hallway. As his hand reached the door handle of his daughter's room, Barbara hissed, 'I think Rob's in there too.'

Hugh's open fingers sprang back. He stumbled down the stairs, slamming the door behind him. Barbara, with a smirk on her face, ducked back into her room. She heard the click of a door opening and sounds as if someone had gone to the bathroom. My God, Barbara thought, maybe they were having sex. How was she to handle this? Hugh had obviously opted out of any embarrassing situation.

Dinner preparations beckoned but she had to walk past that door. Barbara made it to the top stair before Rob opened it. In one hand he had the ubiquitous cap; his other rubbed ruffled hair.

'Hi, Mrs H.' Rob made no mention of why he was here.

'Hello, Rob. Didn't know you were coming over today.' Barbara struggled with her inner thoughts. She wanted to demand he get out of her daughter's room but knew confronting the boyfriend was not on. She'd have to set ground rules with Madeline later.

'We ...' Rob started as her daughter flounced across the hallway.

'Met at the Mall. Fell asleep watching a DVD,' Madeline added.

Barbara took in the challenging look and spun back to the stairs. From the kitchen their voices were a murmur until Rob called out a farewell. Only the guilty skulk off quickly, she decided. Carrots, broccoli, mushrooms and zucchini cluttered the sink. As she washed and diced the vegetables too many 'what ifs' about Madeline flicked through her mind. Barbara turned on the TV news to watch other people's dramas instead.

Saturday morning Barbara woke to the sound of voices outside. Raising her head to see out, she realised they came from paddlers on the lake.

She snuck out of bed not waking Hugh and grabbed a robe. At the back of the garage behind a row of boxes lay the surprise for her husband's birthday. With cardboard on the floor, Barbara half dragged the kayak out onto the lawn. Its colour, vibrant as daffodils, made Barbara's pulse race. She loved surprises. Inside she retrieved the hidden card about old golfers never die they just lose their balls. Her pen finished with a flourish, *All my love, Barbs*.

Back outside, she tied a huge bow round the waist of the kayak. Propping the card amongst the ribbon's silver curls, Barbara stood to admire her handiwork. From the lake's barely dimpled surface came a shiver of breeze. She went inside to prepare breakfast. When it was ready she called Hugh and Madeline, her voice echoing up the staircase. In pyjamas and skimpy nightie, her family came into the family room. Barbara deliberately averted her eyes from the view. In a matter of moments her daughter saw what was on the lawn.

'Dad, look.' Madeline's face, alive with excitement, spun her father towards the windows.

'Happy birthday, darling.' Barbara kissed her husband's cheek.

Hugh's face flushed with embarrassment. 'You shouldn't have.'

'Oh, Mum, you've outdone yourself.'

In bare feet, they raced onto the dew-covered grass. Barbara watched Madeline run her hand over the shiny fibreglass while Hugh read his card. Treasuring the moment, Barbara called them into breakfast.

'You can go for a paddle when you're finished. You'll need something warmer on.'

Father and daughter hastily ate scrambled eggs. Suitably attired, they dragged the gift to the water's edge. Madeline held the prow while Hugh eased into the kayak. With paddle sweeping from side to side, he left rings of disturbed water. Madeline, impatient for a turn, yelled encouragement from the reeds. Barbara almost skipped down to her. She could see Hugh smiling.

After Hugh left for golf, Barbara walked to Narrabeen. Another visit to the café would top off her morning. There had not yet been time for discussion of house rules. She was wearing a warm quilted jacket and comfy shoes. Weaving her way along backstreets, she absorbed weak sunshine. A cloudless sky promised a fine day. Madeline had gone to meet Rob.

A strange-looking fellow walking a dog emerged from a side street. The first thing Barbara noticed was the back of his partly bald head. Long hair fluffed over his shoulders with every stride. His shorts and T-shirt seemed oversize on a small frame as he clumped along in boots.

The dog was a blue heeler tightly grasped on a lead. A car swept by and the animal strained sideways barking at it. Every now and then the man flung his head forward to rearrange his hair possibly to cover his baldness. For some minutes he'd cover his skull with one hand as if to prevent sunburn of the exposed crown.

Barbara, intent on observing, slowed her pace. Intuition warned her not to pass him. The dog trotted happily along but something about the owner's grasp on its lead signalled danger. This made her think about the people in her new neighbourhood. She thought the Northern Beaches was a safe enclave of the middle class. This bloke was a weirdo. What if this area wasn't safe?

Her focus had been on Madeline going back to danger at the university; this was closer to home. Fortunately, when she arrived at Pittwater Road, the bald man crossed and headed for the caravan park. Barbara hoped he was some itinerant who'd move on. Feeling anxious, she crossed the bridge. Several pelicans slept on top of the light posts. Why the huge birds chose to rest there high above the traffic, she couldn't imagine.

Early that evening Barbara, Madeline and Rob sat in the family room dressed ready to go out. Madeline wore a ribbed jumper over jeans. Only a sliver of skin showed when she moved. Rob helped himself to a beer. Hugh was more than an hour late home from golf.

Barbara hadn't told him about the restaurant she'd booked for a family dinner. She'd tried his mobile several times but it was still switched off. No point leaving a message as it would ruin the surprise. Darkness outside made her wonder why he was so late. Hugh wasn't one to linger at the nineteenth hole.

'Where is Dad?' Madeline asked over and over again. Frantically pressing buttons to no avail.

'I'll ring the restaurant to say we're running late.' Barbara made the call. This was the first time Rob was coming out to dinner. Why did Hugh have to embarrass them like this?

Half an hour passed and Rob had found a football replay on TV. Madeline was pacing the room. Reluctantly, Barbara phoned Bob River's mobile. He'd played in the competition. She knew Hugh would see this as checking up on him. Something he hated.

'Sorry to trouble you, Bob but has Hugh left?' Barbara could hear the noisy bar in the background.

'Yeah, Barbara, about an hour ago. Seemed in a hurry to get away. Everything all right?'

'Yes, thanks Bob.'

'Well, Mum where is he?'

'I don't know, Maddy. Guess I should have told him about dinner. You two go along. I'll wait and ring you if I hear anything.'

After they left Barbara poured herself a brandy. Head in hands, she sat at the table trying to fathom where Hugh had gone. She tried his mobile one more time. He wasn't on call. She wondered if he'd been in an accident. But if she rang the hospital all the medical profession on the peninsula would know he'd not come home.

Several drinks later, she stumbled to bed.

In the early hours of dawn Barbara opened her eyes. Blood thumped in her temples; her head ached. Beside her, the bed was rumple free. Hugh had not come home all night.

THIRTY-FOUR

Pain before pleasure, Jill decided, picking up the phone.

'Hello, Mother,' she played with the coiled cord. 'I'm home safe and sound.'

After the usual string of complaints, her mum demanded, 'When are you coming to see me?'

'Tuesday. I can stay two nights then I must get ready for work.'

'That reminds me. I've been saving paper clippings for you. Suppose you haven't heard. Now the cops have found a skeleton. And there's a photo of a detective with a hooker.'

That word unsettled Jill. She finished the call as soon as possible, mulling over these new findings. Mother didn't say if the bones were linked to Katie and Cheryl's murders. Recalling the night before she left, Jill was sure they'd found her sharpened stiletto. And that young bloke had recognised her as a woman. Her stomach lurched. She'd barely got home before being freshly embroiled in the case.

Jill hoped it wasn't Gary in that picture. Confessing what she'd done would be awkward. The police must be surmising a prostitute was involved. All these implications buzzed round her mind, making it more and more difficult to ring Gary. Jill was relieved when his mobile went straight to voice mail. In her huskiest tone Jill told him she was back from the South Pacific. With a cup of tea, she sank onto the lounge and relaxed, cosy in the gas heater's glow.

After a regulated life aboard ship, Jill was pleased to be setting her own agenda again. The holiday still had a dream-like quality. How she'd thrived in the new environment. Energy bubbled inside her. Jill couldn't wait to share the experience with students, finalise her research project and see a certain good-looking detective. For minutes she drifted in a fantasy date with Gary until her gaze fell on Dharani. If only Jill could absorb some of the goddess's serene wisdom. Perhaps Dharani would be more of a confidante than a protector. Enough dreaming, placing her mug on the dusty coffee table, Jill burst into action.

She pulled everything out of her sailing bag onto the bed. A bulging plastic bag of dirty washing was dealt with first. With the washing machine humming away and toiletries back in the bathroom, Jill put other travel necessities back in drawers. Her lacy underwear set, unworn on the holiday, still smelled salty. She hand washed the items, pinning them on the line outside. A cool breeze drove her back indoors. For the rest of the afternoon she cleaned and polished while listening to rock 'n' roll on the radio. Before dusk Jill drove to the local shops for supplies, a takeaway and a DVD. By evening, draped on the sofa, wine in hand; she was back to her old life.

While she was reading in bed, Gary called.

'I want to hear all of your adventures. And the sailing too.' He laughed. 'Dinner Friday night? There's a new place opened in Surry Hills. Walking distance from my place. Night, babe.'

Jill had hardly got in a word or jotted down the details before he was gone. Her pulse raced with excitement. She closed her book and switched off the light. This time, things would be different. What did Gary mean by mentioning his place? Perhaps he had ideas too. Jill thought of her bra and panties sashaying on the line and smiled.

Next morning she fitted in an exercise class before dropping by the office for some books. Jill had plonked a pile on the desk when she sensed the door opening. Duncan stood, silhouetted by the frame. His appearance made her gasp. The changes in him while she'd been away were massive. Skin hung off him. His pallor against the black leather jacket was deathly. And his halitosis was worse than ever. Yet his eyes burned as if his core was self-destructing.

Edging closer, he shut the door. 'You've been away.'

His stare was creepy. Jill kept the desk between them. 'Yes, Duncan,' she answered; worried her tone would convey nervousness. 'You must be really ill.' Her hands shook. Light glinted off his glasses.

Moving nearer, he answered. 'Cancer. But I'm not done yet.'

With what, she thought, as his fingers reached out. Unease enveloped her. She wanted to get past him, run from her office. But he was her boss. Was the threat imagined? Jill remained in control, picked up the books and held them in front of her for protection.

Duncan checked out the titles. 'What are these for?'

'My research proposal. The Kanakas in north Queensland. Family links in Vanuatu.'

Slipping back into professor mode, Duncan retorted. 'So that's where you've been, Jill. Thought you looked surprisingly healthy.' His long fingers stroked his beard. 'We must get together so I can hear all about your trip. My approval will be necessary, you know.'

His knuckle skimmed her cheek. Jill was an insect caught in his web. Fortunately, Paula burst in. She too had changed. Her dishevelled hair and nervy movements made Jill wonder what was going on. Without addressing her, Paula led Duncan out as if he were her patient.

After they'd left, Jill noticed a wet patch on the carpet. Professor Mitchell had lost control of his bladder. Before leaving, she rang maintenance and hoped the cleaners would attend to it. Otherwise her office would reek of urine. How could Duncan continue to work? Why was Paula covering for him? Later that morning Jill managed to talk to Paula alone. 'What's going on with Duncan?'

'Oh Jill, I can't cope with him anymore. Since his mother's died he's been crazy. His own illness is getting to him too. I'm terrified. He could do anything.'

'Paula, stop covering for him. No job is worth it. Go and see the Chancellor. It's time to report Duncan.'

'You're right, Jill, I will.'

Radio blasting, Jill sped down the highway to Canberra. Her car hadn't had a long run in ages. The day was crisp and clear. Sydney's sprawl gave way to paddocks of grazing cows. Country life appeared slower, rambling.

Yesterday's run-in with Duncan still rankled. He was an enigma. Earlier in the year, Jill just thought he was a sleaze. He must have sensed her determination to keep out of his clutches. Paula had provided his titillation. Jill didn't have the slightest interest in an ageing professor. Sleeping her way up the academic ladder had never entered her mind.

She kept hidden her revulsion over the handbag incident. Like any employee in a powerless position, Jill had put up with his behaviour. Also when it came to work-related issues Duncan could be inspiring. The article she'd had published raised her standing in the faculty. He was always hinting she could shine in academia, that he would show her the way. At what price, Jill thought.

A few times Duncan had scared Jill witless. She wasn't sure what he'd do. Before Paula's recent rescue, she'd seen herself fighting him off. She must tell Gary how Duncan was deteriorating. Learning Duncan had terminal cancer was a relief. Dancing around his strange behaviour wouldn't be for much longer. Jill just needed his stamp on her project first.

Canberra's well laid out suburbs were approaching so she checked the route to her mum's retirement village. When Jill parked outside, she noticed the complex had a feel of penury about it. After a lifetime of renting and limited financial resources, Mother had little choice.

A number of two-storeyed buildings with tiny balconies stood before her. Past a bank of letterboxes and straggly native gardens, Jill searched for the right block. A badly pruned grevillea jagged her jeans. She walked up a flight of stairs and along a gloomy corridor. Chiffon curtains covering every window made the place depressingly dark. Jill found the number of Mother's unit and knocked.

Her mum opened the door, unlocked the security screen and gave her a hug. Mother still looked blowsy in a way incongruous with this setting: teased hair with crimson lipstick bleeding into the crevices round her lips. She limped into the room in flat shoes. Arthritis in the knees, she had dispensed with high heels. A stick was propped beside the door. Jill hadn't thought of her as old; she was only sixty-six.

The main room had a couple of armchairs facing the television and a kitchen in one corner. At least the balcony with its three-piece setting faced north catching the winter sun. The two bedrooms were separated by a bathroom, over endowed with handholds. Jill put her overnight bag beside the single bed and joined her mum as she filled the kettle.

'It's quite comfy,' Jill said, searching for the positive.

'All I can afford, Jill.'

Over tea, with Scotch finger biscuits, Jill began the holiday stories. She could see pleasure on her mum's face; this took her mind off her own ailments. Then Jill remembered the gift she'd bought her. She opened the tiny box and lifted the pendant out by its chain. Etched in silver, the splendour of *Dreamsong* brought tears to her mum's eyes.

'Oh, it's beautiful. Whenever I wear it I'll think of sailing the South Seas.'

Happily, Jill had given her something to treasure. They finished their tea and Mother showed her around. The swimming pool was covered during the colder weather but they looked into the change rooms.

'You must lock this door to the office,' Mother said, 'a dirty old man tries to get in when you're dressing.'

'Men still after you in a place like this.' Jill laughed.

Outside, a motorised scooter scuttled along the path. A grey-haired lady in a bulky red cardigan jerked the contraption to a halt outside the main amenities block. The clack of balls drew Jill's attention to couples playing billiards. One of the staff gave Mother a wave as they wove their way back to the sandwiches made for lunch.

Two days later, after shopping trips and hours of inane TV watching with her mum, Jill arrived home. She'd never given retirement villages much thought but Jill was in no hurry to visit again. Watching the old and infirm, hearing of those waiting to die was rather upsetting. Perhaps she'd be a little less impatient when talking to Mother in future.

It took a whole day to complete her research proposal for the trip to north Queensland. Jill had a number of family names to try and locate from the elders in Vanuatu. Pleased with her professional approach, she was sure it would be accepted. This project might even develop into a book, a further step in her career. Jill laid aside the stack of references and planned her lectures and tutorials for the following week. The new semester would absorb practically all her spare time.

Then Jill noticed she had only an hour to get ready for her date with Gary. After a shower, she blow-dried her hair in front of the bathroom mirror, curling shiny strands around the brush. The reflection of her tanned body in the rose-petalled underwear built confidence. Her cheek colour almost matched the blush of the flowers.

Opening the wardrobe, Jill crossed the next hurdle. Her eyes skipped over the flashy red suit she'd worn last time. What a mistake. Tonight she'd go for something subdued and stylish. Jill settled on a tawny top with a beaded neckline and a burnished brown skirt over boots. After dressing, she laid a wool coat on the bed and dashed off to do her make-up.

On the drive into the city, multicoloured skyscrapers' lights put a sparkle into the evening. Jill parked in Riley Street as instructed and made her way through the chilly semi-darkness to the restaurant. Earlier in the year she'd have been too nervous to do this alone. As Jill entered the noisy eatery, Gary got up to assist with her coat. His eyes swept over her. Jill felt a frisson of delight. He was wearing an impeccable sports coat over a flashy shirt.

'Jill, you're looking great. Must have been some holiday.'

They sat. 'Just marvellous. Good to see you.'

A waiter with an interesting shaped goatee handed them menus, picked up the wine, flipping the opener in the manner of an expert. He pointed out the specials board and left them to make a selection. The restaurant was long and narrow with a high ceiling. Columnar lights hung above. Surrounded by the incessant chatter of other diners, the place lacked intimacy.

Jill chose Atlantic salmon on a kumara mash. Gary ordered oysters to start then barramundi. Because they'd already been through that awful getting-to-know-you phase, they chatted amiably. The sauvignon blanc was fresh and fruity. Jill raved about the islands, the people on the boat and the joys of sailing in the Pacific.

'And what about the fellas? All those steamy tropical nights,' Gary interjected.

'Mm,' Jill said, stalling, 'no one special.' Surprisingly, he was sussing out competition. Perhaps he believed all that holiday romance stuff.

Gary covered her hand with his. Then their meals arrived, the waiter placing the square plates with a flourish. Her fish was delectable. Jill asked Gary how the case was going, told him of the photo Mother had saved. A twinge of apprehension showed on his face then vanished.

'Oh, Cyndi,' Gary waved his hand as if the whole thing was passé. He continued with the story how he'd met her with a dead client.

'Do they think a prostitute is somehow involved in the campus murders?' Jill gripped the stem of her wine glass, thinking of the discarded stiletto.

'There's been a certain shoe found. But I remembered where I'd seen it before. No one else knows its relevance.' Gary reached for her hand once more. 'Ralston, my boss, would kill me if he knew what I'd asked you to do. You shouldn't have been on campus at night. Far too dangerous. Let's put the matter behind us.'

'I should also tell what's happening with Duncan.'

Gary put a finger to her lips. 'Later.'

Relieved, Jill smiled and nodded. After their plates were cleared, Gary leaned across the table. Their lips touched momentarily. Desire seared through Jill's body. Two plates of tiramisu arrived. Jill wondered if the tasty dessert would be a precursor. Gary suggested coffee at his place. They strolled there, arm in arm, through the wintry air.

Once inside the door, his kiss was slow and searching. His musky smell made her dizzy. Jill slid off her coat. Gary directed her to the lounge as he went to put the kettle on. She heard him duck upstairs. Possibly he'd left the bedroom a mess. Although, this room looked tidy enough: TV remotes in a row, papers in a rack and cushions at jaunty angles. There was even a gorgeous bonsai on the coffee table.

'Milk, sugar,' he asked.

'Maybe later,' Jill murmured, pulling him closer by the tie, his after-shave an instant aphrodisiac.

Then he led the way upstairs. Two candles on tall stands illuminated the bed. Their pale flickering seemed perfect as if he'd suspected Jill wasn't the bold 'lights on' type of woman. It wasn't the sparse male room she'd expected. Above the bedhead was a stunning painting of the sea, foaming in the fury of a storm. She could almost feel the water surging towards her and hear again the bow wave of *Dreamsong*.

In the gentle glow they helped each other undress. They slid into clean sheets and snuggled up. As Jill lay on his chest, breathing in his masculine smell, Gary told her about a mate who was into aphrodisiacs.

'He used honey and ginger. Really sticky on his pubes. Then his source told him, "No, you fool. You eat it." '

They shook with laughter. Then Gary raised his face above hers, their lips barely apart. Jill could see the wanting in his eyes seeking culmination of the evening. Her lips met his, eager and sensual. They changed position. Her tongue traced his nipple, tasting his skin. She ran fingers over his muscular frame hesitating before his most intimate part. He led her hand further and then expertly rolled a condom over his erection. His touch, gentle but persistent, brought her to a juddering peak before their bodies melded.

Sometime after, Gary's breathing told Jill he was asleep. She closed her eyes but despite a languorous feeling a deep yearning in every cell of her body kept her restless. In her mind Jill knew she wanted more than great sex. That word 'love' rolled in like a sea mist.

THIRTY-FIVE

'Morgue time. C'mon, Rich. Ruggeri's at the autopsy.' Sanderson raised his eyebrows in surprise. 'Says Hazo is a fan of Dr Arabella Steele. Can't think why. I'm not looking forward to another encounter with that frosty forensic anthropologist.'

Fyurk kept pace with his superior all the way to the car park. 'At least a pile of bones won't be gory.'

The vehicle's engine revved to life. Sanderson drove over the coathanger, as the Sydney Harbour Bridge was colloquially known, pleased the afternoon rush from the city had not begun. Devoid of pleasure craft, the harbour looked grey and cold. Only ferries left fanned wakes. When this case was over, he'd steal away to somewhere warm.

Fyurk brought Sanderson's attention back to the present. 'I've started reading *Death's Acre*, the book Ruggeri put me on to. Didn't realise so many in our line of work are ignorant as to what happens to bodies after death.' He opened the glovebox to find a tissue. After a loud snort the ball of paper ended up in his pocket.

Sanderson's glance caught his offsider's smile as the compartment snapped shut. He wasn't going to mention his Chick Kit again or its lack of use in recent times.

'You'll get to see plenty of stiffs as a detective. Decomposed ones will knock your sensitive nose for a sixer. Blood everywhere's the worst. Smells like a freezer full of meat gone off.' Sanderson pulled into the

252

street behind the Department of Forensic Medicine and searched for a parking spot.

'Okay, Gary. I'm not questioning your knowledge. But as Ds we're pressured for time and results. We can't study a body for its stages of decomposition. You know, Bass only started his experiments in 1981.' Fyurk's enthusiasm was cut off as Sanderson got out and slammed the car door.

Along the dim corridors of the morgue, Sanderson recognised the familiar smell of formalin. Fyurk's new shoes squeaked on rubber tiles.

'Jot down anything relevant, Rich. We don't want to miss clues.' Notebooks and pens in hand, they entered the autopsy room. Ruggeri looked up and gave a wave. Hazelton's apron was clean for once, Sanderson noted.

'Afternoon, Detectives.' Dr Steele addressed them in a tone suggesting their tardiness had not gone unnoticed.

Sanderson muttered a reply, refusing to make eye contact. Instead he examined the neatly laid out skeleton on the stainless steel table. Ruggeri had been here throughout the painstaking process. The Coroner required at least one officer to watch a post mortem to verify the chain of evidence. Photographs of wounds, blood samples and even stomach contents from a particular body had to be labelled and checked. As head of the forensics team, the Italian spent longer in this room than he did over cappuccinos.

He started with the skull. Empty eye sockets weren't much use, Sanderson thought, remembering the vivid green of Cheryl's eyes. They'd have to confirm the ID before eye colour would be revealed. Beside her head lay a mat of dark hair. Around the assembly of bones, leaf litter fragments speckled the usually clean surface. The remains of an exposed hand had several phalanges missing. Sanderson wondered whether a dog had chewed it. Near the feet were two plastic bags of soil. The contents of one was brown and crumbly, the other was darker as if oil had been added. He wanted to explain to Fyurk that this greasy residue would have been under the decomposed body. Reluctant to step into her territory, he waited for Dr Steele to commence.

'Dr Hazelton has filled me in on significant details from the other victims.' Pointing at the neck region, she continued, 'Gentlemen, see the tiny fracture of the hyoid bone. That indicates strangulation.'

Sanderson scrawled a note before her clipped tone went on.

'No hair was recovered from the pubic region which may match the pudendum removal in previous cases. However the victim might have had no pubic hair for cosmetic reasons.' Dr Steele's voice remained perfectly calm.

His mind flashed to Cyndi's Brazilian. Sanderson couldn't imagine discussing this part of a woman's anatomy with the anthropologist.

Ruggeri interjected, 'Sando, as you know we've got enough to tell us the victim was female, possibly early twenties. Similarities of the modus operandi show this could be an earlier kill. Dr Steele plans to take dental X-rays and consult with the forensic dentist so we can start tracking dental records.'

'I could run a check on missing persons,' Fyurk offered. 'Do we have an estimated time of death?'

Dr Steele's ponytail flipped as her face turned to him. 'Insect casings of dermestid beetles were found. They feed on the hide and hair. Dr Levy, your entomologist, consulted with me on site. Considering the weather and the shallowness of the grave, our estimation puts the time of death sometime in January this year. Gentlemen, you realise in midsummer an exposed body can skeletonise in a month.'

'Thank you,' Sanderson said, 'you've been most helpful.' He noticed Hazelton was fidgeting and sensed the pathologist was eager to start on another sheet-clad body behind him.

'Sorry for the delay, Hazo. We'll let you get back to work.'

'It's been an interesting morning.' A smile hovered on Hazelton's lips. 'Saw your picture in the paper.'

He gulped. Sanderson hadn't expected his misdemeanour to be raised here. The moment Dr Steele's face reddened, he knew she'd seen it too. The anthropologist spun on her sensible heels and left the room.

'Thanks, mate.' Sanderson stared at Hazelton across the skeleton. 'Guess we get to work identifying this body.'

Ruggeri and Fyurk chuckled as they left the room. The forensics bloke was holding a paper evidence bag.

'What's that?' Sanderson asked.

'Fragments of a yellow top, Dr Steele believes. There was no evidence of other clothing around the burial site. This is going to the exhibits room.' Ruggeri smoothed his dark hair and put his cap on.

Pocketing his notebook, Sanderson pulled out his mobile. 'How are the crime scene photos coming along? I'm bringing in a profiler. We'll need the exhibits out to run him through the case in the morning.'

'I'll be there to help Ruggeri, Gary.'

'Good one.' Sanderson searched the phone till Max Brown's name appeared and hit call.

The answering voice sounded businesslike but he could hear waves breaking in the background.

'Can you believe that?' Sanderson said, 'Max is at the beach. Says sand jogging is part of his fitness regime.'

Fyurk looked up at steely clouds moving in from the south. 'He won't stay long. That's about to dump a heap of rain.'

'Well boys, get that incident room up to scratch. See you there at ten in the morning. Perhaps our behaviour expert can sniff out where we're going from here.'

He watched Fyurk and Ruggeri set off in the forensics wagon before unlocking the Commodore. The drive to his office would be slow. Traffic on Broadway had already built to a barely moving mass of vehicles. Sanderson turned on his wipers as Fyurk's predicted deluge hit. He hated the way darkness fell so early in winter. After he attended to his final chores of the day a run would be impossible. Too wet. Too dark.

No longer did he have the chance of a sexual hit with Cyndi. Ralston had made it quite clear risky dalliances were not on. Sanderson wondered if Cyndi would ring him as the weeks passed. Everything seemed bleak except the encounter in the cot with Jill. That would have to move slowly, he figured. Sanderson couldn't face the rowdiness of the pub. Sport on Foxtel and a bottle of Jack Daniels would see him through the night.

On the way to his office, he recognised Janine walking towards him. 'You look tired. Where's Richard?'

Sanderson straightened his tie. 'The incident room. How was your dinner out?'

'We had a lovely meal, thank you.'

Sanderson watched a tinge of pink come into her face. She knew he wanted more information. Her expression told him it wasn't going to happen.

'I'm glad you two have got together,' he said, 'Rich is a decent bloke.'

Janine smiled. 'I agree.' She slipped past him and out the door.

Sanderson slumped in front of a computer scanning the list of missing persons around January. Teenagers and geriatrics dominated. Usually young women were regulars but at that time nothing threw up a match with their victim. He was puzzled. Prostitutes and drug addicts were rarely reported. But he figured their recent find was most likely a potential student. Perhaps, some lass from the country had come to see the residential college. Surely family would be waiting to hear from her. No use letting scenarios run through his mind. A young woman had ended up dead on campus and he had to deal with it. Tomorrow he'd check all students enrolled for the year. He'd bet more than one hadn't turned up for some reason or another. By the time he'd updated all the case notes his shoulders ached.

Once home, Sanderson took off his gun and locked it away. He hung his suit on a hanger but left it out to air. The morgue's odour would be gone by morning. After showering and dragging on a tracksuit, he traipsed downstairs to the kitchen. His mood didn't lighten much when he saw the contents of the fridge. He microwaved left over Indian takeaway and opened the whiskey. Splashing the brown liquid over clinking iceblocks, Sanderson raised the glass. A large swig sent a warm blast straight to his guts.

Juggling his plate of indefinable curry, the glass and bottle, he made it to the sofa. He switched on the TV and settled in for the night. His gaze rested on the bonsai tree in its blue and white ceramic dish. Its drooping leaves made him feel guilty. It's just a bloody dwarf tree, he told himself. But for Sanderson it was a constant reminder of a fallen colleague. His best mate. Knifed outside his favourite pub. And he hadn't been there.

Sanderson removed the plant from the coffee table and poured another glass. His mood was as low as the level in the bottle when he finally stumbled to bed.

In the early hours of dawn Sanderson woke to the noise of thumping on his front door. Bleary eyed, he opened it to see his agitated offsider.

'No one could get hold of you. Your phone's off.' Fyurk marched in.

Blood thundering in his temples, Sanderson followed him down the dim hallway. Seeing the mess on the coffee table, Fyurk shook his head.

'Phew, you did hang one on.'

Beside the almost-empty bottle was Sanderson's mobile, switched off due to a flat battery.

'Shit,' he said, 'so what's the big drama.'

'We've been called to a homicide at Glebe. Domestic violence. Get your gun. The uniform cops are there but haven't found the culprit.'

Sanderson rubbed his forehead. 'I feel lousy. Can't they get someone else?'

'The other team are off on stress leave. You're the closest.'

With a sigh he climbed the stairs. 'You'll have to drive, Rich. My head's too bad.'

Minutes later, the Commodore flew under the sandstone arch near Central Railway Station. Fyurk radioed they were on their way and flicked the siren on for good measure.

Sanderson, head in hands, felt a surge of adrenalin clash with last night's grog as the car's tyres squealed on every curve.

'Take it easy,' he moaned, 'or I'll chunder all over the dash board.'

Fyurk turned off Glebe Point Road into a narrow backstreet. Sanderson strained in the dim light to read street numbers.

'There,' he pointed to a patrol car ahead skewed across the road, lights flashing.

As they got out a constable approached. 'Woman. Deceased. Front room. Had a bit of a deco round the back. Think the bastard's shot through.'

'You searched inside?'

'Sure, Inspector.'

The squat cottage's peeling paint and cracked pathway screamed neglect. Sanderson could see a light through the curtains.

'Keep an eye out front,' he said to the constable. Then he signalled Fyurk to go down one side passage as he headed for the other.

He took out his Glock in unsteady hands wishing away his hangover. The side gate needed a shove to get its rusty hinges moving. Weapon stretched before him, he moved as soundlessly as possible, eyes alert. Sanderson felt his stomach muscles tighten. Detectives rarely drew their guns at crime scenes.

Before rounding the back corner of the house, savage growling assaulted his ears. Sanderson hoped the bloody dog was tied up. Claws scrabbled on concrete. A huge alsatian launched itself towards him.

'Christ,' he muttered, firing several shots with resounding cracks.

As the sound resonated in his ears he watched the beast falter mid-leap, checked by the velocity of the bullets. It fell at his feet, tongue lolling between glistening canines. Rising sun broke the clouds as he lowered his gun. Sanderson stepped over the dead dog and rounded the corner to see Fyurk finish cuffing a bloke face down on the grass. A constable raced up, Glock wavering. The man on the ground turned his head, spit blasting from his mouth. 'What'd ya kill me fuckin' dog for? Bloody coppers!'

'Keep an eye on this piece of shit, Officer.' Sanderson was nervous around inexperienced cops. He didn't want any more guns going off.

Fyurk checked out the side passage and returned. 'Nice shot, Gary. He charged out of that shed. Couldn't stop him setting the dog onto you.'

Sanderson pointed the barrel of his Glock skywards, blew across the end. 'Sure sobered me up.'

Flashing blue and red lights washed Sanderson's face as he leaned near the driver's open window. 'Take him to the station. He can cool off in the cells. We'll be along to question him later.'

One of the constables shoved the thug's head down as he pushed him into the patrol car.

Gunshots drew a crowd in suburbia. Neighbours were milling outside their residences. Fyurk ran the blue and white chequered crime scene tape across the front of the property, tying it to fence palings. Sanderson left him standing guard at the gate while he went into the cottage.

The woman's body was lying twisted between a table and a sink overflowing with dirty dishes in the brightly lit kitchen. Her blood-smeared face was staring directly at an uncovered light globe hanging from the ceiling; eyes open, pupils fixed and dilated. A wide-blade kitchen knife protruded from the region of her heart through a pink fluffy dressing gown, sliced and blood stained from the ferocious attack.

'Christ,' he muttered, wondering how many knives like these became murder weapons. Sanderson was careful to avoid stepping in blood congealed on the linoleum. From the spatter patterns and defence wounds on her hands and arms she'd put up a hell of a fight.

Whistling softly, he imagined the scenario that led to her death. What could a woman possibly say or do to deserve this? It riled him to see such domestic carnage. That creep at the station better have some answers. Sanderson still felt queasy with fright after the bastard set that huge alsation onto him. He'd charge him for that as well as murder. If he hadn't dispatched the animal in a timely fashion he could have been in hospital. At the thought of a savage mauling, he shuddered. He glanced around the dismal kitchen taking in the old Kooka stove and grimy fridge covered in gaudy magnets.

The tramp of boots announced the arrival of the forensics team.

'Hi, Ruggeri. Early start for you too.'

The Italian saluted, his cap askew over black curls. 'Fyurk tells me you've had an interesting morning.'

'Yeah. I feel like shit.' Sanderson indicated the woman's body. 'Seems a pretty straightforward homicide. Let's hope the bastard's prints are all over that knife. And his dead dog's out the back. Better tell the body snatchers to take that as well.'

'Will do, Sando.'

Ruggeri snapped on gloves as a colleague's camera whirred and flashed.

Outside, a constable relieved Fyurk of the running sheet. The two detectives strode up to Glebe Point Road.

'If I don't have a coffee I'll die,' said Sanderson then related the scene inside the cottage.

'I jumped the fellow as he came out of the shed. Stank to high heaven of booze.' Fyurk traipsed into the first café on the busy street.

'You must have downed him quick. Fit bugger, aren't you?'

'Sure, Gary. Been pumping a bit of iron. Perhaps I need more target practice. Not sure I could have tidied up that dog as well as you did.' Fyurk laughed as a horn blared and Sanderson rubbed his forehead.

The coffee came strong and hot. Sanderson sipped then spoke, 'We'd better get back to the station and interview that mongrel before he gets a lawyer. Must be prompt for Max at the incident room.'

'Righto, Gary.'

THIRTY-SIX

Alone in bed, Barbara felt a flush rise up her body until her neck flamed. She threw off the doona. Was this menopausal or a panic attack?

Hugh's uncreased pillow brought back her dilemma. She sat up, resting against the bed head and fanned her face. Where was he? Never in twenty years had he failed to come home without telling her. Was he dissatisfied with her, with life?

She pulled the doona up, her fingers tracing over the brocade. If Hugh was called to a medical emergency he always rang. The bedside phone had remained annoyingly silent. She picked it up and checked for messages. There were none. Then she remembered that other time he'd left one on her mobile.

Skeltering out of bed, she found her handbag and retrieved the phone. Again: 'There are no voice messages.' Back under the warm covers, she dialled his mobile to find it still switched off. This was so unlike Hugh. Had she really been focused on his behaviour during the house building? Maybe there were signals she'd missed.

Barbara's mind flashed back to when he'd bought those designer jeans. Most uncharacteristic behaviour. He wasn't a man who cared about clothes. Unless, all of a sudden there was someone he was trying to look good for. Was he really having a mid-life crisis?

One of the women in the hospital had lost her husband to that. Bronwyn told her the final sign was having his teeth bleached. Hubby wanted his middle-aged smile white when he looked at his younger par-amour. How they'd laughed at that.

'Silly old git,' Bronwyn said, 'they change jobs, houses or wives in an attempt to feel life hasn't passed them by. Some go for the trifecta.'

Barbara found herself clutching the mobile like a lifebuoy. Numbness crept over her as she recalled the scene at work. Hugh hadn't shown any real enthusiasm for the new house. Was that because he didn't plan on staying? And the jibes at her roly figure could indicate he had a slender replacement. With a sickening feeling, Barbara confronted the thought of being left for a younger woman.

Life didn't seem fair. Signs of middle age had arrived: putting on weight, greying hair, facial lines, saggy flesh and loss of libido. Barbara felt she'd looked after herself as well as she could. Sure exercise was not her thing but her hair and clothes presented well. In the bedroom department she was not always as welcoming to Hugh's advances. That was pretty normal in most marriages, she'd heard. And she shouldn't have to compete with some young bimbo.

Women twenty years younger had all the advantages. Barbara sighed. With a surge of anger she threw her mobile on the doona.

The perfume on Hugh's shirt, the continual late nights and ever-increasing number of conferences began to add up. The name of her adversary reared into her mind. Lisa. Hugh's nurse of all people. How banal. Poor Lisa going through a marriage break-up. Sensitive Hugh, always there to help. And no doubt drawn into God knows what.

Barbara didn't even have Lisa's home number so she could confirm her suspicions. Easing out of bed, she drew aside the curtains. The sun's rays striped the smooth lake. Its brightness made her blink. Two pelicans swooped low over the surface like fighter planes. Despite the calm scene, she remained in turmoil.

On hearing the click of the front door, Barbara crept onto the land-ing. Hugh placed his shoes near the inside mat. He turned and began tiptoeing up the stairs without seeing her.

'Where the bloody hell have you been?' exploded Barbara.

Hugh stopped, his startled face staring up at her. 'Shsh,' one finger at his lips, the other pointing to Madeline's closed door.

'Don't shush me.' Barbara gripped the railing, her knuckles whitened. 'I want an answer.'

Her husband's face took on a demeanour as if dealing with a difficult patient. She wasn't giving him a chance. Pressure built in her head.

'Tell me where you've been all night,' Barbara shrieked, her voice rising to hysteria.

Hugh bounded up the last few stairs attempting to push past her. The nearby door opened.

'What's going on?' Madeline framed the doorway, concern flooding her face. Looking from one to the other, she flung tousled hair over her shoulder.

'Go back to bed, Madeline.' Hugh's tone was short and sharp, 'and Barbara come into our room. We'll deal with this in private.'

'Private eh. So we don't want Madeline to know what Daddy's been up to. She'll find out soon enough.' Barbara followed and Hugh closed the door behind them.

'Now calm down, Barbara. Let's discuss this civilly.'

'Civil! You don't come home all night? You don't phone and can't be contacted. You've been with that Lisa, haven't you?' Barbara trembled, her toes scrunched into the carpet. Tears threatened to staunch her rage.

'As a matter of fact I have,' Hugh answered.

She threw herself at him, battering her arms on his chest. 'You're having an affair with that bitch.'

Hugh held her off, his reply sounding distant, even detached. 'Well it has gone further than I expected.'

Barbara halted, staring through teary eyes. She could feel him drawing away from her as if through some vortex. Despising Hugh as she did that minute brought the only retort she could think of. 'Get your things and get out.'

Reefing the door open, she ran downstairs, continuing out of the family room onto the dewy lawn. Her bare feet halted at the water's edge. Arms wrapped around her nightie, she shivered in the wintry air. Sun scintillating the lake's surface brought little warmth this early in the morning. A kayaker, dipping his paddle rhythmically, swept past her beyond the reeds. Bewildered, she just couldn't face going into the house again.

Barbara listened for noises, heard a door slam and a car revving off. Hugh had gone. As cold seeped into her, she saw Madeline in the kitchen. Only then did she remember her daughter was going away today.

On hearing Barbara coming in, Madeline glanced up from her cereal bowl, spoon poised mid-air.

'Mum, what's wrong? I've never seen you and Daddy fight like that.'

'I don't want to go into it right now, Maddy.' Barbara smoothed her nightie. 'I'd better get dressed. Rob will be here soon. You'll have a lovely week at the holiday house.'

Madeline hesitated. 'If Dad's not going to be here should I stay home?'

'Of course not, darling. It's only a week and you're back at uni. I'll be all right.'

Barbara climbed the stairs to change. She heard Madeline let Rob in; their chatter sounded subdued. What would her daughter tell him? Washing her face, she noticed her eyes still revealed she'd been crying. With her teeth clean and hair brushed, she felt fresher. Madeline, humming in her room, collected her bags. Barbara descended to see them off.

In the kitchen, Rob stood at the sink staring out over the water. He was wearing his cap backwards as usual. Barbara ignored a flash of annoyance as he turned towards her.

'Hi, Mrs H,' he began before his voice dropped to a whisper. 'Sure you don't mind Maddy going?'

'No, Rob. You youngies go and enjoy yourselves.'

Bags slung from her shoulder, Madeline appeared. Barbara gave her a hug and the trio walked to the front door.

'Bye,' the couple echoed.

'Have a good time,' Barbara called after them as they strolled down the drive.

She closed the door and leant against it. Alone, the events of the last 24 hours seemed unreal. Barbara had seen husbands leave their wives on the TV and at the theatre but couldn't believe it was happening to her. And Madeline going away made it so much worse. Lethargic, she took a deep breath and staggered to the kitchen.

While the coffee machine hissed, she found her cache of Tim Tams in the pantry. Barbara ate the lot. A sprinkling of chocolate crumbs adorned the tabletop. Her caffeine shot, strong and hot, built her resolve. I'll get through this, she thought.

Barbara filed back over the morning's events in her mind. Where had Hugh gone? She supposed Lisa was still in her townhouse. Perhaps it was already set up as a love nest and he'd been welcomed. Give it a few days, Barbara told herself. Hugh would return saying he loved her. But what if he didn't come back?

Her whole life had changed in an instant. Maybe building the house and moving had been too much. She'd been so sure of Hugh's happiness when he paddled his birthday kayak. Now such an exciting start in their new home would be forever tarnished. Slumping in her chair, Barbara felt drained.

For the rest of the day, she wandered from room to room not able to concentrate on anything. Beau, her sole companion, followed forlornly. She realised dogs sensed moods more than people expected. A new decorating magazine on the coffee table caught her attention. She sat, cuddling Beau and picked it up. Flipping through the pages of designer decors seemed so meaningless at this moment. Here she was in the stunning new house she'd always dreamt of and she felt numb. Devoid of any satisfaction.

Her husband gone and daughter away, Barbara again sought solace in the kitchen. She found a box of Lindt chocolates. The sound of crinkling cellophane, the rush of creamy sweetness on her tongue sidetracked her negative thoughts. Barbara folded some washing and ironed a top for work, eating a chocolate to reward herself for each job completed.

At dusk she took a bottle of white wine and a cheese platter onto the balcony. She'd consumed nothing but the sugar hits all day. Good eating and exercise slipped her mind during bad times. Barbara drank and watched light fade over the lake. The skyline changed from orange to mauve to indigo. Cold evening air circled around her. The bottle drained; only a smear of brie remained on the platter.

She did not light the candle but sat enveloped in darkness as deep as her mood. Thoughts of the two people she loved most crowded her mind, alcohol blurring the scenes. When thoroughly exhausted, Barbara staggered inside and prepared for bed. The mess of her life made suicidal tendencies surface. Knowing there were no bottles of sleeping pills was a relief. She might have taken them. Then she thought of Madeline. How could she possibly leave her?

Collapsing onto the carpet in the bay window, her body hunched over, Barbara sobbed. The fibres absorbed her misery. She cried and cried losing all track of time.

The shrill tone of the phone aroused her.

'Hello,' she muttered. Hugh was needed for some medical emergency. 'He's not here. Try his mobile.' Barbara crawled into bed.

Kohl circled the rims of Barbara's eyes in an effort to conceal the damage from crying the night before. She checked her make-up in the rear vision mirror before leaving the car. With a brave face, she walked into the physiotherapy block.

At the sight of Bronwyn, Barbara thought she'd crumble but bit her lip instead. Delicately balancing friendship and firmness, Bronwyn ran this section of the hospital with a deft touch. But for the onset of arthritis, Barbara would have been in her position. She was grateful Bronwyn deferred to her experience.

'How was Hugh's birthday? Did he like the kayak?' Bronwyn's glance was cursory.

'He loved it. So did Maddy. She's away with her boyfriend this week.' Barbara picked up the clipboard on her desk.

'Wow, just the two of you in the new house.' Bronwyn filled the kettle then raised her eyebrows.

'Actually,' Barbara hesitated, 'I'm alone. Hugh's on another conference.' She found the lie slipped out easily.

With a wicked smile, Bronwyn replied. 'We should have a girlies' dinner one night.'

'Maybe.'

Barbara knew she hadn't sounded enthusiastic. Only weeks ago she'd wished to be included. If she went along could she maintain the charade?

Bronwyn checked her watch.

'You've got the updated list for the shoulder group?'

'Sure.' Bronwyn passed it to her.

'I'm off to the pool then. See you later.' Barbara's tone of forced cheeriness brought a wry smile to her superior's face.

Along the corridor, Barbara's footsteps echoed. She still felt shaky. Bronwyn must be wondering what was wrong. Barbara had to hold herself together. With determination, she strode into the bright room. The familiar pungent odour of chlorine hit her. Moisture from the hydrotherapy pool beaded the high windows. Her heavy black sneakers ruffled the artificial grass on the floor. Wearing navy shorts to the knee and a white polo top, Barbara advanced on the group, clipboard ready.

She ticked off most of the names and instructed the men and women to change into bathers, shower and enter the water. Rows of plastic chairs were draped with their belongings. Near the far wall, a woman sat knitting, waiting for her husband. His grey shoulder sling was on the chair beside her.

Barbara had taken over this group of shoulder reconstructions and repairs when the department had decided to use the pool. The patients used to come in grumpy and go home worse after treatment. Exercising in the warm water didn't hurt as much, the physiotherapists had been told. The staff could also see their charges enjoyed chatting and sharing experiences as they bobbed around the pool.

Voices resonated around the room as more of the group entered the water. Barbara was about to start when a woman came in with a carer. Her hands gripped the walking frame as her stockinged legs eased forward. The woman's eyes conveyed her terror of falling. She obviously had new knees and Barbara told the carer she'd have to wait till after her group.

Easy-listening music helped her focus as she stood at the pool edge. Dealing with adults who were no longer sure of their bodies was a constant here, Barbara thought. Her patients circled slowly with just their heads above water. One man was totally bald; a woman had her hair coiled in a bun. Barbara explained an appropriate exercise to each one in turn. Several were up to using a kickboard; others could not raise their arms at all.

On the towel-covered table adjacent to the pool, Barbara moved limbs through their range of movement. To her amusement, patients called it the rack. Each person's wet skin felt slightly different. Some retained muscle tone; others displayed flabby dimpled flesh. The woman with the coiled hair let out a small shriek. Those in the pool cheered her on. Working through the pain to regain movement was all part of the challenge.

Barbara directed the bald man to a chair. Handles hung above it on ropes through a pulley. Shakily, he gripped them, raising one arm then the next. Hands on hips, Barbara watched his technique then moved back to the pool. By day's end she found work therapeutic. Not only had she made progress with a number of patients, her own troubles had receded. Barbara stopped at the Noodle Bar to buy dinner on the way home.

The following day she slept late. Once or twice in the night she'd reached for Hugh only to feel a cold void. In a peach gown and tangerine slippers, Barbara slipped into the kitchen. Once Beau was inside, he bounded towards her. His alert eyes shone; pleased to see her. Amazing, she thought, how dogs could lift your spirits. After a tummy tickle he sniffed his bowl. She tinkled some pellets into it then cooked herself some porridge. Liberally sprinkling brown sugar over it, she added a flood of milk making caramel swirls. She ate as if ravenous then brewed a strong coffee. The machine's familiar sounds made her morning feel normal.

After Barbara cleaned up, she found herself staring into the refrigerator. Sparsely filled shelves were unlike the usual family-full appearance. She opened the vegetable crisper to limp broccoli and mouldy beans. There was nothing appetising for a meal. Shutting the door with a whoosh, she delved into her pantry hidey-holes. Not a Tim Tam or chocolate to be found. With an exasperated sigh, Barbara climbed the stairs for a shower.

Dressed in a cosy tracksuit, devoid of make-up, she inspected the house room by room. In her bedroom, the brocade doona was a lumpy mountain on the bed. Madeline's room was organised chaos. Her bed was made but books, precariously piled, smattered her desk. Barbara noticed a new photo of her daughter and Rob blue-tacked to the wall. A pang of anguish surged through her. Would Madeline stay if Hugh didn't come home? Concerns over her safety now seemed unreal. There were numerous ways to lose a child.

Traipsing through the lounge room with its new suede sofas didn't improve Barbara's mood. Almost everything she saw in her house was pleasing to the eye. She should be congratulating herself on the décor, the superb sense of colour, but without its meaningful people she saw an empty shell. Neither a noise nor the sound of a loved one's voice, made the house come alive. Just her echoing footsteps, hollow and lonely.

Barbara's urgent desire to escape forced her outside. She thought of going somewhere but felt far too fragile. Even a comment from a shop-keeper might cause a tearburst. She dragged a chair into the middle of the lawn and sat staring at the lake. Sheltered from the wind, she could hear its whisper in the casuarinas. The winter sun had little warmth but the glinting lake mesmerised her.

Plagued by all the probable changes in her life, her mind skittered in all directions. From frowns to wet cheeks, Barbara's face displayed her feelings like an actor. The thought of Hugh in the arms of his younger nurse made rage rise in her throat. It brought forth a line she'd use if she got the chance. 'You should be thinking about superannuation not sex.' Hugh was in his mid-fifties not the prime of his life.

That evening, Barbara found some cheese and crackers. She opened a bottle of wine. All too soon it was finished. Insensible, she stumbled to bed. At some stage in the night, Madeline rang waking her from a stupor. Barbara, aware of her slurred responses, offered the excuse of sleep.

Her week passed like knitting: knit one, day at work, purl one, day at home. What unravelled her façade was telling Bronwyn why she couldn't go out to dinner. Her work colleague registered shock at her revelation.

'But if Hugh doesn't come back,' Bronwyn said, 'you'll have to sell your beautiful new home. Oh, Barbara. It means so much to you.'

Hanging up, Barbara struggled for control. As soon as she could trust her voice, she made an appointment to see her GP. Dr Barton was a level headed man who'd been the family doctor for years.

Chairs lined the waiting room. They faced a square table full of jumbled magazines. A baby snuffled in its capsule on the floor in front of a young mother. An old man puffed past Barbara to a seat.

'Mrs Harper. Come in.'

She saw Dr Barton's kindly eyes and followed his flecked jacket into the surgery.

'Now what can we do for you today?' he asked.

Barbara sobbed as she spluttered an explanation. She gripped the Gucci handbag noticing with shock her badly chipped nails.

Dr Barton twiddled his pen, possibly searching for words of reassurance.

'Men of Hugh's age think life is passing them by. Suburbia and slippers is no match when a younger woman shows interest. However, many don't want to throw everything away.'

Barbara's face lit up. 'Not long ago he said he didn't want change in his life. I thought Hugh was happy.'

'Well, Barbara, that's a good sign,' the doctor sat forward. 'Bide your time. Don't do anything rash. He may see the error of his ways. In the meantime, I'll prescribe something to help you through.' Dr Barton printed out a script and signed it with a flourish.

'Thank you, Doctor.' Barbara stood as he opened the door.

'Take those. Cheer up. Madeline will be home tomorrow.'

Hope swept through her. Barbara paid the bill then dropped by the chemist. The pills were tiny and blue. She popped one as soon as she got home. With Beau trailing her from room to room, she embarked on a barrage of cleaning.

At midday, she slumped onto the lounge and turned on the TV. A blonde was spouting about affairs with married men. That's not what she needed, Barbara thought, an exposé on infidelity. Absolving herself of all responsibility, the blonde said she was single. It wasn't her fault married men were unfaithful.

The host of the show, a prim brunette responded, 'If less women played around married men would have to go home.'

'Exactly,' Barbara answered, switching off the set before the bimbo irritated her further.

Barbara wielded the vacuum cleaner with newfound ferocity. Locked in her own misery, she'd failed to think how the new circumstances were affecting Hugh. He'd always seen himself as a pillar of the community. Yet she'd read recently that most people thought less of a man who strayed. And it seemed all the more sordid that his paramour was also his nurse at the practice. Perhaps his patients would signal their disapproval by drifting away. Bet that hadn't entered his mind when jumping into the cot with Lisa.

Next day she kept up her cleaning frenzy. Barbara wanted everything right for Madeline's homecoming. She didn't know whether the pills or the physical exertion were making her feel so much better. Parading around now she gained satisfaction from perfectly poised cushions in the lounge and gleaming granite bench tops.

Across the lake she could see market stalls set up. On impulse, she showered, dressed smartly and painted her nails in a berry colour. When they were dry, she announced to a listless Beau, 'Walkies.' His bout of exuberant panting made her laugh. Barbara attached his lead and they set off.

Darting here and there, Beau sought out new smells. Barbara paced herself accordingly thinking back to when Madeline first started walking. Those tottering steps of discovery were a precious memory. Now, so many years later, her daughter was away on holiday with a boyfriend. She wondered where the years had gone.

When they crossed the bridge at Narrabeen, Beau yapped at a pelican settling on a pole. A fishermen in a tin dinghy zoomed under, its outboard reverberated beneath Barbara's feet. Fluttering flags announced the stalls. One featured historic photos of the local area. She studied some of the pictures looking for landmarks that had been there more than fifty years ago. Just one suburb further north at Mona Vale was where the coaches used to stop. Barbara found that era hard to imagine considering the rumble of vehicles on Pittwater Road metres away.

Enjoying wandering from stall to stall, Barbara came across some jewellery. She was immediately drawn to a glass bead bracelet in colours of teal, turquoise and aquamarine. Nestled in black satin, it captured the colours of the sea. The young saleswoman, whose head was swathed in a scarf, scooped up the bracelet.

'Try it on,' she said, unfastening the catch.

Barbara held out her wrist, delighted by her choice. She paid and walked on wearing her precious acquisition. Before heading home, she bought a medallion of fillet steak and a variety of vegetables for a Mediterranean salad. Beau's little legs worked overtime as Barbara walked faster. Once inside, he lapped some water then snoozed on his cushion. For the first time in a week, Barbara cooked a meal and with a wine sat to watch a movie.

Sunday afternoon, Barbara drove into the garage, the boot laden with supplies for Madeline's return. When she saw the kayak, the urge to drive over it surprised her. How satisfying to hear the sound of snapping fibreglass, to see a mess of jagged yellow pieces. But something stopped her. Another idea skipped into her mind.

Minutes later, Barbara dragged Hugh's kayak over the lawn to the lake's edge. She remembered the morning she'd given it to him. Happiness at seeing her husband and daughter enjoying the craft. Standing among the reeds now, she was unsure. The water chilled her ankles. At worst she'd take a dunking. Steadying herself in the yellow cocoon, she paddled off finding her rhythm. Water plipped and splashed as she glided across its mirrored surface. Air, crisp and invigorating, egged her on. Sky faded to indigo in the west. Barbara looked ahead to the tree-clad shore feeling euphoric. The whole lake opened up to her as if she'd begun a journey.

Later that evening, Barbara was pleased with the semblance of normality as Madeline came in the front door. Refreshed and relaxed, her daughter was vibrant. Her bag slipped to the floor and Barbara was encircled in a big hug. Although the homecoming tugged at her emotions, Barbara remained positive and bright.

The following evening Madeline was late home from a lecture. Barbara caught her daughter searching the kitchen drawer.

'What are you looking for?'

Madeline's face was a ghostly white; her eyes darted in fear. 'That alarm thing you bought.'

'Why? What happened?' Barbara felt a stab of concern.

'I ... I thought someone was after me. The uni's put in safety stations where you can press a button for help. I ran to one. They're brightly lit. Then I wasn't sure.' Madeline showed a bewildering mix of emotions.

Barbara located the personal alarm. 'It's a good idea. Perhaps you shouldn't go to any night lectures till they've caught the person.' She pushed hair back from Madeline's eyes.

'I don't know, Mum. It's so scary there at night.'

'Get a good night's sleep, darling. We'll see in the morning.' Barbara went up to her bedroom, every step one of dread. Murder was back haunting her thoughts.

THIRTY-SEVEN

As Jill drove into the car park on the first day of semester her faculty building loomed large before her. Her trip to the Pacific had given her new confidence. She couldn't wait to slip anecdotes of her travels into lectures and tutorials. With her research proposal in her briefcase she strode into the lift.

She hurried past Duncan's office to avoid seeing him after the scene last week. Paula's door was open so she entered. Duncan's assistant was looking more herself: tidy hair, luscious lipstick and manicured nails.

'Is he in?' Jill whispered, pointing next door.

'No. Medical tests. Don't you look wonderful?' Paula eased back her chair as if ready for a chat. 'That winter tan … you're the picture of health.'

Jill sat down resting her briefcase against her leg. 'Did you talk to anyone about Duncan?'

'I went to see the Vice Chancellor. Considering Duncan's medical condition they're reluctant to take his position off him.' Paula raised her eyebrows; she'd obviously hoped her difficult situation would soon be over.

'I don't know how you've put up with him, Paula. But I can't anymore. I'll see the Vice Chancellor too. I need to go higher for approval for my research project and can back up your story.'

'I agree. Duncan is too ill to work. I'm hoping for our sakes the hospital keeps him there. Let's have a coffee soon.' Jill stood up to leave. 'Perhaps I can help with your research.'

'Thanks, that'd be great.' Jill hesitated in the corridor. She was glad to see Paula better. Such a savvy lass eager to help people.

'Oh Paula,' she added, 'I'm having a certain detective round for dinner. I'm not much of a cook. What's a hearty winter meal you think would be good?'

Paula's eyes twinkled as her face broke into a smile. 'Sanderson's a bit of a dish himself. Lucky you. I'd use a slow cooker. Lamb shanks and vegetables. You can't go wrong and your place will smell scrumptious as he walks in the door.'

'Thanks so much. Great idea.' Jill swept into her office with plans of action whirring in her mind.

'Just to give you a glimpse of the Pacific,' Jill said as she dimmed the lights in the lecture theatre ready for her PowerPoint presentation. A photo of *Dreamsong* under full sail appeared. She heard whispers of 'Cool' and 'Wow' from the students as scenes of islands, dark-skinned children and markets were shown. With her audience thoroughly engaged Jill continued her Pacific history lecture.

Her visit with the Vice Chancellor was short. Hiding behind his glasses, the elderly man was reluctant to talk about Duncan. He fussed with folders on his desk. Jill felt there was little point in outlining her boss's behaviour. Academia was a slow-moving environment. Jill decided to change tack.

'Professor Mitchell is too ill to make decisions so I'm leaving my research project in your hands.'

He nodded and waved her out. Jill could feel herself smiling as she entered the glass-roofed cafeteria. Action was exhilarating. Her career was ready to move on without Duncan. As she sipped her coffee she spied a top hat on a nearby table. The object activated a twinge of guilt. She'd once thought Liam might have been involved in the murders on campus. In the joy of returning to the job she loved after her holiday Jill had forgotten the dark shadow over the university.

Liam appeared from the crush of students in the queue. 'That lecture was fantastic. Those photos of the tallship. Like you took us there. Can't wait to hear more.' His meat pie almost jiggled off the plate.

'Thanks, Liam. You'll hear more in our tutorial this afternoon. And you'll be pleasantly surprised by your exam result.'

'Great. See you later.'

His encouragement seeped through her. If only the cops could catch the killer all would be right in her world. If only Gary would ring she'd ask him for dinner. Detectives still had to eat. Jill wanted to ask about the skeleton that had been discovered during her absence.

On her way home she swung by the shopping centre to purchase a slow cooker and the accoutrements she needed for the meal. Winter darkness descended by the time she entered her apartment. Leaving the icy air outside Jill turned on the gas heater. The huge box with her new appliance dominated the bench. She put away the carrots, parsnips and zucchini. Her refrigerator hadn't seen that many healthy vegetables in quite a while.

She scanned her living room. It looked cosy and stylish. Her gaze stopped at Dharani, her exotic Thai goddess head. 'Am I doing the right thing bringing a man here?' she asked aloud. Jill was almost sure the goddess gave a wink of approval when the phone rang. Sanderson's voice brought a thrill of recognition. Before she knew it he was coming for dinner on Wednesday evening. She danced into the kitchen and poured herself a white wine. One super night of sex did not a relationship make but the delectable Detective Sanderson was back on the menu.

He arrived with a spectacular array of tiger lilies and a bottle of red wine. Wearing a suede jacket and black jeans, he kissed her on the cheek.

'Something smells fabulous,' he said with his signature wicked grin, 'reminds me of mum's home cooking.'

Jill showed him the slow cooker, its glass lid dotted with drops of condensation. 'It's been simmering slowly all day.'

'So have I,' he said, opening the bottle. He poured the vibrant red merlot and their glasses clinked.

'To us,' Jill murmured. She led the way to a cheese platter on the coffee table and served him some gooey brie with pear paste on a biscuit.

Sanderson ate while surveying the room. 'Not really the staid apartment of an academic.' He laughed.

She watched him rub fingers over Dharani's nobbled head.

'In fact,' he added facing her, 'this place is full of surprises.'

Pointing to the goddess, 'She's a recent addition. My protector. And I confess I'm not much into cooking. The meal was Paula's idea.'

Another smile flickered across his face. 'So if it kind of cooks itself you don't need to be slaving away in the kitchen?' His brown eyes intently locked on hers.

'No,' she stammered.

'In that case …' Sanderson took her glass and placed both on the coffee table. He drew her into a lingering kiss.

She sensed their bodies close and hungry for each other. He led her down the hallway finding Jill's bedroom lit by a solitary lamp. Unzipping her dress, he let it slip to the floor. She was wearing her lingerie set of black lace and tiny bows. Sanderson's appreciative glance made her blush.

'Mmm,' he whispered, 'nice tan.'

Jill slid his top off and ran her hands over his chest. 'Not bad yourself,' she said. Kissing his neck she let her tongue trace his sternum as she unbuckled his belt. The response of his smooth hands made her tremble. As they ended up on her bed she had one last thought before giving in to the sensations. How wonderful to have a lover who knew what to do.

Later, over dinner they talked sailing. With a little too much wine, Jill felt she may have romanticised her Pacific holiday.

'You know what we should do?' he said, caressing her hand, 'when this case is over we could steal away to Fiji and sail those small catamarans.'

'Bliss,' Jill replied imagining them frolicking together in the sun. She placed warm apple pie in bowls and drizzled custard over for their dessert.

They were ensconced on the lounge, snuggling into each other when his mobile disturbed them. Gary raised an eyebrow. 'Sure, boss.' He killed the call.

'Bugger,' he said, 'Ralston's had a few too many. Wants to see me pronto about the case. I'll get Fyurk to pick me up. Sorry, babe. It's been a great night.'

Minutes later he was gone. Jill eyed the dirty dishes. Not the only one with a shit for a boss, she thought. Homicide was a demanding mistress. Still Sanderson was the most exciting man she'd ever crossed paths with.

THIRTY-EIGHT

Sanderson was examining photos of the skeletal remains of their latest victim when Max arrived on time. The profiler was wearing board shorts and sandals although it was mid-winter. His tawny hair stood up in clumps as if recently gelled. Max looked nothing like the academic he was. Dressed this way, he'd disappear amongst his students.

'Glad you could tear yourself away from the beach,' Sanderson said with a smirk on his face.

'Healthy body, healthy mind,' Max quipped, 'you detectives take life far too seriously.'

'You think corpses are fun, Max? Now, how about concentrating on what we've got here so you can lead us to our killer.'

Sanderson showed Max the crime scene exhibits in order of occurrence. Signing them all out of the exhibits room had been a pain.

'Bet that threw a spanner in the works,' Max said, pointing to the most recent photos. 'Finding a skeleton means our bloke's been killing longer than you figured.'

The detective's fingers tapped the table. 'Sure did. From the first two victims we know he overpowered them in dark places at night. We think he spent more time with Cheryl; the mutilation didn't appear rushed. But he had her in a storeroom. Not likely to be disturbed.'

Max, hands clasped behind him, sauntered past the display boards. 'Can I have some copies of the key shots?'

'Sure, I'll get Fyurk onto it.'

'Have you identified the skeleton yet?'

'I have to check student records at the uni. How about I show you the crime scenes?' Sanderson felt they hadn't discovered anything concrete so far.

'Fine,' Max replied, 'but I'll need all you've got on the victimology of Katie and Cheryl to see if there are any patterns.'

Sanderson phoned Fyurk, detailing Max's requirements. The profiler followed him out to the car park, sneezing loudly.

'Got a tissue?' Max asked, settling in the passenger seat.

Sanderson hesitated then reached across, grabbed a few and snapped the glove box shut. Not before Max's prying eyes had seen some of the contents, he guessed. Shrinks made him edgy. He spent the rest of the drive thinking Max was looking at him strangely. The last thing he needed was a psychologist probing his private life.

He steered their conversation back to the university.

'Scary when murders happen on campus,' Max continued. 'Such a large conglomerate of mainly young people. Serial killers, typically young white males, see them as fertile grounds. Remember that girl murdered at Sydney uni? Her killer was never found.'

Max's long fingers kept scrunching the used tissues as they entered the grounds and parked. Leaving the pathway, Sanderson led Max to the culvert, his shoes collecting mud.

'There,' he pointed at the huge drain, 'Katie's body was inside.'

The profiler scrutinised the area. Sanderson wondered if Max re-ran the crime in his mind. Could a theorist pinpoint the behaviours to lead them to the right person? He just didn't understand how all this psych stuff worked but Max's tips had been too valuable in the past to disregard his advice.

No longer a repository for a body, the drain now looked harmless. A steady stream of water swirled through its base due to recent rain. Sanderson's memory flashed back to that steamy day in March. The recalled image of maggots jostling in Katie's throat made him want to throw up. Without a hangover he had cast iron guts. He inhaled deeply to quell the rush of saliva. The smell of damp earth, the lack of sun made him colder by the minute. Patiently, he waited for Max to finish.

During their brisk walk to the dock area behind the cafeteria, Max peppered him with questions. Sanderson indicated the dumpster and the storeroom used by Cheryl's killer. He elaborated on Wilson's involvement and the drug link. Max took his time again as if committing the scene to memory.

'Okay,' Max said, 'last site.'

Sanderson led him around the jungle of buildings, past car parks to the bushland near the residential colleges. He showed him a remnant of crime scene tape tied round a tree then forged into the scrub.

Warily placing his feet, he detected movement ahead. Sanderson hesitated, signalling Max to stop. A bright flash lit up the gloomy bush.

'F ... ing reporters,' Sanderson whispered before looking into another blinding flash. 'Get that camera out of my face. Who the hell are you?'

'Phil Easton from the *Telegraph*. Didn't mean to upset you, Detective Sanderson.'

The ginger-haired reporter lowered his camera. Sanderson took an instant dislike to him. The bloke stood his ground, a sickly grin on his face. His trousers were two sizes too small, Sanderson noted. Knowing who he was meant this was probably the culprit who took the shot of him with Cyndi.

'Get out of here, Easton.'

'Whoa,' the reporter raised a pudgy hand, 'just doing my job. Finding a skeleton makes this whole thing more macabre don't you think?'

Easton directed the question at Max, who remained silent. The profiler knew better than to play with the media. Sanderson figured the reporter had no idea who his companion was. Hiding his annoyance, he expected Max's identity would be splattered across the tabloids by tomorrow.

'We won't be discussing the case with you, Easton. Just shove off and let us get on with it.'

'Sure thing.'

With the sound of snapping sticks, the cameraman disappeared through the trees.

'Sorry, Max. We managed to keep the media out of here till the remains were recovered. They couldn't get a shot from the chopper. Trees too dense.'

'No worries.'

Max circled the shallow gravesite. Most of the disturbed soil had been tamped back in place. Dead leaves had already begun to conceal it. Soon the ominous shape would blend with the surroundings.

Sanderson didn't disrupt the profiler with his own questions. Max might be trying to see into the killer's mind and in some way intuit his motivation. His scrutiny of this deserted crime scene made Sanderson anxious. Had Ruggeri's mob found all the physical evidence? Somewhere close, beneath gum leaves may be an earring lost in the victim's struggle. Objects associated with skeletons could identify them; provide a lead into their story.

When Max was finished, they walked back out.

'I'll get a cab back so you can go check those records, Sanderson.'

'You sure?'

Max nodded. 'Give me a day or two with the material.'

Sanderson watched the profiler stride off to the entry gate. Every time he saw Max he was left with a feeling of inadequacy. The psychologist's demeanour gave so little away. Perhaps Max felt mere detectives weren't capable of higher thinking. He wiped his muddy shoes on the grass. At the administration office he flashed his badge and began searching the enrolment records.

There were two girls from out of Sydney who hadn't turned up to start the year. He jotted down their details and made it to his car before a rainsquall hit. Huge drops speckled the windscreen as he made the first call. The girl's mother told him she'd taken up an offer at another university. The second call was to Lismore.

'Mrs Schofield. It's Detective Sanderson here. Just checking if you're Karla's mother.' His fingers tapped the gear lever.

'She's not in trouble with the police, is she?' The woman's voice taut with fear.

'No but can you tell me when you last saw Karla?'

'Not since she left in January. Her father didn't want her to go to uni. There was a helluva row. What's this about?'

Sanderson's pause was too long.

'Karla's all right isn't she. She's not ...'

He explained the reason for the call. The mother's distraught response hit him like a jab to the ribs.

Back at the office, Sanderson made a coffee to have with the snack he'd bought on the way. He interrupted Fyurk and Janine's chattering before retreating to his desk. That couple would have an advantage if they made it, he thought. Cops often married cops or nurses as they understood the demands of the job and could cope with shift work.

Fyurk came in; face red. Sanderson decided not to have a shot at him. Still, he wanted all his offsider's concentration on this case.

'Got a possible ID on our latest victim. Karla Schofield from Lismore. Turned up in January to study politics at Phillips uni. Her mother hasn't heard from her since. Some blow up in the family.'

'Guess that's why she wasn't reported missing, Gary.' Fyurk sat down, spinning his chair back to his desk. 'I gave Max all he wanted.'

'Good one, Rich. I'll see if Dr Steele can get DNA from those bones. The parents are coming to Sydney. A DNA swab from them will help us verify it's their daughter. And we'll need dental records.' Sanderson fumbled for his mobile.

'You'd think the parents would be in touch considering what's gone on at the university.' Fyurk's raised eyebrows showed exasperation.

'Karla's from a country town. Some yokels avoid what's going on in the world.'

'But it's been all over the papers.'

'We don't know who Karla's parents are, Rich. Maybe they're not the paper-reading type.'

Sanderson's call to the forensic anthropologist was brief. From the tone of her reply his request was obviously an imposition.

Fyurk watched his face and waited till he finished. 'Who looks like they've been sucking lemons?'

'The Iron Maiden,' said Sanderson, 'should stick her bones where the sun don't shine.'

Fyurk's laugh, loud and throaty, made him grin.

The mugshot of himself and Max was front-page news. Sanderson felt his startled expression did not do him justice. Max's demeanour betrayed nothing. Easton had also extracted a press release from Ralston.

'Bloody journos,' Sanderson muttered, scanning the columns of print. The public were now in on the latest developments in the case. The skeleton was probably another student. Taskforce Artemis had maximum use of resources as they closed in on The Campus Killer. Max's successes as a profiler were lauded.

Sanderson let out a snort of disgust as Fyurk entered his office. He gestured to the newspaper. 'You'd think we'd done nothing when you read this rubbish.'

Fyurk placed two steaming mugs of coffee, one on either side of the desk. 'Yeah, Gary. Figured you wouldn't be too happy.'

'Let's hope we crack something today. Max is due any minute.' Sanderson sipped his warming drink. His gaze took in the ornament of the fornicating pigs. He hadn't given Cyndi a thought for weeks. She hadn't rung him either. His ego had taken a slight dent. But that was before his night out with Jill. Gone was the timid academic he'd met earlier in the year. She was all woman and surprisingly sexy. Goes to show, he told himself, never believe first impressions.

Janine's tap on the door was tentative. With raised eyebrows, she ushered in Karla's parents. 'Detective Fyurk, there's an urgent report just come in.' She beckoned his offsider to follow leaving Sanderson to deal with the couple alone. Something about the way Janine and Fyurk moved off together told him they were now an item.

Schofield had the appearance of a hardened drinker: enormous belly, red-veined nose and a pronounced tremor in the hands. His wife, by contrast, was like a wraith. A grey cardigan enveloped her, covering a loose floral dress. Sanderson felt she was trying to disappear.

When he asked her the colour of Karla's eyes, Schofield interjected. Mrs Schofield cringed. Now he knew why this woman hadn't contacted her daughter. Her husband was a bully. Maybe years earlier she'd had an opinion of her own but submission had become her survival mechanism. Sanderson sat opposite the couple explaining how to take a swab of the inside of their cheeks.

Fyurk called Sanderson to the door. 'Gary, just had a call from Dr Steele. She's compared Karla's dental records with the victim's. It's not a match.'

Before Sanderson could reply, Schofield turned on his wife, voice raised. 'Told you. The bitch used this uni idea to piss off.'

The senior detective just wanted the pair out of his office. Leaving the kits unopened, he edged around Fyurk. 'Mr and Mrs Schofield, sorry to bring you all the way to Sydney. But hopefully your daughter is safe and sound elsewhere. Come with me, perhaps you'd like to file a missing person's report.' He could see the relief in Mrs Schofield's eyes.

'Bloody wild goose chase,' Mr Schofield muttered.

Sanderson walked ahead of the couple, reached the counter and handed them over to the duty officer.

Fyurk had a fresh coffee waiting on his desk.

'Thanks, Rich. That bloke was a low life. Bet Karla stays missing. Her mum's suffering though.'

'A bullying bastard, Gary. There's plenty of them out there.'

'Sure is. So that report means our skeleton remains a Jane Doe. Another box of bones left in the morgue. And there's a story in every one of them.'

Max surprised him by arriving in a trendy suit carrying a leather briefcase. Sanderson thought he recognised the Italian brand but was not inclined to talk threads to a profiler. Max looked like a corporate raider. With a crisp click of catches, the psychologist withdrew a thick report and deposited it on the desk. Max's slender fingers rested on the pile of paper, as he remained standing.

'Now gentlemen,' he commenced, 'let's get on with my offender profile.'

Sanderson felt Max was bunging it on a bit but Fyurk's attentive stare stopped him from saying so.

Max continued, 'You know the usual stuff. Serial killers are generally young white males.'

Fyurk interjected, 'Can you give us an age?'

Max frowned. 'I never give an exact age only a range. As you're obviously new to this, Fyurk, I'd better include a warning here. Profiling is not a science. It's more about directing the investigation than solving it. You can't rely on it solely and often it's only sixty per cent right although my figures are often higher.'

Sanderson watched a look of wariness creep over Fyurk's face. Some of the eagerness had been knocked out of him. Fidgeting with his pen, Sanderson hoped Max would get back on track.

Max's eyes shone with renewed enthusiasm. 'What we've got is a killer with a two month cooling-off period. Katie was in March, Cheryl in May and the skeleton in January fits in. If we don't find him we'll have another victim within a month. Serial killers don't stop. We need to understand his unique characteristics and thought patterns. Look at who he killed, how and then work out why.

'From all we've got so far, I'd say he's organised. He carried a braided rope for strangulation and a scalpel for the post-mortem mutilation. Both young women were overpowered at night. He's working an area he knows, the uni campus. Has there been a history of rapes? Some trigger is usually required to move on to murder. I'd estimate he's intelligent. Probably thinks he's smarter than the cops.'

Sanderson let out a guffaw. 'Don't they all.' Max was impressive in this speciality. Sanderson took a swig of cold coffee and put the mug down. Sun slanting through a high window was suddenly obliterated by dark cloud. The resulting gloom prompted him to turn on the gas heater.

Max waited. He'd covered an adjoining desk with other material from his briefcase. Sanderson knew at a glance this included a map of the campus, crime scene photos, reports, statements and the victimology information.

Fyurk's gaze swept the paper maze as well. He's probably wondering how Max could absorb all the data of the case in two days. His nose twitched. Fyurk reacting to the smell of Max's aftershave? Rather overpowering, Sanderson thought.

Max's authoritative voice filled the room once again. 'Three things drive killings like this: power, anger and sexuality. Our offender is so angry at women he's cutting away their sexuality. Removing the pudenda after he's killed them fulfils his ritualistic fantasy. You two have heard the dominant or neglectful mother thing, right? Well this bloke's behaviour points to serious psychological abuse. But we won't find that out until after he's caught. What we need to do now is go through all the suspects. Their means, method, opportunity and relationship to the victim.'

'Ah,' said Sanderson, 'Rich, bring over a clean whiteboard and a set of markers.' Comfortable with his familiar method, the senior detective joined the others.

'Ready fellas,' Max's marker squeaked a name in blue on the shiny surface. 'Liam. The psych student. Could fit the bill.'

'Except he had a perfect alibi for Katie's murder. Visiting sick mum out of town. So no opportunity.' Sanderson added a red cross beside the name.

'We can eliminate Liam. He had black hair though. That's the only thing you've got from the probable killer.' Max retrieved his list of exhibits.

'Right but it's not enough to get DNA from. The test would destroy it so we're keeping it to match with a suspect when we bring him in.' Sanderson chewed the end of his marker.

'Mm,' Max hummed. 'No DNA. Your case isn't strong in evidence. What about the prof's prints on the cellophane? That puts him near the first scene.'

Fyurk rushed in, 'We never considered the old fuddy duddy a suspect. That was for elimination. He's a smoker. Was at a staff do in the vicinity before we found the first body.'

'A good detective never discounts anyone.' Max's comment came as a rebuke.

A flicker of discomfort passed over Fyurk's face as he removed his jacket. Sanderson, unwilling to let their session slide into personal differences, jumped to his offsider's defence. 'Come off it, Max. Rich is proving to be a bloody good detective. He's the one that noticed the similarity of eye colour and picked up the fragrance the killer uses. That snoz of his comes in handy.'

'All right, Sando. No need to get defensive. Have you checked where every suspect was the day after Katie's murder?'

Sanderson moved uncomfortably, shaking his head.

'You'd be surprised how many killers don't show up to work the next day,' Max added.

Fyurk jotted a note then eyed Max suspiciously.

'What about Liam's room-mate?' Max asked. 'Tim isn't it?'

Sanderson nodded. 'We kept them both under surveillance for a while. The drug squad have given Tim the once over. He's been getting dope from Wilson.' An uneasy silence followed. Had he discounted the insipid druggie? His red hair didn't incriminate him. Once Liam was off the hook should they have concentrated the investigation on Tim? Doubt crept in. But Wilson had loomed large as their prime suspect.

Max had four names on the board. He ran his hand through gelled hair then rested his fingers on the corner of the desk. Sanderson knew the profiler wasn't privy to every lead they'd explored. Nevertheless Max's direct stare was challenging.

Noticing the oily residue Max's fingertips left on the surface, momentarily diverted Sanderson's concentration. The atmosphere in the office was becoming clammy. He strode over to turn the heater off.

Back at the whiteboard, Max confronted him. 'Have you checked alibis for Tim on both nights?'

'No,' Sanderson replied.

Fyurk was already writing. He looked up at Max. 'The killer must have stalked both girls if he selected them on green eye colour. Unless that's just a coincidence. And I think he used Lily of the Valley to excite himself. Perhaps that was the precursor to mutilation.'

'Possibly,' Max replied. His thoughtful expression brought quiet again.

Sanderson scraped the toe of his perfectly polished shoe against the whiteboard's stand. He no longer felt he'd handled this case as well as he could. Max seemed to be finding holes in their procedure. Sanderson would have to stop gap these before the next major review.

Max cut in. 'There's no great mention of this scent thing. It's an old-fashioned one. Perhaps the cruelty goes back to his grandmother. Smell is the most powerful at evoking memories. The killer may even have used it to provoke attacks. We'll come back to that. Now, I agree Wilson appears to fit the bill. He's working class and they're the most likely mutilators. He'd probably been supplying both girls with drugs. Were they going to squeal? Could he have killed them?'

'That's where we're stuck, Max. Wilson had the means, method and opportunity as well as a relationship with both victims. The skeleton presents a problem. As yet it's unidentified and we have no further leads as to who it might be. Wilson didn't start working at the uni till February but could have been living nearby. Came over from New Zealand, has a record but we don't have any actual evidence linking him to the crimes. He has shown a propensity to violence.' Sanderson underlined Wilson's name on the board.

'The only thing,' Fyurk added, 'when we had him in for questioning on the drug thing he went right off when we mentioned the murders. That's not like a psychopath. They can describe what they do to victims in an unemotional way. That's the only thing about him I thought doesn't fit.'

'Good observation. You may be right. I'm certain we're looking for a psychopath. But you both may be finding connections where there are none. Something's strange about this case. Sando, what's the story on the sharpened stiletto?'

Sanderson felt his face flush. 'Rich, can you go get us fresh coffees?'

'Sure, Gary.'

As soon as his office door slammed, Sanderson explained Jill's involvement. The shoe was a furphy.

Max smiled. 'Rather interesting extra-curricular activity wouldn't you say? Are you sure I shouldn't add Jill's name to the board? That'd be a first. A woman serial killer mutilating young women.'

On Fyurk's return, Sanderson brought his finger to his lips. Once again, he squirmed under the psychologist's scrutiny. But Max seemed willing to leave the shoe buried. Max's face, clear skinned and healthy, was a perfect foil for his incredible mind. Fortunately, Max intimidated Fyurk who wasn't about to ask what he'd missed.

Max numbered the suspects and added the numeral five. For one horrible moment Sanderson thought the profiler was going to do as he'd threatened. Instead he added the word, STRANGER.

'That's unlikely, fellas. Remember you can't pick an offender from just speaking to them. The police often meet them in the first twenty-four hours but fail to realise their importance to the case.' Max put down his marker and retrieved his briefcase, refilling it with everything but his report. He straightened his psychedelic-striped tie: bands of cerise, lime and cobalt. 'You're looking for someone with power or control over others. If you chase up those loose ends and sift through my profile I'm sure you'll find where to go.'

Fyurk shook his hand. 'Max, that was brilliant.'

Max's serious countenance came close to another smile, Sanderson thought. 'Thanks, Max. Your input will prove helpful as always.' Something the profiler had said was already nagging at his brain.

THIRTY-NINE

Barbara slept late. Wearing a lilac tracksuit, she meandered into the kitchen to see Madeline scoffing cereal. Her backpack provided a pillow for Beau's head. Madeline's sneakered foot wiggled amongst the dog's tummy curls.

Noticing a flyer on the bench top, Barbara read the words Divorce Seminar.

'Maddy is this for me?'

Her daughter glanced up, spoon in mid-air. 'Yeah. Thought you might go today. It's at the uni. Mum, you really should get on with your life. You can't just work and look after me.'

Barbara, at a loss for words, watched her daughter finish her breakfast. Before Madeline left through the front door, she called out, 'If you go, Mum, give me a buzz on the mobile.'

Stunned, Barbara hadn't thought how Madeline viewed the changed circumstances. Fancy her daughter urging her to move on. Did that mean Madeline felt her father was never coming back? Barbara had taken it one day at a time and was finding new strength. She put the piece of paper down. 'Yes,' she murmured, 'I'll go.'

Once showered and dressed, Barbara clipped on her new bracelet. She would enjoy wearing its sea colours. Sitting in the lecture theatre at the university, she doodled on her notebook until the speaker arrived. A woman of a similar age edged into the seat beside Barbara. She gave a little wave and an all-enveloping smile. Barbara responded thinking the woman's frizzed curls framed a welcoming face. A voice boomed into the microphone demanding their attention.

A few other interchanges during the lecture piqued Barbara's interest. At the end, the woman presented her well-manicured hand. 'I'm Sarah. We should do coffee. I have a feeling we're going to be friends.'

'So do I,' Barbara replied. 'Friends are good if we're to survive this divorce business.'

'Friends are good anytime, Barb.'

They both had short blacks. An hour later, Barbara had to drag herself away to meet Madeline outside the library. The things she had in common with Sarah astounded her. Their conversation was as natural as if they'd known each other for twenty years. With every step, Barbara assured herself Sarah would become a close confidante. How life could throw up wonderful surprises at the worst of times.

When Barbara kissed Madeline's cheek, she became aware of excited voices.

'Mum, there's word they're about to arrest the killer.'

'Thank God, Maddy. Now we can stop worrying.'

Barbara felt Madeline's arms around her. She returned the hug. Madeline stood back and added, 'Oh, Dad rang me a while ago. The girlfriend's kicked him out. He wants to come home.' Her daughter's smile betrayed happiness.

'All right. I'll ring him.' A flicker of indescribable emotion raced through Barbara. It seemed the new house would become a family home after all.

Sanderson's organisational skills were tested to the limit. A frantic twenty-four hours followed for every member of the taskforce. Fyurk was due in his office in ten minutes.

A flurry of reports fanned across his desk. He'd recalled Max's advice to question everything as if you're wrong. Each new piece of information was slotted into position on the whiteboard. His shoes propped on the desktop, hands clasped behind his head, Sanderson sifted through new scenarios confident he could close this case.

When Fyurk marched in, Sanderson couldn't believe it was the same young man he'd been assigned earlier in the year. From shiny shoes to smart tie, his offsider was as well groomed as any D on the squad. Sanderson took some pride in the transformation but no doubt Janine had played a part as well. He could forget comparing him to Dave. Nothing could bring his colleague back. He'd just have to cherish the memory of the best bloke he'd ever worked with. Fyurk removed his jacket and hung it beside Sanderson's.

'You're not going to believe this.' Fyurk sat down rolling his chair towards the desk. He read from a file '... was discharged on Wednesday. Gary, that means Tim's alibi is secure. He was in hospital at the time of Katie's murder. Suspected hep C. So he's the druggie we expected.' Fyurk jumped up, grabbed a red marker and placed a red cross beside Tim's name then another near Wilson's.

'Hang on,' Sanderson cut in, 'we haven't enough evidence to finally eliminate him.' His feet hit the floor. Frown lines furrowed his brow.

'Yes we have.' Fyurk flourished another report. 'It seems Wilson was at the snow the weekend of Cheryl's death. All here. Lift tickets and meals on credit cards. Phone records.'

'Are you sure, Rich?' Sanderson's voice raised in excitement.

His offsider nodded vigorously.

'That means Garbage Boy is in the clear.'

'Sure does, Gary. Told you I didn't figure his reaction when he thought we had him for the murders. Psychopaths aren't so volatile. No wonder he clammed up and wanted a solicitor. Must have been shitting himself bigtime.' Fyurk spun the marker in his fingers. 'That means ...'

'Mitchell,' Sanderson filled in. He punched the air. 'Bloody good work, Rich. I couldn't convince Ralston yesterday to push the magistrate for a search warrant. He's been an arsehole. Wanted everything we were looking for. I told him braided rope, duct tape and pudenda.'

'Did he get the warrant?'

'Finally, this morning. Should be here soon. Before we head off to the professor's abode I'll ring his research assistant to check his whereabouts.' Sanderson made the call while watching his offsider peruse the crime scene photos on display.

'Not answering,' said Sanderson, 'I'll try Jill's mobile.' Again he pressed buttons then shook his head. 'It's off. She must be lecturing.'

'Hope they're all right. If Mitchell's our man he could have gone berserk at the uni.'

Fyurk's words and worried expression brought a lather of sweat to Sanderson's brow. He'd had an inkling about the professor ever since Max went on about the killer seeking power and control. Mitchell was the power freak in that history faculty according to Jill. Those working around him had been forced into accepting his weird behaviour.

Sanderson felt a wave of guilt wash over him. He could have warned Jill last night but the very nature of his job demanded he have evidence before acting on suspicions. He'd never forgive himself if he'd put Jill's safety at risk again.

Fyurk stared at him.

'You'd better be wrong. Still I'll send some uniforms to secure Mitchell in his office and locate Paula and Jill.' Sanderson's mobile ran hot.

'Good idea, Gary.' Fyurk grabbed both jackets as they charged out the door.

In the Commodore, Sanderson sped up the highway towards Killara. Wind buffeted the car in the gale force conditions. Fyurk directed him down several back streets before pointing out the professor's house.

A substantial blue brick with manicured lawns and an unimaginative garden, thought Sanderson. The place had an aura of old-moneyed respectability which made him suspect the professor had inherited the family home. He rang the bell. The door opened slightly. A timid woman peered at them.

'Mrs Mitchell. We're Detectives Sanderson and Fyurk. We have a search warrant to look over this property.'

The woman appeared confused. 'Has my husband done something wrong?'

'Not at liberty to say, M'am.' Sanderson waved the warrant. 'Does your husband have anywhere particularly his own?'

'He has a workshop behind the garage. I'm not allowed in there but I can give you the key.' She invited them inside. Inhaling the musty smell of old age, Sanderson followed. The lounge room was dim with curtains drawn. He wanted to reef them open along with the windows and let the strong westerly clear the air.

Fyurk's eyes were riveted on a woman's portrait above the fireplace. 'Fine looking woman. Striking green eyes.'

'Yes,' the professor's wife replied, 'that's Duncan's mother. Keeps an eye on us from the grave.'

Sanderson found the remark strange. Mrs Mitchell ushered them into her husband's study before handing over the key. She indicated out the back then retired to her recliner rocker, pulling a crocheted rug over her knees to resume watching the soapies.

The detectives glanced around the book-lined room and opened desk drawers. Nothing seemed out of the ordinary. The study revealed Mitchell as a methodical man. Fyurk picked up a miniature print in a gilt frame. On closer examination he found it was an image reproduced from the Kama Sutra.

'A hint of a sexual fetish,' he said, showing it to Sanderson.

'Maybe. Let's see what's in the workshop.'

The first thing Sanderson saw inside was an ancient workbench, its timber greyed and stained from lifetimes of use. Curls of pale wood, like discarded hair, lay on the worn surface. In one corner a chair faced a bar fridge, which had a small TV on top.

'The professor's retreat,' Sanderson said, checking out the shadow board of tools and the shelves. He reached for an elongated varnished box as Fyurk interrupted him.

'Gary. Look.'

His offsider had a coil of braided rope in one hand and a roll of duct tape in the other.

'Bingo,' said Sanderson, placing the box on the workbench. He snapped on latex gloves and opened the lid. Red satin lined the compartments. He lifted out what appeared to be a piece of crinkled leather until he saw the hair attached.

'His trophies,' murmured Fyurk. Pointing into the box he added, 'and there's his favourite perfume. Bet his mother used it. Makes you wonder what abuse led him to all this.'

'Sure does, Rich. Our professor is one sick killer. We'll lock this place up till I can get Ruggeri here. Come on, let's hightail it to the uni.' They didn't go back through the house.

Jill arrived at work early. All was deathly quiet on her floor. On the desk was a duplicate copy of the research project she'd given the professor, a single word emblazoned across the front page: denied.

'Ahah,' Jill muttered, now feeling vindicated at going behind Duncan's back. She'd used his illness, hinted at unwarranted behaviour. The grant was now secured so she could proceed. Jill wasn't looking forward to the inevitable confrontation when he found out what she'd done. Control was Duncan's passion.

She located the pile of exam papers and left for her tutorial. As Jill walked into the room, she shivered involuntarily. A sense of déjà vu struck her while glancing at the chair she regarded as Katie's. Then Liam spoke as he flipped his top hat onto a nearby desk. 'Jill, you must tell us about the South Pacific.'

'Later, Liam. And now for the good news.' Jill scanned the faces of her students as she handed out their papers.

Madeline gave a shriek of delight at her result. 'I'm so enjoying this subject.'

'Perhaps we should drag you away from medicine,' Jill teased.

Liam piped in, 'I'd dump psych any day if I could do history with you forever.'

Jill blushed. This sort of adoration was rare. But it was some kind of payoff for inspiring students. 'I'm just happy Liam you believed in yourself and did so well.'

Following the tutorial, Jill was amazed at how easily she'd slipped back into academic life. Her trip to the South Seas hovered in her mind like a fantasy. As she meandered past the fountain, the bubbles were a hideous crimson. Another student prank?

Her phone rang.

'Jill, want you in my office. Now.' Duncan's tone seethed with anger.

Her stomach tightened. All she could hear was the sluicing of water. She had to get away from the fountain but her feet refused to move. How had he found out so soon?

Jill took a few tentative steps towards the history building. She tried to think of a defence. Duncan knew she'd reported him. She'd heard his fury on the phone. But he was still her boss. She had to face him.

Hands clenched, she stood in the lift. Jill went to Paula's office first. It was empty. Hoping like hell Duncan's assistant was in there, her knuckles tapped on his door. It was flung open. Duncan wrenched her inside then locked the door.

'How dare you go over my head,' he yelled, spittle ejecting from his mouth.

Jill raised her hands. She said nothing. The agitation in his dark eyes stopped any words. Duncan launched himself at her. She felt his arm encircle her neck. Jill tried twisting her body out of his grip. They fell to the floor. She gasped for breath as the pressure on her windpipe increased. The smell of his leather jacket and some horrendous perfume filled her nostrils. His knee pressed into her back holding her down.

Her head skewed to one side, she could see another face on the floor. What was Paula doing there? So still. Her eyes open, not blinking. Realisation struck Jill. Duncan had killed Paula. Adrenalin surged through her. Jill struggled, contorting her body in a frenzy to escape. For a moment she thought his hold weakened. Then he grabbed her flailing arm and pinned it with his other knee. Pain seared her limb.

In a haze she heard loud thumps, splintering timber. Duncan was reefed off her. Metal clinked as a policeman helped her into a sitting position.

'You okay?' he said.

Jill nodded, rubbing her throat. She could see the other cop had Duncan handcuffed to his chair. His glasses askew, he sat stunned. Jill had made it to her feet as Sanderson appeared in the doorway.

He hugged her. 'The nightmare's over,' he whispered, 'you all right to wait in your office?' An officer escorted her out.

Sanderson watched Fyurk check the assistant's body for vital signs.

'Too late for this one.'

The other officer returned, filling them in on what they'd found. Professor Mitchell was rigid in his chair; the cops poised either side of him. He appeared to be in a trance. Fyurk's nose twitched as he stared at the damaged elbow of the man's black leather jacket.

'The scent, Gary, it's all over him. And look at his jacket. That piece of leather wasn't from Cheryl's boot.'

Sanderson nodded. The professor's hands were fists. The hair on his forearms had stiffened with blood. Facing their killer at last, Sanderson noticed something unfathomable about his eyes. They revealed a soul Sanderson was reluctant to see.

Professor Mitchell's eerie tone chilled him, 'You've come about the girls.'

ENDS

ACKNOWLEDGEMENTS

Most thanks go to my writing group for their help and suggestions in developing this novel. I also thank Greg Reid, a retired police prosecutor, for his police stories. Partners in Crime, an organisation for crime writers and readers, was of great assistance during the writing of this book. Listening to professionals involved in and around criminal investigations was inspirational and fed my fascination with crime.

ABOUT THE AUTHOR

Rob McWilliam

Rob worked as a science teacher before turning to writing then taught Creative Writing on Sydney's Northern Beaches for more than 20 years. Rob independently published a first crime novel *House of Shadows* in 2002.

As Meeting Convenor for Partners in Crime, Sydney from 2005 to 2009, Rob sourced expert speakers to provide authentic material for *Malevolent Desire*. An award-winning short story writer, Rob is currently working on another novel.

Interested in writing techniques? Follow Rob's blog – robmcwilliam. wordpress.com

www.ingramcontent.com/pod-product-compliance
Lightning Source LLC
Chambersburg PA
CBHW060406260626
47160CB00006B/2455